10 Ways to Accidentally Fall in Love

Emmy Sanders

Beta Reading by Christie, Jen & Maxie of Smut Readers Society, and Marie Reynard

Editing by M.A. Hinkle

Proofreading by Willow and Lori Parks

Cover Design by Natasha Snow Designs

ISBN: 9798989542079

For everyone who rooted for Brad's story. You asked for it.

Contents

Note to Readers

Despite the word "watersports" being used a whopping 11 times in this book, there are, in fact, no watersports of the non-nautical variety. Enjoy!

Chapter 1

BRAD

If there's one thing I love, it's getting a good sweat going. The kind you feel trickling down your balls. The kind of slick heat you achieve after a rigorous drill sesh with another man.

Or gal. Or enby pal. Honestly, being a gym-bro has nothing to do with gender. It's about *dedication*. Comradery.

It's about doing it together.

"Fuck yeah," I cheer, holding up my hand for a high five as Cas finishes his rep. His palm meets mine without hesitation. The dude is a stellar gym-bro.

"That our last set?" he asks.

"Unless you want to go again?" I say, dropping into a lunge so I can stretch out my hips. "I could probably bust out one more round."

Cas checks the time on the wall. "Actually, I should get going. I have class in an hour."

"Yeah, Cat-man. No worries." I hold up my hand again. "Smash that physio class. And give Birdie a hug for me, will you?"

He huffs a laugh before slapping my palm. Such a good dude. I never would have met the guy if it weren't for my best friend. The Birdie to my Bee. My kindergarten bestie turned lifelong brother. Birdie and Cas started dating not that long ago. And now? Now they're a unit, and I'm... Well, feeling a bit like a third wheel, if I'm being honest.

Not that I'll let that get me down. I'll happily be the front end in a tricycle sitch with my best friend and his boyfriend any day. There are no two guys I trust better to have my rear.

I let out a sigh as Cas heads off toward the locker room. The next second, a soft voice asks, "Birdie?"

Spinning to my right, I find a total gym-dude standing nearby. Tall, beefed up but not in a downing-steroids-in-his-smoothies kind of way. Dark brown hair, brown eyes, super nice smile, and some scruff. Honestly, the guy kind of reminds me of a teddy bear, only leaner. And far less hairy.

"What's one step under a bear?" I ask him.

His smile goes crooked on one end. "An otter?"

"No, man, you're definitely bigger than that. Mountain lion, maybe?"

"I...don't think I'm a cougar," he says tentatively, that smile still on his face. He holds out his hand. "Joey."

"*Dude*," I say, clasping his palm. "Joey Kangaroo! That's *perfect.*"

"Is it?" he asks, sounding unsure.

"Definitely. Kangaroos are strong, bro. I mean, seriously, look at these hammies." I give the side of his leg a slap in demonstration, my palm stinging in the aftermath. "*Damn.* Pretty sure you could crack my neck in half with those things."

And shit. Now he's blushing. I didn't mean to embarrass the guy.

"Sorry. I'm Brad," I say quickly, realizing I never gave him my name. "Nice to meet you, man."

"You, too," he says, finally letting my hand go. "You, uh, never answered my question."

"Oh, right. Birdie. Yeah. That's Jason. We're super close. Used to live together, you know? But now he's with Cas, the guy who was just here."

"Ah," he says sympathetically. "That must be hard for you."

"It *is*," I say, glad he gets it. "I'm happy for him—don't get me wrong. But I miss the dude. We still see each other all the time, but I'm on the outside now. It's different."

"You're still friends?" he asks.

"Oh, totally. We're Birdie and Bee."

He gives me a curious look, and I realize, *yeah*, that probably makes no sense.

"Jason's mom called him Jaybird, which became Birdie," I explain. "And I'm Bee, the little flying dudes? Bee for the letter B for Brad. We've been friends a long time."

"That's...sweet," he says, and he seems to mean it. "Sounds like you've been through a lot together."

"Yeah," I breathe out.

Sharing nearly your entire life with a person is bound to make you close. You see the good and the bad. You go through hard times and joyous ones. Jason's my man, and he always will be. He's been there for me without my ever having to ask. I never really had much of a family of my own, but Jason was that for me. Still is.

So, yeah. We've been through a short lifetime together. But it's no surprise things are changing. Jason found *love*.

Maybe, someday, I can find that, too.

"Are you new here?" I ask Joey before I can get stuck too far inside my own head. "I've never seen you before."

"Just moved to town."

"No shit? You wanna work out sometime?"

That smile lights his face again. It's a good smile. Kind. "Yeah, I'd like that a lot. Can I have your number?"

"Yeah, man. Ready?" He nods, phone out now, and I rattle off my digits. "Text me anytime. I work out most days. Need to, considering I sit for eight hours. I get a little antsy, you know?"

"Office job?" he asks, slipping his phone away.

"Kinda? Except I work from home. What do you do?"

"Construction."

"No way! With the tool belts and everything?"

He huffs a laugh. "Yep."

"*Dude*. I dated this girl once who had this, like, costume for Halloween? The belt was hot as fuck. She wore it while we..."

Aaand there go his cheeks again.

"Too much?" I say, nodding to myself. "Too much."

"You're fine," Joey tells me, but I'm pretty sure he's just being polite. I know I have a tendency to come on strong. Here I am, meeting a brand-new gym-bro, and I'm being crass without meaning to.

"Tell you what. I'm gonna leave while we're on a semi-high note," I say, appreciating Joey's responding chuckle. "And you go ahead and text me if you still want to meet up. I promise I won't talk about my past exploits again."

His smile is soft. Sweet, almost. "Deal. And Brad? I will text."

"Cool, man." I hold out my hand, and Joey clasps his palm with mine.

Fuck, there's nothing like making a new friend.

Letting Joey go, I grab my water from the bench where I left it and head off toward the locker room. I'm still caked in sweat, so I make quick work of dropping trou and showering off, lingering only long enough to finish singing "Bohemian Rhapsody."

Song's the tits.

When I come out of the shower, I end up running into Joey. He must have been finishing up his own routine.

"Hey, man," I greet because ignoring him would be plain rude. He's at a locker a little ways down from my own, his eyes going wide when I drop my towel.

"Uh, hi," he says.

I pull my briefs up, hopping a little when they stick to my damp legs. Joey coughs.

"All right?"

"Yep," he says quickly.

"It'd suck if you're getting a cold."

"No, I'm good. Just a…thing. In my throat."

I nod, getting my shirt over my head and grabbing my towel to do a quick dry of my hair. All set, I grab my bag and shut the locker.

Joey watches me as I head his way. I stop in front of him and hold up my fist, and he slowly bumps his own into mine.

"See more of you soon, Joey Kangaroo."

I add a wink for my new gym-bro, and he makes a sound like something is still stuck in his throat.

"Yeah, uh… See ya, Brad," he replies roughly.

Poor dude. He's probably coming down with something.

Slapping his shoulder, I make my way out of the locker room and gym, humming once I set off along the Las Vegas sidewalks toward home. I have a few things to finish up this afternoon: a couple bugs to fix in the newest video game the company I work for is designing and some emails to reply to from the folks in admin. And then I'll likely cap off my day by logging some game time in one of my favorite co-op shooters.

After that? Dinner. Alone. Maybe browsing a dating app? It has been a while since I've had a girlfriend, and, admittedly, I miss it. I miss spending time with someone. Learning everything there is to know about them. First kisses and warm cuddles on the couch.

I miss companionship.

Now that Jason has moved out, I'm truly on my own. I'm just Brad, twenty-five-year-old single dude, game designer, gym-goer, and coffee aficionado-slash-addict. Yeah, Jason and I will always be friends. We'll always be Birdie and Bee.

But he has Cat-man now. And *holy shit*. The cat who caught the canary. I never noticed that before.

I chuckle to myself as I unlock my door. What else goes with Bee? A flower? That sounds...mildly creepy when I think about the implications.

No. I'm just Brad. For maybe the first time ever.

And I'm okay with that. I am.

But I think it's time to figure out what I want my life to look like beyond my super-sweet job and my brolationship with Jason. I don't want to be alone forever. I want to find my eventual *Mrs*. The flower I'll stick my...yeah, nope. Still creepy.

The whole romance part might take time, but at least I accomplished something today. Something pretty damn big on this journey to self-discovery.

Step one in Brad's Guide to Finding Himself and Falling in Love:

Make a new friend.

Nailed it.

Chapter 2

JOEY

"Joey, need that drill?"

I pass it over to my cousin. "All yours."

"Thanks," he says, getting the wall anchors put in for the cabinets we're installing. "What're you doing, anyway?"

I puff out a breath, eyes returning to my phone. "Trying to work up the courage to text that guy I was telling you about."

"From the gym?"

I nod.

"Just do it. What's the worst that could happen?"

My mind flashes back to the way Brad so brazenly dropped his towel in front of me in the locker room after giving me his number. Either he's incredibly lacking in self-consciousness, which is a distinct possibility. Or he's advertising the fact that he's down for a good time.

And it's not that I wouldn't be into that. *Eventually.* But I'm nearly thirty. I'm at the point in my life where I'm looking for more than just a good time.

"I'll do it later," I tell Iggy, slipping my phone in my pocket. "I shouldn't be texting on the clock, anyway."

He makes a *psht* sound. "You know my dad won't care. So long as we get the job done, you can take breaks as you need them."

"Still, I'll stick to flirting when I'm not on Uncle Johnny's dime."

Iggy huffs a laugh, shaking his head at me. Maybe my uncle really wouldn't care, but the truth is I don't know him all that well. My parents divorced when I was young, and I stayed in New Hampshire with my mom. Iggy is my cousin on my dad's side. Before moving to Nevada a couple weeks back, I saw him a cumulative handful of times throughout my entire life. Same with Johnny.

But with my dad having passed last year and my uncle extending the offer, once again, for me to come join the family business, I thought maybe it was time I got closer to my relatives. They never had an issue with my sexuality, after all.

That was only my dad.

"Hey, where do you want to grab lunch today?" Iggy asks, hefting the frame of the cabinet into place.

I step up on a stool beside him to tighten the screws. "Tacos?"

Iggy smirks. "Oh, really? Tacos again? Don't suppose it has anything to do with the view from that particular restaurant?"

"There's no telling if Brad will even be at the gym," I point out.

"Uh-huh," my cousin mutters. "You've been moon-eyeing him all week, Joey. *Just text him.*"

I push Iggy's face away, shaking my head when he laughs. At least connecting with my family has been pretty great. Even if Iggy is a bit of a shit-stirrer.

After we get the rest of the custom-made kitchen cabinets installed, Iggy and I head out for lunch. Neither of us bothers changing out of our dusty work clothes, but we do wash up a bit. We're not heathens.

My leg bounces once we're seated at the restaurant, our table affording us a nice view of the gym through the window. Iggy snorts, but I pay him no mind.

It's not that I've been *stalking* Brad. Truly, I haven't. But I caught sight of him last week in nearly this exact same spot, and...*fuck*. It's like I was struck on impact. The guy was smiling while doing *burpees*, of all things, his eyes bright and his enthusiasm infectious even from across the street. And when he tossed his head back, laughing at something his friend was saying? I had the distinct thought that *Christ, I'd give anything to hear him laugh for me like that*. This guy I didn't even know.

Maybe it doesn't make sense, but attraction doesn't always. I had to introduce myself. Get closer. *Try*.

Luckily, I happened to be in the market for a new gym.

I don't know why I'm hesitating now. He gave me his number. Invited me to work out with him, at the very least. It's a no-brainer.

"Hey, is that him?" Iggy asks.

My breath catches as Brad walks past the windows at the front of the gym. He appears to be alone today as he settles in for some stretching on a mat beside the free weights.

I debate for all of two seconds before pulling out my phone.

"*Yes*," Iggy hisses.

I type out a quick text to the number Brad gave me, not letting myself second-guess.

Me: Hey, this is Joey. Still up for that workout?

I watch as Brad pauses, tugging his phone from the pocket of his shorts. His face lights up, and Iggy slaps my chest from across the table. My heart hammers as Brad types his response. It only takes a second before my phone chimes.

Brad: Joey Kangaroo! Yeah, man. When are you free?

I have to wait for our waiter to take our order before typing back. I'm not even sure I ask for the tacos I like, preoccupied as I am.

Me: Would Friday after five work?

"What's he saying?" Iggy asks, sipping his water.

"We're figuring out a time to meet."

I nearly fumble my phone when another text comes through.

Brad: Works for me! I live down the street, so text me when you're on your way, and I'll walk over. Can't wait to see you!

"We're meeting Friday night," I tell Iggy, nearly lightheaded with the way my pulse is still racing.

My cousin slaps my chest again. Repeatedly.

"All right, all right," I mumble, batting his hand away, even as my lips quirk.

"Look how excited he is," Iggy says, sounding amused. "He's like a puppy."

I glance out the window again. Brad has a huge grin on his face as he stretches his hamstrings, his head bobbing back and forth like he's singing a tune to himself.

He does look like a puppy, if said puppy had the most gorgeous green eyes I've ever seen and the sleekly muscled body of a grown-ass man.

If Brad is this excited, though… Well, maybe this could mean more to him than a quick fling after all.

I try to quell my own ridiculous smile, but I'm not sure I manage it. I shoot Brad one more text before setting my phone aside, determined to keep my cool until Friday.

Me: Looking forward to it.

When I get to the gym Friday after work, my eyes sweep the room on autopilot. I don't see Brad, but he texted that he was on his way, so I drop my bag off in the locker room while I wait for him to arrive.

I'm just settling in to warm up at the treadmills when I spot him heading my way. *Christ*, he's pretty. Those light, piercing eyes framed by thick, dark lashes. The expressive eyebrows and lips seemingly always tipped into a smile. The dark hair and coarse stubble that makes him look older than that boyish grin would suggest.

"Hi," I say rather eloquently, waiting atop my treadmill as Brad comes to a stop in front of me.

He holds up his hand for a high five. "Joe-bro! How's it going? You look good," he says rapid fire, blatantly eyeing me up and down in a way that has my pulse tripping. "Not too tired after your day?"

I dutifully slap his palm as I sort through his greeting. "Not too tired," I assure him. "You look good, too."

"Thanks, man." He shoots me a smile as he steps up onto the treadmill next to mine. "I'm glad you texted. I needed this. Been on my ass since breakfast."

Brad starts up his machine, and I follow suit, setting the pace for a slow jog. "What is it you do, exactly? For your non-office office job?"

He snorts a laugh. "I work for this gaming company called DreamWyld. Ever heard of it?"

"Uh, yeah," I say slowly, wondering who hasn't. "*Run, Run, Ricochet?* I love that game."

"Dude! Me, too," Brad says, jogging now beside me. "It's my favorite. I helped design it."

"Holy crap," I say, startled enough for my feet to miss a step. I recover quickly. "That's...awesome."

"You think so?" he asks, shooting me another grin.

"Yeah," I tell him, meaning it. I can't even imagine the complexities that go into video game design. "So you get to, what, play video games all day?"

"Yup," he says, nodding his head several times. "Well, mostly. There's some other stuff in there, too, but I stay pretty rooted to my computer, you know? Which is why this feels *so nice*."

I chuckle at his happy groan. I'm not sure I've ever heard anyone as enthusiastic about working out as Brad.

"How about you?" he asks, barely out of breath. "Do any screwing today? Screw...drivering? Wait, no. Drilling! Drill any holes today?" He pauses before muttering, "Why does that sound so odd?"

"I, uh..." A cough sneaks its way out as I try to figure out what all *that* was. And why I was into it.

Brad looks over at me sympathetically before pulling something out of his pocket. "Dude. Here," he says, holding out a couple...cough drops? "Figured you might need these."

I hop up onto the sides of the treadmill and stare at him. "You brought me cough drops?"

"Yeah, man. Gotta look out for my bro."

Stunned at the thoughtful—albeit unnecessary—concern, I accept the wrapped lozenges. "Thank you," I manage. I'm not remotely sick, but the wink Brad sends me does have me feeling slightly feverish.

"You bet," he says easily.

Fuck. This man. I barely know him, and I'm already wondering what kind of fence he'd like around his backyard. White picket?

Slipping the cough drops into my pocket, I hop back onto the belt of the treadmill. Brad and I jog alongside one another for a while, the sounds of our breaths and slapping feet a constant amongst the echoing clangs and light chatter inside the gym. He called me one step down from a bear the other day, but I'm not that much larger than him. Maybe an inch in height, a little bulkier, sure. But Brad has that lean muscle I've always found myself attracted to.

Honestly, I find every single thing about the guy attractive. Even the way he says *bro*.

I think I might be in trouble.

"You loose enough?" Brad asks.

My head whips his way, and it takes me a *long* second to realize he's talking about our warm-up. "Yeah, uh, I'm good."

"Cool, cool," he says, stopping his machine. He steps off the treadmill and picks up his water bottle, guzzling a bit down. "So, what do you want to do first? Arms? Legs?"

"I'm easy," I tell him. "You pick."

His grin is mildly concerning. "Let's do deadlifts."

Oh boy.

"Do you plan on torturing us today?" I tease as we head in that direction.

He shakes his head, brown hair flopping around a bit. "Nah, man," he says seriously. "I'm not into sadism. Or masochism, for that matter. Giving or receiving pain isn't my thing."

"Good to know," I mumble, slipping that fact away and feeling rather flushed.

Brad goes on, seemingly oblivious to my mental and physical state as he stops in front of the weight station. "*This*, on the other hand..." He starts loading up his weights. Nothing too outrageous. "This, I enjoy."

His grin is evidence of that fact. I wait on the sidelines as Brad gets his barbell ready. Once set, he adjusts his grip and starts his reps. Turns out, deadlifts are a lot more enjoyable than I remember. I wish I could say my eyes aren't glued to Brad's ass as he repeatedly lifts the weights off the ground, but I'd be lying. It's fruitless to even pretend otherwise.

It's clear Brad isn't trying to beat any records or even bulk up. No, he's all energy and boundless joy, like he gets a thrill out of the simple act of exercising. I can't help but wonder, to my own detriment, if he's that enthusiastic in bed.

It's far too soon to be thinking that way—and I dismiss the thought before my body has time to properly react—but I can't deny Brad has me more excited about a potential first date than I've been in a long damn time.

Does he want kids?

"Your turn," Brad says, smiling as he steps aside and wipes the sweat off his forehead.

I clear my throat and get into place in front of the barbell, but Brad's hand on my hip has me stalling.

"You can probably handle more weight than me," he points out. "Want me to add twenty, or do you wanna keep it light? No shame in that. Not trying to pressure you."

"Go ahead and add fifty," I find myself saying.

And *great*, now I'm showing off?

Brad simply grins before grabbing two twenty-five-pound weights. We each attach one, and then I get into place, taking a breath to center myself. It's well under my deadlift limit, but the weight of Brad's stare is heavy on my person.

Brad doesn't distract me as I do my reps, but he's there in the periphery, making quiet remarks like *booyah* and *you got this*. It's weirdly motivating, and I finish my lifts feeling more energized than when I began. Brad is there in an instant, his hand squeezing the side of my neck. My pulse takes off like a rocket, eyes dropping to Brad's lips and that infectious grin, but his grip doesn't linger.

"Yeah, man. That's how it's done!" he says, holding his hand in the air. "Give it to me hard."

Good grief.

Unable to deny him, I slap his palm.

"My Joey Kangaroo," he says happily, that ridiculous nickname I can't help but love. "Come on, let's do another two sets before we move on."

I nod, finding myself smiling right along with him. "Sounds good."

And the strange thing is—it really, really does.

Chapter 3
Brad

Joey's a boss.

The guy is strong. Way stronger than he's letting on, I'm sure of it. Pretty sure he could lift me clean above his head if he wanted.

I chuckle, my mind supplying the mental image of Joey lifting me up like Baby from *Dirty Dancing*.

I eye his biceps as he does some curls. We're winding down at the free weights now.

"Do you think I'd make a good Baby?" I ask him. "Like, the name, not the infant."

Joey gives me a look I'm not entirely sure how to decipher. "I guess," he says slowly. "Although I think it would depend on the person you're with."

I nod. That makes sense. "Think you'd be able to lift me?"

He blinks a couple times before setting down his equipment. "In what capacity?" he asks, voice quiet. "Like, against a wall?"

I purse my lips. "I mean, wouldn't really have the same effect as if I were on top of you, you know? But we could work on it."

Joey leans closer. "Are...are we talking about the same thing?"

I cock my head. *"Dirty—"*

"Hey, Brad."

I look over at the new voice, which belongs to one of my coworkers I rarely ever see, considering I'm rarely ever in the regional office. "Oh, hey, Suze. How's it going? This is Joey."

Suzy barely gives Joey a nod before refocusing on me. "I'm good. Haven't seen you in a while."

"Yeah," I say with a shrug. "You know how it goes. I work from home, so..."

She nods, a small smile on her face. "Sure. Hey, would you want to get drinks again sometime?"

My own smile feels a little brittle. "Still can't, sorry."

"Oh. Okay. Well, I guess I'll see you around?"

I nod, and Suzy walks off, frowning to herself.

"Ugh," I groan, taking a seat on the mat in front of the mirrors. "Hate that."

"What *was* that?" Joey asks, joining me on the floor.

"She works at the office," I tell him. "We went out once a while back. She's pretty and all, but it was one of those things where I knew it wasn't going to work out, so I was honest with her. Told her we couldn't go out again. Hate having to say no a second time."

Joey is quiet for a minute, so I get up and put my weights away. When I plunk back onto the mat, he asks, "Why didn't it work out?"

"Hm? Oh. She was rude to our waiter."

"You... You declined a second date with her because she was rude?" he asks. He doesn't sound miffed by that, more intrigued, maybe.

I shrug. "I mean, yeah, man. I know not everyone in the world is kind. But I get to decide what sort of people I let into my life, you know? I don't want to surround myself with negativity like that."

"Wow," he says quietly. "That's... Yeah, I like that a lot."

"Yeah?" I ask with a grin.

He nods, cheeks a little red from our workout.

I bump his shoulder with my own. "Glad you approve. Now help stretch me out?"

A little puff of air leaves his lips. I think he mutters a *fuck* as I roll onto my back, but maybe he's just worn out? Would make sense if he's coming off a cold.

"If you're too tired, we don't have to..."

"No, it's fine," he cuts in, popping up onto his knees. "What are we doing?"

"Hamstrings, man. They're tight."

He groans quietly, eyes slipping shut for a second as he nods. "Yep. Okay."

Poor guy seems a little off, but I'm not going to push him on it. If he says he's fine to keep going, I'll trust he knows his limits. Besides, it'll be quick, and he doesn't even have to do much. Then we can hydrate, smash some protein bars or something, and call it good.

"All right," I say, thrusting my leg into the air. "Have at it, man."

Joey blows out a slow breath as he eases into place near my ass. He presses against the back of my leg with his upper body and arms, not too hard, just right. I groan at the stretch.

"Fuck, yeah," I mutter. "Can really feel it, you know?"

Joey coughs out an affirmative. Once my first leg is stretched, he leans back, and I toss my other into the air.

"Do me again," I tell him.

He huffs a short laugh, sliding over a couple inches. "Christ, I can't tell if you're doing this on purpose."

I'm about to ask *doing what?* when he presses his weight onto my leg. "*Fuuuck.* Good. Yep. Right there."

"Jesus, Brad," he says, shaking his head a little.

"What?"

Joey's eyes dance with humor, voice dropping as he says, "You're just so fucking tight."

"I *know* it, man. You're telling me. Sorry I'm all sweaty, by the way. I'm getting you wet."

He huffs another laugh, his hand shifting down my thigh for a better hold. "I was already wet. And I don't mind."

"Guess that's what showers are for, huh?" I say, easing out a breath as he lets go of my leg. "Washes away all manner of sins."

Joey gives me a *look* as he stands up.

"I don't mean blood," I clarify, accepting his hand so he can pull me to my feet.

"I...didn't think you did."

"Okay, cool," I breathe, shaking out my limbs. "*Definitely* not into blood. So...showers?"

"Oh, God," he mumbles, sounding pained. "Yep. Let's do it."

Joey and I wipe down our area, grab our water bottles, and head into the locker room. His locker is in the same place as last time, right near mine. I grab my shower stuff and head into a stall. I can't help but hum a little as I wash up, feeling good after the workout. I swear I'd go a little stir-crazy without regular exercise. I love my job. *Love* it. But I can only sit for so long before I need to run a few laps. Or break a sweat in the gym.

At least now I have another gym-buddy apart from Cas. *Oh,* maybe I could get them to double-team me sometime.

Fuck, that'd be fun.

When I get out of the shower, Joey isn't done yet. I dry myself, get dressed, and wait for him out in the main part of the gym. I'm chomping down on a dark chocolate almond bar when he comes out, his hair wet enough for the strands to curl like tiny waves.

"Hey, man. Nuts?" I ask.

Joey blinks at the granola bar I offer him. "Can't, actually. I'm allergic to almonds."

"Oh, shit," I say, whirling around and chucking my half-finished bar into the nearest trash bin. I shove the packaged one in my bag before spinning toward Joey, my heart racing like I just sprinted a mile. His eyes are wide. "Don't get too close, dude. I'm contaminated."

His smile is a slow thing. "It's fine, Brad. I'd have to ingest them to have a reaction."

"Oh, okay. Phew," I puff out. "In that case, don't lick me and we should be good."

"I'll try to restrain myself," he says, sounding amused. "Uh, thanks. For today. This was a lot of fun."

"Yeah, man, it was awesome," I agree. "We should do it again sometime. You know, without the near-anaphylaxis."

The smile that crooks his lips has me feeling bubbly. "Definitely. I'll text you?"

"You better. Quick question before you go. Are you into hugs?"

"Um... Yes?"

With a wide grin, I swoop in and wrap Joey in my arms. I swear there's nothing like a hug between bros. And Joey? He's a great hugger. His arms are big, and he's warm. Plus, he smells nice, like pine or something. I breathe in happily and let out a sigh.

"Um," Joey says, voice soft. "Not that I'm complaining, but how long do these hugs normally last?"

"Another ten seconds at least," I tell him.

He squeezes me tighter.

When we finally part, Joey looks happy. Power of a good hug, I'm telling you.

"Don't forget to text," I remind him.

"I will. See you soon, Brad."

I send him a wink as I toss my bag over my shoulder. "Not if I see you first, Joey-roo."

He huffs a laugh, grabbing the door for me to walk through.

What a cool dude.

Instead of heading straight home, I make my way to Jason and Cas's place. It's not that far, actually, just a handful of blocks in the opposite direction of my own apartment. I don't bother knocking when I get there. I have a key, and they're expecting me, so I open the front door, drop my gym bag inside, and head for the couch at a jog.

"Oh, no. No, no, no," Jason says, trying to scramble out of the way.

He doesn't make it in time.

"Birdie!" I crow, jumping and smushing him into the couch cushions. I smack a kiss against his cheek as he groans.

"Gross," he complains, trying to push my face away. "Stop slobbering on me."

"I don't slobber."

"Then why am I wet?"

"Sounds like a *you* problem," I inform him. "Dude... Stop squirming. You're kneeing me in the balls."

"Then get off me, you giant sack of potatoes."

I let out a sigh. "*Fiiine.*"

I roll to the side, and Jason sits up, scrubbing both hands through his messy blonde hair. He mutters something about me falling in quicksand and finding my ultimate demise, but I spot Cas in the kitchen and hop up to head his way.

"Cat-man!"

"Hey," Cas says with his usual gentle smile. "Pizza sound okay tonight?"

"Uh...when have I ever said no to pizza?" I ask, stopping at the counter. "Ooh. Salami me."

Cas grabs a thin piece of salami and holds it my way. I snatch it with my teeth.

"Stop asking for my boyfriend's salami!" Jason shouts from the living room.

"Touchy," I mutter before raising my voice. "I'm not after your man's salami, Jason. I have my own."

"Don't need to hear about that," he calls back.

Cas shakes his head, layering toppings on the pizza.

"Oh!" I say for the both of them. "Guess what? I made a new friend."

"Yeah?" Cas asks. "Where'd you meet?"

"At the gym, believe it or not. His name's Joey. Super-nice dude."

Jason comes into the room, eyeing me as he grabs a drink from the fridge. "Super nice, huh?"

"Totally. But don't get jealous, Birdie. No one will ever replace you."

He narrows his eyes. *Aw*, poor guy. So jealous.

"He's new to town," I tell them, snagging another piece of salami. "I think he was glad to have someone to work out with, you know?"

"Uh-huh," Jason says. "And were you, by chance, doing that wink thing?"

I frown. "It's customary to wink at your gym-bros, Jason."

"It's...not," he says. "That's not a thing."

"It is," I reply, keeping my tone patient. Dude's not a gym-bro. He doesn't get it. "Just...trust me on this, okay?"

Jason merely shakes his head. "Bee, the one and only time I ever agreed to come to the gym with you, you winked at no less than five guys and two girls. Want to know how many of them checked out your ass? Five guys and two girls."

"What?" I say, shocked. "No way. Really? *No*. Wait... Do I have a nice ass?"

Jason rubs his forehead, looking pained. "I'm not answering that."

"Like you'd even know," I say, trying to glance behind me. *Fuck*, where's a mirror? "You only have eyes for your guy."

Jason gives Cas a smile that's so sweet I nearly swoon. My best bud. Such a sap these days.

"Hey, Cas. Do I have a banging ass?" I ask, spinning around.

Jason practically leaps in front of me. He tries to shove me out of the room, but I hold my ground. "I regret inviting you here," he grumbles, pushing at my shoulders.

"You don't," I shoot back.

"You have a perfectly nice ass," Cas says evenly, not even looking my way.

Jason growls, and I back up fast. I don't want to get bitten. *Again*.

"*Anyways*," I say loudly, skirting around Cas to grab the last few slices of salami. "Joey's cool. And he was *not* checking out my ass, thank you very much. At least, I don't think. And don't worry, Cat-man. He's not replacing you, either. I have plenty of room in my heart for more than one gym-bro. I'm polygymorous."

"That's...also not a thing," Jason says. "You know what? Never mind. I'll stay out of it. But don't be surprised if I send you a big fat *I told you so* in the future."

I reach around Cas to pat Jason's head. "Not everything is about sexual attraction, Birdie." As my ace friend should well know. "Joey's cool. Believe me. I'll make sure you guys meet."

Jason continues doing that narrow squint thing, but he finally nods, swatting my hand away when I try to pat his face.

My phone pings, and I pull it out of my pocket with a triumphant, "Aha! Here he is now." I grin as I read Joey's text.

Joey-roo: Would you want to grab dinner with me tomorrow?

"Dinner with my new bud," I mutter aloud. Jason shoots Cas a look, but I ignore my pessimistic bestie and type back.

Me: You bet! Want to pick me up, or should I meet you there?

Joey-roo: I'll pick you up, and we can walk, if that works?

Sure does. I send Joey my address.

Yep. This is going to be my year—I can feel it. My year to find myself. Maybe try something new.

And my new bud Joey? I think he's just the beginning.

Chapter 4

JOEY

I try to quell my nerves as I stand at Brad's door, but I can't quite manage it. I like the guy. Way more than I should for having hung out with him for all of an hour and a half. I want this date to go well.

Of course, we need to actually go *on* the date for that to happen.

With that in mind, I take a deep breath and knock. Brad already buzzed me up, so it only takes a moment for him to open his door. And when he does, my breath promptly leaves my lungs.

Brad is wearing a black shirt tonight, the dark color setting off his light eyes even more. His jeans fit him snugly in a way that has me fighting the urge to touch. And there's a beaming smile on his face because of course there is.

He's beautiful.

Brad steps into the hall to give me a hug. It doesn't last half a minute this time, but that's okay.

"Joey Kangaroo," he says happily as we part.

"Hi," I manage.

Brad locks his door and turns my way. "Ready to go?"

Fuck, I think so. I nod, and the two of us head down the hall.

"It's, uh, nice to see you," I say, rather belatedly.

"You, too, man. Where are we going?"

"A small steakhouse nearby. Is that all right?"

"Are you kidding me? I love meat in my mouth."

I stagger a step, honestly not sure whether or not he meant for that to sound so dirty. But considering he doesn't even chuckle, I'm leaning toward *not*. Christ.

"Did you, uh, have a nice night?" I ask since it's been less than a day since we saw each other last.

He nods, holding the door open for me. We step out onto the sidewalk as he says, "Yeah. I hung out with Jason and Cas."

I try not to cringe. "That isn't hard for you?"

"What?" he says, glancing over at me as we walk. "No. It's not like they live far."

"No, I just mean because you and Jason used to...you know."

I can't imagine hanging out with an ex is easy, but Brad doesn't seem all that bothered. Maybe he and Jason weren't that serious? Except they've been friends since kindergarten. And they *lived* together. I'm not sure I'd be as unaffected in his position.

"I mean, yeah," Brad says thoughtfully. "I do miss what Jason and I used to be, but I'm happy for him and Cas. Sometimes...we have to let the people we love most go, you know? If it's what's best for them."

Fuck.

"Do you still love him?" I ask. I can't not.

Brad's brows draw together. "Of course. I think I always will."

My throat feels thick as I check, "But you're not *in* love with him?"

Please, God, say no.

"What?" he says, almost alarmed. "Oh, no way, man. No."

My breath rushes out of me. "Okay," I mutter, ridiculously relieved. I should've known Brad wouldn't agree to go out with me if he was still hung up on someone else, but for a second, I'd imagined the worst.

Brad claps the side of my shoulder. "Thanks for looking out. Could you imagine?"

He chuckles, and I shake my head. *No, I can't.*

"Well, thank you for coming out with me tonight," I reply. "I'm glad you're here."

His smile is immediate. "Me, too. Besides, it's not like Jason and Cas want me over at their place all the time. I know I'm a lot to deal with."

I frown at that. "I don't think you're a lot. I think you're just right."

Brad stops right in the middle of the sidewalk, causing me to stumble to a stop myself. "Dude," he says. "I think that's the nicest thing anyone has ever said to me."

My cheeks flush under his guileless stare. But then Brad breaks into a wide grin again and nudges my arm to keep going.

"Thanks, Joey-roo. But just so you know, I won't hold it against you if you change your mind. We only just met."

"I won't change my mind," I tell him. Not possible. Who wouldn't want someone like Brad around, with his boundless enthusiasm and honest geniality? He's pure goodness, even if the things that come out of his mouth are, at times, laced with a ridiculous amount of innuendo. The guy makes me happy. How could I get sick of that?

"Fuck," he mutters almost to himself, stepping around some people on the sidewalk. "I'm really looking forward to that meat in my mouth."

I huff a laugh, glancing over at him. *Yep.* Guileless.

When Brad and I get to the steakhouse, I hold the door for him to walk through. He shoots me a smile as he steps across the threshold. From the way he glances around curiously, I'm guessing he's never been here before, even though it's relatively close to his place. I discovered it myself earlier this year when I came to talk to my Uncle Johnny about accepting a job. The steak truly is top-notch and the atmosphere cozy.

Brad beams when I let my hand graze the small of his back. He seems openly affectionate, which I love. My last boyfriend, over two years ago now, didn't like sharing physical touch in public. I honored that, of course, but I can't deny it'd be nice to hold Brad's hand. To maybe kiss his cheek or sit close, my arm around him as we sat on a bench or shared a meal.

I'm nearly lost in the fantasy when the hostess arrives. I give her my name, and she leads us to a table near the back corner of the restaurant. I pull out Brad's chair before taking my own.

He makes a quiet sound of approval. "This place is *nice*. If you'd told me it was so fancy, I would've dressed up."

"You look great," I tell him truthfully. "I like casual over fancy, anyway."

"Right?" he says, eyes wide. "Give me a pair of sweats and a couch any day, and I'm golden."

I nearly groan at the visual. Brad. Brad stretched out on a couch. Brad in a pair of gray sweats on said couch.

"That's the life," I agree weakly, looking over the menu. "Do you, uh, want something to drink?"

He hums. "Unless they have espresso, I think I'll stick with water. I'm not a big drinker."

"I don't think they have espresso here," I say, skimming the dessert section, "but we can always stop somewhere after if you want."

"Yeah? Cool. Oh, hello."

Brad sits back as our waiter arrives, the man setting down a candle between us. He lights it as he introduces himself. "Good evening. I'm Basil, your server for the night. Can I start you gentleman off with anything to drink?"

"Do you have espresso?" I check.

"We do not," Basil says.

"Then two waters, please. And a few more minutes with the menu?"

He nods before stepping back. I don't miss the upward bounce of his eyebrows as he tips his head discreetly in Brad's direction, though.

Pretty sure Basil and I are both in agreement that my date is hot as fuck.

As Basil walks off, Brad shakes his head. "So fancy," he mutters, a little smile on his face as he looks from the candle to the food options.

"Espresso this late wouldn't keep you up?" I ask, curious.

"Nah," he says with another shake of his head. "I'm a natural night owl. If I'm in bed before one, it's because I have company. *Ooh*, look, they have surf and turf. You're not allergic to shrimp, are you?"

"No," I say, my swallow more than a little rough. "Just almonds."

"Good. Shit, let me know if you wanna go halfsies on anything. It all looks amazing."

Good Lord, he's perfect.

We do end up getting the surf and turf. Plus the swordfish steak. And based on Brad's happy moans, I'm fairly positive I'm getting a pretty good preview into what those pre-one-o'clock bedtime activities sound like.

"Good?" I ask hoarsely.

He nods, chewing, his green eyes closing for a moment before they open again. "Good pick, Joey-roo. This place is awesome. Although you might have to tuck me into bed later. It's the least you can do after stuffing me so thoroughly, if you know what I mean."

He winks, and I cough, nearly spitting out my water.

Brad's face falls in sympathy. "Dude. Still sick?"

"No," I croak. "I'm fine." I frantically search for a different topic as I wipe my mouth with a napkin. Anything that's not me stuffing Brad. "Do you, uh...have any family around here?"

"Ah. No," he says, cutting into his steak again. "Never really had family other than my grandfather, but he's gone now. Pretty sure my parents are out there somewhere, but I never knew them, so..." He shrugs, and my chest squeezes tight.

"I'm sorry to hear that."

"Thanks, but Jason's been like family to me," he replies, which...*okay*. That's a little odd, but Brad goes on before I can think too hard on it. "How about you? Family?"

"Yeah, my mom is back in New Hampshire. The rest of my family is here. Aunts, uncles, a good handful of cousins. We weren't close growing up, but we're making up for lost time now."

"That's awesome, dude. I always wanted a big family. But...*eh*. We don't always get the things we want, do we?"

"I suppose not," I agree. His answer makes me wonder, though... "If you could have any one thing, like a wish without all the potential baggage and repercussions, what would it be?"

Brad's smile tips up, as if he likes that question. He doesn't have to consider it for long. "A good cuddle sesh."

His answer takes me so off guard, it's a moment before I can say anything at all. "Really?"

"Yeah, man. It's been a while for me, you know? I miss, just, like...touching someone. Holding."

Fu-u-uck.

How long would it take to custom-order a ring?

"How about you?" Brad asks, cutting the last of his swordfish into two pieces. "What would you wish for?"

I guess I don't have to think about it for long, either. "Happiness. That's what I want."

Brad's lips tip up again. "I like that. You're a good dude, Joey-roo."

"You're not so bad yourself."

His grin feels like all things right in the world.

When Basil comes back around with our bill, I pull out my card. Brad's eyebrows wing up.

"I can pay for myself," he offers.

"I got it," I tell him. "I invited you out, after all."

Brad doesn't fight me on it. He simply folds his napkin and nods. "Next one's on me, then."

I try to play it cool, but I'm pretty sure my smile betrays me. "Deal."

When Basil returns with my card, he gives me a knowing smirk. We thank him before leaving. Cheeky waiter aside, I don't think this night could have gone better.

It's a little cooler when we emerge onto the sidewalk, but it feels nice. I look for the nearest coffee place. "Still want that espresso fix?"

Brad visibly perks. "Yeah. Let's do it."

The coffee shop is just a block down the street. Brad breathes in deeply once we're inside, following it up with an audible sigh that has me chuckling.

"My favorite smell," he admits sheepishly.

"Tell me the truth," I tease. "Are you addicted?"

He cracks a smile that has me feeling warm. "Yeah, man. Bean stew. I can't go without it."

"Bean...stew?" I ask, mildly horrified.

Brad's eyebrow pops up. "Tell me I'm wrong."

The scary thing is...I can't.

Smile still on his face, Brad steps up to the counter and orders a double shot of espresso to go, plus...whipped cream? "Want anything?" he asks me.

I shake my head, watching as he pays and jokes with the barista, so naturally charismatic it's hard to look away. When he gets his to-go cup of espresso piled high with whip, he turns to me, nose crinkled in happiness.

"Ready?" he asks.

I nod. And nod again, charmed beyond words. Charmed by this man and his whipped cream and the easy yet confident way he walks through life. Charmed by his lack of propriety and how goddamn refreshing that is. Charmed, even, by the tiny cowlick at the back of his head.

I am so completely and utterly screwed.

It's not a long walk back to Brad's place. He waits to drink his dessert espresso until we're close, not wanting to burn his tongue, as he tells me. We keep up a steady stream of chatter on the way, the minutes passing far too quickly.

My pulse is racing by the time we reach Brad's hallway. He's talking about pants now, and how pants are a single item, yet so is a pair of pants, and *isn't that just the weirdest fucking thing?*

It is, and I never considered it before, but all my focus shifts to Brad's mouth as he sips his espresso, a small bit of whipped cream staying behind on his lip. His smile goes crooked when he sees me staring.

"What, uh..."

His words trail off as I cradle his jaw, wiping the whipped cream off the corner of his mouth with my thumb. I linger a little longer than necessary, having a hard time pulling myself away. It takes me a good long second to realize Brad's eyes have gone wide. We're standing so close I can make out all the specks of color in his light green irises.

Fuck, they're gorgeous. *He's* gorgeous.

Brad swallows roughly. "Uh, Joey? This might be a strange question. And I could be way off base. But, uh...are you about to kiss me?"

"I was thinking about it," I admit, voice hoarse. Although I would have asked first.

"Oh," Brad says, letting out a single puff of air before stepping back, the move dislodging my grip. "Oh, shit. Joey... I think... *Fuck*, I think I made a mistake. *Please* don't hate me. Please, please don't. I didn't realize. I just..." He groans, and I shake my head, at a complete loss. "Jason was right."

"I don't understand," I say, my gut sinking somewhere down near the bottom of my shoes. "What's wrong?"

Brad cringes, his eyes sorrowful. "I'm *so* sorry, Joey. I really am. I... I'm straight."

Oh.

Ohhh.

Well, fuck.

Chapter 5
BRAD

Oh no.

Joey looks sad. I don't like seeing Joey sad.

"I'm sorry," I repeat, feeling gut-punched when Joey takes a full step back.

"Not your fault," he says roughly, his eyes downcast as he scrubs a hand through his hair. "I just assumed. But... Hold up, what about Jason?"

I'm thrown. "What about Jason?"

Joey's eyes meet mine again. "Your ex?"

"My... *Ohhh*. Jason and I were never together. Not like that. Platonic bros only."

He looks shaken, and I wish I could give the poor dude a hug. Probably not the best idea right now, though.

"So you're just friends?" he asks.

"Just," I confirm. "Like, super-close friends, but I swear our dicks have never touched. Well, there was that one time, but we were both clothed, and it was an accident. Honest."

He shakes his head a little, and my breath puffs out of me. "So tonight..." he says. "This wasn't a date to you?"

Oh, God.

"No," I say, even as I hate it. "I didn't mean to lead you on, Joey. I'm *so* sorry."

He huffs an almost pained laugh. "You didn't, though. That's the thing. I don't think I ever called it a date. I just…"

He groans, turning around, both hands on his head.

Fuck, it hurts.

"If I were into guys, you'd be my first choice," I tell him honestly.

He groans again.

"Not helping?" I ask.

He shakes his head.

I lean back against my door, my head thunking onto the wood. "*Fuuuck*. I'm sorry. This effing sucks. I was really into you, you know? In a nonsexual way," I rush to clarify. "Like, as friends. Gym-bros. And now I fucked it all up, didn't I? Was it the winking? I thought that was a thing. Jason said it's not a thing. *Fuck*."

Joey doesn't seem to know what to do with any of that, but at least he's facing me again, watching me in that steady way of his. My chest squeezes tight.

"I never meant to hurt you," I tell him seriously. "I'd take it back if I could."

"I wouldn't," he says, making my pulse jump. "I'll still be your friend, Brad."

I jolt upright. "You will?"

"Yeah," he says, even as he shakes his head again. "You're a nice guy. And… I could use a friend here. If it wouldn't weird you out."

"Why would it?" I ask, genuinely confused.

"Because I'm a gay man? And clearly attracted to you?"

Oh.

Kinda flattering, actually. But what about Joey?

"Would it weird *you* out?" I ask.

"No," he says, and that's it.

"Well, I mean… I don't care that you're gay, dude. Jason's queer. Pansexual, specifically. And demi. He liked this one guy back in high school? And this girl in college, but nothing happened with either. And then he met Cas, who's a dude, and that was it, you know? He's all about the D now. Although I think he likes Cas's ass, too, considering the things I've heard through the wall. You would not *believe*—"

"Brad," Joey says, huffing a laugh. And, *fuck*, there's his smile. "I get it. It doesn't bother you that I'm gay."

"Not at all. So…friends?"

Joey blows out a tiny breath. "Friends."

"Hug on it?" I offer before reconsidering. "Or…shit. Shake on it? Foot five?"

He blinks at me. "What's a foot five?"

"Like, you just hold out your foot…like this…" He watches my demonstration but doesn't put his own foot out in return. That's fine. "And then you just kinda *tap*. Right? Like a little side foot five."

He looks as if he's battling laughter. "Don't change, Brad. We can hug on it if you want."

"You sure?"

"Positive."

Relieved, I pull Joey in. He's not that much taller than my six feet, so it's a good fit. Like last time, his arms swamp me, and I let out a breath at the welcome squeeze. I think Joey might be a better hugger than any of my past girlfriends. Which, nothing against them, but their arms were much smaller. And with the exception of Jane, who was wicked strong and, honestly, scared me a bit, they all liked being the ones who were swamped in *my* arms.

I like being on this side of things. Being the smaller one for a change. Feels nice.

Secure.

"You have to tell me if I do anything that makes you uncomfortable," I tell him. "I don't want things to get weird."

His laugh passes near my ear, those thick arms giving me another squeeze. "Same."

"Dude. There's literally nothing you could do that would make me uncomfortable. At least, I don't think. You're a good hugger, by the way. You're all warm, and you smell nice."

"I...smell nice?" he asks.

"Yeah. Would it be odd if I asked what soap you use? Actually, never mind. Matching scents might be a step too far, huh?"

He huffs a laugh. "This is a long hug."

"I *know*, man. It's great. Did you know if you hug someone for at least six seconds, your body releases endorphins that make you happy and calm? And the longer you go, the more endorphins you get. Kinda like sex, probably."

Joey grunts.

"So I figure if we hug for sixty seconds instead of six, we're getting, like, ten times the happiness."

"Makes sense."

Right? And if I can make Joey a little happier after everything that went down tonight, I'll feel better. He said it's not my fault, but *fuck*, I sure feel to blame. There has to be something I can do to make it up to him. He thought he was going on a date, only to strike out with a straight dude.

"*Joey*," I whisper. "I have the best idea."

"I'm...almost afraid to ask."

I lean back, placing my hands on his shoulders. "I'm going to help you find *the one*."

His mouth pops open.

"Yes!" I insist. "It's the least I can do. I'm gonna be your wingman, bro! Say yes."

"I...yes?"

"*Yesss*. You're not gonna regret this. Let's meet up tomorrow. Unless you're busy? I'll make a list. Yep. We've totally got this, dude. Tomorrow?"

"Uh, sure?"

"Okay, good." I give Joey a little shove. "Go home so it can be tomorrow. Wait. One more hug for the road?"

There's another laugh. "I think I'm good."

"Yeah, okay, man. Sleep tight! See you in the morning."

I shut my door on what I'm sure is Joey's excited face and grab a pad of paper. Pen in hand, I flop onto my couch and start a list. Joey's best attributes. Good first dates. Where to pick up guys.

My new bud isn't going to know what hit him.

"Are you a boob or an ass man?"

Joey coughs, his hand going to his chest as I sink into the booth across from him at the diner we agreed to meet at. I was so excited last night I barely slept a wink. "Uh, hey, Brad."

"Hey, my dude. So?"

He takes a long sip of his water before answering. "If those are my options, I guess ass."

I make a note on my pad of paper. "Top or bottom?"

"Jesus Christ," he mutters, cheeks flushing.

"Are you shy, man? It's okay if you are. But the more honestly you can answer, the better chances we have of finding your guy."

Joey looks like he doesn't know whether to laugh or smack his head against the table. Honestly, I'm used to that reaction.

But I'm committed to this. Joey deserves the best, and, like I told him, I'm going to make sure he gets it. Which means finding out everything there is to know about my new friend, including whether he's a *plunder* or *be plundered* kinda guy.

After taking a breath and looking around the fairly empty diner, Joey says, "It depends on the person I'm with."

"How so?" I ask, intrigued.

"I'm fairly versatile," he answers, fidgeting with the handle of his coffee mug. "But I've been in relationships where I've exclusively topped, and I've been in others where we didn't do anal at all. I like making my partner feel good, so, to some extent, I'm going to be into activities that complement whatever they're into."

"*Dude*. That's rad."

"Is it?" he asks, an eyebrow raised.

"Yeah. Your partners sound lucky. Do you like rimming?"

Joey spits out his sip of coffee. I cringe, handing over a few napkins. Luckily, a waitress takes that moment to approach. I ask for more coffee—a pot this time—as well as my own mug. Plus some hash browns with extra ketchup. She nods and walks off.

Joey's eyes meet mine from across the table. They're such nice eyes. So warm and inviting. "This truly doesn't bother you? Talking about gay sex?"

"No?" I say slowly. "People are people, man. Sex is sex. I guess I don't see why talking about other dudes' dicks and assholes should bother me when I have my own. *Singular* dick and asshole, obviously. I'm not, like, doubling up down there. *Whoa*, could you imagine?"

"I'm not even sure I understand what's happening right now," he mutters.

Our waitress returns with a pot of coffee, as well as a mug for me. "Hash browns will just be a minute," she says.

"Thanks," I tell her, pouring my coffee as she walks off. "Would it help if I shared, too? I've never been rimmed, but I love going down on girls."

Joey stares while I sip my caffeine. Perfectly black and oh so delicious.

"Should I expand on that?" I ask, setting down my mug.

"I think I'm good," he answers, crossing his arms on top of the table. "Yes, I like rimming. Both ways."

I make a note. "Do you want kids?"

His lips twitch. "From rimming to kids?"

"We're starting with the big stuff, dude."

He shakes his head, but he's smiling. "I think I maybe would. But only if I end up with someone who feels the same. It's not a deal-breaker for me either way."

I nod, marking that down.

"What's next?" he asks.

I look up at him with a grin. "Balls. How do you like them?"

Joey covers his face. I *think* he's laughing, considering the shake of his shoulders, but on the off chance he's crying instead, I push a few more napkins his way. When he drops his hands, there's a smile on his face, and I breathe a sigh of relief.

"Christ, Brad. I'm really curious about the organization of this list. Uh...if we're talking about my own, I prefer to shave if I'm, you know, sexually active. If we're talking about my partner, it honestly doesn't matter to me what their manscaping habits are."

I nod. That tracks with what I know of Joey. He's pretty down to earth and easygoing. It doesn't surprise me that he's not picky about whether or not his guys have bush, nor does it surprise me that he keeps his own balls in trimmed condition. He's tidy like that.

"I shave," I inform him, in case he's curious.

"I'm well aware," he mumbles.

I nod, lost in thought. "In my experience, people seem to prefer having hairless balls in their mouth more. And since I like my balls being in mouths, it only makes sense to stay smooth. Better chances that way, you know?"

"Oh God," he whispers.

"Do you have a physical type?" I ask next, checking my list.

He blows out a breath, sitting back in his seat as our waitress arrives with my hash browns. I thank her again and dig in. I pause when I realize Joey is watching me.

"Baby frites?" I offer, pointing at my plate.

He shakes his head, biting his lip before saying, "I'm good."

"All right, man. So? Type?"

He blinks, eyes running slowly over me. "Good smile. Because it means he's nice. I like the roughness of stubble on my skin and someone who's sturdy enough where I don't have to be too gentle. Lately... I've had a thing for the color green."

I nod, writing those things down. *Smiley. Masculine. Green eyes.*

"Anything else?" I ask.

"The inside is more important to me," he says. "I want someone like... Well, someone like you."

"Dude," I say slowly, setting down my fork. "That's a super-nice compliment. Thank you."

Joey swallows, looking a little uncertain, so I reach across the table to give his arm a reassuring squeeze.

"We've totally got this, Joey-roo. I'm gonna find you the most wonderful guy. Just you wait and see."

He nods, letting out a soft huff of laughter when I flip to the next set of questions in my notepad. "How many pages do you have?"

"Six, I think? You have time?"

"Yeah," he says, a small smile on his face. "I have time."

"Awesome. Let's talk kinks."

Joey's chuckle is warm, like melted milk chocolate. It makes me feel warm, too, and my resolve to find Joey's person strengthens.

Maybe we met for a reason. Maybe *this* is what I'm supposed to do for my new friend. It's not like it's a hardship. I *want* to help Joey. It feels like a step in the right direction on this winding trail called life.

I flip to a familiar page in my notebook and jot that down.

Step two in Brad's Guide to Finding Himself and Falling in Love:

Do a good deed.

Heck yeah.

I'll be the best wingman Joey has ever had. Mark my words. By the time I'm through with him, he'll be head over heels in love.

Chapter 6

JOEY

"He's straight," I say, dropping my tool bag near Iggy's feet.

My cousin blinks at me slowly, not looking remotely awake enough for this conversation. *Hell*, neither am I. I've spent the last two nights tossing and turning, replaying every single interaction I've had with Brad, wondering how the fuck I could have gotten it so wrong.

My gaydar has never been this faulty.

Finally, Iggy sets down his thermos of coffee and braces a hand on the ladder beside him. "We're talking about Brad?"

I nod.

"The guy from the gym?"

Another nod.

"The one who gave you his number and told you to text?"

I cringe. "He was being friendly."

"That's...quite friendly," Iggy points out.

He's not wrong. The thing is... "I can't fault the guy, Iggy. He's... I don't know how to explain it. He's just *good*. He wanted to make a friend, and he doesn't even realize how half the stuff he says sounds. And *fuck*, I just like him, okay? I do, and I know it's a bad idea, but..."

"But?" Iggy prompts.

I groan. "I told him we could remain friends. And he's trying to set me up."

"The straight man you're crushing on is going to find you a date?" he says flatly.

"I *know*, okay?"

"Do you?" Iggy says, finally cracking a small smile. He laughs lightly, shaking his head. *I know the feeling.* "You realize this is going to blow up in your face, right? Like...the more time you spend with this guy—"

"I *know*," I repeat. "But he's just... He's just Brad."

"That literally means nothing to me."

I sit on an overturned bucket and drop my head into my hands, scrubbing my face. A second later, Iggy's palm lands on my shoulder.

"There, there," he says, patting me twice.

"I've never crushed on a straight guy before, Iggy. I thought I was smarter than this."

My cousin crouches down in front of me. We look a lot alike. Same dark brown hair and eyes. Same easy-to-maintain stubble. Even similar builds. "Are we positive he's straight?"

I let out a breath. "He says he is, which is all that matters."

My cousin thinks on that for a moment before nodding. "And you're determined to be his friend?"

I groan again. "Yes?"

Iggy shakes his head, standing back up. "Well, don't say I didn't warn you. But hey, who knows? Maybe Brad will find you the perfect guy."

He's the perfect guy. Except for the tiny little *teensy* matter of his sexuality. And the fact that, no matter my own feelings, Brad could never love someone like me.

I drop my head again. I'm so royally screwed.

After allowing myself another minute to wallow, I join Iggy and the rest of our small crew for the day. Hanging drywall is a decent distraction from my thoughts, but when my phone vibrates over and over in my pocket around noon, I have a sneaking suspicion I know exactly who's rapid-fire texting me. I make it all of five minutes before breaking and checking my messages.

Brad: Joseph-broseph, my man!

Brad: Are you busy tonight?

Brad: If so, clear your schedule.

Brad: You're going on a date.

Brad: You might want to shave your balls.

Brad: Unless you don't put out on the first date! Not trying to pressure you, dude. You do you.

Brad: Could you imagine being able to do yourself? I've heard some people can self-fellatio, but shit, man. I'm not that bendy. Are you that bendy?

Brad: You don't have to answer that.

Brad: Shaved balls or not, get excited. I think you're gonna like this guy!

Brad: I bought you lube.

I take a deep breath. Hold it. Let it out. Laugh a little. Then a lot. When my tears have dried up, I rub my aching chest.

100 percent screwed.

I must be a masochist. I didn't know this about myself, but I don't have any other explanation for why I'm meeting Brad outside a restaurant. For my date. With another man.

"Joey Kangaroo!" he calls. "You look banging!"

I don't have time to respond—or cry—before Brad is greeting me with a hug. It takes me a second to realize he's counting up from one.

"...five, six," he says, letting me go. "Are you ready to get wooed?"

"Is...that what's happening?" I ask, not actually having been given any details about my date tonight. Nor did I ask.

Ignorance is bliss and all.

Brad's face dips into something close to a frown. "Well, it better happen. Otherwise the guy doesn't deserve you."

Oof.

"Don't settle for less than you're worth, Joey-roo."

"Are, uh... Are you coming inside?" I ask around the lump in my throat.

Brad huffs a laugh. "No, man. I'll wait for you out here. Could you imagine? Me crashing your date? Oh! Here. Your lube."

I accept the sixteen-ounce bottle of lube Brad passes me, wondering if I'm dreaming. Or if, perhaps, this is a nightmare. "Um... Where am I supposed to put this?"

Brad frowns down at my pockets. None of them are big enough. He spins me around and pats my ass. "Huh."

Hallucinating, maybe?

"Okay, I'll hold on to it for you," he says. "Just text me if you need it."

"While I'm inside the restaurant?" I question. "On my date?"

Brad shrugs, like it's perfectly reasonable that I might need sixteen ounces of lube on my first date inside what appears to be a mom-and-pop Mediterranean restaurant.

"What, uh...what's this guy's name?" I ask, feeling slightly faint.

"Oh! Lewis. He's five-foot-eleven, a self-described twunk, and he's really excited to meet you. No green eyes, sorry about that. They're uncommon, did you know?"

I did.

"Where'd you find him?" I ask, my concern starting to grow. Honestly, I don't know why it took this long.

Brad waves me off. "It was easy. I just started a dating profile for you on three different sites, mined through about six dozen messages, and decided Lewis was the place to start. Do you know how many dick pics I got sent, dude? One was wearing a hat. The dick. Not the guy. Don't worry—it wasn't Lewis. Good luck!"

Brad shoves me toward the door, my thoughts stuck on the *many* dick pics he was apparently sent. In a single night. While trying to find me a date.

Was he analyzing which ones he thought would be best for me?

The idea is alarming. Oddly gratifying. More than a bit confusing.

The door to the restaurant jingles as I pass through. Belatedly, I realize I have no clue what Lewis looks like beyond *five-eleven twunk*. As it turns out, it's not difficult to spot him. He waves, a giant smile on his face. He clearly recognizes me. Which begs the question...

When did Brad get my picture?

I head Lewis's way, my mind racing a mile a minute. Admittedly, I don't have high hopes for this date, but I try my best to paste on a smile regardless. Lewis deserves me leaving everything else behind and making an effort tonight.

And, maybe, I deserve that, too.

"Hey," he says, standing as I approach. "Joe, right?"

"Joey, actually," I tell him, although it's not even close to the first time someone assumed Joey is a nickname, as opposed to my legal name. "Joe is fine, though. You're Lewis?"

He nods, his gaze raking over me as the both of us sit down. "Shit, you're even hotter in person."

"That so?" I ask carefully.

"Yeah. You could hardly see your face in your profile pic."

What in the hell did Brad post?

"I'm glad you agreed to meet," Lewis goes on. "It's so hard to find guys who are into the same thing as me."

I swallow, filled with equal parts dread and curiosity. Curiosity wins out in the end. "And, uh, what would that be?"

Lewis gives me a secretive grin. "Watersports."

Oh, God. Oh dear God.

When I leave the restaurant three and a half minutes later, Brad does a double take.

"Dude, you're done already?" he asks, eyes widening as I grab his arm. I lead him around the street corner, out of sight of anyone coming or going from the restaurant. In particular, Lewis.

"I told you I liked boating," I say, letting him go.

He nods. "Yeah?"

"Which, I assume, you put as enjoying 'watersports' in my profile?"

"Yeah?" he says again, slower.

I let out a breath, a small laugh escaping with it. "He wanted me to piss on him, Brad. You know...*watersports?*"

His eyes ping wide. "Oh, my god. Is that... Oh, no. I owe Belinda the biggest apology. *Dude*, I didn't realize." He cringes. "I take it you didn't want to piss on him?"

"No," I say plainly, huffing another laugh. "I did not."

Although the ridiculous thing is, if Brad asked me to piss on *him?* I'd probably agree. Hell, I might even be into it. Just the idea of him standing in the shower, water dripping down his back and ass stuck out as he waits for me to mark—

Nope. No, no. Shut it down.

"Damn," Brad says, sounding bummed. "That's too bad. Poor Lewis."

"Uh-huh," I mutter, scrubbing my face for what feels like the hundredth time today. "Poor Lewis."

"Oh, man, no," Brad says, stepping closer and rubbing my arms in a soothing manner. "Joey, we'll find you your guy. This was just the first attempt. A blank shot, if you will. Don't...don't worry. Next time, it won't be a dry run."

I let my arms drop. Brad is smiling at me encouragingly, and it's all I can do not to kiss him. Not to take his face in my hands and just...kiss him for every goddamn thing I'm worth.

Instead, I ask, "Can I see the picture you posted of me?"

"Sure," he says, pulling out his phone. He flips the screen my way after a minute of tapping.

The shot is taken from behind. I'm in the middle of a sumo squat, a barbell resting on my shoulders, my gym shorts clinging obscenely to my ass, and my thighs straining with the move.

Good grief. I suppose it could be worse. Somehow.

When I look up, Brad is still smiling at me.

"When did you take this?" I ask, although it must have been when we worked out together.

"The other day at the gym!" he answers. "Look at your form, man. Beautiful."

My heart thumps painfully.

"Hey, Brad? Think we could grab some dinner?"

Before I faint.

"Oh, sure, dude! Yeah, you're probably hungry. Sorry again about Lewis. The next one will be better, I promise. I'll switch that whole watersports thing to motorboating. No way to confuse that."

As Brad grabs my arm, leading me around the corner and in the opposite direction of the Mediterranean restaurant, I wonder what it is I'm doing. Iggy is right. This is bound to go badly for me. Yet I can't make myself stop.

Don't even want to.

"Thai?" Brad asks, stopping in front of a takeout place.

I nod in agreement, and he opens the door, waving me in with a grin. Brad and I order our food and get in my truck to head to his apartment. It's a little surreal stepping through his door, considering the last time I was here I was striking out with a straight man.

This time, I follow Brad inside. His place is neater than I expected it to be. Maybe it was a poor assumption on my part, but based on Brad's chaotic energy, I figured his home would reflect the same sort of mayhem. He does have a couple controllers out on the couch and more than one coffee mug sitting on the low table in front of it. But, otherwise, everything is clean and tidy.

Brad swings into his kitchen. "Drink?" he calls.

"Water?"

He returns with two bottles, our food hanging off his arm. Brad bypasses the dining table, so I follow him into the living room, taking a seat next to him on the couch.

"How'd you get into construction?" Brad asks, setting our drinks and food down on the coffee table. I have no clue what he ended up doing with the lube, but I'm afraid to ask.

"It's a Delgado family trade," I tell him, accepting the to-go container Brad passes me. He opens up his own before giving me an expectant look. "My dad and uncle co-owned the business before my dad passed. We never got on well, me and my dad. At least, not after he and my mom divorced. But...I always liked the idea of construction. Of working with my hands and building something from nothing. Always loved the smell of sawdust, too. It reminds me of my childhood, I guess. Or at least the good parts."

Brad nods before saying, softly, "Delgado. That's your last name?"

I nod, and he whispers it—"*Joey Delgado*"—like he's testing the syllables on his tongue. I shouldn't like that so much.

"And you?" I ask.

"Bradley," he answers before taking another bite of his food.

I pause, my fork halfway to my mouth. I set it back down. "Your name...is Brad Bradley?"

His head bobs in a nod.

Oh, good Lord.

I have to ask... "And your middle name?"

"Ulysses," he answers, easy as pie.

I take a slow breath. Expel it. Hold back my laugh. "Your full name is Brad Ulysses Bradley?"

"Sure is," he says, shooting me a grin. "What's your middle name?"

"Francis," I tell him.

He hums. "I like Joey-roo better."

Clearing my throat, I say, "You realize when you call me that, you're basically calling me a baby kangaroo-roo?"

Brad pauses, considering that, before a smile splits his face. "*Dude.* That's awesome."

I huff a laugh and pick my fork up again. "Whatever you think, bub."

His eyes widen to a ridiculous degree. "B-U-B. Bub. Holy crap! I never realized." He lets out a small laugh, sounding so pleased my chest warms. "That's pretty perfect, isn't it?"

"It is," I agree, trying not to think too hard about why the endearment felt so good to say. Nor why this right here feels like an infinitely better date than my brief meeting with Lewis, even though this isn't a date at all.

No, I don't linger on any of that. I enjoy my dinner beside Brad Ulysses Bradley, and when he asks me to tell him more about construction, it's all too easy to let the hours while away.

Chapter 7
BRAD

"On a scale from one to ten, how sexy is a 'stache? Seven? Eight?"

Jason looks up from his lunch slowly, blinking at me.

"No? Okay, is it more or less sexy than..." I check my notes. "A 'dick guaranteed to rearrange your guts.'" I grimace. "Yikes. Do people like that?"

"Are you reading porn bios?" my friend asks. "Please, *please* say yes." After a second, he adds, "Although I'd have questions either way."

"It's not porn. I'm trying to find the perfect guy for Joey," I explain patiently. I swear, sometimes it takes a minute for Jason to catch up.

"And Joey's perfect guy either has a mustache or a mega-dick?" he questions.

"Ugh," I groan. "You're right. Neither is good enough. Guess I'm back to square one."

Jason shovels a bite of salad into his mouth, the hospital cafeteria bustling around us. His nursing schedule can be a bit chaotic, so I'm lucky he had time for an actual lunch break with his bestie—aka me—today. I'm not too proud a wing-man to accept help from an outside source.

Especially when said source has more hands-on experience with dick than me. Jason's tally might only be two, but that's still one more than I've handled. My one, obviously, being my own.

"You really like him, huh?" Jason asks, pulling me from my phallus-centered thoughts.

"Uh, *yeah*. I already told you that. He's my Joey Kangaroo."

"Mhm," he hums. "And what does this kangaroo look like?"

I sit back against the hard plastic of my chair as I pull up the mental image of Joey from our gym sesh last night. He was wearing shorts like usual, the blue ones, not the gray. And even though we struck out earlier in the week with Lewis, he seemed in good spirits.

"He's like... If niceness were a man," I say. "His eyes are warm like brownies. And he's all muscly in a kinda soft way? Like a loaf of challah. Add some chocolate sprinkles on top for his hair, and there you have it."

"Sounds...edible," Jason mumbles.

"Do you think I should add that to his bio?"

Jason drops his head into his hands with a groan. "*Ithinkyoushouldbitehim.*"

"What?"

He lets his palms hit the table. "Did you seriously make him a dating profile? Is that what this is?"

"Yes?" I say slowly. "What else am I supposed to do? Walk around with a sign that says 'Me and dude-friend looking for some guy love'?"

"Don't do that," Jason says quickly. "Why not try, I don't know... A gay bar?"

"Huh," I say. "I hadn't thought of that. That'd be fun. Queer dudes know how to dance."

Jason appears to be biting his tongue.

"You all right?" I ask.

He nods.

"Your face is a little red," I point out.

"I'm just wondering how honest I should be," Jason says. "I said I'd stay out of it, but it's *hard*."

"Hard," I say with a chuckle.

"Je-sus," Jason groans, sliding his lunch tray to the side. He crosses his arms on top of the table, looking serious. That face has me sitting a little taller in my own seat. "Okay, here's the thing. You've always known you like girls, right?"

"Yeah?"

"Right. But have you ever...*tried* looking at a guy that way?"

"What way?" I ask. "Like, imagining them with boobs?"

Jason blinks. "No. Like imagining a guy. With *you*."

"Doing what with me?"

His eyes narrow. "Are you being purposefully obtuse? *With* you, with you, Bee. I dunno. Going down on you, maybe? Or you fucking them?"

I consider that for a moment. Joey is the first guy that pops into my head, but a flash of him down on his knees feels so wrong, it immediately pops back out again. I shouldn't be thinking of my friend like that. It's not right.

I try a different guy instead. Some random dude sitting at a table a little ways away. I mentally rearrange him, bending him over the surface. Pushing his scrubs out of the way? Wondering if his thighs are hairy or a little on the smoother side, like Joey's.

Shit.

I try again, focusing on the rando, trying to imagine myself with him. I just...can't.

I shake my head. "You know I'd have no problem being into guys, Birdie. I'm just...not."

He looks at me for the longest moment before nodding. "Fair enough. So what's your plan for Joey's next date?"

"Boudoir photoshoot."

Jason chokes on air. "What?" he squeaks.

"You know, like a fun little sexy meet-cute for him and his date," I say with a grin. "I already booked the couple's session."

"Does Joey know?" he asks.

"Not yet. I can't wait to see his face."

"Good God," Jason mutters, standing. "I have to get back to work, but do me a favor? Would you just...keep an open mind?"

I always keep an open mind, but I nod regardless. "Yeah, man. See you soon."

Jason gives my shoulder a squeeze—which basically translates to a hug coming from him—and heads off. I collect my things and do the same. I have some work to finish. And then?

Then I have a date to pick.

"Where are we?" Joey asks, looking around the front section of the shop I lead him into. It appears to be a waiting room, which makes sense. They probably have the boudoir sets in a private area in back.

"We're at your next date," I tell him.

"Yeah," he says slowly. "I got that. But...what is this?"

"Question. Did you shave your balls?"

Joey blinks at me.

"Hello," comes a voice from the back. A second later, a woman steps out through a pair of dark curtains, giving us a smile. "Hi there. I'm Gianna. Are you two my next session?"

"He is," I tell her, giving Joey a tiny shove forward. "The second will be here any minute."

Gianna looks Joey up and down as Joey glances back at me, eyes wide. "What is this?" he whispers frantically.

I just give him a grin. "You're gonna *love* it. Trust me."

He doesn't look sure, but my phone pings, so I step away as Gianna leads Joey over to a check-in counter. My stomach sinks when I see the message from Joey's date.

He has to bail.

Fucking fuck.

I message the guy back quickly, but it's a no-go. Something about waiting in line for concert tickets?

I curse a couple dozen times inside my head before blowing out a breath. No, this is fine. The photoshoot is already paid for, and we're here, so I'll just...do it myself. No big deal. Joey will still have fun. And I'll make sure to personally vet his next date before approving him for my Joey-roo. Anyone who can so casually leave him hanging isn't worth our time.

Decision made, I slip my phone into my pocket and turn around. Joey and Gianna are gone, so I wait. It only takes a moment for Gianna to return. She gives me an expectant look.

"So, *slight* change of plans," I tell her. "Looks like I'll be the second person after all."

Gianna smiles, waving me toward the counter. "Wonderful. If you don't mind me saying so, you two would make a lovely couple."

"We would, wouldn't we?" I agree with a wistful sigh.

If only.

Gianna has me sign a waiver, and then she leads me back through the curtains to a dressing room, where a few garment bags are hanging in front of a mirror. "You have a couple outfit options. There are pictures with each so you can see how everything is worn. Just let me know if you have questions. I'm happy to help."

"Sure," I say, eyes going a little wide as I look at the pictures attached to each bag.

Gianna leaves me to it, closing the curtain behind me. Tentatively, I unzip one of the garment bags, taking in the complicated set of belts and straps that appear to be a stand-in for actual clothes.

Thank fuck I shaved my balls.

It takes a good few minutes, but I finally get my outfit in place. It reminds me of a vintage fifties look, like what a man might have worn under his suit back in the day. Leather straps run from a belt around my waist to garters at my thighs. Smaller straps lead down to the high, fancy, herringbone socks I'm wearing. My briefs are ridiculously short, leaving my upper legs bare. And I'm shirtless.

But I have a bow tie. That's something.

When I pop my head out of the curtain, Gianna gives me a smile. "Ready for the next step?"

The next step, as it turns out, is doing my hair. Gianna uses a combination of product and heat to set my hair in finger-waves. The whole effect really does make it look as if I fell out of the past.

Rad.

Gianna gives me a smile once done, meeting my eye in the mirror. "Ready to see your partner?"

Oh my God.

"Yes. Yep, show me."

Gianna leads me down the hall. When she slips another curtain to the side and waves me forward, I lock eyes with Joey.

He immediately starts coughing.

"*Dude*," I breathe, stepping forward. "Look at you."

Joey is wearing a ridiculously tiny set of briefs, same as me. But instead of complex garters, he has a simple band around each thigh and suspenders that run over his shoulders. I'm so caught up in our coordinating outfits, I don't realize at first how wide Joey's eyes have gotten.

Right.

"Ah," I say as gently as possible. "So, um. Turns out your date couldn't make it. Sorry, man."

I wince apologetically, but Joey only shakes his head, his mouth open.

"So, I figured I'd step in?" I go on. "Didn't want to leave you hanging, J-roo."

"Brad," he says hoarsely.

And *fuck*, he's upset, isn't he? Of course he is.

"I know, but it's okay," I say, heading over and sitting on the chaise beside him. "We're not going to give up. So we had another strike. That's only two. Next time, your bat is definitely going to make contact with some balls."

Joey starts rubbing his face.

"At least you look awesome," I tell him, giving his thigh a few slaps. "I mean, *Christ*. Look at these gams. You should be proud, man."

Joey drops his hands, his cheeks a little red as he meets my eye. I stop patting his thigh and give him an encouraging smile, but he only blinks at me.

My gut drops. He's still not happy.

"If you don't want to do this, we can call it off," I tell him, keeping my voice low. Gianna has graciously been giving us some space, setting up her photography equipment in the corner of the room while we talk. I'm sure she'd understand if we had to bail. She's already been paid for her time, either way.

Joey lets out a breath. "It truly wouldn't bother you?" he asks. "To be put in compromising positions with me in nothing but your underwear?"

"First, it's not *my* underwear," I note, even though I know that's far beside the point. "But, *dude*, like I told you before, there's literally nothing you could do that would make me uncomfortable. So no, it wouldn't bother me. Why would it? You're my...my Joey-roo."

He seems to come to some sort of conclusion because he nods and licks his lips. "Yeah, all right. Let's do it."

"*Yesss*," I hiss, holding up my hand. Joey gives my palm a quiet slap.

"You boys ready?" Gianna asks.

"Yep," I say happily. "Let's take some classy-ass sexy photos."

Joey huffs a laugh beside me, and I can't help but beam.

This will be a first for me. I've never been professionally photographed, but who better to do it with than my new bro? It's good to try new things. How can you know whether or not you'll end up loving something unless you try?

I think, maybe, that should be a focus on this journey of mine. Self-discovery starts with, well, *discovery*, after all.

I don't have my notepad, but I make a mental note.

Step three in Brad's Guide to Finding Himself and Falling in Love:

Try something unexpected.

Yeah. This is going to be great. I can feel it.

Chapter 8

JOEY

I'm not in the habit of trying to seduce straight men.

There's a difference between helping someone who's curious to explore their sexuality and outright disrespecting a person's spoken truth.

But Brad has given me the green light to touch him during a goddamn boudoir photoshoot while we're in our underwear, and I'm not going to pass up that chance. If nothing comes of it, that'll be that, and I'll find a way to get rid of this kernel of hope I've held on to when it comes to Brad.

But while I have the opportunity, I'm going to do everything in my power to make him see me in a different light.

It might be fruitless. It might not lead to anything changing.

But what if?

I have to try.

Brad has a grin on his face as Gianna positions him atop the chaise. He looks...stunning. Drop-dead gorgeous. Like everything I want and thought, however briefly, I might be able to have.

It doesn't escape my notice that, in the beginning, when I thought Brad was flirting and being overly forward, I wished he would slow down enough that I could get to know him before intimacy came into play.

Now? It's all I can do not to kiss my way up that bare stomach of his. *Fuck*, he has an outie. The cutest little outie belly button I've ever seen on the most wickedly beautiful man.

I'm doomed.

"All right," Gianna says, giving me a little tug. "Right here, sweetie."

I go where our photographer tells me, sitting beside Brad's legs. He's on his back on the chaise, an arm behind his head, his other along the low back of the chair. One leg is out straight, the second bent. Gianna brings my hand to his bent knee, and everything in my core draws tight.

"You'll stay here," she tells me. "And look at your companion as if you want to eat him. Which shouldn't be hard."

Not in the least.

"Perfect," she says, stepping back. "Stay there, gentlemen. Smaller smile, please, Mr. Bradley."

Brad tempers his smile, his face twitching a few times until he seems to manage something that looks less like a manic grin. I flex my fingers against his skin, and his smile pops wide again.

Gianna huffs a small laugh, but she starts taking pictures. I can't look away from Brad. His briefs are the same rusty red color as my suspenders, his socks dark gray. The garters that run up and down his thighs are black leather. And his bow tie. I want to replace the material with my hand. Or, even better, my tongue.

"Dude," Brad says quietly. "Have you done this before?"

"No," I say thickly. "Why?"

"You're a natural. You look intense, man. Hold up. Let me just..." He clears his throat and closes his eyes, attempting to blank his face, but as soon as he opens his eyes again and looks at me, that smile returns. "Fuck, I suck at this," he says around a chuckle.

"I like your smile," I tell him, sliding my hand a little further up his thigh, fingers hooking in the garter straps.

He shivers, and my pulse takes off.

"You guys are doing great," Gianna assures us, coming in to move Brad's foot atop my thigh. I take in a centering breath as his legs spread wider with the movement. I want to grab hold of his garters and tug him onto my lap.

"Can you imagine doing this with a stranger?" Brad asks me. "I guess I can see why it'd be a good test, you know? To see whether or not you have chemistry."

"And us?" I ask, my fingers drifting over his skin.

He frowns slightly. "Well, we're not strangers," he says, this man who's known me for all of a few weeks. "So it makes sense that we're smashing this."

I huff a laugh as Gianna continues to move around us, taking pictures.

"I'll have you two switch now," she says, letting her camera hang around her neck. "Here."

I let go of Brad's leg as Gianna repositions us. This time, she has Brad kneel on the chaise, his legs braced a good foot apart. She has me go down to the floor.

My blood heats as I kneel in front of Brad, the position incredibly intimate with his cock so near to my face. Gianna sets my hands right where I want them: on either side of Brad's hips.

For once, he's not smiling. He's looking down at me with a small frown, the space between his eyebrows furrowed. He seems distracted as Gianna moves his arms, having him cross his hands behind his back, leaving him at my mercy.

I can't decide whether or not I want him to notice I'm half-hard.

Brad swallows as Gianna steps back, the shutter on her camera making a soft click. Neither of us speaks this time. I graze my thumbs along his hip bones, my gaze shifting down from his face to his chest. Down to his defined abdomen. To that little outie belly button and the way his briefs cover his cock. I inhale a soft breath, wanting so badly to lean forward. To nuzzle against him and run my nose along his cock. To shift his underwear to the side so I can take his balls into my mouth the way he likes.

I want to touch him. To taste. To swallow whole.

But I don't. I never would, not even close. Not unless he wanted me to.

Bringing my eyes upwards, I find Brad watching me, his mouth parted the tiniest bit. He doesn't break my gaze, isn't self-conscious about being appraised or seemingly bothered by said appraising being done by a man. He's open and un-abashed, and I don't know if I'll ever be able to add *curious* to the list, but I pray for it.

"Mr. Delgado," Gianna says softly, breaking through my thoughts. "Why don't you grab his wrists?"

Gladly.

I run my hands around Brad's hips to the curve of his ass, where his hands are resting. His skin is warm as I encircle his wrists, the move bringing me closer to his crotch. I can feel his pulse feathering beneath my thumb, the crack of his ass beneath the other.

If this were real, he'd already be naked. I'd hold him here as I showered him with affection. I'd take his cock into my mouth, let him thrust his hips, but I'd control the pace, not allowing him to come until he'd been edged for long enough that his orgasm would be crushing in its intensity. He'd shake and shiver in my arms, falling apart for me and me alone.

He'd smile when it was over. I know he would.

Brad's eyes slip down my body. I have no doubt he can see the erection tenting my briefs.

"Dude," he nearly whispers, eyes flicking to Gianna before coming back to me. "It's okay. Perfectly normal response."

I hum, letting my thumb stroke over the top of Brad's ass. His eyes widen.

"Okay, we'll move on now," Gianna says.

She has us do another few poses, each one having Brad and me connected in some way. He never once shies away, never flinches. The entire session is an exercise in restraint.

When our hour is nearly up, Gianna has me sit on the chaise, my feet touching the floor. She has Brad settle on my lap.

"Okay, Mr. Bradley, you're going to wrap your arms over his shoulders," Gianna says. "Yep. Like that. Have one hand splayed on his back. Yep. The other in his hair. There you go."

Gianna heads around behind me, and I close my eyes. Brad's soft breaths pass near my ear, and my fingers hold tight to his back. For a moment, I let myself enjoy the heat of him and the feel of his chest against my own. I let myself imagine, even, that the possession I feel in his grip is real.

Knowing this is it—my last chance—I slip one hand down to his ass and turn my lips against his neck. It's not so much a kiss as a press, but it's enough. I inhale him. Breathe him in. The scent of the pomade in his hair overwhelms his usual smell, but it's still there, a subtle note underneath it all.

His grip in my hair tightens, his chest rising against my own.

"You guys did wonderfully," Gianna says, her voice as good as glass shattering for the way it causes Brad to flinch away from me. He carefully steps off my lap, and I let him go. "You can go ahead and change back, and I'll get a flash drive ready for you to take home with you."

"Thanks," Brad says before giving me a small smile. "That was good, right? Kinda fun?"

"Yeah," I tell him, cataloguing every inch of him while he's still in front of me. Even though I know I'll have pictures to remind me, it won't be the same. "This was a really inventive date idea, bub. You did good."

He flushes with happiness, looking so lovely it physically hurts.

"Shall we?" I ask.

He nods, and we head out through the curtained doorway. I watch him slip inside his changing room before stepping into my own. As I unclip my suspenders and toss my briefs into the provided laundry bin, my mind stays on Brad. It's pathetic, really, the way I imprinted on him like a duckling. I don't know how to turn this infatuation off. How to stop *wanting*.

I told myself this would be it. That, after this, I'd let it go.

I don't know how.

Could it work, being friends with Brad? Could my feelings fade, given some time? Surely they would.

I hang on to that hope as I leave the dressing room, waiting for Brad in front of the sample photographs I first assumed were art on the walls.

A boudoir photoshoot.

Only Brad.

"Hey," he says, joining me, a grin on his face. His hair is still wavy and styled, quite the visual contrast to his t-shirt and jeans. "I can't wait to see our pics, man. I'm gonna hang one on my wall."

It takes a second for his words to compute. "You...want to hang a half-naked picture of us on your wall?"

"Yeah, why not? I've never had my picture taken professionally before. Feels like a big deal."

"What if someone sees it?" I ask.

He cocks his head. "And?"

"I mean...they'd probably assume we're together."

Would that not bother him?

Brad simply shrugs. "Sounds like a *them* problem if that's an issue."

I can't formulate a single response before Gianna sweeps through the curtain. "Here we go, fellas," she says brightly, holding out a thumb drive. "Your photos."

Brad accepts it with a thanks.

"I have to say," Gianna goes on, "you two were wonderful to work with. I think Mr. Delgado is lucky his date didn't show."

Brad shakes his head. "Nah, I'm the lucky one."

Ah, God.

"Thanks again," he says. "I know who to call if I ever need more pictures taken."

Gianna gives me a smile as she squeezes Brad's shoulder. "Maybe an anniversary session?"

I want to scream *he's straight!* Instead, I bite my tongue as Brad huffs a laugh.

"Maybe someday," is all he says, his face falling slightly. He recovers quickly, shooting me a smile. "Ready to go?"

"Yeah," I tell him, even though I want to know what that flicker of sadness was about. Is a long-term relationship something he wants? Something he's looking for?

We thank Gianna one more time before heading through the door.

"Hey, you doing anything tonight?" Brad asks, unlocking his car with the fob.

Don't do it. Fuck, don't you dare.

"Hanging out with you?" I propose.

His grin is swift, and it hits me with the force of a sledge-hammer. "Yeah, man! We can check out our photos. And then wanna play *Run, Run, Ricochet*? I think I found a glitch earlier, but I didn't have time to investigate it before I picked you up. We should probably get some dinner, too, huh?"

I nod weakly, getting into the passenger seat as Brad suggests different food options and gets us on the road. There's a smile on his face as he drives, chatting animatedly and glancing over at me every once in a while when it's safe to do so. But he's not looking at me any differently after having spent an hour nearly naked in my presence. There's no longing in his gaze or intentional innuendo in his tone when he mentions an Italian restaurant he likes with meatballs that are small enough for him to fit two in his mouth at a time. Or, as he calls it, *double balling*. He doesn't seem remotely affected by the fact that I was touching him in a way friends rarely ever do and looking at him with what I'm sure was unrestrained lust. I don't think he even noticed.

Nothing has changed. Not for him.

Which means, somehow, I have to find a way to let it go.

If only I knew how.

Chapter 9
BRAD

Why are they called cum gutters?

Sure, the muscles that lead down in a V toward the dick are like a big glaring arrow advertising the goods. But it's not like jizz actually comes from a guy's hips and travels down to their...

Wait.

Joey's abs flash back to mind, including the deep V that disappeared below the line of his briefs. If he—*or another dude*—were to jerk off and come all *over* his abs, the jizz would run down those muscles like—

A coughing fit disrupts my rather vivid imagination, ending in me nearly spitting my coffee all over the table. Luckily, I manage to swallow.

"You all right, Brad?" Marley asks from behind the register. I'm at Hyped, my go-to coffee shop to work at when I need a change of pace from my usual view, aka the inside of my apartment. Jason used to be a barista here before he became a full-time nurse. The entire place smells like bitter roast coffee. My favorite.

"I'm fine," I manage, the coughing starting to subside.

I was just picturing cum sliding down my friend's abs. No big deal. Nothing to see here.

"Need a top-off?" she asks.

"What?" I practically yell. "Nothing's coming off my...*top*."

Marley squints at me. "Coffee?" she says slowly.

Oh, good God.

"Right," I say, huffing a laugh. "Coffee would be great, thanks."

Marley has a bemused expression on her face as she comes around the counter, a carafe of deep brown heaven in hand. "Your fuel," she says mildly, filling my cup. "You sure you're good?"

"Have you ever had inappropriate thoughts about gutters?" I ask her.

Marley pauses, blinking at me. "Honestly? No. Can't say I have."

"Yeah," I say with a sigh. *Pretty sure there's something wrong with me.* "Thanks, Marley."

She gives me a nod before going back to work, and I check the time. *Shoot.* I'm going to be late.

I chug the rest of my coffee, wincing as it scalds my throat on the way down, and then I close out my many work applications and shut my laptop. Once my things are packed, I head out the door. I have to swing by my apartment first, not wanting to leave my expensive computer in a locker at the gym. Thankfully, I'm only two minutes late to meet Joey.

"Sorry," I heave, catching my breath after the short jog here. Joey is already positioned at a treadmill, another dude in the spot next to him. "Lemme change, and I'll join you."

"No rush," Joey says, giving me his usual warm smile.

The guy next to him eyes me up and down, as if he thinks I'm considering challenging him for the honorary best bud spot next to my Joe-bro. I mean, not that I didn't consider it for all of a second. But I'm not that petty.

I could take him, though.

I make quick work of changing into my workout clothes, unfortunately realizing partway through that I forgot to grab underwear. Not a big deal. The goods like to breathe, anyway.

When I get back out to the main part of the gym, Joey and the other guy are chatting. I hop up on the treadmill nearest, having to look past the stranger to see my friend. Joey cracks a smile when I wave.

"So what do you do?" Other Dude asks Joey.

"He's in construction," I answer, sending Joey a wink. "Knows his way around the ol' nuts and bolts. Really good at...screwing?"

That doesn't sound right.

"At least, I assume," I go on quickly. "I haven't experienced it firsthand yet, but I'm hoping one day Joey will show me his equipment."

Other Dude seems surprised, but he quickly turns his attention back to Joey, whose eyes are wider than normal. I frown, going over what I said.

"Actual construction?" Other Dude asks.

Joey huffs a laugh. "Yeah. With the tool belts and everything."

"Nice. I'm in finance," the guy says, as if he expects Joey to be impressed. Joey nods, but he doesn't look overly dazzled, and, for some reason, that makes me feel better.

I up my treadmill speed so I'm jogging at a nice clip. I'm hot after my rush to get here, so I grab my water bottle, chugging a bit before spraying some on my face to cool off. The water dripping down my neck feels like perfection, so I rub it back around to my nape, groaning a little.

When I look over, both men are staring at me.

"Needed to hydrate," I explain.

Joey looks a touch red. How long has he been warming up?

"Want me to do you?" I ask, holding up the water bottle.

He shakes his head. "I'm good," he practically croaks.

Shit, I hope he's not coming down with something again.

Other Dude looks between the two of us before refocusing on Joey. *Not like I wanted to give him my water anyway.*

"Have you been to the bar across the street?" he asks.

"Which one?" I cut in. There are several. "The whiskey bar? The dive? The gay bar with the sketchy-as-fuck back rooms? Not that I've been in the back rooms," I say, giving them a wink so they know I'm not bothered by those sorts of activities.

Joey lets out a slow breath, but Other Dude amps up his jogging speed, so I do the same. Not that it's a competition, but *shit*, a good race really gets the blood pumping.

"I haven't been," Joey answers, although I'm still not sure how he knows which bar the guy was talking about. "I'm new to town."

"Ah," the guy says. "You should check it out sometime."

Joey nods, but he doesn't commit. Is he worried about going alone?

"I can take you," I offer, giving him a beaming smile.

It's then Joey's gaze slips down my body. He trips, making a choking sound that has the other guy following his gaze, and *ah*. Yeah...

"Forgot my underwear," I tell them, realizing exactly where they're both looking. Chuckling, I add, "You know how it goes."

They continue staring.

Other Dude slows his treadmill after a moment, hands on either side of his machine. "I don't have a chance, do I?" he asks Joey.

Joey stops his own machine, looking almost apologetic, although I'm not sure why. "It's not... He's not..."

"It's fine," the guy says. "I get it. Have a good one."

Joey mumbles, "You, too," as the guy walks off.

I stop jogging, not having a clue what just happened, but Joey looks mildly distressed. "You okay?" I check.

He abandons his machine and plunks down on a bench nearby, so I do the same. His hair is the tiniest bit damp as he turns to me, and I have an urge to just...rub away his sweat. Which is weird. So I don't.

"Bub," Joey says quietly, the nickname lighting me up inside. It feels like ours. Like something that's just for him and me. "You do realize, as my wingman, you're supposed to *find* me dates, right? Not scare them off?"

My mouth drops open as it dawns on me what he's saying. "That dude was flirting?"

"He was flirting," Joey confirms.

"Oh my God," I whisper, looking around. The guy is long gone. "I didn't even realize! He wasn't very good at it."

Joey huffs a laugh. "Well, how could he compete when your dick was waving an enthusiastic hello?"

I snort. It was kinda like he was waving. "J-bae, my dude, any guy of yours is going to have to get used to my dick being around. So, clearly, he wasn't the one."

Joey blinks at me.

"We need a code!" I realize.

"A code?"

"For when a guy is flirting and you're interested. Should it be a word? A gesture?"

"I can think of so many words," Joey mumbles.

"What about 'green'? You know, like the stoplight system? Green means you're good to go."

Joey gives me an odd look. "Do you use the stoplight system often?"

"I mean... I drive, so yes?"

His lips twitch. "Sure. That works."

"Awesome. So now we just need to find a guy. Hey, wanna head to that gay bar after this? They have nachos, so we can get some grub and scope out future Mr. Delgados. Just...maybe avoid the back rooms, dude. They are *not* clean."

Joey rubs his temple. "Have you *actually* been in the back rooms?"

"Honest mistake," I tell him. "I thought there was candy."

He starts to laugh, quietly at first, and then a little harder. "God, Brad. Don't ever change."

My chest warms at the simple fact that Joey likes me for me. It's rare to find that. To find someone who accepts you for who you are. Who doesn't ask you to change. Doesn't even want you to.

"You're a good guy, Joey Francis Delgado," I tell him. "I'm glad you're my friend."

Joey drops his hand, looking at me for the longest moment. Those brownie-warm eyes are comforting, and I give him a small smile in return. His gaze slips to my mouth before skipping away.

Finally, Joey bumps his shoulder into mine. "Same goes for you, bub. You're quite possibly the best guy I know."

Well, shit.

"I kinda want to hug you right now," I admit. "But we're both a little sweaty. I mean, *I* wouldn't mind, but—"

Joey gives me a hug without hesitation, his massive arms wrapping around me tight. It's the absolute *best*, and I squeeze him back happily. I hear him chuckling as I count to six.

"Should we do something macho now to reassert our masculinity?" I tease as we lean apart.

"Please don't say de—"

"Deadlifts!" I cheer.

Joey groans, but he gives my shoulder a slap as he stands, which I take as enthusiastic assent.

When our workout is finished less than an hour later, we hit the showers. I don't even realize I'm mumbling Queen until I hear Joey hit a high note in the stall next to mine.

"Dude!" I gasp.

He laughs loudly before singing another line. I'm so impressed, it takes me a second to catch up, but then I'm singing along with him, the both of us going back and forth about *letting him go*. When Joey gets to *mamma mia*, I lose it.

Joey makes it out of the shower before me, already dressed and zipping up his bag as I emerge. "I'll wait up front," he says, heading around the corner of the lockers.

I get dressed, still sans underwear, and meet him near the glass doors a few minutes later, a grin on my face. "So are we slamming some nachos or what?" I ask, swinging my bag over my shoulder as Joey holds the door open for me. So polite. "And then we can find you some dick!"

The guy passing on the sidewalk looks over in alarm.

"Don't make it weird," I tell him. "No one likes homophobia."

He moves along swiftly.

Joey shakes his head, but there's a smile on his face as he lifts the hem of his shirt to wipe away the moisture that's already accumulated on his forehead. It's fucking hot today, so no wonder. Of course, the move reveals the sculpted planes of his stomach and the V muscles that, uh... That...

Um.

I nearly jump out of my skin when Joey says my name. "Brad?"

"I wasn't thinking about testing my theory!"

He looks alarmed by the volume of my voice. "What theory?"

"It's, uh, nothing. Gutters, though, they're useful, you know? The way they...function. You ready to go?"

He's still looking at me oddly. "Sure. Want to throw your bag in my truck?"

"Yeah, that'd be great," I tell him. Definitely don't want to drag my sweaty gym clothes to the bar. "This is gonna be awesome, Joey-roo. We'll find you a boomer in no time."

"A...boomer?" he says in some concern, the both of us heading toward the parking garage.

"Yeah, like a daddy kangaroo?"

"Brad." He huffs a laugh. "Are you telling me I should get a Daddy?"

I frown over at him. "I mean, I guess it doesn't have to be a dad specifically. I just mean a guy, you know? Don't worry," I say, waving a hand through the air. "Leave everything up to me. I guarantee you'll be giving me the green light before the night is over."

Joey's laugh feels like warm caramel on a cool vanilla sundae. *Oh.* I should definitely add that to his profile.

Yeah.

We've got this in the bag.

Chapter 10

JOEY

When I contemplated hitting a gay bar with Brad, countless scenarios entered my head. Having to watch Brad bend over a pool table. Having to watch him swallow down a hands-free blowjob shot in an attempt to be inclusive or some such nonsense. Having to explain to countless men, even, that the handsy guy I was with was, in fact, only my friend. And straight to boot.

Not once did I consider the fact that I'd have to watch Brad be hit on. Over and over again. And that he'd have no clue.

"No, man, my hammies are all right, but check out Joey," Brad says, slapping my leg hard enough for my cock to kick. "Can you imagine having these things around your neck?"

Oh, good grief.

"I don't know," the cute twink says, giving Brad a flirty smile. "You look like just the right size for me."

The blatant come-on flies right over Brad's head. He just smiles politely and says, "What a nice thing to say. Thanks."

"You guys together?" the twink asks, raising an eyebrow my way that seems to indicate he certainly wouldn't mind that.

"Not like that," Brad says, leaning closer and wrapping an arm around my shoulder. "Joey's just my dude. My bosom buddy. My baby kangaroo-roo."

"Your...baby kangaroo?" the guy asks, sounding appropriately confused.

Brad winces. "Yeah... Maybe don't call him that. It's mine."

My heart thumps, the traitor.

"Hey," Brad says at a whisper, his lips near my ear. "What are we thinking here? Green, yellow, red?"

The twink looks between the two of us before his eyes settle on Brad. "Are...you his Dom? Because I'd totally be into that."

Oh, Jesus.

"We're going to grab drinks," I say loudly, hooking my hand around Brad's arm and standing. He scrambles to keep up.

"Dude," Brad says on our way to the bar, "he didn't even appreciate your legs. I think that's a hard pass, don't you? I mean, what's his problem? You've got great legs."

I'm about to ask Brad to please stop bringing up my legs—not to mention scenarios in which he's between them—but I pause at the last second. When we arrive at the bar, I turn to him, my pulse feathering.

Don't do it. Don't you dare ask.

"Yeah?" I say, despite knowing better. "What else?"

Brad cocks his head, not looking remotely put off by me asking what else about my person he appreciates. "I mean, your everything, man. You give good hugs, and your eyes are warm and always nice. You're strong, so you could probably carry someone out of danger if need be. And, as I've heard from many, *many* guys tonight, you have a great ass. Which, *dude*, you do. Even I can admit that."

Am I having a heart attack?

"Plus," Brad goes on, utterly serious, "you make people happy, Joey. You're calm and patient and genuinely kind. You're flexible in your thinking, but not so much that you'd compromise your morals. And I'm not sure if you know this, but sometimes you smell like sawdust. Like those happy memories you mentioned from your childhood. I could see that becoming someone else's happy memory, too, you know? You're a catch. Inside and out. And someday, you're going to make the right guy very happy."

Holy fuck.

Just... Absolute fucking fuck.

"You smell like the ocean," I tell him hoarsely.

His face brightens. "Yeah, that's my body wash. Thought it was kind of nice. I've never been."

I nod, my throat tight. "It's, uh...another of my happy memories."

That smile of his softens. "You and your watersports."

I huff a pained laugh. "Hey, you want to get out of—"

"This stool taken?"

Brad grins over at the newcomer, giving me what I'm sure he thinks is a subtle prod. "Nope!" he says brightly. "You two go ahead and...converse or whatever. I need to use the bathroom anyway. Not for anything weird. Just...normal stuff."

I sigh as Brad walks off, not sure whether I should laugh or scream. "If you were hoping to talk to him instead of me, no hard feelings," I tell the guy.

He eases onto the stool next to me, a smile on his face. Admittedly, he *is* attractive in a suave sort of way, with his suit jacket and expertly styled hair. He looks confident, a trait I appreciate.

"Actually," he says, "I was trying to get your attention. Is it working?"

Yep, *definitely* confident. "Not sure yet," I tell him honestly. Because I know—I *know*—I can't fixate on the man currently in the bathroom doing not-weird stuff, but my heart is having a hard time listening to what my head knows.

That if I keep this up, I'm bound to get hurt.

"Fair enough," the guy says, looking, if anything, pleased by my answer. He probably likes a challenge. "Sit with me? I'll buy you a drink."

Deciding I have nothing to lose, I nod and take a seat.

"Alan," he says, holding out his hand.

"Joey."

He grips my palm longer than necessary before flagging down the bartender. "What'll you have, Joey?"

"Whiskey. Neat."

His smile is almost victorious. Smug, even. It's been a while since I've had someone so blatantly pursue me in this way. I can't help but wonder if he'd be just as dominant in every facet of his life or if he's the kind of person who needs to let go of the buttoned-up routine every once in a while. I try to imagine that. Try to let myself get lost in the fantasy of taking over, fucking him so hard and fast that he loses all composure. And I just...can't.

That would have done it for me before. Big time. But now, all I can see in my mind's eye is Brad's laugh and his smile and the ways the two of us could have fun. *That* fantasy is one that's all too easy to settle into, as impossible as the reality of it is.

And I don't think it's going away anytime soon.

"So, Joey," Alan says, sliding the drink the bartender poured my way. "What do you do?"

"I'm in construction," I tell him.

His eyes slip down my torso, appreciation there, but he doesn't have time to say anything more before a familiar body plops unceremoniously onto my lap. I look in surprise at Brad, who loops his arm over my shoulder with a grin.

"I'm back," he says.

"I can feel that," I reply.

He laughs. "No seats, man. Don't mind me."

Brad turns away as much as he can while sitting on my lap with his arm over my shoulder, and Alan gives me an unimpressed look. *Yeah*, no doubt he's not a fan of Brad's special brand of codependence.

I simply shrug. "If it's a problem, that's a problem."

Alan appraises me for a long moment before nodding and slipping off his seat. Brad catches him walking away and gives me a frown. "Oh no. No luck?"

"Nah," I tell him, wrapping an arm around Brad's waist. "But that's okay. I think I'm done here."

"You sure?" he says. "It's early still. I bet we could find some stud for you to sink your drill into. Get it? A *stud*?"

Brad's waggling eyebrows have me laughing, despite his terrible attempt at construction-related dirty humor.

"I'm sure," I say, tossing the rest of my whiskey back. "Besides, I had a thought."

"Yeah? What's that?"

It's a bad idea—the absolute worst, really. But knowing that doesn't stop me. "You mentioned wanting someone to cuddle with."

Brad goes still. "Are you proposing what I think you're proposing?"

"Cuddle sesh?" I offer.

His responding smile has me feeling things I have no right to. "*Dude*, you're not going to regret this," he says, slipping off my lap. "I'm such a good cuddler—you have no idea. You're going *down*."

I banish that mental image immediately. "You realize it's not a competition, right? We're on the same side?"

He *pfts* as we walk toward the door. "That's what you think. But just wait until you feel what my hands are capable of. I'll have you flat on your back in no time."

I swallow thickly.

Brad and I hop in my truck and drive the short way to his apartment. He keeps up a companionable stream of chatter on the way, talking about the forestscape he's designing for work and his other gym buddy Cas, who's helping coordinate a 5k charity run.

He never seems to run out of words, and I find myself hoarding every scrap of information he gives me. Even if I refuse to acknowledge to myself why that is.

Once we reach his place, Brad unlocks the door and flicks on the light. "Bed or couch?" he asks, slipping off his shoes and setting down his bag. "Bed has more room if you're good with it."

It doesn't have to mean anything.

"Bed," I answer, too weak to stop myself.

Brad nods and heads down the hall, and I follow like the lovesick puppy I am.

Just like the rest of his place, his room is not what I expected. The walls are a dark slate, nearly black, the curtains the same color. In contrast, his headboard and sheets are white, and his comforter is a serene gray. He flicks on a lamp, bathing the room in a gentle glow.

"I have trouble sleeping sometimes," he says, giving the curtains a little tug to make sure they're blocking out the streetlights. "This helps."

I assume he means the darkness. I get it. The whole effect makes me want to sink onto his bed and ignore the rest of the world for a while.

"So, uh," he goes on, turning to me with a grin. "Top or bottom?"

I bite the inside of my cheek.

"Or sides," he adds quickly. "I'm good any way."

I'm sure he is, but I rein in my wayward thoughts. "Whatever you prefer, bub."

His smile widens, and he jumps onto the bed. Literally jumps. The comforter gets skewed when he lands on it, but Brad doesn't seem to care. He settles on his side and waves me in.

I feel like the character in every horror movie who walks into the darkened cave when they know danger is lurking. There's a voice inside my head screaming, *"What are you doing? Don't go in there! Turn away! Run, you idiot!"*

Yet my feet carry me forward anyway, and my knees hit the bed. It feels almost unbearably intimate as I lie down opposite Brad, his piercing green eyes inches in front of me. He doesn't appear to have any reservations because he inches forward immediately, going low so his head fits tucked neatly underneath my chin. He wiggles his arm beneath my own so he can loop it around my back, his fingers settling near my nape as he lets out a happy hum. I feel like I can't take a big enough breath, my lungs refusing to cooperate, each hint of sea salt air I get off Brad making it harder to inhale fully.

He's everywhere. In my lungs, my arms, my head.

"Are you close with your mom?" Brad asks, his fingers stroking the back of my neck.

I hum roughly. "Yeah, she's great. My biggest worry in coming here was having to move away from her. But we talk all the time, and she was really supportive of me getting to know my relatives."

He nods against my chest. "Was your dad homophobic?"

It surprises me that he picked up on that. Although I'm not sure why, considering Brad has shown himself to be a good listener.

"He was," I say, rubbing Brad's back in slow strokes. It feels nice. Too nice. "He could tell I was gay before I came out, and he started trying to *man me up*, you know? But my mom wasn't having that. I was ten, eleven? They began arguing a lot, and, eventually, my mom filed for divorce and full custody. My dad never fought it. He packed up and moved back here."

Brad's fingers tighten against the back of my neck before loosening. "I like her already."

I huff a small laugh, the implication of that *already* pinging around in my mind, as if Brad is certain he'll meet my mother at some point.

I don't argue it.

"But the rest of your family is supportive," he says, connecting more dots.

"Yeah. My aunts and uncles and cousins, they've all been great. My Uncle Johnny made it very clear they didn't share my dad's beliefs when he offered me a job. I'm not...*glad* my dad died, of course. But I *am* glad to have the opportunity to know this side of my family."

"I get that," Brad says softly. "Sometimes I wonder about my parents. But they didn't want me. And they didn't want me to know them. So I haven't gone looking. I imagine, if things were different, I'd be happy to meet them, too."

Ah, God.

"Bub..."

"No, don't," he says, giving my neck a firmer squeeze. "I'm fine. My grandfather and me were never close, but he stepped up and raised me when there was no one else. And I'm grateful for that. Plus, I had Jason."

"Your Birdie."

I can hear the smile in his voice when he says, "Yeah. The Birdie to my Bee. You'll meet him at some point. He's kinda quiet, but it doesn't mean he doesn't like you. It just means he's thinking. Family isn't always given, you know? Sometimes it's earned. And I think that makes it all the more important. Choosing to love? I don't think there's anything greater than that."

I don't speak for the longest time. I can't.

"Jason's lucky to have you," I finally manage.

He lets out a small laugh. "He's a good dude. Not much of a cuddler, though. So this is nice. Thanks for being here, Joey-roo. I'm lucky, too."

I ease out a breath, realizing, at some point while we were talking, that we shifted positions. Brad is lying on top of me now, wrapped around me like a koala.

"Told you," he nearly whispers. "Got you on your back, didn't I?"

My chuckle shakes Brad, and he laughs with me. "You're good," I concede. "This, uh...this is what you wanted?"

He deflates with a happy sigh, even though he was already perfectly relaxed to begin with. "Yeah. This is perfect. Pretty sure I could fall asleep just like this."

Yeah. Pretty sure I could, too.

I never thought I'd fall into bed with a straight guy.

I can't seem to locate my regret.

Chapter 11

Brad

There's an art to endurance. To making yourself last. Sure, hydration and protection are important. They keep you safe. But if you want to cross that finish line in tip-top form, it's all about being *limber*.

"You, uh...really want those hamstrings stretched, huh?" Joey says, standing beside me as we prep for the 5k charity run.

"Yeah, man. Don't wanna cramp before the end."

"Sure, sure," he says, hands in the pockets of his hoodie. It's early still, but Joey's wearing sunglasses and running shorts, ready to go. Dude's prepared.

"Did you put on your sunscreen?" I check, standing upright and grabbing the mini-bottle of protection I stashed in the pocket of my shorts.

"I'm good," he says before huffing softly. "You couldn't have gotten lube that small?"

"Oh shit," I say in realization. "I left that in the alley."

Joey laughs, his cheeks doing that squish thing they do when he's happy. "Someone got a nice surprise."

"Heh. Guess so."

There's a crackle of a speaker a second before someone's voice carries over the crowd, announcing that the run is about to begin. I haven't spotted Cas yet, but I'm sure we'll catch him at some point.

I give Joey's arm a slap. "C'mon. Let's raise some money for kids."

Joey and I step toward the white starting line where everyone is congregated. I'm about to ask him if he wants to grab brunch after this, but as I open my mouth, he grabs the hem of his sweatshirt and tugs the material cleanly over his head.

I break into a sudden and rapid coughing fit instead.

Joey whips his head my way, concern etched across his features. "All right, bub?"

"You're... You, uh..."

Joey's shirt is cropped above his belly button. It almost looks like he took a pair of scissors to a regular tee, which may be the case. And with his sweatshirt now tied around his hips, all of his stomach muscles are on full display. Which...is fine. Not like that's a problem. A *distraction* maybe, for some people.

I look around, but no one seems to be paying Joey any mind. In fact, plenty of people are shirtless or in sports bras. Of course Joey's outfit is no big deal. Nothing at all to be concerned about.

So why is my heart racing so damn fast?

"Fine," I manage, giving myself a shake. Totally fine.

"If you're sure..."

"Yep!" I say cheerfully. "Ready to eat my butt?"

Joey's eyes flare wide.

"Shit, that wasn't right," I mutter. It only takes a second to click. "*Ah.* Ready to eat my dust?"

"Did you just combine that with the phrase 'kick my butt'?" Joey asks.

"Sure did."

He nods. "Yep, that tracks. Bring it, Bradley. You're going down."

I grin as the announcer starts the run, a bell chiming just after. Joey gives me a shove backwards before taking off, and I bark a laugh, chasing after him. I catch up quickly, and we settle into a good, swift jogging pace similar to our warm-ups at the gym. It's a nice morning, the sun not yet high enough for us to be baking.

"Think they'll have donuts at the end?" I ask.

Joey glances over at me. "Why would they?"

"I don't know. I thought that might be a thing."

"Have you done many 5ks where that was a thing?" he asks curiously.

"I've never actually finished a 5k."

He looks surprised by that. "Really? Why not? You've run that far before, haven't you?"

"Well, sure," I tell him. "But, you see... The first one I did, there was this restaurant advertising bacon breakfast sandwiches, and I got a little sidetracked."

Joey laughs.

"And then the one after that, this woman next to me fell and skinned her knee. And that was it, man. I had to bow out."

"Wait, why?"

"Blood," I explain. "Can't do blood."

I shiver just thinking about it.

"Huh," Joey says. "Well, when we get to the end of this one, you can find out if there are donuts."

"I hope there are, but if not, you're buying."

He shoots me a smile. "Deal."

Joey and I run in silence for a while. A good eighth of a mile, in fact.

"Do you want to get married?" I ask him.

Joey trips, eyes wide as he recovers and looks over at me. A few people move around us as I give Joey's shoulder a steadying hand.

"Geez, dude. You good?"

He nods, huffing as we settle back into our running pace. "Uh, crack in the ground," he mutters. "You mean that generally, don't you?"

How else would I mean it?

"Yeah, I figure it's a pretty important compatibility measure," I point out. "You said kids are flexible for you, but some people have pretty firm beliefs about marriage. Probably something your wingman should know."

Joey is quiet for a minute. I wave at a cute toddler in a stroller as we pass.

"I'd like to get married if it feels right," Joey finally says. "It's not a deal-breaker for me if the person I'm with doesn't want that, but... I guess I always hoped I'd walk down the aisle one day. For so long, someone like me wouldn't have been able to. And although every single person should have the same inherent rights as human beings, it doesn't change the fact that queer individuals face scrutiny every single day, simply for being who we are. I don't want to take for granted the effort we've gone through to be seen and accepted and be able to do something as simple as proclaim our love in front of others. And I want my partner to know I wouldn't ever take them for granted, either. So, yeah, I'd like to walk down that aisle. It'd mean a lot to me for so many reasons."

My chest feels tight as I take in the earnest expression on Joey's face. He's such a good guy—solid and sweet and immensely thoughtful—and he deserves to have that. To find someone who will share his dream.

"Joey," I say seriously, "don't settle, okay? We'll find someone to walk down that aisle with you."

His smile is soft. "How can you be so sure?"

I shrug before wiping the sweat off my forehead. "Because I'm determined. I promised I'd find you your guy, and there's no way your guy won't want to give you everything you deserve. He's out there; I know he is. I'll hook you up, J-dawg, even if it's the last thing I do."

Joey's lips twitch. "You're starting to sound like my pimp."

"Your marriage pimp!" I say with a snort. "Can that be my official title?"

"It'll go right on the certificate," he deadpans. "And J-dawg?"

I cringe. "Yeah, that one didn't land. Don't worry, Joey-roo. Won't happen again."

He chuckles. "Sometimes I wonder if you're even real."

A frown pulls at my lips, an uncomfortable sensation settling in my gut. "What do you mean?"

Joey squeezes my arm as the both of us swerve around a slow-moving jogger. "I don't mean it in a bad way, bub. It's good—believe me. You just..." He goes quiet for a moment before saying, "Most people put up walls, whether or not they intend to. But you're just *honest*. You're honest about who you are. It's a rare quality."

I chew on the inside of my lip, my feet rhythmically pounding the pavement. Joey's do the same beside me.

"I've never seen the point in pretending to be anyone but who I am," I tell him. "Maybe it's stupid, not protecting myself. I do get hurt sometimes. But if you spend your life building walls, you might miss out on the people who'd see you for who you are. I don't want to miss out on that."

I nearly stumble when Joey tugs me to a stop. He pulls me in for an unprompted hug, and my heart kicks, my chest feeling tight where we're pressed together.

My buddy Jason has never been big with physical affection. At least, not with me. And that's fine. It's not the way he's hardwired.

But Joey is different. He doesn't hesitate to give me hugs or a touch to let me know he cares. I've never really had that outside of the occasional girlfriend. And maybe it's because it's been a while since I've had one of those, but Joey's arms around me feel like the best sort of comfort.

I could get addicted to it if he let me.

He gives me another squeeze before letting go. "Like I said, you're a rare gem, bub. As for those assholes who'd hurt you? Let 'em try. I have a hammer, and I know how to use it."

"Whoa," I breathe. "Joey. Did you just threaten bodily harm for me?"

He chuckles, clasping my neck. "Seriously, don't stop being you, okay?"

I must be grinning like a fool because Joey shakes his head, looking fondly exasperated. Or maybe just fond. His shirt, I notice, is sticking to his chest now, sweat creating a damp spot on the fabric. My brain does a funny little blip when a bead of that sweat slips out from underneath the hem, the single drop rolling over the hills and valleys of Joey's stomach. It heads down, down, down, toward—

"Ready to keep going?" Joey asks.

"Yep!" I say much too loudly, practically jumping. We settle back into a swift jog, my heart rate elevated. But that's normal, right? Perfectly normal for cardio.

I frown a little.

"Did you know not all animals sweat?" I say. "Like dogs. They pant to cool down. Or air their crotch."

I catch Joey's raised eyebrow before refocusing ahead.

"Could you imagine if we were like dogs?" I go on, huffing a laugh. "If we just stopped wherever we were and spread 'em all willy-nilly? Just *whoop*, flat on our backs, whip out the goods. Really ventilate those shafts, you know?"

Oh, good God, what?

"Brad," Joey says, a chuckle in his tone as I wince. "Maybe not the best place to be discussing...shafts?"

"Right," I say quickly, looking around at the families we're passing. I clear my throat. "I wonder if kangaroos sweat."

"This kangaroo sure does," he says, confirming he's the absolute best.

I grin, but as soon as I look over at him again, my gaze slips down to his stomach, and I snap my head forward.

"Yeah," I cough out, wondering what it is about all that bare skin that—"*Oh.*"

I beeline toward a street vendor nearby.

"Brad?" Joey calls, his footsteps following me. "We'll have time for bacon sandwiches when we're done."

I shake my head, but I don't bother stopping to explain it's not bacon sammies I'm after. I'm too transfixed by the most magnificent thing.

I tug out my wallet as I stop in front of the vendor's stall. "The pink one," I tell them, still catching my breath.

They nod, plucking the item off the rack and handing it over. After they run my card, I turn around with a massive grin on my face.

Joey looks perplexed.

"Hold still," I tell him, stepping forward with the bright pink fanny pack in hand. I wrap it around his stomach, the click as it locks into place strangely satisfying. After adjusting the strap so it's snug, I step back and look him over. "Perfect."

Joey, I realize, is watching me with a strange expression, and my excitement starts to fade.

"You don't like it?"

"No, it's good," he says quickly, his eyes sweeping over my face. "I just... Thanks, bub. I love it."

My grin is back in full force. "You bet. Ready to finish this run?"

"Let's do it."

I stand back as Joey jogs off ahead of me, nodding to myself. Yeah, that's way better. Now his stomach isn't so...empty. Plus, the dude looks phenomenal in pink.

"Coming?" Joey calls, turning and jogging backwards.

I get my feet into gear.

It's not long before Joey and I reach the end point of the 5k. It wasn't a grueling run by any means, nor a competitive race, but attendants at a stand near the finish line cheer for the people crossing, and it makes me feel proud of our accomplishment.

"Water?" Joey asks, hands on his waist as he walks over to one of the tables where wax paper cups wait. He hands one over, and I have just enough time to down it before I hear my name called.

"*Brad.*"

I give Cas a big wave as he approaches. "Hey, man!"

"You guys just finish?" he asks, giving Joey a smile. Cas is a good dude that way. Always nice, always welcoming.

"Sure did," I tell him, squeezing Joey's somewhat sweaty shoulder. "Cas, this is my man, Joey Kangaroo. Joey, this is Cat-man."

"Nice to meet you," Joey says.

Cas shakes Joey's hand. "You, too. Thanks for coming out today. I appreciate you both helping with this fundraiser."

"Of course!" I tell him happily. "I got a lot of pledges from the people at my office. They were really enthusiastic, actually. I didn't realize my coworkers were so excited about charity."

"Did you ask for donations in person?" Joey asks, a small smile on his lips.

"Sure did. Why?"

His smile widens. "Bub... You realize you're incredibly charming, right?"

A warm sort of fizz sets off in my stomach. "You think I'm charming?" I ask, unable to hide my grin.

Joey shakes his head, looking amused. "Ridiculously so. I'm not surprised your coworkers couldn't say no to you."

"Huh," I say, weirdly happy that Joey thinks I'm charming. I've been called *too much* plenty of times. But charming? Not that. At least, not that I'm aware of. "You're not so bad yourself, my kanga-dude."

He gives me a cheek-crinkling smile.

"Well, thanks again," Cas says, drawing my attention his way. "If you guys are hungry, there's some fruit just over there."

"Aw, man," I mumble sadly. "No donuts?"

Cas looks confused. "No donuts, no. I need to take care of a few things, but it was nice to meet you, Joey. I like the fanny pack."

"Isn't it great?" I agree, slipping my finger under the band and giving it a little tug.

Joey makes a strangled sound, the muscles in his stomach tensing. I glance at his face, wondering why he seems so off, but he's focused on Cas. "Um. Nice to meet you, too," he says.

"See you soon?" Cas asks the both of us.

I let go of the fanny pack to hold up my hand. "Yeah, man. You know it."

Cas slaps my palm before heading off.

I sigh, eyeing the fruit. "I suppose we should get some sustenance?"

"Yeah, that's fine," Joey says, sounding distracted. Dude's probably just hungry. I get it.

Once we reach the snack table, Joey picks an apple, and I grab a banana.

"You're still buying me donuts," I remind him, peeling my fruit.

"Yep."

"I deserve some sugary carbs."

"Bananas are sugary ca—"

Joey cuts off into a round of choking, and I look at him in alarm, quickly finishing my bite.

"Dude, you all right?" I ask, stepping forward to slap his back.

"You just...you went for it, didn't you?" he says, voice hoarse.

It takes me a second to understand he's talking about my banana, half of which is now gone. "If they're really small, I can usually get them in one go," I tell him proudly. "But this one's a beast. Two-biter for sure."

He wheezes a little.

"You okay, man?" I ask in concern, rubbing his shoulder. "You look rough."

Joey nods tightly. "I'm good. Promise. This was, uh...a really nice morning."

"It was, wasn't it?" I agree. "Thanks for helping me finish my first 5k, Joey-roo."

His chuckle is soft. "My pleasure. But I'm pretty sure you did it all yourself."

"Maybe so. But you were there with me. And I'll always remember that."

Joey's expression is hard to make out behind his sunglasses, but the small smile that graces his face makes me feel like I did something right. "Ready to get those donuts?"

"*So* ready," I tell him, tossing my banana peel in the trash.

Maybe it was my feet that carried me across the finish line, but you can never discount the encouragement people give you along the way. And Joey? He's one of the most encouraging people I know. He makes me feel powerful, like I could do anything I set my mind to.

In fact...

Step four in Brad's Guide to Finding Himself and Falling in Love:

Accomplish a goal.

Done.

I ran my first 5k.

I wonder what else I could accomplish with Joey by my side.

Chapter 12

JOEY

I stare at the text that's ready to send to Brad, my nerves a jumbled mess. I don't know why I'm so tied in knots over what should be a simple invite to hang out.

Yes, you do know, my brain so helpfully replies.

I tell it to fuck off and hit send.

Me: Want to come to a BBQ at my aunt and uncle's this afternoon?

Brad's reply is almost immediate.

Bub: Yeah, man! I love BBQ. What should I wear?

I huff a laugh.

Me: Anything you want. Although you might want to bring your swimsuit. They have a pool.

Brad doesn't respond right away. Not for a long while, in fact. I'm starting to get concerned when my phone finally chimes.

Bub: Okay.

Just *okay*? That's odd.

Me: Want me to pick you up or send the address?

Bub: Come get me. That way, I'll feel fancy.

I snort.

Hold on...

Me: You're not going to ride in back and pretend I'm your chauffeur, are you?

Bub: No?

My smile is ridiculously big as I leave my house and head toward Brad's. His apartment is across town, but the trip passes quickly, even as my palms start to sweat. I tell my body to cut it out. This isn't a date. Brad is my friend. Period.

My friend, who I'm bringing to meet my family.

Shit.

When I pull up to the curb, Brad is waiting for me. He hops right in my truck, settling in the front passenger seat, thankfully not the back.

"Joey-broey," he says in greeting, smiling like always. "I'm so ready to choke on your meat, it's not even funny."

"What?" I cough out.

"Your family's barbecue," he says as if it's obvious. "I'm *starved*. You caught me before I had a chance to eat lunch."

"That's, uh, good," I manage, easing into traffic. "That you didn't eat yet, I mean."

Brad nods before mumble-singing something about meat on his tongue. It's distracting, to say the least.

My Aunt Margot and Uncle Johnny's place is nice, a two-story home in a suburban neighborhood with big, manicured lawns. I park on the side of the street before grabbing my bag from the back.

Brad unceremoniously thrusts his swim trunks at me. "Here. Put these in with yours. I don't want to meet your family while I'm holding my speedo."

"It's hardly a speedo," I note, even as I put it in my bag.

"Same diff," Brad says. "Feels weird, you know? I want to make a good first impression."

My pulse kicks, Brad's concern over meeting my family making me feel so many things I probably shouldn't be feeling for this man. "My family will love you, bub," I assure him. "You don't have to worry about that, all right?"

He sends me a grin, but there's a relieved edge underneath it. "Duh. Of course they will. Haven't you heard? I'm *charming*."

"Christ," I mutter, unable to stop my own grin. "You're going to let that go to your head, aren't you?"

"What? *Nooo*. Why would I do that? I'm a good boy, Joey."

Brad bats his eyelashes at me, and I have a hard time remembering why I can't simply...kiss him. Kiss him and never stop.

My voice is hoarse when I say, "Then be a good boy for me and get out of the truck."

Brad blinks, his mouth falling open. "Dude. Did you just use your sex voice on me?"

"What?" I squeak.

"That was...that was not your normal voice, man."

"I don't know what you're talking about," I lie, zipping up my bag.

He squints at me. "You're not getting sick again, are you?"

"Perfectly healthy."

Brad places the back of his hand on my forehead, apparently checking my temperature. Then he squeezes my bicep a couple times, for reasons entirely unknown.

"Fine," he relents, opening his door. "But if you get sick, I'm gonna wrestle you into bed and tie you down. And you'll take it. *Happily*. I can't have my baby roo feeling blue. Heh. That rhymed. You coming?"

Good fucking grief.

Swallowing down my "not anytime soon," I follow Brad out of the truck. I nearly reach for his hand and have to forcibly remind myself that's not what this is.

That Brad isn't...*mine*.

Brad is all smiles as we round the house toward the backyard. It looks like most of my family is already here. I see Johnny and Margot near the grill, Johnny manning the meat as Margot sips what looks like a margarita. Iggy is punching his brother Reggie on the arm. My cousin Sonia is lying on a pool float while her husband watches over their young kids. A couple of the other kids are running around a tree, trying to spray each other with squirt guns. And that's just the start of it.

"Whoa," Brad breathes. "Your family is *huge*."

"Okay?" I check, knowing he's not used to that sort of thing.

He nods, his smile genuine and bright.

Margot is the first to notice us. "Joey!" she calls warmly, walking over across the grass, her heels somehow managing not to sink into the earth. She's wearing a wrap-style dress over her swimsuit, and when she gives me a hug, she smells like coconut sunscreen. "So glad you could make it, honeybunch. Who's this handsome fella at your side?"

Brad beams.

"This is Brad," I tell her. "My...friend. Brad, my Aunt Margot."

Brad doesn't hesitate to give my aunt an enthusiastic hug that has her eyes going wide in delight. She wraps an arm around him with a smile, her drink held out to her side.

"So nice to meet you, Mrs. Delgado," Brad says politely, the two of them separating.

"Well aren't you sweet. But please, just call me Margot. Would you boys like drinks?"

I check in with Brad before giving my aunt a nod. "That'd be great, thanks."

"Of course. Come, come," she says, waving us back toward the grill. "Johnny, our Joey brought a *frieeend.*"

Oh boy.

My uncle gives us a grin, his eyes squinted against the sun and his grill tongs held in one hand. "That so? Handsome fella."

"That's what I said," Margot responds with a laugh, slapping her husband's shoulder.

Brad looks positively gleeful.

Oh boy.

"His name's Brad," my aunt adds, pouring premade margarita mix into two glasses.

"Well, it's nice to meet you, Brad," Johnny says, holding his free hand out to shake. "If you've got our Joey's approval, you've got mine. You like chicken?"

As my uncle pulls Brad over to the grill, Margot hands me a drink.

"He's just my friend," I whisper.

She tweaks my cheek. "Sure, hon."

I sigh, startling when someone careens into my back. At least I have a tight hold on my drink. "Iggy," I say in greeting.

My cousin pats my shoulder a couple times before stepping around in front of me. He has an eyebrow raised. "You brought your gym-bro?"

"Don't judge," I say, voice quiet as I cut a glance Brad's way. He's talking excitedly with my aunt and uncle, looking utterly at home. "I just... I can't quit him, Iggy. I don't want to."

His expression turns almost contemplative. "I'm not judging. I just don't want to see you get hurt is all. He's still..."

"Straight?" I fill in. "As far as I'm aware."

He nods, lips pursed. "Hmm. I don't suppose he knows you have feelings for him?"

I don't bother telling Iggy I *don't* have feelings because there's no point. I think the only person unaware is Brad himself. "He knows I was attracted to him," I say, which is true. Even if it doesn't quite answer his question.

And even if that attraction never went away. Not even close.

Iggy nods, but a sudden "Not near the grill!" from Margot has our attention shifting.

One of the kids is near the edge of the hot metal grill, using the side of it as cover for the ongoing water gun fight. Margot tries to shoo him away, but he stays put, doing his best to avoid the high-pressure blasts of water coming from his brother. Before anyone has a chance to herd the kids back toward the lawn, there's a battle cry, and Brad is leaping into the fray.

I watch in...not quite disbelief, really, but awe as Brad wields his own squirt gun he got from who-knows-where and runs after the kids. They both sprint away, trying to avoid Brad's blasts, and he chases after them, a huge grin on his face.

I shake my head, my chest feeling warm. Dangerously warm.

"Who's the hunky stranger threatening my children?" my cousin Alice asks, amusement lacing her tone.

"That's Joey's Brad," Iggy answers.

He steps away as I try to smack him.

"Nice catch," Alice says, sending me a wink before heading back inside.

I sigh. Again.

As Brad plays with the kids, helping keep them away from the grill, I bring out plates and utensils for our late lunch. Brad's shirt is soaked when he finally calls it quits, but his smile is wide and his light green eyes are positively sparkling.

"Did you see that?" he asks, a little out of breath. "Sonny was ruthless, but I totally won in the end. Not that we were keeping score or anything."

"Have a good time?" I ask, even though it's obvious he did.

"*Dude*. That was so much fun. I haven't played with water guns in...well, forever. Hey, where's my drink?"

As Brad heads off to retrieve his margarita, Sonny plops down at the long, bench-style table. He's soaked from head to toe.

"Your boyfriend's pretty cool," he says, helping himself to a handful of chips.

My pulse trips, but I don't have time to correct him before Uncle Johnny calls everyone to eat.

Lunch is a rowdy affair. I introduce Brad to the rest of my family. As my *friend*. I'm not sure anyone believes me, even though it's—*sadly*—the truth. Everyone, unsurprisingly, is smitten. Plates of potato salad and corn on the cob are passed as hands get messy with barbecue sauce. Most of the kids barely eat a thing before they're up and moving again, not wanting to waste a perfectly good day of play.

"No pool for thirty minutes," Sonia calls to the lot of them. She shakes her head gently before facing the table again. "So, Brad, what do you do?"

"Oh," he says, wiping his mouth with his napkin before giving my cousin a smile. "I'm a game level designer with a focus on world design for DreamWyld, a company that produces massively multiplayer online video games." When no one says anything, he adds, "I make virtual trees?"

"He helped create *Run, Run, Ricochet*," I fill in, still impressed by that fact.

"Seriously?" my cousin Reggie asks. "Did you make that creepy skeletal forest in level ten?"

"I did!" Brad says happily. "Gave me nightmares for months."

Most of my family chuckles, but based on Brad's shiver, I'm pretty sure he's serious.

I give his leg a squeeze, and his smile turns my way.

Dangerous, indeed.

Conversation shifts to construction, as it so often does in this family, and Brad gives me a nudge. "Pass the corn?"

I hand the plate over, and what transpires can only be described as one of the most erotic culinary experiences of my life. Brad rolls the corn over the butter dish, positively coating it before sucking his thumb into his mouth. He cleans the digit—*thoroughly*—while I squirm. Then, ever so slowly, he licks his way around one end of the corn cob, his tongue curling gently over the tip. I forget what my lungs are for. Finally, he takes a relatively normal bite, shooting me a scrunched-face smile when he sees me watching him.

"It was really wet," he informs me.

I'm well aware.

Brad goes back to eating his corn, periodically licking it, sometimes biting. At one point, he wraps his mouth around one end, collecting a few kernels there.

And I thought the banana was bad.

I cross my leg over my knee as Brad sucks butter and salt off his fingers. Out of the corner of my eye, I see Alice shooting me a thumbs-up.

Oh, for fuck's sake.

At least they're supportive.

I'm grateful when our meal ends, having had to watch Brad attack his barbecue chicken with the same relish. I'm honestly not sure how much more I could've taken. Luckily, Brad finishes up, wiping his hands on a napkin. He gives me a nudge once done.

"Bathroom?" he asks.

I nod. "Come on. I'll show you."

I grab my bag on our way into the house, and then I lead Brad down the hall to the first-floor restroom.

"Here," I say, passing his swim trunks over. "You can change now if you want."

"Oh," he says, sounding a little surprised by that. "I, uh... Sure. Don't we need to wait thirty minutes, though?"

I huff a laugh. "I'm pretty sure we'll be fine. I won't let you drown, bub."

He gives me a tentative smile, taking his swimsuit. "Okay. I'll meet you out there."

Right. I take my cue and step back, heading for the upstairs bathroom as Brad shuts the door.

I make it back outside first and help clean up a bit as I wait for Brad. He emerges after a good ten minutes, fidgeting with the hem of his shirt. His swim shorts—*not* a speedo, thank God—are in place.

"You good?" I ask, not used to seeing him so twitchy in a way that looks almost...nervous, as opposed to due to an excess of energy.

"Sure, sure," he says quickly, eyeing the pool. Sonia and her kids are already in it. "So we just...get in the water?"

"Unless you don't want to?" I check.

"*Pft.* No, it's fine. Good. Yep. Just, uh, don't toss me in, okay?"

"Of course," I say, frowning after Brad as he heads toward the pool. He stops at the edge, sitting down and gingerly extending the toes of one foot into the water. After a second, he puts both feet in.

I ease down next to him, twisting around and dropping into the pool, knowing it's best done fast. The cool water is a shock to my system, but considering the heat today, I welcome it. Brad has a grin on his face when I break the surface.

"Feels good," I let him know.

He nods, but he makes no move to jump in. He does strip off his shirt, however, prompting my gaze to skitter away.

I swim for a bit while Brad sits with his feet in the pool. Sonia is floating again, and her kids are wading in the shallow end, floaties on their arms. When it's been over ten minutes and Brad still hasn't moved a muscle, I head his way.

"Everything okay?" I ask, settling my hands on either side of his hips.

He spreads his legs a little to give me space between his knees, a move I try not to read too much into. "Yeah," he says. "It's just…"

"What?" I prod gently.

He leans a little closer before saying, "I don't know how to swim, Joey."

I try to keep my shock from showing, but I'm not sure I manage it. "Why didn't you say so?"

"I was embarrassed."

"It's nothing to be embarrassed about," I assure him, even as my gut twists. "Shit, bub, what if you'd fallen in?"

His lips turn up the slightest bit at the corners. "You said you wouldn't let me drown."

Well, that's the absolute truth.

I take a quick breath. "Want me to teach you?"

He looks around again, and it's not hard to guess why.

"None of them will judge," I promise. "And they don't even have to know. We can start in the shallows, and I'll lead you out to the deep end, okay?"

Brad looks into my eyes for the longest time before nodding. I ease back as he hops to his feet, heading around to the other side of the pool. My pulse is thundering as I swim his way, although I'm not even sure why. It's just swimming lessons.

But it's Brad. Trusting me.

He's confident enough as he walks down the steps into the pool, even as he shivers. I try not to stare too long at all that exposed skin, instead focusing on making sure he's comfortable. I meet him where the water starts to get deeper.

"Ready?" I ask quietly. I'm pretty sure Sonia will clue in to what we're doing, but I'll still try my best to make sure Brad isn't self-conscious about it. "Just hold on to my arm, and I'll do the rest, okay?"

He nods, taking my arm and walking forward as I step backwards toward the deep end. As soon as we get to chest height in the water, Brad scrambles, all but attaching himself to me. I brace as he wraps his arms over my shoulders, his legs curling around my waist.

"Sorry," he whispers frantically. "Sorry, sorry. I freaked."

"It's okay," I assure him, rubbing his back as my heart thrashes wildly.

"Can we just...go out like this? Just...hold me? Please?"

Oh God.

"Anything you want," I tell him. "But we don't have to go out at all. We can stay right here in the shallow end if you'd prefer."

He shakes his head. "No, I want to. I need to get it over with. Just...face my fear head-on, you know? And I'm safe with you. I know that. You'll keep me safe, Joey."

I've always considered myself a fairly level-headed person. I don't act on instinct, instead considering my options and carefully choosing the best course. The most rational one.

But there's nothing whatsoever rational about allowing myself to fall for a straight man. And yet I'm not even trying to stop it. I only tighten my arms around Brad and promise what I know to be true.

Will I keep him safe?

"Always."

Chapter 13
BRAD

Joey starts moving backwards once I stop strangling him with my limbs. His eyes stay on my face, making sure I'm okay.

I give him a clipped nod.

As soon as his feet leave the pool floor and we start to float, my legs tighten around him on instinct.

"It's okay," he says soothingly, using his arms to keep us at the top of the water. "Relax your legs, bub. I've got you, okay? Just...relax for me."

I do. It takes concerted effort, but I finally relax my death grip on Joey's waist.

"Good," he says, voice low. "Can you let go? Just for now. Float with me?"

He chuckles when I shoot him a glare.

"Christ," he whispers. "I don't think I've ever seen you make that face."

"It's my *you're being an idiot* face. Usually, you're not an idiot."

He gives my leg a tiny pinch, and I squawk.

"You don't have to let go of my shoulders," he says. "Just unwrap your legs and float with me. It'll be easier, I promise."

I don't like the sound of it, but considering I also don't want to drown Joey—*and myself by proxy*—I unwind my legs. One at a time. Slowly.

"There you go," he says, giving me a big smile that makes me feel better. Until he adds, "What a good boy."

"Don't mock me," I grumble.

"I'm not," he says with a soft chuckle. "You're doing good. I'm going to swim backwards now, okay? Just let yourself be tugged along."

I can do that. Easy peasy. *Go with the flow.*

Joey starts to move, and I inhale sharply, clinging to him harder.

"Watch the neck," he rasps.

"Fudge," I mutter, loosening my arms. "Sorry."

"It's fine," he says. "Look, you're doing it."

I open my eyes to realize he's right. Not that *I'm* doing much of anything. But Joey is paddling us around, and I'm along for the ride like some sort of barnacle. A barnacle that's essentially lying on top of him.

"You're my own personal Joey-float," I say with a huff of laughter. "And I didn't even have to blow you." A second passes—the quietest second in existence—before I hastily add, "*Up.* I didn't have to blow you up."

He chuckles, his eyes practically sparkling as he swims around the deep end of the pool. "Nope. I'm all prepped and ready to go."

I squint at him. "Was that an anal joke?"

Joey sputters, the both of us sinking several inches in the water before he recovers, at which point I'm certain I've already died. "We're good," he says, his palm settling at the back of my head.

"Both hands in the water," I eke out.

He obliges, letting go and paddling with two arms again. Once I can breathe, I realize my face is pressed up against Joey's chest. He has surprisingly little hair, and I idly wonder if that's natural or if he shaves.

Comfortable enough, I stay put. Joey is warm, even though the water is cool.

"Want to try floating on your own?" he asks.

"No."

"Okay... How about kicking your feet?"

"I'm good."

He huffs a laugh, the motion making his chest rise. His pecs are on the larger side, I notice. It's not even that I haven't seen them before, but it's certainly the first time I've had an up-close and personal view of one.

I've always loved tits. I love lying on them, all soft and squishy, like pillows. Love tracing their curves with my fingers or tongue. Love sucking on them, even.

And *holy mother of God*, I am *not* imagining sucking Joey's pec.

Fucking—

"Brad," Joey says in alarm as I unintentionally flail away from him. He grabs hold of me before I can sink, and I'm back to clinging, my legs around his waist, my pulse trying to convince me I'm having a heart attack. "Are you okay?"

"Fine," I breathe, so not fine.

Joey keeps one arm around me as he paddles toward the edge of the pool. He grabs on, keeping us stable as I catch my breath.

I'm suddenly acutely aware of the fact that my crotch is pressed against Joey's. That I'm wrapped around him almost intimately. That he's a gay man who, once upon a time, thought we were going on a date.

I don't know what he sees on my face—have no clue what emotions I'm broadcasting—but Joey's eyes dip down, to my mouth maybe? And then he twists in a way that forces distance between us.

"Here," he says, guiding me to grab on to the edge of the pool.

I do, transferring my weight, watching Joey's expression. What was that emotion just then?

"You boys okay?" Sonia calls.

I shoot her a quick thumbs-up. "Yep. Just fine. I'm not a very good swimmer," I admit.

Sonia smiles softly. "That's okay. It took my kids a long time to be comfortable enough to even try. You're doing great."

I give her an appreciative nod before resting my chest against the smooth tiles lining the pool, my arms on the sun-warmed concrete above. Joey is quiet next to me, and I glance at his profile, wondering why I never noticed how well-defined his pecs are. Not that it's a surprise. He's a fit dude.

Fit yet soft.

"You like challah?" I ask him.

His brow furrows as he looks my way. "Sure?"

"Yeah," I say quietly. "It's nice."

Joey clears his throat. "Want to try floating in place? Just a little?"

I give a slow nod. "Yeah. Might as well give it a shot."

Joey pushes off from the edge with an encouraging smile. He explains to me what to do. That he'll help support my arms while I get my bearings. That, once I feel comfortable, he'll let me go. That I should use my arms and legs as needed to keep myself in place.

Sounds easy enough.

Turns out floating in place is fucking hard. But Joey makes it fun. After several attempts, I manage it for about three seconds before grabbing for Joey's arm.

"You're getting the hang of it," he says.

"Sure," I agree. "Now I know if I go overboard at sea, I'll have just enough time to panic before slipping under."

Joey's expression is almost reproachful, his lips twisted into a wry smile. "You'll get it," he says. "It just takes time. Want to try floating on your back instead?"

"Oh, hell no," I say, immediately wincing as I check where the kids are. I lower my voice, even though they're far away. "Heck no. You never turn your back on a foe, Joey."

He stifles a laugh. "Fair enough."

"I do want to try going under, though. Could you hang on so I don't sink to the bottom?"

"Sure," he says, clasping my arm tight.

I grab his elbow as he holds mine, and then I let myself drop, which takes more effort than I thought it would. I don't open my eyes under the surface, not sure how the chlorine would feel, but I do blow a couple bubbles, my hair feeling as if it's floating around my face. It's nice, the sensation of weightlessness, Joey's hand like a tether keeping me from floating away.

When I kick upwards, Joey gives me a tug. I break the surface with a grin, wiping the water off my face. Joey looks...serious, almost. He's not smiling.

"What?" I ask, not liking a not-smiling Joey.

He shakes his head, his eyes skimming over my face. "Nothing, bub. Want to get out or stay a while?"

Noticing a couple of Joey's cousins heading toward the pool, I decide my swimming lesson is probably done for the day. "Would you hang out with me on the kiddie side?"

He nods, motioning me toward his back. With a grin, I loop my arms over his shoulders and hang on as Joey swims to the shallow end of the pool. I let go once my feet can touch the bottom.

"I'll grab us some water," he says, diving forward with a few powerful strokes before standing upright, his waist clear above the surface. Water cascades down his shoulders and back, along his spine, over the fabric sticking to his—

"*Ahh*," I murmur, looking away. What is *wrong* with me? A bro does not objectify his fellow bro's ass, no matter their gender.

Sonia makes an amused sound. "Thirsty, hun?"

"Yeah," I admit. I am kinda parched. Good thing Joey is grabbing us drinks. "He'll be back soon," I let her know.

"I can't imagine he'd be able to stay away for long," she says. "You two are absolutely adorable, by the way. It's good to see my cousin happy."

Heh. That's...nice.

"I want to see him happy, too," I land on.

She gives me a smile, and I head over to the stairs, taking a seat half in the water as Iggy and Reggie cannonball into the deep end. Iggy sends me a wave that I return.

When Joey comes back, handing me a bottled water and taking a seat beside me, I remember what I forgot to mention earlier.

"Hey, are you free Thursday night?"

"Think so," he says. "Why?"

"I found you a date," I tell him excitedly. "A really good one. I've been talking to this guy for over a week, and I think you'll really like him."

Joey is quiet, his hand suspended mid-twist on his water bottle cap.

"Unless you already have plans?" I say tentatively. "We could probably move it to another day. I haven't bought the tickets yet."

"Tickets?" he says, voice even.

"Yeah, a baseball game. Thought that'd be fun. I know you've been watching some of the games since moving here, and Logan is a big sports fan."

"Logan," he repeats.

"Yeah," I say again, giving Joey's foot a nudge with my own under the water. "Everything okay?"

He finishes uncapping his water, downing a couple sips before facing me. "You really want me to go on this date?"

I frown. "Of course. You didn't think I'd forgotten about being the best wingman ever, did you? I'm not planning on letting you down, Joey-roo."

He searches my face for a moment before nodding slowly. "All right. I'll give it a try."

"That's the spirit," I say, tousling his wet hair some. It's so much fun I do it again, running my fingers through the strands until they're sticking up straight.

Joey, I realize, is watching me with an odd expression.

"Sorry," I mumble, smoothing his hair back down. "So, Thursday?"

"Thursday," he agrees.

I mentally pump my fist. Thursday night, Joey and I will meet Logan. And who knows? Maybe my friend will fall deep in love.

It's late when Joey drops me off. We stayed at his family get-together all afternoon and into the evening. Everyone was so nice and welcoming, and I completely understand why Joey is happy to be here with them.

It makes me happy *for* him.

I take a quick shower to wash the pool off me before plopping onto my couch and calling Jason. He's been busy all week, so we haven't had a chance to talk.

"Hey," he says.

"Birdieeeee," I crow.

"Oh Lord."

"Guess what? I swam in a pool today. Well, sorta. I didn't swim so much as *assisted glide*, but it was awesome. Joey's teaching me. He said we can go back anytime."

Jason is silent for a beat, and I pop a chip into my mouth.

"Teaching you?" he finally asks. "What do you mean?"

"He's teaching me how to swim."

"You...you don't know how to swim? How didn't I know that?"

"I dunno," I say with a shrug. "Guess it never really came up. Not like we ever went to the beach or anything."

"I..." He trails off with what sounds suspiciously like a growl. "The fuck. I feel like a terrible friend for not knowing that."

"Hey, man. It's okay. Not your fault. I bet you didn't know I like having my face sat on, either. Some things just don't come up in conversation."

"Bee," my friend says slowly. "The fact that you're putting queening and not knowing how to swim in the same category is—you know what? No. It's not weird at all. I don't even know why I'm surprised. So you saw Joey again today?"

"Yeah," I tell him, eating another chip as I hitch my heel up on the coffee table. "I see him most days, actually. It's nice. I like spending time with him."

"That so?" he says, drawing out the words.

"Mhm. Not that I don't like hanging out with you, too!" I make sure to add, not wanting the dude to get jealous again. "It's just different. He's my baby kangaroo. But don't call him that."

"I...wasn't planning on it."

"We're going on a date Thursday. Well, not him and me, obviously. Us and Logan. *Him* and Logan, but I'll be there."

"Sure," he says faintly.

"I'm not leaving anything up to chance this time," I explain. "I even vetted the guy. *Extensively.* We've been chatting every night for days."

"Sure," he says again, slower. "You weren't talking to him through Joey's dating profile, though, were you?"

"Yeah?"

There's a brief pause. "Please tell me he knows he was talking to *you*? Not Joey?"

"Oh, yeah, man," I assure him, to which Jason puffs out a breath. "I just explained I'm Joey's new bud and that I needed to make sure he passed muster before I let him at the goods. So far, he has. He's nice, is open to marriage and kids, seems pretty cute, has a stable job doing tax prep, and he's even got green eyes."

"Joey likes green eyes?" Jason asks.

"Yep. Honestly, I think this guy might be the winner."

And then, once Joey has his man, I dunno... Maybe I could focus on dating again, too. It's kind of slipped my mind as of late.

"Can I ask you something?" Jason says, sounding serious.

Uh-oh.

"Sure?"

"Say Joey and this guy hit it off," he says. "Maybe they start dating for real. And, maybe, Joey has less time for you. Would that bother you?"

I take a second to truly consider it, even as my gut churns uncomfortably.

"I mean, it'd suck, but I want him to be happy," I answer. "I guess if that means I come second, I'd just have to be okay with that, right?"

Jason makes a small sound of acknowledgment, but the question sticks with me.

Because I don't want to lose Joey's time.

And, even though it makes no sense whatsoever, I don't want to come second.

Chapter 14

JOEY

"Joey-roo!" Brad says the moment I open the door. "Look! Look what I got you."

He's holding out a fanny pack.

In bright yellow.

With the name *Brad* written in jewels across the front.

"Is that...bedazzled?" I ask.

"Did it myself," he says proudly. "C'mere."

Brad doesn't wait for me to step forward, instead swooping in to wrap the fanny pack around my midsection. It clicks into place, and he tugs my shirt a few times, as if needing to make sure everything is settled just so.

I look down at the ridiculous piece of adornment. I want to hate it. I want to hate it so bad.

"Pretty snazzy, right?" Brad asks, peeking around my shoulder. "Hey, your place is nice."

"I'll, uh, give you a tour sometime."

"Maybe later if we get lucky, huh?" he says, waggling his eyebrows before his face does something complicated. "Wait, no. That doesn't make sense. I wouldn't stick around if Logan came back here. Heh. No, that'd be weird. Let's go!"

I follow Brad to his car in a bit of a daze. It takes me longer than I'd like to admit to realize Brad is *also* wearing a fanny pack. A neon green one. And on the front...

"Bub," I say slowly. "Does that have my name on it?"

Brad grins, stopping near the front of his vehicle. *Joey* shines in gaudy jewels on the front of his fanny pack. "Yeah, man! We match. Matching packs."

"Shouldn't we be wearing our own names?" I ask, more than a little bewildered.

He scoffs. "No way. Like this, everyone will know we're besties. Bros gotta look out for each other's fannies, dude."

I...have no words.

"Did you get Logan one?" I ask, not sure what I want his answer to be. Frankly, I know hardly anything about this Logan, but Brad assures me he's a winner.

Brad looks abashed. "I didn't think of it. Do you think he'll mind?"

Will Logan mind that his date is wearing the name of another man? A man who happens to be attending said date like an overprotective chaperone, who's touchy-feely and cares so damn much it's palpable, even though his feelings are painfully platonic?

"Should be fine," I assure Brad, despite knowing we're bound for disaster.

As it turns out, Logan seems...nice. His eyebrows rise as Brad greets him near the entrance to the stadium, his gaze flicking down first to Brad's fanny pack and then to my own. But there's a smile on his face when he and Brad embrace as if they're best of friends.

Logan steps forward once they part, introducing himself before Brad has a chance to do the honors. "Logan Carmichael."

I accept his outstretched hand, unable not to take him in at least a little. He's handsome; I'll give Brad that. It's as if Brad took a list of his own attributes and found someone who matched. Logan has dark hair, stubble, what appears to be a leanly muscled build under his team t-shirt and jeans, and his eyes are green.

In any other circumstance, I'm sure I'd find Logan quite appealing. But with Brad standing beside him, smiling at me in that way he does, there's simply no comparison.

"Joey Delgado," I say, trying to offer my best smile.

I have to at least *try*, right?

"Nice to meet you, Joey," Logan replies, his eyes roaming over me. A smile quirks his lips. "Should we head in?"

Brad produces our tickets from his fanny pack with an excited grin. "Let's do it."

We make our way through ticketing and past the concessions to our seats on the main concourse. Unsurprisingly, I end up sitting in the middle, between Brad and Logan. The stadium hasn't quite filled up yet, but it will soon enough.

"Brad tells me you work for your uncle's construction company," Logan says.

I give him a nod. "That's right. We do residential work, mainly remodels and custom jobs, like cabinetry. You're a tax preparer?"

His smile tips up on one end. "I am. Exciting stuff, huh?"

I chuckle. "Hey, I never said it wasn't. Do you enjoy it?"

"I do, actually. In a lot of ways, it's predictable, which I like. It doesn't keep me at the office after five."

I hum. "Not married to the job, then."

"No," he says simply. "It wouldn't be my first priority."

I understand what he's saying, and admittedly, I like it a lot. I want my future partner to be present, to enjoy spending time with me and building a life together. I don't want our jobs to come before our relationship.

A slap on my thigh has me turning my head. Brad has a huge grin on his face, and it hits me like a sucker punch. Because for a second, just a second, I'd forgotten he was there. He shoots me a thumbs-up, clearly happy Logan and I are getting along, before focusing on the field. The players are out now, warming up.

My throat feels tight as I force my gaze off the side of Brad's head.

"Have you lived in Vegas long?" I ask Logan.

"My whole life."

"Hey, me, too!" Brad says, reaching across me to offer my date a high five. "Vegans for life, man."

A laugh falls from my mouth. "I don't think we're called vegans, bub."

He *pshts* me. "You're new. You don't know."

Logan, looking amused more than anything, slaps Brad's proffered palm.

"Heck yeah," Brad says, plunking back into his seat. I'm not sure if he realizes his hand is resting on my leg now, but he doesn't move it.

"Where were you living before?" Logan asks me.

"New Hampshire."

"Ah. Were you near the coast or more inland?"

"Right on the coast, actually. I miss the water quite a lot."

Brad snorts beside me, and I'm more than certain he's recalling the *watersports* incident. I give him a warning flick on the leg, which prompts him to pat my face like I'm a dog.

"That's a pretty big change," Logan notes. "From the coast to the desert."

"But worth it," Brad says, not even looking our way. "Joey's a family man. He's got a lot of love to give, you know? And of course he loves his mom, too, but he's not the type of guy to turn his back on anyone. It's admirable, and I think his family knows just how lucky they are to have him here."

My heart thumps viciously.

"Besides," Brad goes on, "he has a pool at his disposal now, so he can satisfy the urge to get his trunks wet anytime he wants. Logan, you like footlongs?"

"What?" I sputter.

"Hot dogs?" Brad says slowly, looking between the two of us. "Or cheesesteak? Popcorn? I'll grab us some food. What do you want?"

Jesus Christ.

"Uh, anything is fine," I mutter.

Logan lists something I don't hear past the pounding of my heart, and Brad nods. He gives my leg a squeeze before getting up and sidestepping out of our row, the jewels spelling *Joey* glinting on the front of his fanny pack.

"He's sweet," Logan says.

The sweetest.

"Does he go on all your dates?"

I open my mouth to tell him *of course not* but realize I can't. "He, uh... He's made it his mission to be my wingman. He's pretty committed."

Logan hums, and I wonder what he truly thinks of Brad's presence tonight. He doesn't seem upset, but I suppose if he and Brad have been talking for the past week-plus, he probably knew what to expect, at least a little.

The two of us chat a bit about our families as the first pitch is thrown, the noise in the stadium increasing. Logan is easy to talk to, but despite him ticking all my theoretical boxes, I find I'm simply not invested in the date like I should be.

Of course, I know why that is. And when my oblivious, oh-so-committed wingman returns a minute later and my heart races at the mere sight of him, I wonder if there's simply no getting over Brad.

"Look," he says excitedly, passing a burger and fries off to Logan before handing what appears to be an entire pizza to me. Then he holds up his prize. "They had corn dogs."

Oh no.

Brad looks ridiculously happy as he retakes his seat, the breaded hot dog on a stick in his hand. I know, beyond a shadow of a doubt, I should look away. I should absolutely look away.

I don't.

Brad's tongue comes out to play first, licking a broad swipe up the entire length of the corn dog—base to tip—in an effort to collect the ketchup that's dripping down the side. Before retreating, said tongue flicks across the top, a sight that has me stifling a groan. And then, if that wasn't enough, he proceeds to stuff half the thing in his mouth like there's a medal at stake for eating it in as few bites as humanly possible. Even Logan sounds impressed by the display.

That probably shouldn't bother me as much as it does.

When a cheer goes up around the stadium, I whip my gaze away. I put all my focus into the game as I eat my pizza, knowing I can't be taken by Brad's tongue or his mouth or the happy noises he made as he practically choked on his footlong. I can't be thinking about his enthusiasm or wondering how advanced his deep-throating skills are. I *can't.*

I shouldn't.

A curious hum has me turning Logan's way. "You have a little something," he says, making like he's going to touch my cheek.

"I got it," Brad cuts in loudly, tugging me around by the chin. He holds my face as he wipes a napkin across the corner of my mouth, his brow furrowed in careful concentration. Once done, he gives me a beaming smile, and *fuck*. It feels as if my heart might beat right out of my chest.

You're perfect, I want to scream at him. *You're killing me. Kiss me, kiss me, kiss me.*

Oblivious to my inner turmoil, Brad's touch feathers away. Logan clears his throat, and I try to control my racing thoughts.

"So," my date says, his burger and fries gone now. "Can I ask about the matching bags you guys are wearing?"

"Our fanny packs?" Brad says happily, crowding into my space again. Not that he went that far away to begin with. "They're awesome, right? Look at this."

Brad unzips my fanny pack, an action that has no right to turn me on, and pulls out chapstick, gum, and even a tiny bottle of hand sanitizer. I had no clue he put those things in there.

"Super functional," he says, zipping it back up. "Plus it really accentuates Joey's waist, don't you think?"

Brad proceeds to stroke my stomach above the fanny pack almost absentmindedly, and my core clenches tight. Logan, rightfully so, doesn't seem to know what to say. He watches Brad's hand move over my shirt before lifting his gaze to me, an eyebrow subtly raised.

I don't know what to say either.

After a small eternity, I shift Brad's hand away, not sure how much more of his platonic fondling I can handle. He doesn't seem perturbed. But he does grab a slice of pizza off the box in my lap, sending me a wink before taking a bite.

As the innings pass, things only get weirder. It starts when Logan gets up to use the restroom, taking our trash to toss out on the way. Once he's gone, Brad starts fiddling with my fanny pack again, loosening and tightening the strap, making sure the buckle is clasped tight, shifting my shirt around until it's lying flat. Seemingly satisfied, he leans back and nods.

"My name looks good on you," he declares, casual as can be.

I practically choke.

Brad starts singing Beyonce's "Single Ladies (Put a Ring on It)" under his breath, complete with hand motions, and I wonder if this is a fever dream.

"Hey, wanna switch seats?" he asks after a minute.

I eye him curiously, but he's watching the game again. "Why?"

"This is a good spot. Great view. Figured you might want to enjoy it."

"We have nearly the same exact view," I point out. "I'm sitting right next to you."

He shrugs, far bouncier than usual. His leg keeps moving. "Logan seems nice."

"Which you already knew," I say slowly.

"Well, sure," he says. "But sometimes people can be different in person. He's great. Just *greeeat*."

"What's with the tone? Is there something you don't like about him?"

He waves a hand through the air. "*Psh*. What? No. I picked him for you, didn't I? I did good."

He nods to himself, but he looks...off. Distressed, almost.

"Bub, if there's something I should know—"

"Hey, you're back!" he practically yells, moving his knees to the side so Logan can pass.

"I am," Logan says, giving me a perplexed look. Honestly, I have no answers for Brad's odd behavior. Including the fact that the moment Logan retakes his seat, Brad leans his shoulder firmly against my own. I look over at him, my pulse spiking, but he's watching the players.

Does he even realize what he's doing?

As the game comes to a close, Brad's leg is back to bouncing. He seems antsier than I've ever seen him.

"Everything all right?" I ask, leaning his way and speaking quietly. People are getting out of their seats now, filtering out of the stadium.

"Yeah. Of course," Brad says. "It was a good date, right? You had fun? With...Logan, I mean?"

"It was great," I assure him, although I would have enjoyed it more if it was just me and Brad, a thought I refuse to linger on.

He shoots me a tiny smile.

"Ready to go?" Logan asks, peering our way.

I nod.

Brad is extra jittery as we head toward the exit, the three of us moving slowly through the crowd. He keeps glancing over at me, grinning a little too widely when I catch his gaze.

When we finally make it out of the stadium, Logan stops me with a touch on my arm. "Could I have a word? Alone?"

Brad jumps away from us. "Oh! Of course. I'll just, uh, wait over here. You two talk. About stuff. Alone. Yep."

Brad trots off, only glancing back once he's a respectable distance away. If I didn't know better, I'd say he looks upset. But he turns his face away so quickly I wonder if I only imagined it.

"Joey," Logan says, recapturing my attention. "You need to tell him how you feel."

My gut sinks like a stone.

"Don't apologize," he says before I have a chance to do exactly that. He huffs a small laugh, brushing his hair back. "He's possessive of you. You realize that, right?"

"It doesn't mean anything," I tell him hoarsely. "He's..."

"Straight?" Logan says, an eyebrow raised. "So he told me. But he's into you. And, frankly, I'm not surprised. I had my suspicions. Which is why I can't fault you for going on this date while you have feelings for someone else. I went on it knowing someone had feelings for you."

My mouth opens and closes. "Why?" I finally manage, not knowing how to refute his claim that Brad has feelings for me.

He can't. He doesn't. Does he?

Logan shrugs a little. "I couldn't *not*. After the way Brad talked about you... I had to know. And he was right. About everything. I would have liked getting to know you, Joey."

"But not now?" I ask.

His smile is almost amused. "Tell you what. If things don't work out between you two, then yeah, give me a call. But I doubt I'll be hearing from you."

I have no clue what to say. I don't *want* to hope. I hate the way my heart is racing and how my mind is spinning, trying to figure out if Logan is right. I'm not sure I can trust my instincts when it comes to Brad because I never would have thought he was straight in the first place. His flirting doesn't mean anything. Neither does his open affection or proprietary fanny packs.

He's just...Brad.

And if I admit I have feelings and he doesn't reciprocate them? We won't stay friends. Brad wouldn't want to hurt me like that, I know it. And I don't want to lose him. I'm not ready.

Might not ever be.

"Joey," Logan says quietly. "I really think you should tell him."

I nod, but I've never been more conflicted in my life.

Crushing on a straight friend is one thing. Admitting you're interested in them romantically? That you want...*more?*

In what world does that possibly end well?

Chapter 15
Brad

My chest is in a vise as I watch Joey and Logan embrace. It's a quick hug, far below the six-second threshold, but it still feels as if it lasts forever.

It shouldn't bug me. I shouldn't want to run over there and forcibly shove them apart.

Fuck. What is wrong with me?

I chew on my fingernail as they say a few more words to each other. When Logan steps away, shooting me a quick wave before heading off, my heart soars. Is he leaving?

I *definitely* shouldn't be relieved by that. In fact, I'm fairly certain that makes me the worst wingman ever. But I don't care. Not right this instant.

I make my way back over to Joey, trying to gauge whether or not he's happy about Logan's departure. He's watching him leave with a furrow in his brow.

"Hey," I say once close, aiming for upbeat. "So, uh, how'd your talk go?"

Joey's gaze shifts my way, something indecipherable in his expression. "Fine."

I nod. "Cool, cool. I take it he's not coming back with us?"

He shakes his head slowly.

"Okay," I say as breezily as possible, even as I sag in relief. "That's probably good, right? You're looking for more than casual, so..." I let my sentence hang, not really wanting to consider Joey and Logan fucking. "Did you guys set up another date?"

"No," Joey says quietly.

I ease out a breath before grinning in what I hope is a reassuring manner. "There's still time, right? Plenty of time. I have his contact info, so if you want to—"

"Brad," Joey cuts in. "Let's head home, all right?"

"Yeah," I say quickly. "Sure."

Home.

Joey is quiet as we drive back to his little bungalow. He told me he's renting the place for cheap in exchange for doing some repairs. By the look of things, he's already been hard at work.

The outside of the house is dark blue, the trim a freshly painted white. There's a section of porch that looks brand new, the wood still bright and unstained. A rocking chair sits atop it, right near the front door. Joey uses his key to let us inside, and I kick off my shoes before taking everything in.

The place is...adorable. That's the best word I can come up with. The entryway is a gentle sage color, the living room off to the right cream. It's clear Joey did some work inside, as well, because one of the walls has white streaked across it, like he patched it up and has yet to repaint it. Further down the hall is a dining room with a big bay window and the kitchen, also a sage color. The back of the house looks out over the small backyard, where a patio and portable fire pit sits.

I turn back around, heading for the stairs I saw at the front of the house. Joey's bedroom must be on the second floor.

He laughs as I zip past. "Feel free to look around," he calls after me.

"Thanks," I yell back.

I find the bathroom first. The walls are a deeper green than the color downstairs, emerald maybe, and the floor is done in black-and-white tiles. Next is a closet. Boring. Joey's bedroom is at the end of the short hall.

I peek my head in, nearly gasping when I see the dark navy walls and the giant bed adorned with a good dozen pillows.

"Oh my God," I whisper, pushing the door open wider and stepping inside. There's a gray-and-white rug at the foot of the bed, super soft to the touch, and the curtains must have blackout linings because hardly any light is peeking through.

It's *perfect*.

"I liked how dark your room was," Joey says from the doorway. "Thought I'd do something similar in here."

"You painted it this way?" I ask, surprised by that.

He nods, walking toward the dresser and removing his fanny pack. I make a small sound of mourning, even though it's *fine*. Not like he can wear it twenty-four seven. Or he *could*, but it probably wouldn't be comfortable. I suppose his stomach looks good without it, too. *He* looks good. Any which way, really.

The strong thighs. The thick core. His lovely face, and the big arms that feel so perfect wrapped around me. I'm not a small guy, but Joey is bigger, and he makes me feel protected. Safe. Which is probably why I like having those arms around me so much, right? Like, *really* like it. Love it, even. Want it more than anything.

"Brad?"

I startle, realizing Joey is talking to me. "Sorry, what?"

He shifts on his feet, eyes aimed toward the ground. "There's something I wanted to ask you."

"Oh no," I mutter aloud, my stomach dropping.

Joey stills, meeting my gaze. "What? What is it?"

"You have the voice. I did something wrong, didn't I?"

"What? No," he says quickly.

"I was rude tonight, wasn't I?"

"No, not rude. Just..."

"I was hogging you," I say, that hollow space in my gut growing. "*Fuck*. I'm sorry, Joey. I didn't mean to. I just... Logan was there, and... I don't know. I just wanted..."

"Hey," Joey says, walking closer. "It's okay, bub. I'm not mad."

"You're not?"

"No," he says, reaching for me. "Of course not. Come here."

I blow out a breath, practically falling against Joey's chest as his arms wrap around me tight.

"I'm sorry," I whisper, burying my face against his shoulder. "I don't know what my problem was."

Joey exhales roughly, his hands rubbing up and down my back in a soothing manner. My own slip under his shirt, settling on his skin. He's warm. So very warm. "It's okay," he says again, his voice a little raspy.

"I probably shouldn't come on your dates anymore, huh?" I say, even though I hate it. I don't want Joey going on dates without me.

Jason was right. I *do* want all his time.

"I've been the worst friend," I mumble.

Joey inhales a sharp breath, his stomach dancing under my fingertips. I'm not sure when my hands moved to his front, but his stomach is just as warm as his back. He feels *good*. Solid and strong. But comfy, too. I wonder if he'd be up for cuddling again. Maybe he'd even let me get rid of his shirt this time so we could be skin to skin. I could crawl on top of him, soak up his warmth. Lie on that cozy chest of his and trace his abs with my fingers or the tip of my—

I still, my thoughts coming to an abrupt halt, my heart pounding so hard in my chest I swear I can hear it.

"Joe?" I croak. "Would you excuse me for a minute?"

"Yeah," he breathes.

Slowly, I pull my hands out from under Joey's shirt and take a step back. I don't meet his gaze as I slip past, heading out of the bedroom. I make my way swiftly down the stairs, walk outside, and jog around to the back of his small garage where I'm out of view. My hands shake as I pull my phone from my pocket.

Jason doesn't answer my call. *Fuck.*

Okay, okay. He's probably working. It's fine.

I let out a breath and try Cas next.

"Hello?"

"Oh, thank God," I whisper. "Cat-man, you've gotta help me."

"What's going on?" he asks, sounding calm. Cas is always calm. I appreciate it more than I can say at the moment.

"So, uh...you know Joey? My gym-dude? My...*other* gym-dude?"

"Yeah," Cas says. "We met, remember? At the 5k?"

"Right," I say on an exhale. "Um. I think I like his stomach."

There's a pause on the other end of the line. I've never done well with pauses.

"Like, I want to taste his belly button?" I explain. "Or come on his abs. Maybe both? *Oh shit.*"

"Okay, breathe," Cas says. "You know that's perfectly fine, right?"

"But he's my friend," I hiss. "It's pretty rude to imagine painting his stomach, don't you think?"

"Painting his stomach with... No, I got it," he says. "You know a lot of relationships start as friendships, right?"

"Sure," I say slowly. "But... I've never wanted to come on a dude before. What if it's just...I don't know. Some kind of primal urge? Like, some sort of caveman *this is my friend so I'll mark him as mine* thing?"

Cas is quiet for a couple seconds. "I really don't think that's a thing."

I groan.

"It kind of sounds like you might be attracted to him," Cas points out.

Yeah, it kinda does.

"Jason is going to be pissed he missed this," he goes on, sounding fond.

"Yeah," I mutter. "He'll yell. Lovingly, of course."

"Of course," Cas agrees.

I heave out a breath. "Cas... I don't get it. I've never been interested in a guy before. What's going on?"

He's quiet for a moment. Finally, he says, "I think sexuality is a lot more fluid than people assume. And even if you do swing primarily one way, I think there's always room for the exceptions. The people that just...*do* it for you. It doesn't have to be more complicated than that. Have you talked to him about how you're feeling?"

"No," I admit, voice quiet. "I just realized, so now I'm hiding between his garage and a shrubbery. I don't know what to say."

He huffs a laugh. "Maybe start with something other than creaming his abs."

"Holy fuck," I whisper. "Why does that sound so hot?"

Cas laughs again. "Hey, if you have questions about any of this, you can always ask, okay? I'm not telling you you're one of us now. That's for you to decide. But if you do join the rainbow, it might be a lot to figure out. Jason and I will be here if you need it."

My throat feels stupidly tight. "Thanks. You're a good dad."

Cas sighs, but it's an amused sound. "Good luck, okay? You're pretty fearless, Brad. I don't know if you know that. But you are. You can do this."

I want to believe him, but it feels *big*. Not just maybe being into a guy for the first time in my life, but being into *Joey*. He's my baby kangaroo-roo. My gym-bro. My friend.

What if he doesn't feel the same?

Holy shit. What if he *does*?

"I, uh, should probably head back inside," I tell Cas. "Thanks for answering the phone."

"Of course. Let me know if you need anything?"

"I will. Later, dude."

"Bye, Brad."

I hang up and slip my phone back in my pocket.

So I like Joey's abs. And the way he feels pressed against me. Not to mention his pretty brown eyes and his smile. Such a nice smile.

Maybe I like *him*. Maybe I should...explore that.

Oh God.

I let myself back into Joey's house and close the front door quietly behind me. I don't hear him moving about, so I make a quick detour into the kitchen and fill up a glass with ice water, gulping a few mouthfuls down.

I can do this.

As I head back upstairs, I construct possible conversation starters in my head.

Hey, Joey. Turns out I might be a dab queer.

Joseph-broseph. Question. Do you like cum play? Asking for a friend.

Joey Kangaroo. Can I hop on you?

Jesus Christ, I'm screwed.

When I get to the top of the stairs, the bedroom door is closed. "Joey?" I call out.

"I'm in here," he yells back.

I nod, taking a breath and bracing myself. Then, I push open the door.

"Holy—"

Joey is facing his dresser, wearing abso-fucking-lutely nothing except for a teeny tiny jockstrap. His ass is just...right there. It's right fucking there. All naked and smooth and—

Joey spins upon hearing my voice, his eyes widening in alarm. I'm already stumbling backwards, mumbling a, "Sorry, sorry," when my heel gets caught on a floorboard. Before I know what's happening, I'm going down, the glass of ice water in my hand spilling all over me like an expertly timed cold shower. I'm so stunned by the turn of events I don't move a single muscle.

"Shit," Joey hisses, rushing over. He drops down beside me. "God, bub. Are you all right? Did you hit your head?"

My mouth moves uselessly, my gaze slipping down Joey's chest and stomach to the rather sizeable...bulge staring me in the face.

"Duuude," I breathe. "You're practically naked."

"I was changing," he says calmly, slipping his hand underneath my head, like he's checking for damage. "I didn't think you'd walk in on me."

"Yeah," I mumble. "My bad."

"Are you okay?" he asks again.

"Uh-huh. You're wearing a jock."

"*Brad.*"

"Yeah," I say quickly, snapping my gaze up to Joey's face.

He appraises me for a long moment. "You sure you're good?"

"Yep," I squeak. "Didn't hit my head. I promise."

He nods, letting out a breath. "Okay. Let me put on some clothes."

Joey stands up, turning around. And I promptly choke on my tongue as his ass—as *he* walks away.

Fuck. It's not just his stomach I want to paint.

I force my gaze off those bouncing cheeks and sit upright, my pulse hammering. As Joey pulls on a pair of sweatpants, I get to my feet and grab a towel from the closet. I dry my face before taking off my poor dampened fanny pack. Setting it aside, I tackle the mess on the floor, grateful the glass didn't break.

"Here," Joey says softly, squatting down beside me. He tugs me around to face him and starts rubbing another towel over my hair, his gaze soft.

"You're, uh, not upset I walked in on you nearly nude?" I ask.

He huffs a small breath. "No. You've seen me changing in the locker room at the gym plenty of times."

Yeah. I guess I just never really *noticed*.

I swallow heavily as I let myself look. *Truly* look. For maybe the first time ever.

Joey's eyes are locked on my hair as he dries me off. He has thick lashes. Dark, too. The brown of his irises is...really quite beautiful. Like a tiny autumnal starburst. His hair has a bit of curl to it. Not much, just enough to make it look tousled, even when dry. And his stubble, a bit longer than my own, suits him. I can't help but wonder what that coarse hair would feel like against my skin. Would it burn?

I shiver, my gaze slipping down to Joey's loose-fitting tank top. It's gaping just enough for me to get a hint of his pecs and the definition of his obliques. He's in good shape; that much I already knew. But even though Joey has a physically demanding job and is a regular at the gym, he's not all rock-hard muscle and popping veins. He has a little padding, which I love all the more. I know from experience how comfortable he is to lie on.

My gaze slips a little further down. To his sweats. And the way the material is pulled tight because of his squat. *Fuck.* Knowing what's hidden under only a thin layer of gray...

"Brad," Joey says quietly.

"Yeah," I rasp, realizing the towel has stopped moving over my hair. I force my gaze upwards.

Joey looks...perplexed. Which I get. I was just checking out his junk. And what can I possibly say to explain it other than the truth?

Cas said I'm fearless. I don't know that I've ever thought of myself as such. A little impulsive, maybe. Prone to following my instincts first and asking questions later.

Well, maybe I shouldn't start overthinking things now. After all, I'm trying to find myself, right? And I can't travel down a brand-new, possibly *exciting* road without planting my heel forward first.

Step five in Brad's Guide to Finding Himself and Falling in Love:

Be brave.

Here goes nothing.

"Hey, Joey?" I say, trying not to let my nerves show. He waits patiently. Always patient. "So, uh, it turns out I really like your face. And, if you're still amenable, I'd very much like to greet your tonsils with my tongue."

Joey blinks at me, the towel falling from his fingers.

I cringe.

Yeah, that could've gone better.

Chapter 16

JOEY

"I'm sorry," I say slowly, positive I must have misheard. "You want to greet my...tonsils with your *what?*"

"Tongue?" Brad answers, not sounding sure.

I take a breath and stand up, feeling dizzy. "Are you... Are you saying you want to *kiss* me?"

"See, it sounds so much better when you say it," he mumbles, frowning.

"Bub. Are you serious?"

He winces a little and stands, his hair an absolute mess, the front of his shirt still wet. "I am serious. Would you still want to kiss *me?* I know that was a long time ago, and your feelings might have changed since then, but—"

His words cut off when I take his face in my hands. My inhale is shaky, my heart pattering along as I hold Brad's gaze. His eyes, so very green, are wide open and staring right back at me. There's no question in my mind.

I don't know who moves first. Brad tugs my shirt, I back him into the wall, and then my lips are on his and everything is narrowing down to *him.* The softness of his mouth, his chest bumping mine, his smell, his taste, the sound of his surprise.

"Fuck," Brad gasps, pulling me closer.

His mouth parts, and I don't hesitate. I dive in, swallowing down his moan, relishing the way his fingers tighten in my shirt. He's perfect—*perfect*—and I'd consume him if I could. I'd take him down my throat, keep a piece of him inside me always.

"Joey," he breathes, those two syllables spurring me on. His head thunks against the wall when I drop my lips to his neck, sucking on the sensitive skin there. "*Haaah.*"

His fingers find my hair, and I'm back at his mouth, nearly shaking with my want for him. When did this happen? What changed? Is this real? He wants this, right? He's so sweet. *So* sweet. God, I'm mauling him. I need to pull back. I need...

Brad's startled sound has me backing off in an instant, our lips parting with a smack. He looks dazed, his hair in disarray, pink coloring his cheeks.

"I'm sorry," I say, my breath coming short. "Was that too much?"

"No, no," he answers quickly, his gaze slipping downward. "It's just, uh... Ho-hooo-ly shit, is that a big hammer you've got pressed to my hip."

I step quickly back, cursing my carelessness. Brad's gaze stays zeroed in on my crotch, his eyes wide.

"He's a gregarious fellow, isn't he?" he says with a nervous laugh. "Just really wanted to pop up and say hello."

"Sorry," I repeat, adjusting myself as best as I can.

Brad blinks. "*Hoo,*" he says, seemingly shaking himself loose. He runs his hands through his hair, taming the strands somewhat. "I guess I'm kind of flattered, you know? Just...don't expect that thing to fit right away. Christ."

I blink after Brad as he swipes the fallen water glass off the floor, along with his fanny pack, and starts making his way down the stairs.

"You have coffee?" he calls.

I'm not sure I have a single functioning brain cell left after that.

I find Brad in the kitchen, rifling through my cupboards. "Let me," I say, grabbing the coffee from the pantry. I keep one eye on him as I portion the beans into the blender, my pulse flitting about wildly. He's looking out the window to the backyard, a contemplative expression on his face.

Once the coffee is ground, I dump it in the filter and turn on the pot. It starts to spit as I face my houseguest, not knowing what to make of his mood or...*this*. Any of it.

"So, uh," I say slowly. "What, um..."

"I think I was jealous," Brad says.

"Jealous?" I ask, my pulse kicking back up.

"Of Logan."

Oh fuck.

"Um, yeah?" I say.

He nods, still looking out the window. "Here's the thing. I didn't like him having your attention, you know? Which is pretty shitty of me, considering I set you up with the guy. But...every time you were looking at him, it pissed me off."

Oh, God.

"So, uh, the kiss," I say hoarsely. "Was that because you wanted my attention on you?"

Brad's head whips my way. "What? No. I wasn't... I wasn't trying to *manipulate* you, Joey. Did it feel like that to you?"

"No," I say quickly, grabbing a mug from the cupboard. "The kiss didn't feel fake. I'm just trying to understand what's going on here, bub. I don't want to make assumptions."

I fill up Brad's mug now that his coffee is ready, the silence stretching painfully in the few seconds it takes before Brad speaks again.

"I don't have a perfect answer," he says. "All I know is I understand cum gutters now because of you, and I'm pretty sure I'd like to test yours out if you'd let me."

The mug of coffee hits the floor, and Brad jumps back, avoiding the spray of liquid that coats the hardwood.

"Oh no," he mumbles, bending down to grab the miraculously intact mug. "Bad night for drinks."

"You...you *what?*"

Brad looks up at me. "I'm attracted to you, Joey. At least, I'm pretty sure I am. I've been having a lot of thoughts."

"Thoughts about me," I say weakly.

"Yeah," he answers, standing up. He hands me the mug, and I get my feet into gear, pouring him a new cup before grabbing a roll of paper towels for the spilled coffee. I wipe up the mess as quickly as I can.

Brad sips his coffee as I wash my hands.

"So, uh, the kiss," I begin again, my thoughts a jumbled mess. "That was a test?"

His face scrunches. "Not a test, no. More of a...confirmation."

I think I need to sit down.

I can hear Brad following me into the living room, his footsteps soft. I feel as if I'm rolling. Flipped upside down and lost at sea, unsure of which way is up. When I plop onto the couch, Brad sits beside me.

"I don't really know how to do this," he says, voice quiet. "I've never been interested in a friend before, let alone a guy. I'm in uncharted territory here. And I don't even know...I mean... Would you even want to...*you know*...with me?"

"Yes," I say immediately.

Brad blows out a breath. "You sure didn't have to think about that long."

I slip off the couch and kneel in front of him, my hands on the outsides of his knees. His mouth opens as he looks down at me, his chest rising and falling with his breaths.

"Whatever you're thinking about? Whatever you want to try? Try it with me."

"Joey..."

"I won't put pressure on you," I tell him seriously. "I won't push for anything you're not sure about or ready for. You're safe with me, and you can explore with me."

"But what if I end up hurting you?" he nearly whispers.

"Why would you hurt me?" I ask, pressing a trembling kiss to the top of his knee.

He eases out a breath. "Because, once upon a time, you asked me out on a date. And I had no clue. You were in this before I was, Joey, and... And I don't want to treat you like an experiment because you're my only single, queer friend."

I close my eyes, resting my chin on the knee I just kissed. "Would you rather experiment with someone else?"

"No," he says immediately. His fingers thread through my hair, the touch so soft it hurts. "I don't... I can't even... I don't want anyone else."

I open my eyes, meeting his gaze. "Then try with me," I say thickly. "It doesn't have to be anything more than you're ready for. I'm not putting expectations on you, bub."

His brow creases. "So, we'd be...what? Bros with bennies?"

I huff a laugh, hands tightening on his legs. "We can call it that. And if you decide it's not for you? That's fine. Sometimes people are just curious."

The look he gives me is amusingly stern. "Joey Kangaroo, my dude, my guy, I think if the things I'm envisioning you doing while you're down on your knees are the opposite of off-putting, then I'm not as straight as I thought I was."

It's embarrassing how quickly my cock swells at that. I'm almost grateful he can't see it.

"Besides," he goes on, leaning forward, the move bringing us closer. "Being queer isn't the part that scares me."

"No?" I ask, throat tight. "What scares you?"

"The thought of losing you," he answers, just about doing me in. "I couldn't stand to lose you, Joey."

"Give me a month," I all but beg. "A month to show you what it could be like. And then, after that, we reevaluate. If things get weird..." I take a breath, expel it. "Then we stop. We don't risk our friendship."

He nods slowly, looking lost in thought. I loosen my grip on his knees, inching my hands up his thighs and holding on tight.

"No Logans," he finally says, a hard edge to his voice. "He was nice and all, but I don't want you with anyone else. Just me."

Fuck.

"No one else," I agree hoarsely.

"And you tell me if I do something weird," he goes on. "I don't know what. But if there's some gay sex line I cross, I gotta know, man. Like, can I lick your nipples?"

My breath puffs out of me. "Mhm."

He nods. "Okay, yeah. Good. Just be patient with me. I mean, I don't even know how to take dick, dude. I'm pretty sure I'll need to stretch a lot first. Like really warm up, you know? Because *fuck*. Things are tight back there."

Oh, Jesus.

"You, uh...you'd want to try that?" I ask, pretty sure my voice sounds like gravel by now.

"Yeah, man. I want to try everything with you. Just, uh...maybe we can ease into the masterclass-level stuff?"

"We can definitely take it slow," I assure him, setting my forehead on his knee.

"You all right?" Brad asks, petting the back of my head.

"Mm."

"You sure?"

"Mhm."

"You're kinda just hugging my legs, Joey-roo. You need a cuddle?"

I stand up, wrapping my arms around Brad's shoulders and taking him down to the couch. He laughs under me, his arms coming around me tight as I tuck my face against his neck.

"I like this, you know," he says. "You on top of me. Smothering me. Feels good."

Fuuuck.

I rub my nose over his skin, breathe him in, nip gently.

"Oh, shit," Brad whispers. "There's Greg again, huh?"

I pause, my lips on his neck. "Did you name my dick Greg? As in...gregarious?"

"Yeah?"

"Of course you did," I mutter, unable to stop my laughter. I pull back enough to see Brad's face. He's grinning up at me, looking so damn happy my chest swells like a balloon. "I'm gonna kiss you again. Sound good?"

"I think I can handle that," he says, lips quirking.

I lean down, catch those lips, soak up his moan.

Slow. I can definitely take things slow. I have a month to prove to Brad he should be mine.

For tonight, I'll prove I can learn his mouth as well as I know the man himself.

"Let me get this straight," my cousin says. "Or not so straight, as it were. Bros...with benefits."

"That's right," I answer.

The sound of the miter saw puts a temporary halt to our conversation, but I can feel Iggy's gaze on me as he waits. Once I hand him the piece of trim I cut, he says, "But you're half in love with the guy already."

"So?"

"*So*, seems kinda risky, don't you think? How are you supposed to...*cash in* on your benefits without feelings getting involved?"

I grab the rest of the boards we cut to size, and the two of us head back into the house we're remodeling. Even though no one on our crew has an issue with my sexuality, I still lower my voice.

"I don't expect my feelings to stay out of it," I tell my cousin. "Not in the least. But there's no world in which I pass up what Brad is offering. Do you know what kind of courage it takes to come out to someone? He asked *me* to kiss him, Iggy. No wasn't an option."

"Look," he says softly. "I like the guy. I do. And frankly, he was all over you at the barbecue, so I'm not doubting that his intentions are sincere. I just worry..."

"That he'll experiment with me and move on?"

"Well, yeah," Iggy says.

I nod, bending down and lining up one of the trim pieces before hammering it into place. "It's a risk I'm willing to take. This is brand new for him. It's a lot to take in and come to terms with. The last thing I want to do is scare him off by asking for forever. You know what he told me?"

"What?" my cousin asks, squatting down next to me.

"He said he didn't want anyone else, Iggy. Just me. So this means something to him, too. I'm sure of it. The very least I can do is give him a minute to adjust. The rest will come."

"You sound so sure about him," he says, the beginnings of a smile forming.

"I am," I admit. "If there's one thing I'm sure about, it's him."

Iggy shakes his head, but he doesn't look upset. "I'm not going to say I get it, but I'll support you. And if Brad breaks your heart, well... Let's just say he won't be invited to the next family barbecue."

I huff a laugh. "How utterly vicious of you."

"Man, I might look like a pit bull, but you know I'm nothing but a Shih Tzu on the inside, all fluffy and soft."

"You forgot yappy," I put in.

Iggy punches me on the shoulder. "Am not, you dick. You know what? I take it back. I hope Brad crushes you."

"You do not," I say, motioning for another piece of trim.

Iggy hands one over. "No, I don't. But I'm not *yappy*. I enjoy conversation. There's a difference."

As Iggy and I finish installing the baseboard on the main floor of the house, my cousin rambling all the while about the difference between talking *to* someone and talking with them, I can't help but smile. It's not that this life is all that much different than the one I had in New Hampshire. I'm still doing the same sort of work, still filling my days with sawdust and the smell of varnish. Still working out in the evenings and watching TV or playing the occasional video game to relax.

But it's all the in-between that's so much richer than it was before. My family has grown. The work I'm doing is more fulfilling now that I'm working for people I know and care about.

And, of course, there's Brad.

Maybe we are just bros. For now.

And maybe being the explorational plaything for a bi-curious man I'm half in love with has the potential to backfire horribly. In theory.

But he asked to kiss me. *He* asked.

That means something.

So I'm not holding back. Brad wants to confirm his attraction to me?

I'll give him all the proof he could ever need.

Chapter 17

Brad

"You absolute asshole!"

I pop off my couch, looking over in alarm as Jason storms into my apartment like the place is on fire. Before I can open my mouth to ask what's wrong, he tackles me onto the couch cushions.

"The fuck," I squeak.

"You *dick*," he says, grabbing a pillow and shoving it on my face. "I can't believe you told Cas about your big gay revelation before me!"

"Are...are you trying to smother me with a pillow?" I mumble into the fabric.

"We're supposed to be *friends*."

"We are," I groan.

"*Ugh.* You're not even struggling," he complains, pressing the pillow against me harder before tossing it away. "It's no fun if you don't struggle."

"Whoa," I breathe. "Birdie, that was grim."

He swats my chest before flopping onto the cushion next to me and crossing his arms. "So? Was it okay?"

"Wait, what?" I ask, sitting upright.

"Did he treat you with respect?" he practically huffs. "Was it *good*?"

Slowly, it sinks in what he's asking. "Oh my God," I whisper. "You precious baby bird, you *care*."

Jason scowls at me.

"You *love* me," I say in glee. "Admit it. Tell me you love me and care about me and want to make sure my queer deflowering was everything I'd hoped and wished it would be."

"I regret everything," he moans, dropping his head back against the couch.

I pat his face. "You lovely little dumpling, Joey and I didn't have sex."

He stills, and I pull my hand away before he can bite it. "You didn't?"

"No. Don't get me wrong—we *will*. And very soon, I'm guessing. I mean, I've never had a dick down my throat, but it can't be that much different than a banana, right? Greg's definitely a two-biter, but I'm gonna work on it. You know I love a challenge."

Jason's face is pinched. "Who's Greg?"

"And *dude*, I really don't know if I'm a drill or be drilled kinda guy, but I'm looking forward to finding out. So I need you to tell me everything you know about lube. And douching. Oh, and do you think Joey and I should jump straight into handcuffs or save them for a special occasion? Birdie? Where are you going?"

"Need a drink," he calls from the kitchen.

"Grab me a refill? Pot should be full."

Jason comes back into the room with a soda and the coffee carafe. "Can't believe I'm still enabling your addiction," he mumbles, filling my mug.

"Stuff of life," I say happily, sighing around my sip.

"So... You two didn't have sex," Jason says, sitting back down and popping the top on his soda.

"Nope. Just kissed."

"But it was good?"

"Yeah," I say, my smile spreading. "It was good."

"And you're feeling okay about everything?" he asks me seriously. "About liking Joey?"

"It's the easiest thing," I admit, still stuck on that. "I don't really understand why *now*, you know? I don't know why it's him. But..."

I think over how to explain it to my friend.

"I think I liked him first. As a person. And maybe that made it easier for me to consider what a physical relationship between us might look like. And I'm not saying all relationships need to include sex because of course they don't. But I *do* like Joey's body. I like looking at him. I like being close to him. I *really* like kissing him. And, I mean, *shit*. Have you seen the dude's hammies? You haven't, but trust me, they're *thick*. And don't even get me started on his stomach."

"Wasn't planning on it," he mutters.

"My point is I know I want him. I do, even though I'm still having a hard time conceptualizing certain things. But I think that's because I've never done it. I've never tried, you know? And I'm a hands-on learner, always have been. So maybe it makes sense that none of this clicked before him. Because I've never really *touched* other guys the way I've touched Joey. He's very touchable."

Jason rubs his face. "This is going to be a thing now, isn't it? Me hearing about you and his—"

"What do you think his dick looks like?"

"Yep. There it is." Jason huffs a breath before setting down his soda. "I'm only going to say this once. And believe me—it'll be as uncomfortable for me as it is for you."

I snort. "Doubt whatever it is will be uncomfortable for me."

He levels me with a *look*. "I'm going to say it because it's my duty as your honorary brother."

"Aw, Birdie."

"Oh my God, let me get this out." He takes a breath and rushes on. "You never, *ever*, have to do anything you don't enjoy. And I know you know that. But if you try this whole...*be drilled* thing, it shouldn't hurt unless you want it to. So take things slow, don't skip the..." He makes a choking noise, sounding as if he's dying. "The foreplay. *Jesus Christ.* Use fingers, his or yours, to stretch the muscles. You can even try toys if you want. Or—*fucking hell, my life*—his tongue. Lube. Condoms. Don't forget those. And seriously, Bee, tell Joey if anything doesn't feel right. And what? Why are you smiling at me?"

"Joey would never hurt me," I tell him. "I'm not even worried about that."

He eases out a breath. "Okay. Good. That's good."

"But tell me more about this tongue thing. I can do that to his ass?"

Jason drops his face into his hands.

Yeah. I think this whole queer-awakening thing is going smashingly.

There's a pep in my step when I arrive at the gym late Saturday morning. It's been a whole thirty-six hours since I last saw

Joey. He had a busy day yesterday, so we couldn't meet up. But now that it's the weekend, he's free as a bird.

I whistle to myself as I stash my gym bag, getting a few odd looks tossed my way that I pay no mind to. Nothing could get me down on a day like today.

I'm just stepping up on a treadmill to get my warm-up started when Joey walks in. My heartbeat trips, a smile forming on my face in an instant...

And then I about *die*.

Joey is wearing the shortest short-shorts I've ever seen on any human and a cropped tank top that shows off every single inch of his V. His bag is at his side, not impeding the view in the slightest, and, if anything, the way his arm muscles are popping from the weight only adds to the picture. And as he walks my way, giving me a breathtaking grin? I start to worry I may get my first ever gym-boner.

"Joe," I breathe, clutching the sides of my treadmill tight since my knees no longer seem to be functioning. "What are you..."

"Hey, bub," he says easily, coming in to give my temple a kiss. "Let me store my bag, and I'll join you."

Joey walks off, and my head swivels to follow him.

"Oh, fuck," I mumble, eyes dropping straight to his ass. "Is that some cheek?"

Joey disappears around the corner, and I take a moment to shake myself loose.

So Joey is hot. I already knew that. Not like it's a big deal if he wants to show it off a little. Or a lot. He *should* be proud to display those thighs and that artisanal stomach. Not to mention the little trail that leads down below the band of his itty-bitty shorts that I most definitely want to follow with my—

"*Taaa*," I cry, pulse kicking as Joey hops up on the treadmill next to my own. "Joe-bro! My kangaroo-boo. How's it hanging?"

My eyes, incidentally, drop to his crotch, and I quickly avert my gaze.

Joey looks amused as he turns his treadmill on. "Feeling okay?"

"Me? Oh, just swell. Not that I'm *swelling*. Gosh, no. None of that. Because it'd be inappropriate. At a gym. Which...heh. Swole. It's kinda the same but not at all, you know?"

And *oh my God*, someone stop me.

Joey chuckles, as if he actually followed that train of thought, and starts off at a jog. My eyes slip down again. *So much thigh.*

I get my own machine moving as Joey asks, "Have a good day yesterday?"

"Oh, sure," I answer, thinking back over the past twenty-four hours. "Lots of nuts." Joey lifts a quizzical brow, and I hasten to add, "Not my own! I wasn't, like, jerking off all day."

Only once. Okay, maybe twice. Three times tops. While thinking about Joey and his abs.

I wheeze. "The nuts were for the squirrels."

"The squirrels?" he asks.

"For the game I'm designing," I explain, thankful when my heart rate starts to come down. "Most people probably don't think about it, but there's a lot of detail that gets layered into the background of video games. Especially in ones like ours that are more visually realistic. Stuff like squirrels, deer, falling leaves, pinecones on the ground... Anything to make it feel more lifelike."

"And you're the one who designs all that," Joey says, sounding almost proud. Which is...nice.

"Well, I'm one of the people," I correct. "It's a team effort."

He hums. "What's your favorite part? Of your job, I mean."

I consider that as my feet slap against the treadmill belt, Joey's doing the same beside me. "Testing, I think. Not just in-design simulation, but actually creating a character, going into the game, and exploring it. I like looking at how everything has come together. Experiencing what we've created. Not to sound all *Matrix*, but when people play our games, they see exactly what we intend them to, right? They see the world we've built. When I play...I see all the components, all the code and carefully constructed webs that hold it all together. And I guess I really like that part. Because it reminds me that real life is the same."

"How so?" Joey asks, watching me curiously.

"Just...people," I say with a shrug. "We have so many systems running at the same time under the surface. There's a lot we're feeling and thinking and going through, but when you look at a stranger moving throughout their day, you don't see that. You're not thinking about *their* life. You're thinking about them in relation to you. It's good, I think, to remember we're all real under the surface. And the way we treat each other matters."

Joey holds my gaze for the longest moment, never breaking stride. "Shit, bub," he finally says, shaking his head slightly. "You're pretty remarkable, you know that?"

"You really think so?" I ask, feeling warm and...*fuck*, I don't even know. Like I could run another ten miles easily if I have Joey there to encourage me.

"Yeah, I really do," he answers. "Now what do you think—should we run a bit longer or move on?"

"I'm all warmed up," I tell him, shutting off my machine as he does the same. "What do you want to do today? Legs? Arms? Core work—*oh my good freaking God.*"

"All right?" he asks.

I cough. "Yah. Good. You're just, uh, bent right over there, huh?"

"Legs are a little tight."

"Sure, sure," I say, swallowing, my eyes taking in the curve of Joey's ass. His hands are reaching toward the ground, the tips of his fingers touching his toes. His ass is... "Cinnamon buns, you know? They're pretty good. Round and...tasty."

Joey shoots me a look before hugging his calves, digging into the stretch, his head practically between his legs. *I* want to be between his legs.

"So, uh, what are you doing after this?" I ask, wondering if I sound as desperate as I feel and praying the suggestive "me?" I heard was only inside my head.

Joey stands upright and shakes out his limbs. "I'd like to get a little work done at my house this afternoon. Do you... I mean, would you want to come over? I don't know that it'd be all that interesting, but—"

"Yes," I say excitedly. "Yeah. Yep. Count me in. Do I get to play with your hardwood?"

There's a long beat of silence before Joey's lips twitch. "You're talking about my floors, aren't you?"

"What else would I be—*Oh.*"

"Oh," Joey repeats, grinning. He steps in close, fingertips pressing lightly to my stomach, his breath passing near my ear as my own hitches. "Either way, bub, the answer will be yes."

With that, he walks away, leaving me gaping at the wall of windows.

"Joey!" I hiss, spinning after him, nearly stumbling when I catch sight of the strong lines of his lower back glistening with the smallest hint of sweat. I swallow down my spit and catch up to him. "You... You can't just say stuff like that while I'm wearing gym shorts."

"No?" he asks mildly, looking rather pleased with himself.

"No way, dude. That's, like, Boner Bro Code 101. Everyone knows nylon is off limits. What...what are you doing?"

"Leg press."

"In *those*?" I squeak.

Joey gives me a smile I'm pretty sure is part wickedness as he settles onto the machine, his legs up near his chest, those tiny shorts leaving absolutely nothing to the imagination. *That's definitely some cheek.*

"Are you wearing a jock?" I breathe reverently.

Joey smirks, and *yep*. It's official. I've left the mortal plane. It's the only explanation for why I feel suddenly weightless, the only sound in my ears the whoosh of air and clouds around me.

"At least you're in my Heaven," I mumble.

"What?" Joey asks around a laugh, starting his reps.

"Just that I'm fairly certain you're a literal angel, and I've never been between a guy's thighs before, but I'm a little jealous of that empty space between yours."

The machine clunks loudly as Joey comes to a halt, his whole body going still. "Shit, bub."

"What?" I ask, mildly alarmed.

"It's just... I'm not used to hearing you say stuff like that on purpose," he says. His lips twist as he asks, "Is it the shorts?"

"I mean...they don't hurt," I admit, gaze traveling over Joey's quads and then up to his exposed stomach before reaching his eyes. "But no, Joey. It's not just the shorts. I'm pretty sure it's a you thing."

He blows out a breath, dropping his head back for just a second before he seems to shake himself off. "Okay. How about a cease-fire on the flirting and the eye-fucking until we're done with our workout. Otherwise, you're not going to be the only one with a gym shorts problem."

I grin, eyes pinging back down to Joey's crotch. "That so?"

He points at the leg press machine next to him. "Get to work, Bradley. Only good boys get cuddles."

"*Dude*," I say, not sure whether I should be appalled or awed. "You're holding cuddles ransom?"

Joey snorts, adjusting his feet and starting his reps again. "Not ransom. Just think of it as...motivation."

"Well, I'm motivated," I mutter, taking a seat next to him and hitching the bottom of my shorts up, trying to show as much skin as Joey. He grunts. "So. Motivated."

Joey's gaze flickers with amusement and something far more heated as I begin my own leg presses. Turns out exercising while horny kind of sucks.

It's a relief when we finally wrap up our workout. I'm sweaty, tired yet wired, and *really* looking forward to going back to Joey's place.

"Want me to grab us lunch on my way over?" I ask, holding the door into the locker room open for Joey to walk through. "I can pick up sammies or something."

"Sure," he says. "Thanks, bub."

"Don't mention it. It's the least I can do in exchange for you teaching me the ways of the...hammerer. The screwer? *Christ*, maybe my first lesson should be woodworking terminology."

Joey snorts a laugh. I'm about to add a joke about him teaching me how to *work wood* in more ways than one, if he knows what I mean, when my words dry right the hell up. Because Joey unceremoniously tugs off his crop top. Clad in only the skimpiest shorts known to man, he grabs his toiletry bag, a towel, and heads toward the showers.

"Meet you after?" he asks, a coy lilt to his words.

"Um," I manage.

Joey smirks. Without even closing the curtain, he hangs up his towel, sets his bag on the ledge of the shower, and drags his shorts down to his feet.

I choke, Joey's ass framed by that jock directly in my line of sight. He turns just enough for me to see the outline of his clothed cock, *winks*, and then closes the curtain.

I think, quite possibly, I'm really going to enjoy my foray into hardwood.

Chapter 18

JOEY

I beat Brad back to my house, which isn't a surprise. To say I'm excited for his arrival would be an understatement.

Despite the flirting at the gym, I'm more than happy to let Brad set the pace between us. I'm in no rush for things to progress physically.

But the fact that Brad wants to hang out, doing something as simple and mundane as house renovations with me on his weekend? That means a lot.

I change into a pair of old jean shorts while I wait for him to arrive. When my phone rings and I see that it's my mom, I answer.

"Hey, Mom, how's it going?"

"Hi, my boy," she says happily, her soft voice so very familiar. "Things are good here. What are you up to?"

"I'm about to do some work on the house," I tell her, heading down the stairs.

She hums. "What's today's project?"

"The wainscoting in the dining room. Either refinishing it if it's in good enough condition or scrapping it for new."

"Well, if anyone can fix up some boards in need of loving repair, it's my little carpenter."

I smile. My mom never begrudged me wanting to follow my dad's footsteps into construction, despite the obvious divide that grew between us. She's always supported me following my dreams, just as she supported my decision to move here to Vegas.

"I'm hardly little anymore," I point out needlessly.

She *pshs* at the same time as I hear the front door open and close. My pulse kicks up as Brad's voice rings throughout the house.

"Honey, I'm home."

"And who might that be?" my mom asks in my ear.

"That's my...Brad," I answer, holding the phone away from my mouth before calling, "In here."

Brad comes sauntering down the hall and into the kitchen, a big smile on his face. When he sees I'm on the phone, he raises an eyebrow.

"My mom," I tell him.

Brad nods, and before I know what's happening, he's plucking the phone out of my hand. He sets the call on speakerphone as I blink in shock.

"Mama Delgado?" Brad says cheerfully. "Hi. Hello. I'm Brad, Joey's new bestie."

"Is that so?" my mom asks, sounding amused. She knows perfectly well who Brad is to me. There aren't many secrets between me and my mom. "It's nice to meet you, darling."

Brad beams, mouthing *darling* at me. "Same! Sorry we can't meet in person. I give great hugs. Just ask Joey."

"In that case, I'll have to take a rain check," she says gamely. "Are you helping Joey with the house today?"

"Oh, for sure," Brad answers. "Brought some lunch, too. Can't have my baby kangaroo going hungry."

"Your...baby kangaroo," my mom says slowly.

I drop my head.

That...*was* still a secret.

"It started because of his legs?" Brad tries to explain. "Like, kangaroos have strong legs, right? And so does Joey. And obviously he needed a name."

"Obviously," she agrees. "Do you have one?"

"In general or Joey-specific?" Brad asks, setting the phone on the kitchen table as he starts pulling our lunch out of a to-go bag.

"I suppose specifically from my son."

Brad nods, even though she can't see it. "I'm his bub."

Silence. And then, softly, "That's sweet, darling."

"Isn't it?" Brad says, looking at me with a happy grin. "Joey's a sweet dude."

Lord.

"Will you be coming with my son next weekend when he visits?" my mom asks.

Brad's eyes swing my way, wide, as he mouths, "*Motorboating?*"

I snort before clearing my throat. "I, uh, haven't had a chance to ask yet," I tell my mom, speaking next to Brad. "But you're welcome to join me. It's my mom's birthday."

Brad perks. "If it's not an imposition," he says, even as he's grinning.

"Not at all," my mom answers. "Come. I insist."

Brad's palpable excitement makes it hard to remember this won't be my...*boyfriend* meeting my mom. Not yet, at least.

"We should probably get to our lunch," I say.

"Of course," my mom replies. "I'll see you soon, Brad."

"Can't wait. It was really nice to meet you, Mama D," he says before handing my phone over.

I click off speakerphone, bringing the device to my ear. "Mom?"

"I love him," she says instantly.

I glance Brad's way before walking further into the kitchen. "It's still—"

"Early. I know. You told me. Doesn't mean I can't hope for my son."

I let out a sigh. Brad is pulling his chair out now, our sandwiches sitting atop their wrappers on the table. "I hope, too."

She hums. "I'll let you get on with your date."

"It's not a—"

"Toodle-oo! Love you."

The line goes dead, and I huff a laugh. Ever the optimist, my mom. After filling two glasses with water, I join Brad at the table. He shoots me a closed-lip smile as he chews his sandwich.

"Your mom is nice," he says once his mouth isn't full.

"Yeah. She's the best, really."

He nods. "So are we driving over?"

I pause, lips quirking. "You want to go on a forty-hour cross-country car ride? Twice?"

He shrugs. "Could be fun. Ooh! We could stop at a bunch of those weird roadside tourist traps, like the country's biggest ball of yarn or a wax sculpture museum featuring D-list celebrities."

"*Or*," I propose, chuckling, "we fly, and it takes a fraction of the time. I'd only planned on staying the weekend, anyway."

"Sure," Brad says easily, sandwich hovering in front of his face. "That works. I suppose now is as good a time as any to pop my plane cherry."

He bites into his sandwich, and I stare at him, my own food remaining untouched. "You've never flown?"

"Never had a reason to," Brad mutters. He shoots me another small smile. "But hey, it'll be an adventure. Like the pool! You know, a lot of my firsts are turning out to be with you, Joey-roo."

He chuckles, but I flush hot. At the implication of trust, maybe? At the memory of Brad clinging to me in the water? At another first we recently shared. His first kiss with a man. And what other sorts of *firsts* he's expressed interest in.

"As long as you're sure," I say, shifting in my seat. "We could drive if you'd rather."

"Nah, it's fine," he answers, giving my foot a nudge under the table. "Now eat up so we can screw." His eyes widen, and then he coughs. "Fool—*tool* around. *Christ*, you know what I mean. So you can show me your tool. Your *hammer*. Oh my God, what is happening?"

I laugh so hard my eyes leak.

When Brad and I finish up our lunch, I head out to the garage to grab my tool bag. Remembering something Brad let slip when we first met, I grab my belt as well, slinging it around my hips.

Brad is waiting in the dining room when I get back inside, looking as if he's inspecting the wainscoting I told him we'll be removing.

"You're right," he says, running a finger over the flaking wood. "It's in pretty bad shape, huh? How do you even repair something like this?"

"Sand it down," I explain, setting my bag on the floor. "Hopefully, the wood itself is in good enough condition that we can simply repaint it after."

"So I *will* get to play with your hardwood," he jokes, spinning my way, only to practically fall over his own feet. His eyes shoot impossibly wide, his gaze settling on my tool belt. "*Joey.*"

"You did ask to see my hammer," I say, patting the tool at my hip.

Brad lets out an airy, "*Yeah*. Yep. It, uh...looks good. Very girthy. And stiff."

I huff a laugh and pull it free. "Here."

"You want me to hold it?" he asks, voice high.

"If you want. I'll loosen the panels, and you can pry them free."

"While you...wear that," Brad says, gingerly taking the hammer from my grip.

"While I wear my tool belt, yes."

My lips twitch as Brad continues to stare. The fact that he's not even trying to hide his newfound interest is a heady fucking thing.

"Remember what I said before?" I ask.

He meets my eye, cheeks a little flushed. "Um. Which thing? You've said a lot."

"I'm safe," I remind him. "You can *try* with me. Touch me. Do whatever you want with me."

His cheeks darken. "Whatever I want?"

"Within limits," I amend.

"Right," he says a little roughly. "No watersports."

I chuckle, taking a step closer. Brad tracks the movement, his breathing picking up. "What I mean, bub, is that you're looking at me like I'm your favorite dessert. If you want to take a bite, you can."

He lets loose a breath before closing the scant distance between us and tugging me in by the back of my neck. Our lips crash together, both of us taking a single second to breathe, and then Brad's hand is in my hair, and mine are on his hips, holding him steady or maybe holding *myself* steady. He kisses the same way he does everything. Enthusiastically. He's light and playful, lips toying with me almost, but underneath it all is a buzzing current of wonder I can feel in the way he jolts when our chests brush together. Can feel it in his soft moan as his fingers drift down to my neck and shoulders, as if he's mapping the shape of me. I can feel it in his breathy exhalation as my own hands, surely bigger than his partners' before, settle at the small of his back.

This is new for him. Exciting. And it makes it all the more clear to me how damn lucky I am to be the one he chose in the first place.

I won't ever abuse that trust. Not ever. Not even if, when all is said and done, Brad goes on his way. Without me.

The thunk of the hammer against the floorboards has both of us jolting. Brad huffs a laugh, our faces still close, his eyes feathering open and latching on to me. "Sorry. Lost my grip."

I give the sides of his waist a squeeze before stepping back and picking up the hammer. "Might want to keep a firmer hand on your tool," I tell him, passing it over.

He snorts, eyes drifting down over me before he faces the wainscoting. He clears his throat several times. "So, uh...show me how this thing is done?"

With a nod and a quick adjustment of my tool belt, I grab a chisel and a mallet and start loosening the boards. Brad follows after me, using the claw of the hammer to tug the nails free and then lightly knocking the panels loose after I demonstrate the process for him. He has a smile on his face the entire time we work, and when I point out the nails he's removing are called brads, he gleefully starts making jokes.

"Fuck, that brad was tight. Really had to wiggle my way in."

"Heh. Wanna watch me hammer myself?"

"Hello, brad. I'm Brad. Prepare to meet your doom, as there can only be one."

I wonder if he'd prefer a spring or fall wedding.

It only takes fifteen minutes for us to strip the wainscoting from the walls. Afterwards, Brad helps me lug the panels outside. I set up my corded sander as he watches on.

"Moment of truth," I tell him, lowering my protective goggles so I don't get dust in my eyes.

"Do it, my man. Give that wood a good hard rubdown."

I look over at a frowning Brad.

"Why is everything wood-related so dirty sounding?" he mumbles.

With a laugh, I start up the sander. It doesn't take long to find out the wood is still in great condition beneath the cracked, flaking paint. Of course, with the uneven texture of the wainscoting, it's more trouble to remove the topcoat. But, after doing all I can with the sander, I grab some loose sandpaper to get in the crevices.

"Wanna do this part?" I ask Brad.

"Fuck yeah," he says, trotting over.

I grab an extra pair of goggles from my tool belt, settling them in place over Brad's light green eyes. There's a flutter in my chest as he grins at me. A tug in my groin I can't quite control. It's me who pulls him close this time, smacking a kiss against Brad's lips that causes him to grin wider.

"My, my," he says, tone teasing when I let him go. "Does working wood turn you on, Joey-roo?"

"Doing it with you sure does," I admit.

He looks pleased by that. Happy. And the fact that Brad has gotten comfortable enough to flirt with me makes it all too easy to tease him right back.

"You're up, apprentice. Show me how you stroke your wood."

Brad squints at me. "Is this, like, a kinky roleplay thing? 'Cause I could get into that."

I snort, but apparently he's only getting started.

"*Ooh*, Joey, your belt is *so big*. Please, teach me how to hold your drill. Oh! No, no, wait." He clears his throat dramatically, and I can't help but bite my lip. With a lift of his chin, he says, "I've got a Brad right here you can tap. Shit, that was good."

My smile feels ridiculously wide, my chest bubbly and warm. "Hey, bub?"

"Yeah?"

"I've tapped a thousand brads, but not one of them measures up to you."

He gapes at me. "*Dude*. That was smooth."

"Just like this wood will be when you're done rubbing it."

He busts out laughing. "Holy fuck. You picked the dirtiest profession."

"Somehow," I say slowly, "it's only dirty with you."

Brad preens at that, looking quite proud. With the sun beating down on us, I wave the one and only Brad Ulysses Bradley forward and show him how to get the sandpaper into the tight corners of the wainscoting.

By the time we're done, the wood has been smoothed back down to its natural glory, and I wonder if I've ever spent a day better than this one.

Chapter 19

BRAD

Things I've learned in the past several hours.

One. Joey looks just as hot in a tool belt as he does wearing a fanny pack. Maybe hotter, although honestly it might be a toss-up. The dude is *fine*, not a sentiment I've had the privilege of thinking before him.

Two. Woodworking is dirty as fuck. Case in point. There's a machine called a bench grinder. I'm still not entirely sure what it does. Joey started explaining the high-speed flex shaft, and I tuned the rest out. Not my fault, really. My brain was...elsewhere.

Three. This Brad most definitely wants to be tapped. Maybe not *fucked*-tapped. Not yet, at least. But perhaps our dicks could tap together? A little meet-and-greet? That's a thing, isn't it? We could do our *own* bench grinding.

Oh, fuck. There goes my brain again.

"Brad?" Joey asks, pulling me back to the present. He's wrapping the cord around his sander. "You okay?"

"Yep," I reply quickly, wiping my hands off on my shorts. They're a bit dusty, but not nearly as coated as Joey is. There's a fine layer of sawdust covering the man's entire torso and arms. Those thick arms that were rhythmically working the sander for the past hour. Back and forth. Stroking over and over and—

"*Oh*," I breathe as Joey grabs the hem of his t-shirt, tugging the material over his head. I swear time slows as he shakes it out, the muscles in his arms and abdomen rippling, his tool belt pulling his shorts dangerously low as sawdust floats through the air around him like glitter catching the light. "It's like the start of a porno," I whisper.

"What's that?" Joey asks, tucking his shirt into his waist-band.

"I was…just wondering…when you want to start painting," I say, not sure if I should admit to Joey that he's officially re-placed the cut-off-jean-shorts-wearing, tool-belt-wielding women from my fantasies with, well, the real-life image of *him*.

Is that bad bros-with-bennies etiquette? Fuck if I know.

"Painting can wait until tomorrow," Joey says, plucking his protective eyewear off. "We've done enough for the day. Want to hang out for a bit? We could play games. Cook some dinner, if you want?"

"Uh, yeah. Definitely," I tell him, a little distracted by the flex of his arms as he puts his tools away, not to mention that V that disappears below the edge of his waistband. I wonder if his cock is straight. Curved? Thick, like the rest of him? It sure felt thick pressed against my hip.

"Great," he says, giving me a smile. "I'll just head in and wash up real quick."

"Sure, sure," I say, licking my lips. "Um. Can I watch?"

Joey pauses.

I pause.

"Uhhh," I manage.

"You want to watch me shower?" he asks, standing very still, the brown of his irises dark. Far darker than usual.

Joey said he's here for whatever I want to try, right? Well, right now, what I want is *him.*

Steeling myself against my nerves, I admit, "Yeah, Joey. I want to see you. Touch you, maybe? And I definitely want to watch you shoot all over your abs."

Joey huffs an almost disbelieving laugh. "Fuck, bub."

"Maybe next time?" I agree.

He groans, head tipping back. When he meets my eye again, he stalks forward. My pulse jumps into my throat, my stomach hopping right along with it, as Joey comes to a stop in front of me. His work-roughened hands bracket my neck, his thumbs stroking over my jaw. He looks at me. Simply looks.

"Are you going to kiss me?" I ask, my pulse nearly drowning out my voice.

"Was thinking about it," he mumbles, those same exact words he spoke all those weeks ago when we stood like this outside my apartment door after our non-date date, when Joey wiped whipped cream off my lip and looked as if he wanted to devour me.

It's the same way he looks now.

"Well," I say, breath coming short. "What are you waiting for?"

Joey's lips curve into a smile, and then his mouth is on mine. He smells like sawdust, his skin warm beneath my palms, and I lose myself for a minute. In Joey. In the way his mouth feels impossibly familiar, as if we haven't kissed a mere handful of times before. I lose myself in wondering how many more kisses we could have. How many more days just like this.

We agreed on a month. A month to...explore. To try this out without risking our friendship.

But does it have to end there?

I'm hard and aching by the time Joey pulls back. As if sensing it, his eyes drop straight to my crotch, and he lets out a small whoosh of air.

"Do you want to come upstairs with me?" he asks, giving me the choice. Giving me an out, I suspect.

I don't want out.

"Yeah," I tell him firmly. "I'm ready to make acquaintance with your balls now, if the three of you would be so kind."

Joey's responding laughter feels a whole lot like that future I was just envisioning. I can't help but wonder if his moan will be the same.

Joey leads me up to his bathroom on the second floor, the air between us thick and anticipatory. He twists the shower on while I wait in the doorway.

"Good?" he checks.

I nod quickly.

He loosens his tool belt, the click of the buckle like a gunshot over the soft patter of water hitting tile. I wet my lips, watching as he drags the heavy belt off, setting it on the floor so it's leaning against the wall. He pauses again, watching me, hands toying with his waistband.

"Keep going," I tell him.

He pushes the button free. Unzips his jeans. I ease out a breath as the material drops to his feet, leaving him in black boxer briefs, his cock an obvious presence, tenting the fabric almost obscenely. He steps out of his shorts, shuffling them off to the side to rest near the tool belt.

"Still good?" he asks.

I step forward, the steam from the shower having started to warm the room. "Can I?"

Joey nods, his gaze more hooded than I've ever seen. It's a rush, knowing I turn him on. Knowing he's already hard, willing and waiting for whatever it is I have in mind. Which is, incidentally, a lot. Almost too much at once. Too many things I want to see and try. Too many ways I want to touch him or watch him touch himself. Places I want to taste. Tease. Tongue open.

I let out another breath, hands landing on his stomach before drifting down toward the band of his underwear. I slip my fingers beneath it, dropping down to a crouch as I tug the material down over his cock. It bobs once freed, waving almost proudly, as thick as I'd imagined and perfectly straight. I give the top of it a small tap, watching it dip a mere inch before popping up again.

"Hello, Greg," I whisper. "I'm Brad. It's so very good to meet you."

Joey makes a choked sound above me. "Did you just...give my dick a handshake?"

"It's only polite," I say, tugging his boxer briefs down to the ground. He steps out of them, and I lean back onto my heels, taking him in. All of him, nude in front of me. Bared fully. "Fuck, Joey. You're...you're really pretty."

He sucks in a breath, his cock jerking right in front of my face.

I let out a surprised laugh. "Oh, he liked that, huh?"

Joey swallows, the motion visible. "It's not every day a gorgeous man calls me pretty, let alone while said man is down on his knees."

My heart kicks in my chest, a near-painful thing. "You think I'm gorgeous?"

"More than," he says seriously. "I thought that the first time I saw you laughing, bub. I was pretty stoked when you gave me your number."

I groan, dropping my forehead to his hip. "Yeah, sorry about that?"

"I'm not," he says, fingers threading through my hair. I look up again, and I'm taken aback by the sincerity in his eyes. The softness, even. "It led us here, didn't it?"

Fuck.

I turn my face, eyeing Joey's cock. From this angle, it looks huge. Far bigger than any banana I've had down my throat. I run a finger over the length of it, from tip to base, and Joey lets out a sound that's near a hiss.

"Can I watch you jerk off?" I ask, wanting to see what Joey likes. Wanting to know how he pleasures himself.

"Yeah," he answers. "Anything."

He holds out a hand, and I let him pull me up. Joey steps into the shower while I tug off my clothes. His eyes stay on me, flushing my skin, making my very bones feel as if they're vibrating.

When I step into the shower after him, he tugs the curtain closed. There's a single showerhead situated in the middle of the spacious square stall. Water falls between us as Joey grabs his soap, squeezing some onto his palm. He offers it to me next, and I take the bottle, washing myself with half-focus as I watch Joey's hands run all over his skin. He takes his time, suds forming with every swipe of his palms over his biceps, his pecs, his stomach, down further. His fist glides over his cock once, twice, a puff of air escaping me when he reaches lower still, cupping and washing his sac. He does his legs last before stepping under the showerhead to rinse off. When he moves back, I take my turn, letting the water soak me, my eyes closed against the spray.

"Do you know what I love about being with someone who has a dick?" Joey asks, prompting me to step out from under the showerhead and open my eyes. His hand is around his cock again, moving leisurely.

I shake my head, eyes glued to the movement, my heart racing like I'm on a track.

"The fact that I can *feel* whatever it is they're feeling," he answers. "If they stroke their cock, I can feel it in my own, a phantom touch. Can you feel it?"

He glides his fist up and down in a purposeful stroke, and my entire body rolls in a shiver.

"Yeah," I admit, voice hoarse.

He smiles, a small, mischievous thing. "And this?" he asks, reaching for his balls and rolling them in his palm.

"Yes," I rasp, tingles racing across my skin. I feel strung tight, overly aroused even though I haven't even touched myself. Watching Joey's hand move up and down, watching his dick disappear and reappear piece by piece, watching his thumb swipe over the head, and the hand he has between his legs... I *can* feel it all. Imagine it. It's a circuit of pleasure from him to me in a way I've never experienced before.

But I want to be responsible for his pleasure, too. I want to feel him in my palm. Want to feel his pulse and the throb of his cock against my fingers. *Fuck*, I want to know what it's like to cause his eyes to shutter in bliss. Want to make him tip over the edge and know it was *me* who brought him there.

There's no dismissing who Joey is as he stands in front of me. He's a man, yes. One I'm attracted to. Maybe that should scare me a little or make me pause.

But the truth is the idea of being with a man never bothered me. I just never saw myself with one.

Not until Joey.

"I want to touch you," I tell him. "I don't know what I'm doing, I just... I want it. Can I?"

In answer, Joey lets himself go, and I step forward, wrapping my hand around his cock. Feeling him in my grip is alarming. Not because it's frightening or new. But because of how *right* it feels. This is *my* Joey. And touching him has never, not once, felt wrong.

He sucks in a breath as I stroke him, awkwardly at first until I find the right angle. His hand grips the side of my arm, his other on the shower wall for balance, muscles tensed and his breathing growing more rapid as the seconds pass.

"Bub," he says, voice rough, uneven. My eyes flick up to his, and my breath punches from my lungs.

He looks...awestruck. Utterly bewitched.

"Fuck, Joey," I whisper, his pupils so large the brown is barely visible. "Your dick is in my hand."

"Yeah," he breathes.

"It's just...that's your penis. Like, hello. I'm jacking your erect cock right now."

He groans, fingers tightening on my arm.

"It's a very nice cock," I assure him. "Not that I've had many. Or any. But I like yours a lot."

He sinks his face against my neck, biting lightly, and I jolt.

"*Fuuuck*," I groan out, his stubble and lips dragging along my neck. Across my jaw. To my lips. He kisses me, hot pants against my mouth, his tongue meeting mine as I work him over. I *can* imagine what it's like for him, just as he said, the ghost of it turning me on all the more.

When he stutters out a ragged breath like he's close, my heart leaps.

"Can I touch you?" he asks, as if he wants nothing more.

"Yeah. Yes. *Please.*"

His hand leaves the wall to wrap around my cock, and we both stumble. I end up pressed against the tiles, Joey boxing me in, the tug of his callused grip making me gasp and shiver. It's torture and bliss in one, as oversensitive as I am. As close to the edge already.

"Oh fuck, oh fuck," I mutter, losing my rhythm on his cock.

"Do you know what it feels like to touch you?" Joey rasps, his hand tangling in my hair, his other a relentless dragging pressure that has my balls wanting to unload.

"Yes. Yes, I do," I pant. "Because it's how I feel touching you."

He grunts at that, his cock jerking in my fist, the unmistakable swell of him giving me just enough time to look down before he's shooting over my still-stroking hand. His cum hits his abs, one spurt, two, a third running down his slick skin. I suck in a breath and follow him.

My orgasm hits me like a goddamn medicine ball to the stomach, and I watch, almost out of body, as my cum joins his. It's so fucking erotic, seeing it streaking down, watching it run along those gutters like I imagined that I come again. A second time? An aftershock? I don't even know. But it races through me like a live wire, cascading energy pinging around every corner of my body from my balls to my cock to my fingers and toes. I curl into Joey, holding his shoulder for support, hanging my head and staring through bleary eyes as our cum rolls down his skin.

"Fu-u-uck," I moan. "So very definitely queer."

Joey huffs a laugh, the sound petering into a groan when I lift a heavy-weighted hand to his pec. I trace the firmness of the muscle, running my fingers over and around his nipple. Mapping the shape of him.

"I like these, too," I admit. "I mean, I like a lot about you. But these are, uh...yeah."

Joey's hands slide to my lower back, settling on my ass cheeks and tugging me close. I pull in a breath, the sheer size of him so much bigger than I'm used to. *Everything* about Joey is different than what I'm used to.

"Would you stay the night?" he asks, his lips brushing the side of my head.

"Like a sleepover?"

Another laugh. "Mhm."

"Yeah, okay," I agree, grinning. "Can I use your chest as a pillow?"

A small pause. "If you'd like."

"Very much," I tell him. "But maybe let's stay here for another minute, okay? Because I'm not sure if my legs are working yet."

Joey chuckles, his lips pressing a quick kiss to my hair. I let him hold me against the wall. Hold me up, really. Like any time I'm in Joey's arms, I feel safe. Cocooned.

Precious, even.

We'll need to wash up again to remedy the sticky situation between us. Unfortunate, really, considering how nice my jizz looks on Joey's skin. And then we should definitely make some dinner before either of us gets too hangry.

But for now? I'm content to stay right here in Joey's massive shower, sharing the afterglow.

I just had sex with a man. *This* man. I think I can most definitely add that to my list.

Step six in Brad's Guide to Finding Himself and Falling in Love:

Wade fearlessly into the unknown.
Big. Fucking. Check.

Chapter 20

JOEY

It's my internal clock that wakes me. A quick check of the lightly lit analog above my dresser confirms it's early still, not even eight in the morning.

I glance down at my chest, where a rather warm Brad is using me as a pillow. He's barely moved all night. Or, if he has, he came right back in, nestled in the crook of my arm, his cheek pressed against me, his hand settled atop my stomach.

He said he doesn't sleep well, but he didn't disturb me once. A good night for him, maybe?

I run my hand lightly over his shoulder, the feel of him tucked against me, all smooth skin and warm man, making my throat catch. It feels so...*normal*. Or what I want normal to be. Brad, here in my bed, or me in his. Waking up together. *Being* together, period.

People spend their entire lives searching for this. Trying to find the right person at the right time. To know I've found mine...my right person...without yet knowing if it's the right time?

It's terrifying.

I told Iggy it was worth the risk. And I still believe that. I do.

But I don't know how I'd ever be able to let this man go.

When Brad shifts, I hold my breath, not sure whether or not I want him to wake and shatter this perfectly still moment. He murmurs something indistinct, his fingers skating over my skin before settling at the side of my ribs. Turning his face, he lets out a sigh. He's lying almost entirely on his stomach, a position I'm not sure I could sleep in.

He seems to slip back under, and my tension unwinds, making me realize just how stiffly I'd been holding myself. Perhaps I'm still a little scared. Scared that Brad will wake up and realize exactly who he's with, and that he'll, what...freak out, maybe? Change his mind?

But he didn't act any differently last night after our shower. After the shared orgasms that left me reeling. He was all smiles while we made dinner, ate on the couch, and played video games. And he came upstairs with me afterwards, far earlier than his usual bedtime, claiming the snuggles would be well worth it.

He's initiated every step of this, hasn't he? The first kiss. Admitting he felt something...*more* for me, even if he didn't have a full grasp of what that meant. Asking to watch me touch myself and for him to do the same.

At this point, I don't think the physical is going to scare him. Which means I need to start showing Brad what it is I want us to be. More than sex. More than...bros with benefits.

I need to show him what it would be like to be mine.

When Brad shifts again, making a more alert sound, I rub up and down his arm. He pulls in a breath, face nuzzling against me as he seems to come to consciousness.

"Comfy," he mumbles, his voice sleep hoarse.

I huff a small laugh. "The bed or your pillow?"

"Both," he says, giving the pec he's not lying on a squeeze. My cock, already half-hard, stiffens when Brad starts to rub himself against me, an unconscious movement that has his erection dragging against my leg through the thin fabric of the sleep pants he borrowed. He stills as soon as he realizes what he's doing. But then he turns his head to look down my body and says, "Oh, good. You're up. Hi, Greg."

My laugh this time is mostly breath as Brad skates his fingers down my bare stomach. My cock bucks, and he makes a soft, excited sound, as if the simple fact that he turns me on is astonishing to him.

"Can I?" he asks.

"Of course," I say roughly.

He doesn't slip his hand under the band of my boxer briefs. Instead, his fingers trail over the fabric, he himself scooting ever so slightly to see better. He's still lying on my chest, still looking down, and it kills me not to see his face. But knowing he's watching his hand as it smooths over the head of my cock is arousing in its own right. He glides his palm downward, grip loose, tracing the shape of me.

"God," he says, squeezing a little before making a return trip upwards. "Something about...about holding your dick is like..." He lets out a breath. "Everyone has tells, you know? Signs of arousal. But *this*. There's no mistaking this. And I've never been on this side of the equation before. With someone's dick in my hand. I didn't realize it'd make me feel so..."

The persistent up-and-down exploration of my cock makes it hard to think, but I manage to ask, "Makes you feel what?"

His lips ghost over my pec, a featherlight touch, his fingers tightening in a way that has my hips hitching and a groan reverberating out from my chest. He turns his face toward me, tongue swiping over my skin before bright green eyes flash upwards, meeting mine, startling in their intensity. "Powerful," he answers.

My breath is shaky, my hand flexing on Brad's arm as he shifts again, pushing himself all the way up. His hand never leaves my cock, stroking me through my briefs as he hovers above me, his hair a mess he does nothing to try and tame. He holds my gaze and lowers his lips to my chest, pausing. Waiting.

For direction, maybe? Waiting for me to beg?

"Suck me," I request. Or maybe it's a demand.

He grins—a playful thing that feels like a punch to my gut—before lowering the final half inch required to lick my nipple. His tongue rasps over me, soft and wet, just once. And then he takes me into his mouth.

My head falls back against my pillow. Not just because his lips are on me. His tongue, too. But because of the way he's sucking me like he goddamn loves it. He lets go of my cock, taking my pec in hand, *him* groaning as his tongue rubs and his thumb rolls over my nipples in tandem. He pops free and shifts to the other side, taking that nipple into his mouth, his cock pressing against my hip as he sucks and ruts against me.

"Fuck," he whispers, more to himself than anything. "Fuck, these are beautiful."

My chuckle is hoarse. "I take it you're a boob man?"

"They're not boobs. I know that," he answers, his short stubble bristling my skin as he lays kisses across my pecs. "But still, Joey. They're fucking..." His words dissolve into a reedy sort of moan as he gets distracted, his hand like a hot brand traveling down my stomach. He leans back enough to watch his fingers trace over my skin, seemingly transfixed by every groove and bump he encounters. He runs a path over my Adonis belt, down and then up the V-shaped muscles. "Fuck.

These, too. I'm happy to report your cum gutters are in perfect working order. Ten out of ten, would jizz on them again."

"Glad you approve," I manage, my stomach muscles jumping when Brad's hand finds its way back to my cock. He squeezes me before giving me a couple near-desperate jerks through the fabric of my briefs.

"Why was that so hot?" he asks, me or himself, I'm not sure. "Seeing my cum on your skin. It was like..."

He trails off, and I have to move. I can't lie still anymore. I grab the back of Brad's thigh and tug his leg over me so that he's straddling my lap. He lets out a surprised laugh, but it quickly shifts to a groan as I pull him down and grind up against him.

"Fuck," he mutters, eyes slipping shut.

"Can I try something?"

"Yeah, yep," he husks.

Smoothing my hand under his waistband, I ease his sleep pants down over his ass and free his cock. Then I hastily push down my own underwear until they're around my hips. Brad watches with wide eyes as I spit in my palm.

"What are you..."

I wrap my hand around our cocks, spreading the moisture and giving a squeeze. "Ride me, bub. Come on my stomach. Mark me up all you want."

Brad mumbles another hearty *fuck*, his eyes feathering closed and then opening again as he shifts his hips, testing the movement. He settles into a rhythm easily, letting out little gasps, one after another, as he fucks into my fist, our cocks rubbing together.

"Why does that feel so—*haa*," he breathes, words aborted. "Why—*ahh*. I've never...*fuck*, that's good. Why is that so good?"

Brad's eyes are fixed on our cocks, at my fist wrapped around us, at the way he's grinding against me in an approximation of fucking. His hands plant on my chest, and an electric shock zings from the point of contact straight down to my dick. I start stroking us harder, grabbing his hip and urging him on. The way his body is moving makes it all too easy to imagine he's sinking onto my cock instead. It's too much. Too...

"Joey," Brad groans, fingers flexing against my pecs. "I need you to come. Need you to—*need* you."

With a verbal shove that feels almost physical in its intensity, I fall blindingly over the edge, my cock pulsing in my fist, the rub of Brad's dick against me making me feel as if I'm spiraling down a ravine. I'm weightless, for just a moment, caught in the quick snap of all-consuming pleasure that makes focusing on anything else an impossibility. There's only the complete takeover of my senses and a single breadth in time where nothing else—not a single thing—exists except for this. Brad and me.

The fog clears just in time to register Brad's excited moan as he swells in my hand. His cum lands on my stomach, his chest and abdominals heaving in and out as he works to catch his breath. A tremor wracks his body, motion followed by stillness like the tail end of a sigh.

I let go of our spent cocks, casing Brad's face, not sure what I'm looking for. All I see is...happiness.

Brad lifts his hand slowly, cool air washing over my chest as he trails his pointer finger downwards. It takes me a minute to realize he's not just rubbing our cum into my skin, but...

"Did you just spell out your name?" I check.

He makes a satisfied sound, patting the side of my stomach before hopping up with energy I'm not expecting. "I sure did. Now I need some coffee. Do you want any? I'll start a pot. Hey, what time did you want to paint those boards today? Do you even have paint? If not, we can run to the hardware store after breakfast. *Ooh.* Dibs on asking for caulk. I've always wanted to do that."

Brad is nearly out the door, sleep pants pulled back up over his ass, when he spins and heads back my way.

"Forgot something," he says, one knee on the bed as he leans over me. Hand clasping the side of my neck, he gives me a quick yet enthusiastic kiss. He smirks when he leans back, eyes on my stomach, a smug expression filling his face. Then he twists my nipple and practically jogs out the door. "*Gooood* morning!"

I huff a laugh. And then another. My stomach tingles, our cum drying on my skin, the butterflies below the surface caused by the very same man who casually branded me after coming hotly across my abs.

For a guy who thought he was straight not a week ago, Brad sure has fallen into bed with me with an ease that's surprising and yet...not.

After washing up, I find him in the kitchen, the pot of coffee already brewing. He's humming, looking inside my fridge, dancing a little on the balls of his feet.

"You like bacon?" he asks, shuffling the contents of my fridge around. "Eggs? I assume so because you bought them, but you never know. Maybe you just like cracking the shells and sorting the yolks from the whites, not actually—Oh. Hey."

"Hey," I say, wrapping my arms around Brad's stomach and giving his cheek a kiss. He's still warm, smelling a bit like *us* even though I can tell he washed his hands.

"Standing cuddles?" he asks, closing the fridge door. "I can get on board with that."

I snort. "I think it's called a hug."

"Oh. Heh. Right. I guess I'm just not used to facing away from the person I'm hugging. I'm usually the aggressor, you know?"

I turn my nose into his neck and laugh. "The aggressor?"

"Well, yeah. I tend to be more touchy-feely than my partners. A little clingier, I guess? So this?" He slips his arms back so he can grab my ass, giving me a little squeeze. "It's nice. Very nice."

"Anytime you want a hug," I tell him seriously, "I'll give you one. Be it six seconds long or sixty."

He lets out a happy sigh, leaning back and giving me his weight. His voice, when he speaks, is quieter. "Thanks, Joey. It's underrated, you know? Just...holding someone. Being held. People take for granted what such a simple form of contact can do. But I've always thought... Well, I think I might like it more than sex."

"Really?" I ask, trying to keep the surprise from my voice.

"I mean, don't get me wrong. Orgasms are awesome. Orgasms with you? Really fucking awesome. Like, top notch, dude. And we've only scratched the tip." There's a pause. "The tip of the iceberg? That's a thing, right? Anyways, my point is I really love painting your abs. But..."

I huff another laugh, and Brad moves his hands from my ass to my arms, covering them and turning his face toward me so I can see his profile.

"But orgasms don't last. They just don't. It's all well and good to want someone's body. To enjoy getting off with them. But wanting someone past that? Outside of that? Wanting to share a moment of connection? I think that's pretty great."

My breath leaves me softly, my eyes slipping shut as response after response flits through my head, each far too transparent to speak aloud. How do I tell this man he's quite possibly the loveliest person I've ever met? That I admire him and respect him. That I want him to keep surprising me with his kindness and grace, just as much as I want to hear the rambling words that so frequently fall out of his mouth.

I want to know every single piece of him, top to bottom, inside and out. I want to spend my life learning who he is. Falling, again and again, in small swoops and in large ones.

"I think..." I take a breath and start again. "You said once that hugging releases endorphins that make people happy and calm. Since meeting you, I've been more calmly happy than I can remember being in a really long time. Maybe ever. You're like a hug, Brad. Always. Whether or not we're touching. So if this gives you even a fraction of what you've given to me, then yes. Anytime you want it...or need it...I'm here."

Brad spins, and I loosen my hold, hands coming to rest on his back once he's facing me. We're nearly the same height, Brad just a touch shorter. It makes it easy to look into his eyes, to let him see what he wants from mine.

"Kissing," he says. "That's a benefit, right?"

"Big one," I agree.

"Yeah, good."

Brad's lips are warm as they meet mine. They're soft and sincere. And maybe he's onto something about the importance of intimacy outside of sex. Because what Brad and I are building—what we have been from the start—feels stronger than any other connection I've had. It's a foundation I could see holding us up for years, decades to come if we let it.

Assuming, when all is said and done, this home we're crafting...is one Brad wants to keep.

Chapter 21
Brad

"So explain to me again how this works. Is it going to hurt?"

Joey's lips twitch, but he doesn't appear bothered by my many questions. No, he's utterly calm and serene as he sits beside me in the big metal death trap we're about to go up in.

"It won't hurt," he promises.

"Unless we crash."

Someone in front of us gasps, and I cringe. *Yeah*, maybe should've kept my voice down.

Joey squeezes my hand. "If we crash, you probably won't feel a thing."

I stare at him blankly. "That does *not*, in fact, reassure me. What the hell, dude?"

He huffs a small laugh, pulling my hand onto his lap and looking at me so fondly my heart tries to jump from its cage. "Once everyone is on board, they'll close the plane doors and give us a speech about safety. We'll buckle our seat belts, and the pilot will drive us out onto the tarmac, just like a car."

"A really big car," I mumble.

"Just like a really big car," Joey says, not missing a beat. "Then we'll probably have to wait a little while before it's clear for us to take off. Once we go, it'll feel fast. You'll be pressed back against your seat, and then you'll feel a small swoop in your stomach when we leave the ground."

"Joy."

"It's not so bad," Joey assures me. "Your ears will eventually pop and you might feel some pressure throughout the ride, but it won't hurt."

"And landing?" I ask.

"The same thing in reverse. We'll descend, your ears will clear, you'll see the ground coming closer, and then the wheels will touch down and the plane will slow."

"You make it sound simple. I know it's not simple."

He shrugs. "It is for a pilot. They're trained for this."

I puff out a breath. "Who looked up at the sky one day and thought, 'We should fly like birds! That sounds like a *great* idea. Not dangerous in the least to be so far above the ground.' I don't have wings, Joey. I was not made for flight."

He gives me an odd look. "But aren't you Bee?"

"I... *Fuck*."

Joey laughs, and I groan.

"It'll be fine," he says, twisting my hand in his, the soothing motions of his fingers intended to lull me into a false sense of security, I'm sure. "How about this? Once we land, I'll ensure the trip was *well* worth your while."

I eye Joey's little smirk, my pulse hopping. "Yeah?" Glancing quickly around, I lean closer and ask, "We talking handies?"

He snorts lightly. "Or..."

Or...?

"Or what?" I demand when Joey doesn't say anything else. His eyebrows do a little dance, gaze dropping to my lips, and I suck in a breath. "Blowies?"

His laugh this time is louder, but he only shrugs, as if to say *maybe*.

"Joey," I hiss. "If your lips are on the table, that's going to be a firm yes. *Fuck*. I'm getting a boner."

"At least you're not scared anymore," he says.

"Oh, I'm still terrified. Not of the blowjob," I hasten to add. "Just that I might die before I have the chance to experience what your tonsils can do."

A beep overhead cuts off our conversation, and I reflexively squeeze Joey's hand.

"*Shit*," I chirp.

He makes a soothing sound as a voice comes over the intercom. I pay attention to every word, clocking where the closest emergency exit is, visually planning who I'll have to step over to get there. At least there are no children in the way, so I won't have to feel guilty.

"I'd bring you with me," I tell Joey, even though he's not privy to my internal thoughts. "We could share a flotation device."

His smile is warm.

When the plane starts moving, I realize I'm crushing Joey's hand. I ease up on the pressure, but he doesn't seem to care one way or another. I'm sitting in the window seat, so I have a clear shot of the ground as it passes. We turn onto what looks like a runway... And then we take off.

"You said there'd be a wait," I squeak, squeezing Joey's hand harder.

"Guess we were ready to go," he says.

My reply is something akin to "*ahhh*," and I close my eyes, not wanting to see us leaving the safety of the tarmac. There's a small whoosh in my stomach, a distinct loss of vibration, and then Joey's free hand is tugging my head around. He kisses my forehead, leaving his lips there, and I *breathe*.

"Okay?" he asks after a moment.

It feels like we're still going up. "Uh-huh."

"You're doing good."

"I'm ridiculous," I counter. "I'm a grown man who should not be afraid of flying."

"Hey," he says softly. "It's your first time. Of course it's going to be a bit scary."

"You sound like the girlfriend I lost my virginity to."

There's a pause. "Do I want to know?"

"Probably not," I admit. "There was a lot of emotional crying. On my end, not hers."

He hums. "Look."

Slowly, I open my eyes. The first thing I see is Joey's face an inch in front of mine. There's a small smile curving his lips, and *oh*. So pretty.

I give his cheek a pat.

He huffs a small laugh before nodding toward the window. "Over there."

"Huh?" I say, turning my head. "Are those..."

"Clouds," Joey fills in for me.

I make a small noise.

"You okay?" he asks.

"I'm just gonna rest for a bit," I mumble, closing my eyes and sinking down onto Joey's lap, my legs squished awkwardly against the side of the plane. "Let me know once we've landed?"

In answer, Joey threads his fingers through my hair, stroking gently.

At least if we fall out of the sky, we'll do it together.

"Oh my *God*," I whisper, face pressed to the window of the car. "This is your childhood home?"

"Pretty great, right?"

"Joey. It's *on* the water. I know you're an amphibian, but you didn't tell me you grew up literal footsteps from the shore. Is that a gazebo?"

"A small one," he says, putting the car in park.

"Uh, a small gazebo is still a gazebo, dude. What's that?" I ask, pointing to what looks like a huge shed with windows.

"Guest house," Joey says, opening his door. He climbs out but stops, leaning down far enough for me to see him through the doorframe. "Which means we don't have to be quiet."

Joey winks—*winks*—before heading toward the back of the car to retrieve our bags.

Suddenly, I'm thinking testing out the structural integrity of the guest bed sounds like a stellar plan. But then I see a woman stepping out the front door of the house. At first glance, Joey's mom looks absolutely nothing like him. Strawberry blonde hair, a petite frame, light blue eyes. But then she smiles, big and welcoming, and I see it.

I'm out the door in no time, and Mama Delgado's gaze swings my way.

"Mama D!" I call.

"You must be Brad," she says.

I stop just before reaching her. "Hugging okay?"

She waves me forward. "Get in here."

With a grin, I curl my arms gently around the woman who raised the most perfect man. She smells faintly floral, reminding me of the lemon trees in the regional office when they're in full bloom.

"You were right," she says, giving me a squeeze before letting go. "You give great hugs. It's so nice to meet you, darling. How was your flight?"

"Horrible," I say happily.

She looks momentarily taken aback, but then Joey is setting down our bags and stepping close.

"Mom," he says, tugging her in, looking like a giant compared to her.

Mama Delgado rubs Joey's back, the motion so casually familiar it makes my throat feel tight.

"My boy," she says gently, hands on his shoulders as she leans back. "Look at you. As handsome as I remember."

"It's only been a few months," he points out.

"*Psht.* A lot can happen in such a short period of time," she says, canting her head in my direction and raising an eyebrow.

Joey quickly cuts in. "Can we help with dinner?"

"It's all ready," Mama Delgado says, turning and giving us a wave. "Come, come. Set your bags inside for now. You can get settled after we eat. Brad, do you like seafood?"

"*Do* I," I say, loping after her.

Joey chuckles from somewhere behind me.

The inside of the house is just as inviting as the outside. It's washed in pale blues and seafoam green, oatmeal-colored accents keeping the decor light. Windows overlook the grassy yard out back, a small sloping hill leading down toward rocks that edge the crystalline blue water. A dock leads further out, the sun casting glittering ripples on the gentle waves that lap at shore.

"Wow," I mutter, feeling Joey's heat at my back as he joins me near the windows. "I guess I can see why you miss the water."

He hums lightly. "I do, but… I don't regret the move. And Las Vegas…it's really grown on me."

"Like mold?"

"Like—" He makes a grumbly sound, wrapping an arm around my waist. "Come on. Let's go eat."

Chuckling, I let Joey tug me toward the kitchen.

Plates are set out along the white countertop, wicker stools planted in front. I take a seat next to Joey just as his mom sets a plate of fancy-looking sub sandwiches down.

"Lobster rolls," she tells me.

I groan happily, and Joey huffs a laugh.

As it turns out, lobster rolls are the bomb. Joey catches his mom up on the construction business and his family in Vegas as we eat, and Mama Delgado asks me questions about video game design, seeming genuinely interested. She also asks about how Joey and I met, although I'm fairly certain by Joey's eye roll, it's a topic they've covered before. Even so, I tell her about the gym, leaving out the accidental first date and the whole *your son is teaching me how to buff his hardwood* thing.

I do know some limits.

When Mama Delgado excuses herself to take a call from a friend wishing her an early happy birthday, Joey and I head outside. By unspoken agreement, we make our way to the dock. It's sturdier than I expect, not moving in the least as we walk out to the end, where there's a wider platform. A boat is stationed nearby, held in a big metal frame half out of the water. Joey takes a seat beside me on the dock, letting his bare toes reach toward the rippling waves, so I do the same.

There are a handful of watercrafts out. Speedboats, a sailboat, a couple kayaks. But it's peaceful. Quiet where we are.

"When did you learn how to swim?" I ask.

"I don't really remember it," Joey says, "but my mom said I had lessons when I was one. They started early because of the risk associated with living so close to water, although the yard was fenced at that point. I just remember always knowing how to swim, as far back as my memories go."

"Bet you were cute," I mutter. "Little Joey Delgado in his tiny trunks splashing around in the water."

He's quiet for a moment. "What sorts of things did you do with your grandfather?"

"Ah," I say, leaning back on my hands as I think about it. "Not much outside. He liked puzzles, so we'd do those sometimes. And he had these models he'd build. Architectural ones, like famous buildings. He didn't really want me helping with that, but he'd let me watch. I don't think he knew how to handle me, you know? This kid he wasn't expecting so late in life. But he tried his best."

"Did you ever know your parents?" he asks gently, the words quiet like he's not sure he should ask them.

I don't mind.

"I didn't. Or well, maybe I did, but I don't remember them. They left when I was...three, I think? Some of my earliest memories are actually of Jason. He was..." I huff a laugh, thinking about the scrawny kid I met in kindergarten. How prickly he was but just as desperate for a friend as me. "He was mine. I don't know how to explain it other than he claimed me, and I claimed him, and that was it, you know? I think sometimes you just *know* someone is going to be important to you, even if you don't know how."

"Yeah," Joey says quietly, his gaze intent on me when I look his way. "I know what you mean."

I swallow roughly, not sure whether or not I should read into those words the way I want to. In the end, I settle for my own truth. "There haven't been many people in my life who knew how to handle me. I know I'm...a lot. And maybe that's why I fell into video games, you know? Playing them at first. And then making them. It's a space where imagination is limitless. And perhaps there's no truly perfect world, imagined or real, but when I think of *my* perfect world? Of what I want my life to be? I just want to be happy being me. What I'm trying to say is... Jason was the first person who accepted me as I am. Who made my life a happy one. Now, there's you."

"Bub," Joey says, nearly a whisper.

"I know we haven't known each other for long," I rush on. "But you're one of my closest friends. You're my people now. My Joey Kangaroo. So just...you better get used to me being around, man, because I've already claimed you. And I'm not that easy to shake."

Joey doesn't say a word. Instead, he crushes me in a sidelong hug, the both of us toppling onto the dock. I laugh as he smushes me beneath his weight, not at all displeased about my predicament.

"I guess you kinda like me, huh?" I tease.

He nods against my neck, his stubble bristling me. "Quite a lot, actually."

"Good," I sigh. "'Cause someday soon, I'd really like to find out if I'm a *caulk* or *be caulked* sort of guy."

A beat of silence passes. "Are you talking about—"

"Sexual intercourse," I answer.

Joey wheezes.

"All right?" I check.

"Yeah. Yep."

Yeah. This is a great fucking day.

Chapter 22

JOEY

It's early evening when we finally bring our bags over to the guest house. Although *house* in a generous term. The space is all one room apart from the bathroom, which is sectioned off. The rest of it is open, a bed at the back right and a small kitchenette along the left. Near the front door is a two-seater couch.

It's cozy but still plenty of room for two people for the weekend. Best of all, it's private.

I flick the blinds closed on the windows that face the main house before heading Brad's way.

"*Dude*," he says, looking inside the small fridge. "Is that iced coffee?"

I *might* have told my mom about Brad's caffeine habit. I'm not surprised she had some coffee waiting for him, nor am I surprised by the three bags of high-quality beans on the countertop.

"Look at—*Oh*. Hello there," Brad says.

"Hi," I reply, gently closing the fridge door and backing Brad up against the wall. Surprise and excitement spark in his eyes. It's the last thing I see before my mouth is on his.

Brad groans, hands fisting in my shirt to pull me closer. There's a quick, "Mhm, good," and then his lips are back on mine, all chaotic energy and the boundless enthusiasm Brad seems to carry on his person at all times. There's simply no resisting him, never has been, so I don't even try. I meet his movements in kind, our hands tugging, lips battling, fingers and tongues demanding more. When I palm Brad's cock through his jeans, he jolts and then sags against the wall, words mumbled against my mouth like *yes, that, please.*

I pull back, and Brad makes a noise of displeasure. But then I'm dropping to my knees, and his eyes flare wide.

"Oh my God," he whispers. "Are you gonna…"

"I'm gonna," I tell him, flicking the button on his jeans and dragging down the zipper. Brad pulls in breath after breath as I slide his pants down his legs. His lips look starkly red, his eyes so light they're nearly clear, and I catalogue every inch of him, filing the mental image away for later as I tug his briefs to the floor.

"Oh God," he says again.

I take his cock in hand, marveling at him here before me. How open he is. How unafraid in the face of things that truly matter. How, for a while, I thought I'd never get this. I thought it was a fantasy and nothing more.

Yet now…

Now, Brad is here with me. In this with me. He took a leap, allowing me to catch him, and there aren't enough ways to express to him what that means to me.

"Thank you," I tell him before wrapping my lips around the end of his cock.

His shuddering breath is music to my ears, the feel of him on my tongue heaven. He's the perfect thickness to worship for hours without tiring, but I don't think he'll last that long. Even so, I start now, slipping my lips to the base of him, holding him in my throat reverently, meeting his gaze so he can see there's no hurry in mine.

"Fuck, Joey," he all but whispers. "Look at you. Your mouth is around my dick. Holy fuck."

I hum, encouraging the rambling I've come to love—hell, I loved it from the first moment—and slowly drag my lips up toward the tip of his cock.

"Ah, God," he says, his hands flat against the wall, his chest shaking with his breaths. "No right to feel that good. Holy shit."

I suck on his cockhead for a moment before angling his dick out of the way and going for his balls. There's a *thunk* I suspect is Brad's head hitting the wall as I tongue one, swiping at it before running my fingers along the backside, helping lift his sac for better access. When I pull a ball into my mouth, Brad groans. Loudly.

"*Oh fuck.* Your tongue. That's really good. That's—Jesus!"

I smirk as I manage to get his entire sac in my mouth. I run my thumb along the tip of his dick as I suck him gently, tongue rubbing the undersides of his balls.

"Double balling," he breathes, making me choke on a laugh. He groans in response, his entire body feeling as if it's vibrating. "Fuck, fuck, fuck. *Joey.*"

I let his sac pop free, rolling his balls in my palm as I lift my head enough to lick up the length of his cock. "Yeah, bub."

He looks down at me, pupils blown. "I...don't have a conversation point. That wasn't, like, *hey, Joey?* It was just *Joey,* 'God, yes, man, your mouth is a genius and I like the way you look on your knees.'"

"All that in four letters?" I murmur, tonguing the bead of precum at the tip of his dick.

"*Hah.*"

I snort, taking him into my mouth again. Brad's hips hitch forward, his hand hovering in the air for a moment as he makes an "eh?" sound I think is a question. I nod around him, and his fingers sink into my hair, his other hand still flat on the wall like he's bracing himself.

"Your mouth is a treasure," he gasps. "Pure gold. *Fuck*, you're sexy. Holy shit. I'm gonna come."

I pull off of him, stroking his spit-slicked shaft with my fist. "Where do you wanna unload?"

"What? I don't fucking know, dude! You can't expect me to make decisions right now."

I huff, licking around his head, and he groans.

"Mouth?" he says. "No, face. Abs? *Fuck*. Mouth."

I drop lower, tonguing his sac again, pulling each ball into my mouth one at a time as Brad's grip tightens in my hair.

"*Joey*," he groans, the sound a plea.

Easing upwards, I swallow his cock to the root. Brad cries out, practically humping my face as his orgasm draws near. Keeping my eyes on his, my own watering, I press my fingers back behind his balls, lightly brushing his hole. He sucks in a breath but doesn't squirm away, so I rub more firmly with the tips of two fingers, and Brad comes down my throat with a hoarse, surprised shout.

He bows over me, both hands in my hair now, his cock swelling and releasing against my tongue. I continue sucking, keeping my fingers where they are, moving my hand just enough for the heel of my palm to massage his sac. He looks wrecked, his hair in disarray, his face gorgeously flushed and his mouth parted as he gasps for breath.

When his tension unwinds and he mutters, "Fuck, holy fuck," I ease away, grabbing his hip to help keep him steady and using the neck of my shirt to wipe the spit and cum off my face. A second later, there's a soft tap against the bottom of my chin.

I look up to find Brad staring right at me.

"Sorry," he says. "Just...needed to see your face."

I manage to keep my *fuck* inside. But only barely.

"Here," Brad says, holding out his hand. I let him tug me to my feet. "So, uh. That was, uh... Yeah."

My lips twitch. "Yeah?"

"Big fat yeah. Fifteen out of ten on the blowie. Like, pretty sure I lost consciousness for a second there. What, uh...what do you want?" he asks, tugging me closer. His fingers drift up under the hem of my shirt, seeking my stomach like a homing missile. "I mean, I could totally blow you, dude, but it's not going to be as elegant as that."

"Could I..."

I hesitate, but Brad gives my stomach a poke. "No, tell me."

"Could I fuck your thighs?" I ask, knowing it's the closest I'm going to get to fucking Brad the way I want right now. I'd be inside of him in a heartbeat if I thought he was ready, but we're not there yet. And that's fine.

He doesn't look unhappy with the request. If anything, he looks intrigued. "What, uh... How would we do that?"

Taking his jaw in my hand, I angle his face toward mine. His breath catches, and I close the distance between us, kissing him thoroughly, knowing he's tasting himself on my tongue. The thought is thrilling.

Breaking away, I tell him, "Turn around."

There's another intake of breath, and then Brad twists, kicking his pants and briefs off his foot as he spins to face the wall. I get my own pants down enough for my cock to spring free, and then I spit in my palm. Brad looks back at me as I wet my cock, a soft curse leaving his lips.

Stepping close, I press my lips to his cheek and guide my dick between his thighs. "Okay?" I check.

"Yeah," he breathes.

"Close your legs."

He does, stepping so his feet are pressed together, his palms flat against the wall. I interlace the fingers of our right hands together, bracing my left just below his stomach.

"You're gorgeous," I tell him, punching my hips. He gasps, and I repeat the motion, relishing the sound he makes. "You're good. And kind. And so fucking sexy it kills me sometimes."

"*Joey.*"

"I want you all the time," I admit, the sound of my hips slapping Brad's ass and the feel of his thighs around my dick turning my control into a tenuous thing. "All the time. And I'll never take more than you want to give me. But I'd take *everything* if you let me."

Brad's fingers tighten against mine, and he turns his head. "Take what you need. I trust you, Joey."

The noise I let out is pained. Brad doesn't object when I move my arm up around his chest, pressing him into the wall as I rut against him harder. I hold him to me, my nose at the back of his neck, everything in me riding a razor's edge as I battle not to lose myself. But there's no stopping it. I know I'm already lost.

I clamp my teeth down on Brad's shoulder as I come, my hips pressed to his ass, my cum coating the insides of his thighs as I jerk against him. It's so much, and not enough—not ever enough—and I don't know how to tell him he's ruined me. That I'd take a lifetime of holding him in my arms while my cum dripped down his legs over ever feeling another's touch. I don't want them. Any of them.

It's not logical. To *know* that so soon. To be so utterly sure of it.

But love, well... I don't think it's an emotion that's ever been ruled by logic or reason.

I don't move. Not right away. I keep my arm around Brad's chest in an approximation of a hug, my lips pressed to his shoulder. Our hands are still intertwined, the sound of our breaths mingling in the otherwise quiet room.

"One... Two... Three..." I say between breaths.

Brad huffs a laugh, face still turned toward me. "Four... Five..."

"Six," I finish, bringing my nose up to his hair, breathing in his subtle ocean scent. It's even better than this place, and I let it settle in my lungs, infiltrate me fully.

"You, uh...you're not letting go," Brad says quietly.

"No," I agree.

He hums, shifting just enough for my cock to slip from between his thighs. A curious sort of "huh" follows. "I've, uh, never had someone make such a mess of me before."

"Don't like it?"

"No, no," he says. "It's not that. I just feel...wet? It's kinda hot."

I press a kiss to the shell of his ear. "Does that mean I can come on you again?"

"On me. In me, maybe."

I grunt.

"I mean, we've already talked test results," he goes on. "We're not fucking anyone else. It'd be kinda hot to know your cum is in my ass. For *you* to know. For *me* to know you know."

"Yeah," I manage weakly.

"Would that... I mean, it's not like either of us could get pregnant, so would it be a big deal? To skip the condoms?"

I let out a slow, slow breath. "It's a matter of comfort level and trust," I tell him seriously. "Some people don't like that. And a lot of sexually active queer men wouldn't consider it unless they trust the other person implicitly. Generally, that translates to a long-term relationship."

"Oh," he says, the one syllable sad.

"But I trust you, bub," I continue quickly, pulling back enough to turn him my way. I resist dropping my gaze to his half-naked body, instead keeping my eyes on his as I frame his neck with my palms. "I trust you. And I'd enjoy it. So if you want me to fuck you bare...or if you want to fuck me bare, I'm game."

He swallows somewhat roughly. "I'm curious about it."

"Me fucking you," I guess.

He nods. "That felt good."

"Which part?" I ask, pulling my pants up to grab some paper towel.

"Um... You touching me. And...you behind me like that. I, uh..." He lets out a breath. "You have this way of making me feel small? Not in a bad way. In a good way, as if you're curling around me like a protective bubble. And that's new for me. To be the one being...taken care of? None of my girlfriends in the past took that more...assertive role. And I know being *manly* has nothing to do with who's doing the dicking. Like, roles in the bedroom don't define a person any which way. It's just..."

I wait as Brad collects his thoughts, using the opportunity to wipe up the mess between his legs now that I've done a cursory clean of myself. He gives me a quick thanks, not bashful in the least.

"Here's the thing," he finally says. "I *know* I'll enjoy fucking you. It's a given. But I'm fairly certain you fucking me is going to rearrange my world a little. And I guess I'm kinda looking forward to that."

My heart thumps painfully as I get to my feet. I step close to Brad, unable to keep my distance, unable to stop myself from brushing his hair back and cupping his face in my palms. "I'll make it so good for you," I promise.

He lets out an incredulous laugh. "See? That. That's what I'm talking about. All you have to do is say a few words, and I'm gone. How do you do that? How do you make me *want* you so much?"

"You must kinda like me," I tease, using his words from earlier.

He snorts, his hands on my hips pulling me closer. "Joey-roo, my dude, *like* is not a strong enough word for you."

My inhale is shaky, but Brad goes on.

"I'm a little bit obsessed, to be honest. It's embarrassing. And *ho*, hello, is that Greg again? Thought he went to sleep."

"He must have a thing for beautiful men being open and honest," I tell him, stroking his cheek with my thumb.

"Is that what we're calling filterless now?" he asks, forehead wrinkled. "I mean, I'm not opposed. It's just—*Oh*. Do that again."

I oblige, running my lips along his neck, my stubble bristling his skin.

"Fuck," he mutters, hands tightening on my hips. "You're just...full of...benefits, aren't you?"

His breathlessness has me smiling. "Loads. Why don't we get in the shower, and I'll show you the benefit of having an extra pair of hands around?"

"Yeah, yep. I like your hands. And—*holy shit*. You're carrying me. Like, I'm just up in the air right now as if that's a perfectly normal thing for a guy my size."

I smile against Brad's neck, his arms and legs wrapped around me tight like a clingy koala. His briefs dangle from his foot for a moment before dropping to the floor, the paper towel I used to clean us up long forgotten. I'll take care of it later.

Right now, I have an inquisitive, kind-hearted man in my arms, and I have every intention of showing him that obsession he mentioned?

It goes both ways.

Chapter 23

BRAD

Joey waits patiently as I step slowly down the ladder attached to the side of the dock. It's warm today, the sun out as it's been all morning. After sharing a lovely breakfast with Mama Delgado, Joey proposed going for a swim.

It's not that I'm against that idea, evidenced by the fact that my toes are now dipping into the cool, shallow water. I just have a healthy fear of being swept away in an uncontrollable current and ending up lost at sea, aka at the bottom of it. Never mind the fact that we're at an inlet where the water is relatively still compared to the beachfront just down the road. Caution is a good thing.

As is my nice orange life vest.

It makes getting down the ladder a little cumbersome, but I manage, my toes finally sinking into soft sand, the water up to my knees.

"That's not so bad," I comment.

"Pretty nice, right?" Joey says, a grin on his face as he squints into the sun.

"Oh," I sigh, patting his cheek. "Yes. So, so nice."

His smile gets impossibly wider.

"How far out do you want to go?" I ask.

"Just enough to swim?" Joey suggests. "You can stay a little further in if you want."

I nod idly, walking alongside Joey, one hand on the dock for balance. "Could I, like, float away?" I check.

"Nah," he says easily. "You'd get pushed to shore, not outwards."

"Sure, sure. But what about undertows?"

He smiles at me. "That's a concern at the beach, but not here, I promise."

I nod again, trusting him. As we reach the end of the dock, where the water is halfway up my stomach, wetting the bottom of my life vest, I come to a stop. Joey steps a few feet further, turning so that he's facing me and then pushing backwards into the water. He floats easily on his back for a couple seconds before twisting and dropping under the surface. When he comes up, he's fully wet, reminding me of that day at the pool when water was dripping down his back and over his ass, and I couldn't help but watch the journey.

Was I curious about Joey even then? I must have been. Why else would I have felt guilty for looking at his ass?

"I think I've always been bi," I muse aloud.

Joey's head snaps up, and he stands, walking my way as he brushes his hair back. "Yeah?"

"I mean... I've always been able to appreciate a nice ass. Man, woman, enby, it never mattered. I just... I've only been with women. But I wouldn't enjoy looking at men if I didn't find them attractive, right?"

Joey hums, seemingly weighing his words as his head tilts back and forth a little. "I don't think anyone can say for sure other than you. I think it's possible to find someone objective-ly beautiful without wanting to be with them sexually or romantically. It's like art. You can appreciate it without wanting to take it home."

"Dude," I say, letting out a snort. "Nice one."

He chuckles. "What I mean is attraction isn't always cut and dried. Is it possible you've always had the potential to find a man desirable but just haven't consciously thought about it before? Sure. Or maybe it has more to do with connection than body."

"Huh," I mutter, thinking that over. "Jason is demisexual. Have I mentioned that?"

"You did. Once," he says.

"Sex wasn't something he wanted before Cas," I tell him, positive Jason wouldn't mind me sharing that with Joey. "He's always had a high libido—and please, don't ever ask me to explain how I know that. Our walls were not thick."

Joey huffs a laugh.

"But he didn't want to share that, to get off, with other people. Not until Cas. And even now, there's only Cas for him, you know?"

He nods, looking curious about where I'm going with this. I hardly know myself, talking my thoughts aloud more than anything else.

"I never doubted being sexually attracted to women," I say. "I don't think I'm demi. But I do think, maybe, having a connection with you made all the difference. Because..."

Because I liked Joey before I realized I liked his stomach.

Because sex wasn't the first thing I wanted from him. It was simply to be close. To know him better.

Because the chance I might lose him to the Logans of the world made me confront the fact that my feelings weren't strictly platonic.

Which means...

Which means I wanted a romantic relationship with Joey before I ever wanted a sexual one.

Holy shit.

No wonder I demanded our bros-with-bennies sitch include exclusivity. I didn't want Joey falling for anyone else. *Don't.* Don't want that.

"Bub, you okay?" Joey asks, having moved closer. His hand is sun-warmed on the side of my arm, his lashes dark from the water. His eyes are so fucking pretty it hurts.

Just realizing I'm in a hell of a lot deeper than I thought I was.

I let out a chuckle, hoping it sounds far less manic than it feels. "Fine."

"Does it bother you to be questioning your sexuality?" he asks, entirely serious, like all he wants is to make sure I'm emotionally stable.

Stupid sexy fucking consideration.

"No, it doesn't," I admit, clearing my throat. "Whatever I am, I am. It doesn't matter to me what I was or wasn't in the past, not really. It's knowing myself now that matters. It's just..." I let out a measured breath. "I feel like I should have figured it out sooner."

I don't tell Joey that includes the whole *oops, I kinda want to shack up with my gym-bro in a till death do us part sorta way* realization. At least, maybe I do? But that's not something one blurts before being absolutely sure. Hell, even then, there's probably a standard waiting period, right? Like, at least six months before admitting you want joint bank accounts?

Fuck, I don't know. I never was very good at this relationship stuff, as Jason's many attempts to cheer me up with espresso ice cream after a breakup attest to.

I don't want to fuck things up with Joey. I'm not even *dating* the guy. Not really.

Not yet.

Joey's soothing voice brings me back to the present. To my toes sinking in the sand and the gentle whoosh of the water lapping at shore. "Hey, there's no one right time or right way when it comes to this stuff. Everyone is different, which means everyone's experiences are different. Don't compare yourself to others as a measure of *should have* when it comes to figuring out your sexuality. Or anything, really. You're perfect as you are, bub."

"Damn," I mutter. "You're really good at making me feel good."

He looks pleased.

"Dunno about perfect, though," I add, giving Joey's bare stomach a couple lingering pats as I pass. "But far be it from me to criticize your judgement. Now c'mon, Joey-roo. I need you to bench me into the air and call me Baby."

Joey blinks at me for several seconds before saying, voice questioning, "*Dirty—*"

"*Dirty Dancing*, dude! Yes!"

He shakes his head, but there's a smile on his face as he joins me in the deeper water. I'm pretty sure I hear him mumble something about *owe it all to you*, and I decide, despite the limitations of my body, I'm going to try very hard to have Joey's babies.

I bounce on my toes as Joey gets into place a little ways in front of me, the water high enough that I won't hit the sandy bottom if I fall. When he waves me forward with both hands, I grin and take off at a running start just like in the movie.

Or at least I try to.

"Fuck," I mutter, my legs moving ridiculously slow through the water. "Joey, I'm stuck."

He's laughing.

"No, dude, seriously. I can't run in this."

I pump my arms at my sides as the full force of the Atlantic tries to keep me anchored in place.

"Lift your legs," he calls.

I grunt, getting my knee above the water, and then the other, high-jumping a couple steps as Joey laughs his head off. When I look up, he's doubled over, his hands on his knees under the water.

"Joey!" I hiss. "Places! I'm getting close."

He stands upright, his hands poised like he's ready to catch me, even though I'm still a good five feet away.

"Fuck," I yell, waving my arms faster.

He doubles over again.

Launching myself, I land on top of the water, my life vest carrying me to a waiting Joey. He scoops me out of the water, and the both of us tumble over.

"Stop laughing," I say, laughing. "That wasn't majestic at all."

"Oh my God," Joey manages, getting his feet under him, me still in his arms like a buoyant drowning rat. Once we're both upright, he wipes his face. "Best thing I've ever seen."

"That was the *worst*," I counter. "No one told me you can't run in water."

I can't tell if the moisture on Joey's face is from our fall or his tears.

"What if we skip the running start?" he proposes.

"*Fine*. But you better still call me Baby."

"Happy to," he says, squatting down, his chin dipping below the surface of the water. "Here, climb on."

"I...really want to make a joke right now."

"About…"

"About climbing you like the sturdy tree you are and finding a nice branch to fit between my legs. In case it's not clear, your dick is the branch."

Joey coughs, sputtering around a mouthful of water.

"Jesus, dude. I know you're part merman or whatever, but that doesn't go in your lungs."

"Yeah," he croaks. "Got it. Ready?"

"I was born ready," I tell him, leaning against the hands he has raised above the water. Joey gets a firm grip on the sides of my stomach, right below my life vest, and then he stands.

For a second, maybe two, I'm airborne, my arms out to my sides and an unstoppable grin on my face. Joey calls, "Nobody puts Baby in the corner!" because he's the literal best. And then I'm splashing into the water, a shock of cold surrounding me before I bounce back to the surface.

I roll onto my back, laughing as the sun beats down on my face. Joey appears in my vision, light haloing him like an angel.

"Okay?" he checks, smile wide.

I nod, the water in my ears making everything sound odd. "Pretty sure I can die happy now."

"Let's maybe not do that," Joey says, grabbing me and hauling me upright. I bump into his chest, the vest between us, water dripping down the side of Joey's face and his hair curling in wet swoops like the waves.

There's a stutter behind my ribcage. The briefest feeling of being airborne once more.

Joey's lips taste faintly of salt when I kiss him, like the sea and the sun. He's firm beneath my fingertips, and everything about him, from the already familiar feel of his mouth to the way excitement and warmth skitters down my spine at his proximity, settles me in a way so few things do.

I'd stay lip-locked with the man for the entire day if I could, but I highly doubt Joey's mom would care to see her son making out with someone in what equates to her backyard, adult or not. So I pull back.

Joey lets out a quiet hum, his hands brushing my hair back from my face. "Question," he says, a coy lilt to his words that I like a lot. "How do you feel about...watersports?"

I suck in a gasp. "*Yesss.* Can I drive the boat?"

"Absolutely not," Joey says, letting me go and making for the ladder. "But you can be a good boy and enjoy the ride."

"I... *Hmm.* You know, I'm not usually into the whole *good boy* thing," I point out, following after him, "but you make a rather compelling argument."

Joey grins as he climbs the ladder, his legs flexing and his ass right there, so full and perfectly round, like the most beautiful sweet buns I've ever had the pleasure of seeing.

I want to ice them.

"Coming?" Joey calls, grabbing our towels off the dock.

I blow out a breath.

So very definitely not straight.

Once inside the house, Joey and I make sandwiches to bring out onto the boat. Mama Delgado pulls out a small cooler for us, adding a few drinks and a small container of pasta salad to round out our lunch.

"Have fun," she tells us, giving my cheek a pat before shooing us out the door.

"Your mom's the best," I tell Joey again, the two of us walking back across the lawn, t-shirts on now so we don't get too crispy.

"I know," he says simply.

Joey grabs an inflatable tube from the shed, offering me a ride out to the boat because he's a goddamn gentleman like that.

He holds it steady near the end of the dock. "Ready, sailor?"

"Aye aye, Captain," I reply with a grin. "Raise ye flagpole and prepare to be boarded because this seaman is ready to ride."

Joey blinks at me.

"Yeah," I say slowly. "I just heard it."

He snorts, keeping the tube balanced as I climb on. "For the record, you can jump aboard my flagpole anytime you'd like."

"*Nooo*," I groan, holding the cooler close and glancing over my shoulder. "No sexy talk, Joey-roo. There are parentals about, which means I don't need to be sporting a kangaroo-induced boner."

"Is that different than a regular boner?" he asks curiously, dragging me out toward the boat.

"Far more trigger happy," I explain.

He looks oh so happy about the effect he has on me, the smug, lovely man.

"Just so you know," he says, waist-deep in the water now, "that was *not* my sexy talk."

"What? I thought it was sexy."

He makes a sound almost like a huff, stopping and spinning toward me, his hands on the side of my raft. "Bub, if I wanted to give you a boner, I'd tell you that as soon as you're ready for it, I'll show you what it feels like to have someone inside of you. I'll open you up with my fingers. One, then two, then three, until you're begging to feel how much further I can reach with my cock. I'll introduce you to your prostate, make you ache in the best possible way, and only then will you find out what it's like to be fucked within an inch of your life. And you'll thank me for it."

"Holy fuck," I breathe. "You're a cruel, wonderful man, Joey Francis Delgado."

He tugs me in by the back of my neck, kissing me soundly. "Come on. We've got a metaphorical flagpole to raise."

"Flagpole is already up," I mumble, adjusting myself as the waves pass underneath, a gentle sway I could get used to.

Maybe there *were* signs before Joey. Things I missed or didn't question when it came to men around me. But it doesn't matter. Because this, here and now, is a pretty big deal. In fact...

Step seven in Brad's Guide to Finding Himself and—*fuck*—Falling in Love:

Learn a new self-truth.

I'm bi. And even if I had never acted on my feelings for Joey, I knew that to be true the moment I called Cas from behind Joey's garage. So no, it doesn't matter if Joey is the only man I end up wanting. And it doesn't matter if the labels I choose change over time as our language evolves or as my own understanding of myself grows. None of it will negate the fact that I'm attracted to Joey now. On pretty much every level I could be.

And that my feelings for my gym-bud turned friend turned...*more*...are far more complicated than *not platonic*.

Chapter 24

JOEY

Brad and I stay out on the water for a good couple hours. Despite being on a speedboat and *not* a pirate's brigantine, as I repeatedly remind him, Brad doesn't let up on the "seamen" puns. Nor the occasional flagpole-related joke that's distinctly dirty in nature.

Honestly, I wouldn't have it any other way.

By the time we make it back to land, Brad voicing his enthusiastic approval of motorboating, we're too tired to do much other than eat an early dinner with my mom, watch a movie—*Dirty Dancing*, of course—and head to bed.

And that's precisely where Brad should be now. So when I roll over to find his spot empty despite it clearly being the middle of the night, I sit up and look around.

"Bub?" I call softly, noticing a person-shaped shadow near the kitchen.

He jolts slightly. "Oh, hey. Sorry, did I wake you?"

"The lack of you woke me," I admit, swinging my legs out of bed. "You okay?"

"Yeah. Of course," he says. "Just couldn't sleep."

I hum, scrubbing my face a little before standing.

Brad makes a soft sound. "You don't have to get up."

"I don't mind," I tell him, padding across the floor. "Please tell me you're not drinking coffee right now?"

He snorts, setting down the cup in his hand, the clink of it soft against the countertop. "No, just water."

Brad doesn't object when I wrap myself around him. In fact, he leans into me, a sigh accompanying the relaxation of his shoulders.

"Want to talk about it?" I ask.

He shrugs, his hands worming under my t-shirt. "I dunno. I've never slept well. And it's not the coffee's fault, I swear. I quit it for half a year once to check, and it only got worse. I just..."

He makes a noise that's almost a grumble, and it's so unexpectedly surly, I have to keep my laughter in check.

"I tried therapy before?" he says, almost like a question. "And she said when a person grows up feeling...alone, without their needs for emotional support and safety being met, they may learn habits of self-sufficiency that aren't always healthy in the long run. Like, meerkats have a system of defense, right? There's always at least one on guard, even when the others are sleeping. I guess I just...didn't have anyone to watch my back."

My heart breaks at the casual way in which Brad explains his childhood abandonment. And, apparently, the ongoing problems that stemmed from his parents giving him away to a man who, by Brad's own admission, tried his best but wasn't the warmest. Did he not have anyone to comfort him when he had a nightmare? Was he afraid if he asked too much of his grandfather, the man might give him up, too?

"Is there anything I can do to help?" I ask, my voice hoarse.

"You already help," he says softly. "You're the best sleeping pill I've found, Joey. But... I guess no system is foolproof."

I nod, throat tight. "Want to go for a walk?"

"Yeah?" he asks, pulling back, his face hard to make out in the dark.

"If you want."

"I do. Let me grab some pants," he says, practically skipping away.

The two of us get dressed in the dark, and I grab a flashlight in case a car comes along while we're on the road, though I doubt there will be anyone around at this time of night. With our sweatshirts in place to ward off the chill, we head outside. The moon is a small sliver in the sky tonight, the private road dark without streetlights. But there's just enough light for us to walk by.

I lead Brad in the direction of the park, figuring the swings might help. Maybe it's a silly idea, but he seems to calm with motion.

We're quiet on the way there, but as soon as Brad sees the small playground up ahead, he *whoops* and sprints toward the equipment. There's the swing set—a large, metal-framed thing—and a solitary slide that gets too hot to go down when the sun's out. Brad heads right for the swings, plopping onto one of the black rubber seats, his hands around the chains as he sets into motion.

"Shit," he says, the one word happy and light. "I haven't been on a swing in forever."

"Figured you might enjoy it," I admit, settling onto the one next to him and swaying in place. "Can I ask a question?"

"Oh boy," he says, whooshing past me, his chains creaking slightly where they connect to the frame. "Sounds serious."

"Only a little."

"Ask away, my kangaroo."

I huff a laugh. "Did it not help when you lived with Jason?"

He makes a small sound of acknowledgement, under-standing I'm asking about his sleep, but it takes another few seconds before he answers. "It did a little. But Jason's schedule was so sporadic while he was in nursing school. Some nights, he wasn't even around. And when he was, I mean... It's not like we slept together. He liked his space, which was fine. But knowing someone is there and actually feeling them is different, I guess."

I hum, considering. "Should we make a schedule?"

"A what now?"

"A schedule for sleeping over," I explain. "Some nights at your place, some at mine?"

Brad stops so abruptly, pieces of bark go flying in all directions when his shoes dig into the earth, his swing rotating violently before jerking to a halt. "*What?*"

"Would you not want to—"

"I want," he says quickly. "I just... You'd really do that? Sacrifice your nights for...me?"

"I'm not sure why you're under the impression that spending my nights in bed with you would be a sacrifice, bub, but I'd be happy to share your bed whenever I'm able. Believe it or not, I kinda like knowing you're close, too."

He blows out a breath. "If it's too much, you have to let me know."

"I will. But it won't be."

"I might hog the blankets," he points out.

"I know."

"I'll probably drool on you."

"I know that, too," I assure him.

"I might not always go to bed as early as you."

"We'll figure it out."

"Yeah, okay," he says, and then, "*Ooh*, I'll make a calendar! Color-coded, of course. You'll probably want to keep some stuff at my place, right? I can clear out a drawer. And maybe I could have some space in your closet? You wouldn't mind me stocking some better coffee beans in your kitchen, would you? Your stuff is okay, but honestly, Joey, you could do better. What are your thoughts on a *Star Wars*-themed alarm? I've always thought 'The Imperial March' had a nice ring to it. Joey, you coming? It's bedtime."

Chuckling, I follow after Brad as he makes his way back across the park. He keeps up a running commentary the whole way to the guest house about the *proper* way to turn down a bed and how it makes all the difference for that moment you slide under the sheets. I nod along, not minding whether my sheets are right-side up or crinkled all to hell, so long as Brad is between them.

As soon as we get inside, Brad kicks off his shoes, shucks his sweatshirt and jeans, and falls into bed. He makes a grabby hand I assume is meant for me, so I undress and climb in after him. I've barely made contact with the mattress when Brad forcibly rolls me to my back. He settles over me, legs outside of mine, the entire length of him slotted against me with his cheek on my chest.

There's a stutter beneath his ear. One I'm positive he'd hear if he's listening for it.

But neither of us says a word. In fact, with the way Brad's breathing has evened to a slow, steady pace, I'm more than certain he's out. Just like that.

I swing the sheet over us, knowing, if only he'll let me, I'll do my very best to keep all of his nightmares at bay.

"Here. Suck."

I raise an eyebrow, but Brad simply thrusts his finger closer to my face.

"Suck me, Joey."

"You should...maybe consider rephrasing that."

Brad's forehead wrinkles. "Put my finger in your mouth, suck off the cream, and tell me if I did good."

"Oh good Lord," I mumble, grabbing Brad's hand and directing his finger to my mouth. I lick off the buttercream frosting, rather enjoying the way his lips pop open when I swirl my tongue around the digit. Tugging it free, I say, "You did good, bub."

He preens, even as his cheeks flush.

And the man thinks he doesn't have a praise kink.

Shaking my head, I pass over the dyes. "Pick a color."

"What's your mom's favorite?" he asks before saying, "No, don't tell me. Let me guess."

Brad plucks out the blue and yellow dyes. By the time he's done mixing, the frosting is a soft aquamarine. Honestly, it's perfect.

"Did you get your mom a present?" he asks, starting to spread the frosting over the cake we baked.

"I did. A set of juice glasses with a floral design."

Brad stills, looking over at me. "Am I supposed to be drinking my juice out of special glasses? Is this a thing no one told me?"

I snort. "It's not a requirement."

"Thank fuck," he mutters, going back to the frosting. "At least we didn't get her the same thing."

"*You* got my mom a present?" I ask in shock.

"Duh," he mumbles, concentrating as he shifts the frosting knife to cover the corners.

"Want some help with that?"

He swats my hand away. "You do the flowers. I spread the cream. That was the deal."

"You've gotta stop calling it cream," I mutter.

"You said you like my cream."

"That's not... You know what? Never mind. Yes, I do love your cream."

"Thought so. *Aaand* there." With a flourish, Brad stabs the knife into the bowl of frosting and passes it over. "Your turn."

Huffing a laugh, I transfer the rest of the frosting into a piping bag.

"Where is your mom, anyways?" Brad asks.

"Went to the market to grab some fresh crab," I tell him, twisting the bag closed and carefully squeezing out a flower, one petal at a time.

"The fuck," Brad mumbles. He watches me do another before saying, emphatically, "Those actually look like flowers."

"Yes, they do," I say around a chuckle.

"How... How are you doing that?"

I shrug, continuing to pipe the decorative flowers along the border of the cake. "I liked construction. My mom liked to bake. I picked up a few things."

"Damn," he mutters. "I think you just unlocked some sort of bakery kink I didn't know I had. Hey, Joey. Joey. Joey-roo."

"Yes?" I say, lips twitching.

He up-nods. "You can frost me anytime you like."

I pause, pulling the bag away from the cake as I face Brad. "The one time you don't say cream..."

His brow furrows, but then he gets it. "Fuck! Okay, okay. Hey, Joey—"

"I'm back," my mom calls, the door closing behind her.

Brad's eyes widen. "Cream me, Chef," he says quickly and quietly, leaving me to choke on absolutely nothing as he turns toward the front of the house. "Welcome back, Mama D! Don't come in the kitchen, please. Not because we're naked. Just because there's a surprise we don't want you to see. Promise, we're not naked."

My mom laughs softly while I attempt to get my lungs working again. "How about I leave my bag out here and you come grab it?" she says. "It needs to go in the fridge."

"Will do," Brad says, jogging off to intercept the crab.

"Good grief," I mutter. "I guess I asked for it."

Brad brings the crab into the kitchen, putting it in the fridge as my mom makes a show of passing with her hand over her eyes. It doesn't take long for us to finish decorating the cake. Once the flowers are done, I pipe a border along the bottom edge, and Brad adds three candles on top, one for each decade of life, as he tells me.

"Because surely your mom can't be older than thirty," he yells.

"Number one, I doubt she can hear you all the way outside," I tell him, carefully putting the cake under a large dome to help keep it hidden for now. "Number two, I'm twenty-nine. Which makes that entirely impossible."

He *pshts*. "Your mom is lovely, and she should know it. I'll miss her when we go back."

"Yeah," I say, my chest feeling tight. Not only because *yes*, I'll miss my mom, too. But because of the effortless way in which Brad adores her and has from the beginning, as if there was never any doubt. As if, maybe, he loves her simply because I do. "Why, uh...why don't we let her know the kitchen is open?"

Brad nods, and, after one final check to make sure everything is put away, we head outside. As my mom makes dinner, telling us under no circumstances are we to help because we've done enough, Brad and I take a seat under the shade of the gazebo, him with an iced coffee, me with an iced tea.

"I always wanted to visit the ocean," he says almost wistfully, the breeze ruffling his hair. "Thanks for making that happen, Joey-roo."

"We can come back anytime you'd like," I tell him, meaning it and hoping beyond hope there's a reason for Brad to continue coming back with me after this. After we pass our one-month mark when Brad and I will decide whether or not this is working.

It has to work. It already is, isn't it? I refuse to believe it's only me.

My mom finds us out under the gazebo before long, dinner in tow. Accompanying the crab cakes is a lemon, feta, and tomato orzo dish. As always, the food is delicious, and Brad compliments my mom with genuine appreciation.

Once we're done with our meal, Brad and I clean up the dishes and bring the cake outside. I leave the dome on and jog back into the house for the lighter I forgot. I'm rooting around in the kitchen drawers looking for it when my mom steps inside.

"I love him," she says.

I close a drawer and try another, my heart beating fast. "So you told me."

"And I'm telling you again. He's perfect for you, Joey. He's a light. He'll make you happy."

"He already does," I admit, trying another drawer. "Where's the lighter?"

My mom walks around the counter, opening a cupboard. "Here."

"You moved it."

She shrugs. "Reorganized. You're in love with him."

I nearly fumble the lighter at her blunt assessment, managing to catch it just before it falls to the floor.

"I've never seen you look at anyone the way you look at him," she goes on, her voice soft. "When are you going to tell him?"

I let out a slow breath, holding on to the countertop for support. I could tell her it's complicated, that Brad is more than a friend but not quite a boyfriend—which she knows, if not in precise detail. I could tell her this is new for him, and I don't want to rush him in any way—a fact she also knows. I could try to deny her claim altogether, feign ignorance, but I know there's no use.

The only thing I can say is what I know to be true. "Soon."

She nods, an approving smile on her face. "Come on. Let's not leave him waiting."

Brad gives us a grin when we rejoin him inside the gazebo, and I feel as if my heart might take flight. Before we unveil the cake, my mom opens her presents. She gushes over the petite glassware I got her, tracing the flowers with her fingers and demanding a hug. And then it's Brad's turn. My mom seems just as surprised as me by the gift card to a local restaurant acclaimed for its seafood. Brad gets his own hug and a heartfelt thanks for the thoughtful gift, which has him beaming in response.

When I finally lift the dome off the cake, Brad watches my mom closely, looking as if he might just jitter right out of his skin.

"Oh, what a lovely color," she coos.

Somehow, Brad manages to smile harder.

I light the candles on the top of the cake, Brad and I singing "Happy Birthday" to my mom. It's such a simple thing, a small celebration for a woman who deserves the world, as far as I'm concerned. But being here with these people, the water lapping at the shore and the sun starting its descent in the sky, I feel immeasurably content. Happy in a way I don't remember being since I was a child.

So when we finish the song and my mom says, "There are three candles. Why don't we all make a wish?" I don't hesitate.

I wish...

That I never have to give this up.

Chapter 25

BRAD

I've always considered myself a driven person. There haven't been many real-life foes I've faced that I haven't conquered in some form or another.

There was the Rubik's Cube my grandpa gave me when I was in the fourth grade. It took me a few years, but I solved it.

There was that time I got my car wedged horizontally between two parked trucks with only two inches of wiggle room, but I damn well got myself out without so much as a scratch to either vehicle.

There was even that teacher I had in tenth grade, Mr. Barker, who told me I lacked the discipline necessary to code anything more complex than a game of *Pong*. I sent him a copy of *Run, Run, Ricochet* when it was released.

No, I'm not one to let an obstacle get the better of me. Which is why I'm standing proudly in my bathroom, butt-ass naked, determination spurring me on in the face of my most recent—and possibly wickedest—adversary.

"You. Will. Not. Win," I say firmly.

The enema bulb stares back at me.

"Okay," I breathe, going over the instructions inside the douching kit for the fourth, possibly fifth time. "Clean the bulb. Done."

I give the fucker a squeeze so it knows I have the upper hand.

"Fill with water that's just under lukewarm."

I run the tap, waiting until it feels room temperature, and then I turn it just a touch colder like it says. Don't want to burn the insides, I guess. *Yikes.*

As I fill the bulb, my imagination so helpfully supplies the little dude's shrill shrieks of protest. *Nooo, stop. I can't breathe. You win. I'll do whatever you wa—aaahglrglblr.*

I snort and shut off the tap, checking the instructions again.

"Attach the nozzle of your choice to the bulb."

Slowly, I look over at the nozzle options.

"*Yeah.* I'll take fine tip, thanks."

Making sure not to spill the water, I grab the slimmest nozzle from the box and give it a little wiggle into place.

"There. That looks like the picture. Next up... You may lube the tip of the nozzle if you prefer. Hard yes."

Juggling the items in my hands, I grab the lube, get it open, and squeeze out a small amount onto my fingertips. I coat the tip of the nozzle, my cock twitching as I remember the feel of Joey's fingers pressing against me a couple days ago, back before our return trip to Vegas. That felt pretty damn good, so this should feel...*fine* at minimum, right? My dick is certainly cautiously optimistic.

Granted, it's Joey's cock I'm looking forward to having inside my ass, not this literal douchenozzle. But hey, one step at a time, right?

"Okay. Insert the nozzle. *Hoo, boy.* Not even dinner first?"

No, no. I can do this. *Come on, Bradley*. Easy peasy. Insert and squeezy. The question is...*where* do I do this?

"Standing or seated position," I read. "Uhhh. So it's either stick something up my butt while sitting on the toilet or stick something up my butt while watching myself in the mirror? That's...a choice."

Fuuuck.

"Standing," I decide. "But, shit, what if I...drip? Is that a thing? Can I drip? Jesus Christ, I need backup."

I swipe my phone on and call Jason. I'm more than certain Joey would be happy to help me if he knew I was doing this. But that's the whole point. He *doesn't* know. Because I want to surprise him. And, *maybe*, if I'm being entirely honest, I want to prove to myself I can handle this on my own. Or *mostly* on my own.

"Bee?" Jason answers after only a couple rings.

"Birdie! I need your help."

"What's that echo?" he says. "Are you...are you in the bath-room?"

"Sure am."

There's a beat of silence. "Please tell me you didn't call while taking a shit."

I snort. "No, dude. Of course not. I'm just about to anal douche for the first time, and I don't know if drippage is a concern. But tell me fast because this water is quickly losing its just-under-lukewarm status, and you know how I don't like to be cold."

There's a far longer beat of silence this time before Jason sighs. "I have so many questions, and I'm not sure I want answers to any of them. Hold on. I'm getting Cas."

I bounce on my heels a couple of times as I wait, eyeing the douching bulb that I'm sure is mocking me.

"Shut it," I mumble. "You're about to go up my ass, so—"

"Hello?"

"Cat-man!" I call. "How's it going?"

"Good," he says. "You're on speaker. Jason said you need help with...douching?"

"Yeah, man. So here's the deal. I've got the bulb lubed up and ready to go. It's time for insertion. I just don't know if I should stand or sit."

"Ah," Cas says as Jason mumbles something I can't make out but that sounds suspiciously like *can't believe I'm raising a baby bi.* "First thing. You didn't lube the bulb itself, right?"

"Oh, no. Just the tip," I assure him.

"Good. Because you don't insert the whole thing."

"Right," I huff, looking down at the rather wide bulb. "Yeah, no thanks. Although I suppose if it got stuck up there, Jason could—"

"Nope!" he shouts.

"But you're a nurse!" I counter.

"And I'd refer you to someone else," he says, sounding farther away.

"Where's he going?" I ask Cas.

"Drink," Cas answers. "So, personally, I like to stand in front of the toilet with one foot up on the seat, right? That way you have easy access and can sit right down after."

"That makes sense," I agree.

Better than the whole *stare at my reflection awkwardly in the mirror* plan.

"Another option is doing it in the shower," Cas goes on. "Then you can wash up at the same time."

"Multitasking. I like it. Question, though. How do I, like, hold the water in like it says to?"

Jason must be back because he says, "You just...hold it."

"Right. But *how?*"

"You hold it," he says firmly. "Like...just *hold* it."

"Right," I say again, slower. "But *how* do I do that?"

"I got this," Cas says calmly. "You know when you're worried about passing gas in public?"

"*Ohhh*," I say in understanding. "You just hold it."

"For fuck's sake," Jason grumbles.

"Is he doing that angry, bristly cat thing?" I ask Cas.

"Sure is," he answers, sounding fond.

"Your death will be swift," Jason promises.

"Okay, I think I'm good, dudes," I say happily. "I've totally got this. Wish me luck and a speedy clean-out!"

Cas sounds as if he's saying goodbye, but the call clicks off too quickly to hear the full thing. Sweet, bristly Jason.

"Okay," I say aloud. "It's me and you, you...douche. God, that's weird."

Getting into position, I pop my foot up on the lip of the open toilet, the bulb in hand. I have to kind of...feel around for the right spot. Which is different. Not bad. I'm just not all that used to actively seeking out my butthole. Target acquired. So now I just...put it in.

Yep.

Here we go.

Aaand okay. That's...also different. Just slipped right in there, didn't it? Good, good. The instructions said not to go too far. So right there should be fine. I think? And then I'm supposed to just...squeeze the bastard for up to ten seconds. Which is a pretty big margin in which error could occur, if you ask me. Might as well err on the side of less. It said to flush a couple times anyways.

"Yep. That's decided. We're doing six seconds, bulby, just like any good hug should last. Okay. One, two, *hoo*, that's weird. Three. Four? *Ahh*, five. Six. That's probably good, right? Yep, calling it. Now I just...take you out?"

Hold it, hold it, hold it. And *there*. Nozzle is free.

I put my foot down, bouncing a little before deciding *nope*, no bouncing. No bouncing at all.

"This is so fucking weird," I mumble, trying a shimmy. And okay, maybe no moving whatsoever. How long am I supposed to hold it? Because gravity is doing its job like a motherfucking champ, and this water wants to return to sea.

Leaning over, I grab the instruction sheet, skimming the directions.

"Why don't you say!" I shriek. "What's a 'moment'? That's not a goddamn standard unit of measurement. Are we talking seconds? Tens of seconds? Have I passed the moment mark? Ahh!"

I drop the paper and plop my ass down on the toilet.

"Oh God, oh God, oh—"

Five minutes later, I'm shoving a clean and dried douching bulb into its new home inside the drawer under my sink.

"I'll concede to a draw," I tell it grimly. "I think we can both agree there was no clear winner today."

The bulb stares back at me. Smug bastard.

I flip it off, shut the drawer, and head into the shower.

Yeah.

Semi-nailed it.

"Good, good, right there!"

"You're shouting again," Joey says calmly.

"I can't help it, man! You try being in my position and keeping quiet. Whoa, hold up. Stop."

Joey stops immediately. "Something wrong?"

"This doesn't feel right."

"What do you mean?" he asks, a bit of concern in his voice.

"I don't know. Can you just...look around back?"

"You want me to check the back door?"

"Yeah, man, take a peek at the back entrance. What else would I be—Oh, *fuck*. Need your hands up front. On me, on me!"

Joey's character sprints over, already firing at the zombies quickly encroaching on our hiding spot. But it's too late. We're overrun with nowhere to escape to and not enough ammo to make it through the horde. The screen flashes red, and I drop my controller onto the coffee table.

"*Fuuuck*," I moan. "I really thought we were going to make it to the cache that time."

"We'll get it next time," Joey says, setting his own controller aside and propping his foot up. Our containers from dinner are still out, so I hop up to take care of those before rejoining Joey on the couch, landing with my head on his thigh. I give it a loving pat, and Joey huffs a laugh, his hand sinking into my hair as I scoot even closer, lifting his shirt enough to tuck my nose against his stomach.

True to his word, Joey has spent every night with me this week since we returned from New Hampshire. I'd feel guilty hogging so much of his time, except... He really doesn't seem to mind it. And I've never slept so soundly in my life.

Emotional support cuddle-bro for the win.

Not that *sleeping* is the only thing we've been doing. In fact...

"Well, hello, Mister Gregory," I murmur, turning my face to greet the erection trying valiantly to poke me through Joey's jeans. "We meet again, my friend."

"You can ignore him if you want," Joey says, never one to push or presume.

I snort, even as my insides fizz. "Now that'd just be rude," I mumble, giving Greg a kiss through the fabric. "So, Joey, I've been thinking..."

"Yes?" he says, his breath hitching as I skim my hand up to his pec. *So nice.*

I give him an appreciative squeeze, thumb rolling over his nipple as I go on. "I've been thinking I'd really like to see how much of your dick I can fit in my mouth. And then, maybe, we could try the same with my ass?"

Joey stills, and I turn my face up to see him. He's blinking down at me.

"You'd put your dick in my ass," I clarify, in case that wasn't clear. "Like, fuck me. You...fucking me."

"Yeah, I got that," he says hoarsely.

"I cleaned myself out, dude, and it's been over the hour mark the instructions say to wait, so we're totally good to go. Probably. In *theory*. I gotta say, though, I have a whole new appreciation for bottoms. I mean, that shit takes some serious dedication, you know? Although I'm guessing it'll be smoother sailing the next time around. Now that I know what to expect and all."

"You cleaned yourself out," he repeats.

"Yeah. Surprise? Why don't you seem—*Oh*, hello."

"I am happy," he fills in, the hand he slipped into my pants grabbing hold of my ass. "You're sure, bub?"

"So super sure," I tell him, the feel of his fingertip unerringly finding its target infinitely more arousing than the impersonal plastic of the nozzle I shoved up my ass earlier. "I want—" I huff out a breath as Joey presses against me, just a little. "I want you to do what you promised. I want you to wreck me, Joey. To show me what it can feel like. I'm ready."

Joey's hand leaves my pants as he stands, dumping me unceremoniously onto the couch cushions. For a second, I worry I said something wrong. But then Joey scoops me up into his arms as if I weigh nothing.

"Holy shit," I mutter, wrapping my arms around his neck as he carries me toward the bedroom. "That was impressive as fuck, dude. Is it just my loins, or is it hotter in here?"

"I'll never wreck you," Joey says, his voice rough as he maneuvers me through the doorway. "Not ever."

"It's just an—"

The word *expression* dissolves into a yip as Joey tosses me onto the bed. I bounce once, and then there he is, crawling over me, his crotch slotting against mine and his eyes so earnest I have no choice but to shut my mouth and listen.

"All I will ever do is worship you," he promises, leaning down to press a kiss near my ear. The next one lands on my neck, his stubble making me break out in goose bumps. "I will make you feel good. *Only* good, bub. There's nothing in this world I wouldn't give to you if it's within my power to do so. Whatever you want. Whatever you need, it's yours."

Fuck.

"So," I say a little breathlessly as Joey tugs my shirt aside to place a kiss on my shoulder, "if I asked you to put your fingers in my ass while I tasted your cock, you'd give me that?"

Joey's answer is in the way his lips meet mine, forceful and sweet. "Anything."

And maybe he's talking about our arrangement. About him helping me explore sex with a man for the first time.

But the promise in that one word is enough to have my heart skipping a beat.

No, I don't think he'll wreck me. Not intentionally.

But I'm well and truly fucked when it comes to Joey Delgado.

Chapter 26

JOEY

I feel electrified as I help rid Brad of his clothes, my skin buzzing and my fingertips prickling with hyperawareness. I don't know what it is about this man, but he's had me under his thrall since the moment I met him.

And now?

Now he wants to know what it feels like to be fucked, and he wants me to be the one doing the fucking.

It's a miracle I'm still conscious.

I kiss Brad's chest once his shirt clears his head. Down further. His stomach and that little outie belly button I want to erect a shrine to. Brad huffs a small laugh, his eyes bright as he looks down at me. *Fuck*. He's so gorgeous.

I inch lower, kissing his subtly sculpted abs as I flick open the button on his jeans. Lower still. His cloth-covered cock.

Brad lets loose an airy sort of breath, the kind of sound he makes when we're just getting started and he's still somewhat under control.

That won't do.

I slip his briefs down and take his cock into my mouth. The noise he lets out this time is louder, a moan mixed in with a laugh as he says, "That's supposed to be my job."

"Sucking your cock?" I ask, tugging his pants and underwear off so I can lick a stripe down the length of his shaft.

"Sucking *yours*," he says, his whole body jerking when I take one of his balls into my mouth. "But that's good, too. Keep on."

Gladly. I give his sac some love, using my tongue and lips, sucking each ball into my mouth and then both, until Brad lets out a string of *ah, ah, ah* sounds like he's closer than he wants to be. I let him go, brushing my fingers back along his perineum instead. Brad spreads his legs wider, the invitation clear.

I give his inner thigh a swift kiss before slipping back. "Let me grab the lube."

"Yep," he says, voice choked.

Knowing where it's stashed, I grab the bottle, tossing it on the bed before pulling off my shirt. Brad makes an appreciative sound as I drop the fabric, his gaze intent as he watches me undress. He gives his cock a slow stroke, eyes shifting downward as I tug off my jeans and then my underwear.

"That'll fit?" he asks dubiously.

I huff. "It'll fit."

He licks his lips and nods, and the sight of him naked before me—hand on his cock and body spread out along his pristine white sheets—has me itching to dirty him in every way possible. To lick him from head to toe. To push him onto his stomach and eat him out from behind. To fuck him so hard into the mattress that he won't ever want to leave this bed. We'd stay here, tangled together, making a home that's all our own.

"You're staring," Brad says, a soft smile gracing his lips.

"Because it's you," I answer, heading his way.

He exhales, letting his cock go and rolling fully onto his back as I cover him, my lips meeting his for a long, drawn-out kiss.

I pull back enough to speak. "I want you on top of me. So you can control the pace."

"Yeah," he breathes.

"And while your mouth is on my cock, I'll work my fingers into your ass."

"*Why-y-y* does that sound so much hotter when you say it?" he groans. "Fuck. Yeah, let's do that."

With a snort, I roll onto my back, and Brad hops up. He swings himself around, looking over his shoulder to check my position before easing his leg over my head.

"Oh my God," he mumbles. "Can you see my ass right now?"

"Yes," I tell him, smoothing my hands up his backside. "That okay?"

"Yeah, yep," he says, hands settling to either side of my hips. "Just feeling a bit exposed here. No biggie. Hello, Greg. You're looking very handsome today. Have you always been this...robust?"

Brad's hand wraps around the base of my cock, and I grab the lube to distract myself from how good it feels to have any part of him touching me. Knowing any second his mouth will be added into the mix has me fighting to hang on to my control.

"So, uh," Brad says conversationally, stroking me once. "I've been practicing."

A soft swipe of his tongue has me groaning, eyes slipping shut. "Practicing?"

"My BJ skills."

"On what?" I ask, more curious than anything. I flip the lube open.

"Popsicles," he says, giving me another lick. "A couple bananas. One cucumber."

Oh good God.

"So I'm fairly confident I can get at least half of your dick in my mouth," he says. "But I'm gonna shoot for whole."

I barely have time to brace myself before Brad's mouth is sliding over my cock. I hold on to his leg, back bowing as he takes me deeper than I would have expected for his first foray into dick sucking. He makes a sound, pulling off with suction that has me grunting.

"That's..."

"What?" I ask roughly, using the reprieve to lube my fingers.

"I mean...you're just way more satisfying than a popsicle. Hold on—let me just..."

Brad sinks back down, the wet heat of his mouth sliding over me, the soft, rhythmic sucking nearly doing me in, despite the novice coordination of it all. I'm pretty sure Brad could stare at my dick, ask me to come, and I'd do it. Having his mouth on me?

I don't stand a chance.

"That's really fucking good," I manage to say, my toes curling against the mattress as I do my best to keep myself in check. "Feels fantastic, bub."

"Yeah?" he asks, sounding ridiculously happy.

"Mhm. Just don't bite, okay?"

He makes an incredulous sound. "Why would I—*Ahh*, God. Oh God. That feels so much better than the nozzle."

Brad drops his head forward as I massage his ass, slipping the tip of one finger inside. "Okay?" I check.

"Mhm," he hums, his hand still on the base of my dick, his cheek rubbing the side of it. He turns his head, giving me a halfhearted lick as I press a little further inside of him. "Weird, but good. Keep going."

I work myself past the first knuckle, going slow, in no hurry to rush this. The focus helps take my mind off my cock as Brad licks the head, giving me soft sucks in between sounds of pleasure and small gasps as I start stroking my finger in and out in earnest.

"That, uh," he mumbles, making another sound like a choked moan. "It feels like it *shouldn't* feel good, you know? But it does. I kinda want..."

"More?" I ask.

"Yeah, think so."

I pull out, adding more lube before rubbing against him with two fingers. "You tell me if I'm going too fast," I say. "We can take however long you need."

He huffs, the sound puffing over the head of my cock. "Stop being so wonderfully thoughtful and get your fingers in my ass, dude."

"Bossy," I mutter, lips twitching.

"Oh my God," he whispers. "Am I a bossy bottom? *Holy shit*, am I turning into Alex?"

"Who's Alex?" I ask, slipping one finger back inside of him and then the tips of two.

"Just this guy I know. I'll explain later. *Hah*. Do that again. Again, again."

I ease my fingers in, crooking them, and judging by Brad's moan, the stretch is blooming into pleasure. "Good?"

"Weird," he breathes. "Wonderful. How, uh... How will I know once you've found my prostate?"

I snort.

"What? Why's that funny?" he asks, giving me a slow stroke, his efforts to blow me all but abandoned. I don't mind.

I edge my fingers in a little further, searching, rubbing...

Brad vibrates as if I've shocked him, his ass clamping down on me as he garbles out a surprised, "Oh, holy fuck. Oh fuck. Fuck, fuck."

"Good fuck? Or bad—"

"Really good fuck," he says firmly. "I'm gonna need you to do that again, Joey-roo. Like, a lot. Just don't make me come yet, okay? I have plans for Greg here, and as good as your fingers feel, I'm pretty sure having your dick inside of me is my new life goal."

I huff a laugh, stroking his ass cheek as I work to loosen him with my fingers. "I've never had as much fun with anyone in bed as I have with you," I tell him truthfully.

"*Dude*. Maybe you can tell me about your past conquests when you don't have part of your body inside of mine?"

I still, and he makes a mournful sound. "You're not a conquest," I say seriously.

He pants out a breath, and although I can't see his face, his back rises and falls rhythmically.

"You're not," I say again, needing him to believe me. Needing him to know this, right here, has absolutely nothing to do with notches on bedposts. It's...*so* much more than that to me. And maybe it's not the same for Brad. But I don't want him to ever doubt that he *means* something. Period. "Okay?"

"Yeah, Joey," he says quietly. "I know that. I do. It's just... I don't want to hear about them, all right? The...others."

"Flip over," I tell him, heart pounding.

"Huh?"

"Flip onto your back," I say again, pulling my fingers free.

He whines at the loss, but he does as I ask, climbing off of me and rolling onto his back. His eyes are wide when I crawl over him, settling between his legs. He looks vulnerable in a way he's never tried to hide.

"What I should have said is I love how you make me feel," I say, slipping my fingers back inside his body.

He pulls in a breath, arching his hips, his eyes never leaving mine.

"I should have told you that you make me happy. And that I'm so grateful you trust me in this way."

"*Joey*," he mouths, no sound accompanying the word.

"I should have said you make my life brighter, bub. That every day you're in it is better simply because it has you."

His hand tightens on my arm as I slip a third finger inside his body, going slow. I ease back, running my tongue up his cock, knowing—for me—it's the stretch from two to three that can cause a moment of discomfort. I suck the head of his cock into my mouth, hand resting on his stomach as I do my best to show Brad the best parts of being opened up. How it can feel like so much and yet not nearly enough. How it causes a blaze, an unyielding desire to find out just how much more your body can take. How you reach a point where all resistance is gone, and there's only the knowledge that you'll burn up if you don't do something—anything—to quench the fire.

When my fingers move inside Brad with ease, the man himself shifting and panting, I know he's there.

"Okay?" I ask.

He nods, blinking rapidly, his knees bent and one hand above his head, grasping at nothing.

"Bub? Do you want—"

"Yeah," he breathes, cutting me off. "In me. Now."

I grab the lube, pulling my fingers out to wet my cock. I try to keep my hand from shaking, my eyes raking over Brad as

I reach for his dick next, pumping him a few times to spread the lube.

"Breathe out when I push in," I tell him. "And stroke yourself. It'll help."

He nods, and I slide my fingers back into his body, fucking him with them a few more times to make sure he's ready. The *fuck, fuck, fuck* he lets out assures me that he is.

When I ease free and grab the base of my cock, I meet Brad's eye, checking in. He nods again, the green of his eyes a small ring surrounding black pupil.

I notch against him, pressing gently. His sharp intake has me stalling.

"Don't stop," he tells me immediately. "It's not bad. Promise."

"Stroke yourself," I remind him.

He shakes his head quickly. "Not a good idea. Too close."

"Do you want me to—"

"I said don't stop," he repeats. "Please. I can't... You have to keep going, Joey."

Taking Brad at his word, I press forward. He makes a sound like a *hah*, his neck arching back, his hand trembling on his cock, not moving, only holding. His muscles are tight, and I'm about to suggest switching to fingers for another minute when Brad breathes out, the tension release allowing my crown to pop inside his body.

He says, "Oh. *Oh, oh*," I slip another half inch forward, and then, with a jerk, Brad starts coming over top of his fist.

I watch in absolute shock as he strokes himself through the tail end of the orgasm forced from him, his ass strangling the head of my cock. It's a battle to stay still. To let him ride out his euphoria without moving a muscle, knowing pushing inside of him at this point might only hurt.

But seeing his pleasure? Watching him come apart on only a couple inches of my cock?

It's the most erotic thing I've ever seen in my life.

When Brad slumps flat, he breathes out heavily, a shaky exhale followed by an equally shaky inhale. "Fuck," he says. "Holy fuck. I'm sorry."

"Don't be."

"I can't believe I came that fast," he pants.

"You said you were close. I just didn't realize—"

"No, I know. But seeing your cock and then feeling it press into me... The pressure, and... It just..." He makes a small explosion sound before wiping his hair back from his forehead. "I'm a total bottom, aren't I? Holy shit."

I huff a laugh, my cock so hard it hurts. "I'm going to pull out now, just so you're prepared."

"Wait," he says, grabbing my arm to stall me. "Could you just...come like that?"

"You want me to...stroke myself off and come inside of you?"

"Well, why not?" he says. "It's kinda nice, having you there. So you could just..." He mimes jerking off, adding another explosion. "Or pull out. If you'd rather. That's fine."

"Just so you know," I tell him, sliding my hand over the base of my cock, "there won't be a time where I say no to filling you up."

"You like the idea of your cum in me?" he asks, his eyes bright, his usual smile back on his face. "Is it because you know no one else has ever had the honor?"

Shit.

"Doesn't hurt," I rasp, the tug on my cock mixed in with the sight of my dick still edged in Brad's body hurtling me toward the edge fast.

"Does it turn you on knowing no other dick has been in my body but yours? That no one has staked a claim inside of me but you?"

"Jesus, Brad."

"Come on, Joey. Pump me full. I want to feel what it's like to be marked. Wanna know you're the one leaving a piece of yourself inside of me."

A wave of lust hits me so hard I can't fight it, and I unload inside Brad's body on a grunt. He makes a sound of surprise as I do my damndest not to press inside of him further. My grip on his thigh is probably bruising, so I ease up quickly, stroking myself through the last of my orgasm, my knuckles bumping Brad's ass.

I feel wrung out when it's over, tiny zaps crawling over my skin, the head of my cock still nestled inside Brad's body. I never want to leave.

"That's, uh, way hotter than the enema," he says.

"Oh my God," I groan, chest heaving as I laugh. "I'm going to pull out now, okay?"

"Yeah."

Carefully, I inch back. Brad's brow furrows, but that's all as I slide out of his body, a string of my cum following the departure. I ache to push it back in.

"Okay?" I check.

"Uh-huh."

"You sure got mouthy there at the end," I note, sliding up the bed and lying down beside him, my arm around his middle as I breathe him in.

"I did, didn't I?" he says, sounding impressed. He wiggles a little to get more comfortable. "You must bring out my dirty side, Joey-roo. Can't say I hate it."

I huff a breath, kissing his shoulder. "That felt okay?"

"Uh, yeah? Dude, did you miss the part where I shot off like a rocket the moment the countdown began? We didn't even make it to one, and I was freaking gone."

My insides warm as Brad starts in on his usual rambling.

"Next time, I'm taking the whole thing, man. We'll just have to do less foreplay, or—I don't know—you need to be less sexy or something. *Shit.* I forgot about your blowie! Okay, we're going to work on that, too, because I only got, like, half of your dick in my mouth before you distracted me. Hey, how long do you think your cum will stay in my ass? Do I have to worry about drippage?"

Gold wedding bands or silver?

Ah, well. I guess I have time to figure it out.

Chapter 27

Brad

I fling open the door to Jason and Cas's apartment.

"I took a quarter of a dick!"

My best friend sets down his fork and turns to face me. Cas keeps eating.

"Not a quarter-sized dick," I clarify. "It was a very large dick. Or, well, not *huge*. Little above average? Perfectly sized, in my opinion. Greg is a great dick. My point is Joey fucked me. A little bit. And I liked it."

Understatement. Pretty sure I'm a cock slut now. Who knew?

Jason sighs, the weariest sound I've ever heard in my life.

"Dude, you okay?" I ask, turning to close the door. The woman across the hall has wide eyes, and I give her a smile and a wave before she's cut off from sight.

"What do you mean by 'a little bit'?" Cas asks.

"Oh, like, he got the tip in, and I blew," I explain, heading toward the couch. "But good news! Douching was a huge success. What are we eating?"

Jason makes a disgruntled sound as I squeeze in beside him, but Cas holds up his hand. "Nice job, man. I'm proud of you for being open to new experiences."

"Thanks, dude," I tell him, feeling choked up as I slap his palm. "That's really sweet of you to say."

"Get a room," Jason mumbles.

"I really doubt you want me doing that, Birdie. I like dick now, so—*Ow*, your nails are like claws!"

I wriggle away from Jason's grip, contemplating sitting next to Cas before thinking better of it. I plop down on the floor on the other side of the coffee table.

"So," I say, grabbing a container of fried rice, "how are we all feeling about snowballing? 'Cause it sounds hot."

Jason throws his hands in the air. "I was *eating*."

"And *I'm* curious about sharing jizz through the tender magic of kissing. What's the big deal?"

"Hey, I'm helping put together a bachelor auction next weekend," Cas says as Jason tries to skewer me with his eyes. *Yeesh*. Moody today. "Any chance you and Joey would want to participate?"

"Oh," I say, my gut doing a weird little dive. "Is it, like, auctioning off a date?"

"Not at all," Cas says. "It's any service you want to provide to the highest bidder. *Non*-sexual, of course. Proceeds will help refurbish run-down parks and community centers in the area."

"Damn you and your good heart," I mutter happily. "Count me in. I'll have to check with Joey, though."

"Sure," Cas says easily. "Just let me know by Tuesday."

"Will the guys be there?" I ask, snagging a crab rangoon.

"Most of them, yeah. Why?"

"No reason," I say, a grin spreading across my face. "I just happened to mention Alex to Joey the other day. This'll give me a chance to introduce the two of them."

Jason raises an eyebrow but doesn't comment. Me?

I ponder what sort of service I could offer for Cas's charity auction.

"Do you think people would pay for hugs?" I ask Joey.

He's doing chest presses while I work on leg curls. We'll switch machines once we're done with our reps.

"Probably," Joey answers, his arm muscles doing very nice things. "People pay others to cuddle them, right?"

"Oh my God," I realize. "I could do that! Platonic cuddle sesh. Unless... Would that bother you? If I cuddled some-one?"

Joey is quiet for a long moment, his face set in con-centration or contemplation, maybe. "You're a physically affectionate person, bub. I wouldn't ask you to change that."

The sentiment hits me warmly before I realize Joey didn't actually answer the question.

He goes on before I can bring it up. "I think I'll offer a re-modeling service. I could do kitchen cabinets or whatever the person needs."

"That's a great idea," I tell him, switching to the chest press machine when Joey waves me in. He starts his leg curls. "We both know when it comes to polishing wood, you're, uh... You..."

"Brad?" Joey prompts, lying on his stomach now, his ass in the air and his legs curling behind him.

"Hard," I mumble. "You're hard...to beat! At wood. You're an exceptionally hard woodworker. Very...proficient and stuff. The hammies probably help. Why am I sweating so much?"

Joey huffs a laugh as I do my best to focus on my chest presses and not the way I want Joey to press me between his thighs.

"Hey, so—"

My ringing phone stops me from asking if Joey would be interested in squeezing my head like an exercise ball later. Probably for the best, considering gym-boners are frowned upon. I pull out my phone and answer Jason's call.

"Hey, Birdie."

"Uh... What the fuck is on the wall of your bedroom?" he asks without a hello.

"Dude, you're in my bedroom?"

Not wanting to disturb the other gym-goers, I stand, pointing toward the windows so Joey knows where I'll be. He gives me a nod, and I head that way.

"Yeah," Jason says. "You asked me to drop off your suit. All clean and pressed, by the way. You're welcome for that. Now why am I staring at your nearly naked ass with...is that Joey? Your gym guy?"

"Gym guy," I say with a snort. Sweet, oblivious Jason. "It's gym-bro. And yeah, that's him. Why?"

"Why?" he parrots. "Uh...I thought that'd be obvious. Is this...from that boudoir photoshoot?"

"Yeah, his date didn't show up, so I stepped in. I just got the picture hung up the other day. What's the problem? I thought it looked nice."

"Putting aside the fact that you hung this in your bedroom...or *anywhere* for that matter..." He takes a breath, puffing it out. "Bee. That man is in love with you."

"What?" I nearly screech.

"He is one hundred percent in love with you."

I huff. "No way, dude. That was, like, a couple weeks after we met. We weren't even...*you know* back then. We were just friends."

"Yeah..." he says slowly. "Your friend? He's looking at you as if you're the single most important thing in his life. He has feelings for you, Bee. Big ones. Like, the biggest. So whatever it is you two are doing? This whole friends with benefits thing? It either needs to end or...*not* end. You can't string this guy along."

I look back at Joey, my pulse pounding so hard I can hear it in my ears. He's wiping down his machine, not paying me or my phone call any attention.

"I wasn't..." I try to explain, my thoughts getting jumbled. "I'm not..."

"I know you would never try to hurt him," Jason says, his voice softening. "But if you're not...*feeling* it, you need to cut things off. Before he gets in any deeper."

I clutch my phone tight, unable to take my eyes off Joey. "How'd you know? That you were in love with Cas?"

Jason is quiet for a minute. "It wasn't any one thing. It felt...inevitable. From the very beginning. He was...unlike anyone else I'd ever known. All I wanted was to spend time with him. To know him better. He made me feel strong because I never doubted what I meant to him. I fell in love like the changing of the seasons. Slowly and inescapably. And I knew it because...because I didn't want to look forward into a future that didn't have him."

I let out a breath, wiping at my cheek. "I'm really happy for you, you know."

"Yeah," he says quietly. "I do know. I'm happy for me, too. Do you...do you think you might be in love with Joey?"

Joey himself finally looks my way, smiling softly as he catches my eye. Even from halfway across the room, I can see the warmth in his gaze. The way those brown eyes are impossibly kind and endlessly patient. Is Jason right? Is that love?

I return Joey's smile, even as my gut rolls at the thought of hurting this man in any shape or form. I never wanted that. I don't want to hurt Joey.

"I think..." I say slowly, Joey's words from the other day coming to mind, along with the same feeling of unfathomable fondness they evoked in me the first time around, the swell of it in my chest almost uncomfortable but...not. "I think every day he's in it is better simply because he's there."

Jason lets out a quiet hum. "You do like him."

"So much," I admit, knowing the words aren't nearly enough. "I don't want to break things off. I want..."

Boyfriend seems like such a trite word. I've been a boyfriend before. But none of my past relationships felt anything like what I have with Joey.

Have I been fooling myself? Going along with this whole bennies package out of fear that he might not feel the same way I do? But if he does... If Jason is right...

"I have some thinking to do," I tell my friend.

"Of course. I didn't fuck things up, did I?" Jason asks. "I wasn't trying to be a dick. I just—"

"No," I assure him. "I think I needed to hear it. Thank you."

"Yeah," he says. "I'll see you Friday?"

"Yep. Love you, Birdie."

"You, too, Bee."

I click off the call and slip my phone back in my pocket. Blowing out a breath, I head over to where Joey is waiting.

"Hey," he says as soon as I'm close. "Everything all right?"

"Yep," I answer as chipperly as I can. "I think I'm done here, though. Ready to head out?"

"Sure. Your place or mine tonight?"

"It's a Joey-bode night," I say as we walk toward the locker room. "I just need to take care of something first, so meet you there?"

Joey gives me a searching look, but then he nods.

We wash up in separate showers, like usual, but we end up in front of our lockers at the same time, pulling on our clothes almost in sync. I don't stop myself from looking Joey over, knowing no one else is around to care about my ogling. Joey certainly doesn't seem to mind. He perks up—in more ways than one—as his gaze rakes over me in return.

I didn't see Joey walk in today, having arrived after him, so when he finishes getting dressed and pulls the bright pink fanny pack out of his locker, I choke on a laugh.

"Quite handy," he says, giving me a wink as he clips it on, the jangle of his keys inside evident.

"Fuck," I mutter, that fondness trying to crack my chest open. "Why are you so great?"

"You sure you're all right?" he asks, looking at me in an almost worried way. I don't know why until I register the moisture at the corners of my eyes.

"Fine," I say quickly, blinking and grabbing my things. "See you in an hour or so?"

"Yeah. C'mere."

I step forward, and Joey tugs me in the rest of the way. The feel of his lips against mine is just as intoxicatingly perfect as his arms wrapped around me. I can sense the inexplicable prickling of tears again and forcibly quell them, my hold on Joey's shirt pulling the fabric tight.

I don't know what my problem is apart from, you know, realizing this dude right here is who I want my forever to be with. Which...yeah. I guess that's a pretty big fucking deal.

When Joey breaks from my lips, he doesn't go far. He kisses my temple, his hand on the back of my head keeping me close. There's a small sound that leaves his throat, almost like an aborted word, but then he lets me go.

"Okay," he says softly. "See you in an hour?"

"Yep," I answer, trying to keep my voice steady considering it feels like my entire world has tilted on its axis in the span of fifteen minutes or so.

I shut my locker. Joey does the same. Then we make our way out of the gym.

When I get home, the first thing I do is pull out my phone. It rings three times before Cas picks up.

"Hey, Brad. What's up?"

"I have a favor to ask. This charity auction... Do you have, like, an MC? Someone who presents the bachelors or whatever you're calling us?"

"We do," he says slowly. "Why do you ask?"

"Do you think... I mean, could I introduce Joey?"

After a brief pause, he says, "I don't see why not. Why? What are you thinking?"

"Let's just say this Baby has a plan. And nobody puts Baby in the corner."

Another pause. "*Dirty—*"

"*Dirty Dancing*, my man, heck yeah! Such a good movie."

"It's pretty great," he agrees.

"Okay. I'm gonna let you go. I have a script to write. Another question, though... Are there, like, words I should avoid? Swear words or...other things?"

"Oh boy."

When I click off the call ten minutes later, I sit down in front of my coffee table, knocking a controller aside and slapping down a familiar pad of paper. I flip past Joey's interview on likes, dislikes, family planning, and kinks, as well as my own list of life steps I've been absolutely smashing, and I smooth down a blank page, my pen at the ready.

My hand can hardly keep up with the words forming inside my head, my scrawl messy and barely legible. I do my best to get everything down, knowing I can polish it later.

It's not every day a person professes their undying love.

I'm damn well gonna do it in style.

Chapter 28

Joey

I smooth the hem of my suit jacket as I eye myself in the mirror, making sure I haven't forgotten any part of my outfit. I can't say I've ever been auctioned off in front of a room full of people before, but at least I don't look half bad.

The knock at my front door is expected, as is Brad barging in, followed by his voice ringing out loud and clear. "Coming up, whether or not you're dressed!"

His feet stomp up the stairs, and then there he is, hanging in my doorway, his smile shifting into a frown.

"Damn. You're not naked."

I snort, something knocking around in my chest as Brad steps fully into the room, donned in his own suit and looking rather dapper. "You look great, bub."

"So do you," he says, eyeing me up and down. "Can I see the other side?"

I spin, and Brad steps closer, his hands smoothing over my ass.

"Very nice," he murmurs, giving me a squeeze.

"Hey, now," I say teasingly. "Hands off unless you plan on bidding tonight."

He makes an affronted sound. "I can't sample the goods?"

"Nope."

"Not even a little sample?" he mutters, lips drifting along my neck. He kisses beneath my jaw and inhales. "Fuck, you smell good."

"Do I?" I ask, my pulse stuttering.

"Mm. Like freshly cut wood and man. You smell like you."

I pull in a shaky breath, spinning to face him. His eyes, such a clear green, smile back at me. "You're trouble," I tell him.

He pouts. "I thought you said I was a good boy."

I bite my lip. "Do you wanna be?"

"This feels like a trick question," he says slowly.

I huff a laugh, holding out my hand. "C'mon, bub. Time to offer ourselves up for charity."

The charity auction is being held in a hotel ballroom downtown, just north of The Strip. Neon lights brighten the façade of the building, as well as nearly every business to either side. People pass on the sidewalk as I hand my keys off to the valet, gambling and other entertainment to be had just down the street.

The inside of the lobby is nearly as packed, guests checking in or going out for the night, those dressed in cocktail attire heading in the direction of the ballroom, same as us.

We're almost to the open double doors when someone calls out an excited, "Brad?"

"Oh shit," Brad says with a smile. "Here we go."

"It *is* you," the short blonde guy says, breaking away from the two men with him to launch himself at Brad. It's hard to say who hugs who tighter. "It's so good to see you, sweets. It's been *ages*." Stepping back, the newcomer eyes me. "And who, pray tell, is this gorgeous specimen you brought with you?"

Brad gives my shoulder a squeeze. "Alex, this is Joey Delgado, my kangaroo. But don't call him that. I'd hate to have to fight you. Joey, this is Alex Monroe and his boyfriends. Hey, Finn. Rowan."

The two men with Alex return Brad's greeting, having reached us, and I give my own hello as Alex assesses me. "My, my. And is Joey your...*friend?*" he asks Brad, eyes sparkling in a way that feels strangely familiar, although I'm fairly certain I've never met the guy before.

Brad huffs a laugh. "You could say that."

Alex cocks his head, but another couple approaches, one man with curly brown hair tied up in a bun and the other scowling, his broad frame hugged by his suit jacket.

"Small fry," the scowler says, addressing Alex but raising an eyebrow Brad's way. "Please tell me you're not corrupting the straight boy again?"

"'Scuse you, Grumpy Bear," Alex says, hands on his hips. "When have I *ever?*"

The so-called *Grumpy Bear* holds up one finger and then two. "Cas's going-away party. Countless times at the club."

"Teddy and Kipp's engagement party," the curly-haired one adds. The grump pops up another finger.

"Rude," Alex says. "For your information, I never forced Brad to dance with any of those men. And Dixon, Niko, this is Joey, Brad's friend."

"Funny story," Brad starts. "Turns out, I'm not actually st—"

"Nice to meet you," Niko, the curly-haired man says, not having heard Brad's mumble. "You'll have to excuse...well, all of us, really."

"Do I...know you from somewhere?" I ask, that feeling of déjà vu returning with Niko, same as Alex.

Niko smirks.

"There you guys are," Cas says, coming around the corner. "Come on in. We're getting the bachelors set up in a dressing room."

"*Ooh*, fun," Alex says, winding his arms through each of his boyfriends'. "How much do you think we'll go for?"

"Considering you're priceless," Finn, the redhead says, "I haven't a clue."

"You are so getting laid later, Ginger Bear," Alex says around a sigh. "Grizzly, you wanna be in the middle this time or should I?"

Rowan blushes furiously, the men walking out of sight as Brad gives me a grin, hopping a little on the balls of his feet. "Ready?" he asks me.

"As I'll ever be."

We follow Brad's friends down a hall, settling inside a large dressing room with couches and chairs. An attendant gives us a quick rundown of what to expect from tonight's auction. They'll introduce each of us, one at a time, before calling us to the stage. We'll stand there as bidding occurs. And then, before we go, we'll be given contact information for the winner of our service.

Easy enough.

We're left with bottles of water as we wait, Brad sitting close enough that we're connected from hip to knee. His leg bounces some.

"So, Joey," Alex says, giving me a curious look. "How is it you know our Brad?"

"We met at the gym," I tell him, leaving it at that since it seems Brad isn't out with these people yet. I'm not even entirely sure *who* these people are. "How did you meet?"

"They worked with Cas before he went back to school for his physical therapy degree," Brad answers distractedly, looking toward the doorway. "Oh, there's Jason. C'mon, I need to introduce you."

Brad tugs me off the couch, and Alex's eyebrows pop up. Jason, as it turns out, is a slender man, his blonde hair shaggy, his suit looking a touch too big for his frame. Brad lets my hand go to hold out his fist toward his friend. Jason begrudgingly gives him a bump.

"Right on," Brad says before pushing me forward, as if presenting me. "Birdie, this is my...Joey. Joey Kangaroo, my OG bestie. Don't take it personally. He just got there first."

Jason sighs, but he holds out his hand, eyes almost sharp as he takes me in. "Nice to meet you."

"You, too," I tell him, shaking his hand.

"Look at you guys," Brad says, sounding choked up as he tugs the two of us into an awkward hug. "Best buds already."

"Squished," Jason garbles.

"Gentlemen?" a woman calls, standing just inside the doorway in an incredibly low-cut, sparkling green dress. "If you'll please follow me, we're ready to begin."

Brad lets us go, and everyone starts filtering toward the door. I can't help but notice Brad's gaze on the woman's chest. Jealousy hits, sharper than I'm expecting, as I wonder if she's the type of person Brad would normally go for.

"She's pretty," I murmur, regretting the words the moment they leave my mouth. What am I even doing? *Testing* him?

As if I have that right. We may be...exclusive. But that doesn't make Brad mine. Not yet.

I swallow harshly at the reminder of the ticking clock over my head. Our month is nearly up, which means I need to figure out how to tell Brad I want to extend our benefits...preferably indefinitely.

Brad only shrugs at my comment, looking nonplussed. "Sure, she's pretty," he agrees, shooting me a tiny smile. "But I was just thinking that I like your pecs better."

Alex's head whips our way as that pressure inside my chest eases like a quickly deflating balloon.

"Really?" I ask.

Brad gives my chest a loving fondle. "Yeah, man. Not that it's the outside that counts. I like you for...*you*. You know?"

Fuck.

"Bub..."

"Sorry we're late!" a new face says, careening to a halt just outside the door. Another man stops at a much more subdued pace. "We got caught up in...traffic."

"They were totally boning," Alex says with a snicker before raising his voice. "Kipperoo! Over here. I'll catch you and Teddy up to speed."

The guy who looks like a hyperactive GQ model grins, his hand clasped by the man named Teddy, a gold band glinting on each of their left ring fingers.

I frown, eyeing the one who does in fact resemble a teddy bear. "Do I know him?" I mutter aloud.

Brad snorts.

When we get to the ballroom, our hostess in green guides us over to a few rows of chairs set beside the stage. The room is buzzing with conversation, round tables set up throughout the space, the decor glinting in golds and red. We take our seats, Brad on one side of me, Alex ending up on the other. Jason is directly behind us, Cas busy helping with the event.

"This is so exciting," Alex says, rubbing his hands together.

"No Emil?" Teddy asks, his voice low and gentle.

"No, he and Christian couldn't make it," Alex says, craning his neck. He makes an *ah* sound before pointing at a long-haired blonde man in the crowd who waves back. "But look, Mal is here with Henrik."

Mal says something to the man sitting beside him, who's loosely holding a cane. He lifts a hand in greeting, even as his eyes don't quite settle on us.

"So these are Cas's old coworkers?" I ask Brad.

He opens his mouth to respond when a buzz cuts through the air. There's a soft tap, and then a voice rings out, enhanced through the speaker system.

"Good evening," the man onstage says, standing behind the microphone in a pristine black tux. "Thank you all so much for attending tonight's charity auction. As you know from the packets you received upon entry, we have a wide array of volunteer services being offered today."

The master of ceremonies continues his welcoming spiel, and I take a second to look at Alex again, trying to work out why he seems familiar. He catches me glancing his way and gives me a wink that niggles at my memory. But before I can figure it out, the first bachelor is being called to stage.

The MC introduces Dixon with an extensive and inventive list of his most positive and charming attributes. His offer of a full house cleaning creates quite the bidding war as the blonde-haired Mal repeatedly outbids everyone else in atten-dance. Dixon pinches the bridge of his nose as he goes for an even eight grand to his...coworker? Friend?

"I'm not wearing a maid's outfit," he grumbles to Niko as he retakes his seat beside the stage.

Niko laughs for a solid thirty seconds.

The trend continues, Alex's boyfriend Finn going up on-stage with his offer of website design, Jason with a week of pet sitting, and Alex himself, who pulls over ten grand for...a car wash?

"These people have a lot of money to spend," I whisper to Brad, who nods with wide eyes.

But then he perks. "Oh, here we go."

"Next up," the MC says, "we have Joey Delgado with a special introduction by...Brad Bradley. Is Mr. Bradley here?"

Brad pops up as Alex's head swivels in our direction at an alarming speed. "His last name is *Bradley*?" the blonde squeaks.

Brad jogs up the steps to the stage and exchanges a soft word with the MC. Clearing his throat, he approaches the mic.

"What is he doing?" I mumble to myself, my heart racing.

"Hey, everyone," Brad says, smiling widely and waving at the room. "So, I know this is a little different, but I asked if I could have the honor of introducing Joey tonight. So, uh, here we go."

Brad produces a piece of paper from his pocket, brandishing it to soft chuckles from around the room. He opens the paper, gives the attendees another smile, and starts to read.

"Joey Delgado is twenty-nine years old, six foot one and a half inches tall, the perfect width to fit your arms around for a hug, and he has hair the color of rich chocolate icing."

There's another round of chuckles.

"Oh my God," Alex whispers, leaning forward.

Brad beams. "He's hardworking and passionate, a carpenter since the age of seven, when he carved his first-ever mallard duck out of a hunk of cherrywood."

Holy shit. How did he find that out?

"He's dedicated to his career, his family, and his friends. His likes include the smell of sawdust and the ocean, plus watersports of the nautical variety. Not the...other thing."

Jason makes a choked sound from behind me.

"In his spare time, Joey enjoys flexing at the gym and playing video games with me on his couch. Oh, and he's also allergic to almonds. So if you have the honor of winning his time, make sure to lock up your nuts." Brad winks at that.

"This is amazing," Alex hisses as the crowd chuckles again.

Brad looks down at his paper, pausing briefly before his eyes lift. They meet mine for only a second before he goes on, his voice softer than before.

"There's a lot I could tell you about Joey. That he has a nice smile and a kind word for everyone he meets. That he truly is a great carpenter, and you'd be lucky to have him work on your house. I could even tell you he looks banging in a tool belt, which is the absolute truth."

Alex stills.

"But the thing is...none of that adequately describes Joey Delgado. Because his smile isn't just nice. It's that feeling you get when the sun comes out and your skin warms and all you can do is turn your face toward the source of that heat because nothing has ever felt that good. He *is* kind, but he's also generous and patient and willing to rearrange his entire world just to make the people he cares about happy. And all I want—" His voice chokes off, and my heart stutters, my own lungs seizing tight as I struggle to understand what this is. Brad takes a deep breath, his fingers running along the edge of the paper in his grip. "All I want is to make him happy, too. Because he's one of the best people I know."

"Oh my God," Alex whispers, looking over at me with wide eyes. "Is he... Are you two..."

It's then two entirely unrelated things happen at once.

It dawns on me who Alex is, beyond Brad's friend. He's Tink, a porn star at Elite 8 Studios. Several of these men work there, in fact. Dixon, Niko, Teddy. Cas did, too, as Himbo. And it didn't occur to me until just now.

But that realization doesn't hold my attention for long. Because Brad makes a soft sound of surprise and looks down at his finger.

"Oh," he says into the mic. "That's blood."

"Oh shit," Jason utters at my back.

Brad chuckles nervously, his color draining quickly away as our conversation from the 5k returns to me like a smack in the face.

"This woman next to me fell and skinned her knee. And that was it, man. I had to bow out."

"Wait, why?"

"Blood," he said. *"Can't do blood."*

"That's, uh... Shoot," Brad says in real time. "Um, Joey?"

I'm already out of my seat, the crowd letting out a collective gasp as Brad's knee goes out from under him. My heart is in my throat for the second it takes for me to reach the stage. And as I lunge forward, Brad crumples.

Chapter 29
BRAD

"Morning, Greg," I mumble, shifting as I wake up.

"It's not morning, bub," a familiar voice says, soft and sweet. "And that's not Greg. Just a microphone."

I still, registering the hard surface beneath my body but the warmth under my head. Blinking open my eyes, I find Joey smiling down at me, my head, apparently, cradled in his lap.

"Are we onstage?" I whisper.

He nods slowly.

"Is everyone staring?"

Another slow nod.

I groan.

"Oh my God, are you all right?" Alex asks, appearing in my periphery like a poof of blonde. The next second, Jason is there, too, looking down at me in concern. I can hear a murmur of noise from the audience, but the MC takes that moment to bend down, picking up the fallen microphone.

"All right, folks," he says, cutting through the din. "It looks like Mr. Bradley is going to be okay. Let's take a quick ten-minute break, and then we'll continue on with the auction."

"What happened?" I ask Joey, deciding if I don't look at the crowd, I can pretend they're not there.

"You got a papercut," Jason fills in as Joey brushes my hair off my forehead.

"And passed out, sweetums," Alex adds.

"Yeah," I say slowly, easing myself into a sitting position. Joey helps, rubbing my back as my vision swims. "I don't do well with blood."

"Here," Cas says, having appeared next to the stage. He tosses a box of juice toward Joey, who grabs it and proceeds to open the straw, popping it into the top of the box. "I'll be back with some food."

Joey hands me the juice as Cas heads off to find a snack. I take a few sips, resolutely not looking down at my finger.

"It's a good thing your knight in shining armor is so quick," Alex says, glancing between me and Joey with a knowing expression. "He managed to stop your head from hitting the stage."

"Small mercies," I mumble, remembering the speech I had been giving when I passed out. *Fuuuck.* I didn't even get to finish. "Uh, thanks for the save, Joey-roo."

He squeezes the back of my neck, conversation continuing to buzz around us.

"Uh... Think we can maybe go somewhere a little less...public now?" I ask.

Joey nods quickly, standing and offering me his hand. I spot my speech on the stage beside me and grab it, shoving the paper in my pocket before Joey pulls me up.

"I'll find a Band-Aid," Jason murmurs, hurrying off ahead of us.

Alex sticks close as we make our way off the stage, the rest of the porn star crew giving me worried looks as we pass. I shoot them a reassuring smile and a wave before we round the corner out of the ballroom, heading toward the dressing room we were in earlier.

Once inside, Joey settles me onto the couch. I drink my juice, and Alex goes to grab some water.

"Doing okay?" Joey asks, wrapping a spare napkin around my finger while we wait for Jason to return.

"Embarrassed," I admit. "And a little woozy. Otherwise fine. Sorry I botched your auction intro."

"Hey, I'm not worried about that," he says, his hand on my thigh squeezing gently. "In fact, I... I quite liked what you said. About me."

"Yeah?"

He hums. "How'd you find out about that duck I carved?"

"Your mom. We talk most days."

"Of course you do," he mumbles around a smile. His expression turns a little pensive as he eyes me. "Did you really mean all that?"

I pull in a breath, my pulse hitching and my hand idly running over my pocket where the rest of my speech sits. "I, uh..."

"Found a first aid kit," Jason says, unintentionally interrupting us as he comes into the room. He squats down in front of the couch, holding out his hand. I pass my own over and keep my gaze averted as he tends to my minor flesh wound.

"Water and a snack," Alex announces, the next to rejoin our small group. He hands the items off to Joey. "I should get back out there, but you and I are going to have a little chat later, *Mr. Bradley.*"

The small blonde raises an eyebrow in challenge, and I huff a laugh. "You mean about my newfound appreciation for swordplay?"

Alex's mouth drops open, a look of pure glee taking over his face. "Yes, I mean about that! When did this happen, sweet stuff? Tell me every single detail."

"Well," I start, thinking it over, "first there was Joey's hammies. Or maybe it began with the cum gutter fantasies? You see—"

"Oh my *God*," Jason groans, giving my hand a hard pat before closing the first aid kit. "You're all set."

"We'll talk later," Alex threatens cheerfully on his way to the door. "Remember. *Every. Single. Detail.*"

He waves his fingers in a goodbye, and I turn to Jason.

"I'll live?" I check.

"To be determined," my friend mumbles.

"So...you know a bunch of adult film stars," Joey says, his lips quirking.

"They're great guys," I tell him. "Cas used to—"

"Yeah, I figured that out just tonight," he says.

"Aw, look, Birdie," I say to Jason, who's washing his hands in the sink now. "Another person who's seen your beau's—"

"I dare you to finish that sentence," he growls.

"He's a little possessive," I whisper to Joey.

Jason glares at me.

"*Yikes*. Okay," I say, clapping my hands together. "Lemme smash this pita and hummus, and then we'll get back out there to sell our bodies. Our *services*. We'll sell ourselves for charity. *Frick*. You know what I mean."

The rest of the auction goes off without a hitch. Joey raises an astounding twenty-five grand for his renovation services, likely in part due to my spectacular speech and subsequent fainting. He looks a little awed, but I'm not surprised in the least.

I don't think he realizes just how easily he draws people in, like the smell of cinnamon rolls or, *ooh*, one of those big sunflowers you can't help but stop and stare at. And *holy freaking shit*. I'm his bee!

"Hey," I whisper to him as the master of ceremonies gives his closing speech. "*Pst*. Joey. Joey-roo. Wanna pollinate me later?"

He turns to me slowly.

"You know," I hedge, bouncing my eyebrows. "With your *stamen*. I'll do a little"—I wiggle my fingers—"and you'll give me your sunflower seed."

Alex leans around Joey to stare at me.

"Maybe we should discuss our...stamens later?" Joey suggests.

I snort. "I'm a bee, dude. Not a flower. I don't have a stamen in this scenario."

"Then how would I pollinate—you know what? Never mind. The answer is going to be yes," Joey concedes.

I fist pump.

"So. Amazing," Alex whispers.

As the charity auction crowd starts to disperse, Cas hands each of us a card with contact info for our donors. My winner is named Eugenia Davis. Honestly, she looks like the type of person who could use a good hug. I hope our cuddle session helps her.

"You hungry?" I ask Joey. "I know it's late, but I'm kinda craving dogs."

His lips twitch. "Sure. We can grab some hot dogs on the way home."

Home. I like that.

Neither of us has a chance to take a step, however, before a small body barrels into me. "*So,*" Alex says, strangling me as he hangs off my back. "I was discussing it with the guys, and we decided we should throw you a big gay coming-out party. What do you think? Do you love it?"

"We?" I ask around a grin, even as I struggle for breath.

I can practically feel Alex rolling his eyes. I met Alex and the rest of the Elite 8 Studios cast and crew when Jason and Cas started dating, and it didn't take long whatsoever to learn Alex is a meddling meddler who meddles.

Not that I mind his brand of mischief one bit.

"*Fine*," he says in an exasperated tone. "*I* decided. It was me. Happy? Of course, we don't have to call it a coming-out party if you're not—in fact—out, sweets. Your comfort comes first."

He's also incredibly bighearted.

"Pretty sure I'm out," I tell him. "Not that I made an announcement or anything. Wait... Do people do that? Should I send out cards?"

Joey looks ridiculously fond, an expression that has me smiling back at him on autopilot.

Alex titters a laugh. "Please do," he says, sliding off my back. "The party?"

"I'm in," I agree. "*Oh my God*, wait. Can we get those candy penis necklaces again? The ones you passed out at Cas's going-away party? Those tiny dicks were delicious."

"Honey, I'll get you all the dicks you could ever eat," Alex says solemnly.

"I mean...I can fit a lot in my mouth, dude. So careful with your promises."

He grins, and Joey threads his fingers through mine. My heart skips a beat.

"I'll send you the details," Alex says, throwing his arms around me in a final hug I readily return. He plants a smooch on my cheek before speaking low, for my ears only. "I hope he's your one. You deserve it, Brad."

My throat feels tight as he pulls back, and I give him a smile and a nod. Alex shoots me a little wave, bouncing over to his boyfriends.

Joey squeezes my hand. "Ready?"

"Yeah," I sigh. "Let's go home."

I say a quick goodbye to the guys on our way out of the ballroom. Jason catches my eye, his hand held near his ear as he mouths *call me*. I give him a nod, and then Joey and I head out the door.

It's fully dark outside the hotel, apart from the streetlamps and neon lights. The ever-present bustle of the city is a constant noise in my ears as Joey and I wait for his truck to be brought around. When we get to his place, he suggests eating our hot dogs in the dining room so we don't drop ketchup or pickle relish on our tuxes. Apparently, we're too fancy to eat commando on the couch, which is *fine*.

The wainscoting gleams white in the low light of the room. Looking at it reminds me of the weekend we spent refurbishing it, which in turn brings a smile to my face. Thoughts of Joey tend to do that.

"What's next on the project list?" I ask, tugging a hot dog free from my bag.

Joey raises a single eyebrow. "Bub, as I already told you, I'm not doing renovations naked. Wearing only a tool belt simply isn't safe."

"No," I say around a laugh, although I can't blame his mind for going there, considering how many times I've brought up that very thing. "I'm just wondering what we can work on next."

His lips hitch up at the corner. "You want to help again?"

"If you'll let me," I tell him seriously. "I'm pretty handy with a tape measure, if you haven't noticed."

"Greg and I are both well aware."

I snort.

After a second of consideration, Joey says, "We could replace the porch skirting next weekend if you want."

I grin. "It's a date."

By the time Joey and I make it upstairs, I'm beat. I watch him undress, taking in the view as any kangaroo-watcher would. The appearance of his brief-clad backside has me letting out a soft sigh. *That's the stuff.*

Joey is first to sink into bed, patting his chest in clear invitation. I hop up next to him, my muscles melting as I settle my head on his cozy pec. Joey's skin is warm beneath my cheek, and I idly run my hand over his stomach. His fingers thread through my hair, sifting rhythmically, the only light in the room the lamp on Joey's nightstand.

"You doing okay?" he asks, voice quiet.

"Yeah," I breathe. "Fine. Just tired."

He hums. "It doesn't bother me."

"What's that?" I ask, craning my head up to see him.

"You cuddling someone," he says, answering my question from before. "I won't lie and say I want you pursuing anyone else while we're...together. Men, women, whomever. But... I don't want you to stop being yourself, bub. And I trust you. So even though I hope I can be the person to give you the comfort you need, I'm not going to ask you not to comfort others. Because then I'd be asking you to change. And I won't ever do that."

My heart beats swiftly, a heavy whoosh passing through my ears as Joey's words settle over me. His eyes, although dark in the lamplight, are warm. Always so warm.

"Thank you," I manage, knowing it's not enough.

For someone to tell you repeatedly that they like you just as you are... That they *accept* you, possibly even love you, for exactly who you are...

How do you say thank-you for that?

I settle my cheek back over Joey's heart, his pulse a metronome to my thoughts. There's a soft thrum of *want* running through my veins, as there is anytime Joey is near. An awareness of his body spread out beside me. Of his lips so close. Of the knowledge that with a few choice touches or words I could see his smile, hear his laugh, make him moan.

But, for now, I'm content to stay just like this. Being held by him. Holding him in return and keeping him close. I think there are lots of ways to want a person. And sure, I absolutely want Joey to cover me in so much pollen I need to take an antihistamine. But right now, for tonight, this is more than enough.

For a kid who grew up without comfort, without any real security, it's everything.

Tonight didn't go quite as I planned. I never got to finish reading those words burning a hole in my pants pocket. My attempt to sweep Joey off his feet ended with him, well, catching me as I fell off my own.

But that's okay.

Life is full of stumbles, isn't it? What matters is not giving up.

Step eight in Brad's Guide to Finding Himself and Falling in Love:

Never give up on your dreams.

Our thirty days are nearly over. But I'm hoping desperately that this month Joey and I spent together will be the first of so many more to come. I just have to ask if he wants the same thing I do.

A lifetime of bennies.
A partnership.
Love.
And I think I know just how to do it.

Chapter 30
JOEY

"You're not going to tell me where we're going?" I call.

"Nope," Brad yells from downstairs, sounding exceedingly cheerful for someone who showed up the minute I arrived home from work and shoved me up the stairs like a drill sergeant with the express instructions to shower and get dressed for a night out.

The fact that he didn't join me in said shower was odd enough. Him refusing to tell me what, precisely, this night entails? That has me more than a little curious. It could be anything with Brad.

A specialty coffee run for his espresso with whip.

Announcing my love of watersports to a stadium crowd.

Hell, going down in a shark cage for all I know.

I have no clue what to expect, but I trust Brad. So I head to my closet to grab a shirt.

The moment I throw open the door, I stop still. "Uh, bub?" I call. "What am I looking at?"

I hear Brad bounding up the stairs, a strange beeping noise accompanying him. He walks into the bedroom holding my stud finder, the noise coming from him as he waves the device in front of me. His *beep, beep, beeps* intensify.

"Found you," he says triumphantly.

"You're ridiculous," I tell him, unable to stop my grin. "Did you find that in my tool bag?"

"Yep."

"You didn't get out the—"

"No, I wasn't playing with your drill again," he says, pouting. "I'm well aware we still need to repair the wall after last time."

"Mhm," I say mildly.

"I didn't know it'd start spinning when I squeezed the trigger!" he defends. "I thought the safety was on."

I snort, waving toward my closet. "What's this?"

Brad brightens immediately. "Oh, that's your fanny rack, dude! A rack for all your packs. It keeps 'em neat and tidy. Nice, right?"

"Sure," I say slowly. "But, uh, when did I get so many?"

The...*fanny rack*, as Brad called it, has a good dozen fanny packs tucked into neat rows. Last I was aware, I only had two.

"I *might* have gone on a bit of a spending spree," Brad says. "But you deserve to look pretty, babe."

He pats my stomach, his touch lingering as he looks fondly over the fanny packs.

I don't even tell my traitorous heart to cut it out.

"Should I wear one tonight?" I ask, pulling a shirt off its hanger and shrugging it on.

Brad hems with a prolonged "ehhh" noise, seemingly torn. "I mean, it's not really a pack place. But... Your fannies, man."

"How about I wear one tomorrow?" I suggest, doing up the buttons on my shirt. "Your choice."

"*Ooh*, the 'sexy bitch' one," he says excitedly, his previous woe forgotten. "No, wait. The tie-dye. *No.* 'Cool dad.' Definitely that one. You're a total DILF, dude."

"I'm...not even a dad," I point out.

He *pshts*. "Not yet, maybe."

I'm pretty sure my heart stops.

"We should get going," Brad says, checking the time on his phone. "Are you ready?"

Christ.

"I hope so," I mutter.

Brad drives us into town, drumming his fingers against the steering wheel as he hums along to the music on the radio. He's wearing a long-sleeved green shirt in nearly the same color as his eyes tonight, and when he looks over at me with an instant smile, I'm hit the same way I was the first time I saw him.

He took my breath away then. That smile. The sight of his laugh. The way he drew me in like a magnet, calling to the very iron in my blood to get closer and learn who he was.

He still takes my breath away. I think he always will.

Brad pulls into a parking garage not far from his own apartment, and I wing up a brow.

"Are we heading to your place to play video games?" I ask.

He snorts. "No. We wouldn't have needed to leave your house to do that."

"Gym?"

"Dude. You definitely could've displayed your fanny at the gym. It's not that. Just...trust me?"

"Always," I tell him.

His answering smile is like a sucker punch.

Brad's fidgeting intensifies as we leave the parking garage and walk down the sidewalk past the many businesses on this stretch, both of us weaving around the typical evening crowd. He seems...nervous. Which, in turn, makes me nervous.

Finally, Brad slows, and I look over at a building I recognize. It's the steakhouse I brought him to for our first date. Or, well, what I *thought* was our first date.

Brad stops in front of the restaurant, not yet going in. My heart beats a little unsteadily as his gaze flicks up to me, to the side, and back to me again.

"So, uh," he says, twisting one hand in the other. "I'm not sure if you remember, but it's been a month since we started this whole...bennies thing."

My breath catches, pressure coalescing beneath my ribcage. I exhale slowly.

"And, uh, well... I've been thinking a lot about that," Brad goes on. "About what we've been doing and how we met. And...the future."

"Yeah?" I ask, my voice hoarse.

He lets out a breath and squares his shoulders, meeting my gaze head-on. "I planned a date for you, Joey. The reservation is under your name."

My gut does a slow, *slow* dive. "What?"

"I think you'll really like this guy," Brad says, unaware of how his words are gutting me. "He meets all your criteria, even the green eyes. I promised I'd find you the one, remember? I think this guy could be it."

"I... *What?*"

"What what?" he says, his tentative smile turning into a frown.

"Brad, I... No."

"Huh?"

"*No,*" I reiterate.

"But you haven't even seen who it is," he says, his tone turning almost frantic.

"I don't care who it is," I shoot back. "I don't... I don't *want* it."

This time, it's Brad sounding almost wounded as he asks, "What?"

"I don't..."

I let out a frustrated noise, my pulse so heavy it feels like a drum beneath my skin. I spin away before spinning right back, Brad's wide, green eyes making my stomach clench. My fear, far outweighing my anger, has my voice coming out as a rasp.

"We said we'd talk about it. About...*us*. That we'd reevaluate things once the month was up. I mean...what the actual fuck, bub?"

"Joey," he whispers.

"No, you don't get to just...pass me off to the next guy without a word. It's you and me. I thought we were on the same page about that."

"We *are*."

"Then why are you asking me to walk in that door and go on a date with some man that isn't you? I don't want them. *Any* of them. The only person I want, the only person I've wanted for *months* now, is you."

"Joey," he says again, but the words are already spilling out, and there's no stopping them.

"None of them have *your* green eyes, Brad. None of them will feel the same wrapped around me at night. None of them are capable of being what I need because I'm already in love with *you*. I love you, okay? So no. You told me not to settle, and I'm not settling for anyone but the man I love. I'm not giving you up without a fight, got it?"

The curve of Brad's slowly burgeoning smile takes me momentarily off guard. I don't understand what he has to smile about, but then he says, "*Joey*. It's me. I'm the date."

My exhale is loud. "*What?*"

"I was going to come in once you were seated," he explains, his hand sliding up my arm. "I was trying to be cute."

"You nearly gave me a heart attack," I croak.

"I'm sorry," he whispers, his eyes closing briefly before they're on me again. "You love me?"

Fuck.

"I do," I say, despite the way my nerves are flayed open.

"Good," he says firmly. "Because I'm kinda in love with you, too, dude. And you not feeling the same way would've really spoiled this whole grand gesture thing I'm trying to pull off."

I let out a pained laugh, and Brad tugs me close, his hand anchoring at the side of my neck.

"I don't want you with anyone else, Joey. And I don't want to be with anyone else, either. I'm sorry I fucked this up, but I was trying to tell you thirty days isn't nearly enough time for me. Not when it comes to you. I'd like to share *all* your days if that's something you'd like, too. I can't promise to always get things right. I mean, case in point right here. But I *can* promise I'll always do my best. Because you're worth it. You're my baby kangaroo-roo. And, if you'll let me, I'll be your boomer."

"Fuck, bub," I rasp out, my relief mixing with a heavy dose of joy and so much affection it's physically painful. "Are you saying you want to be my Daddy?"

"Uh..." he says slowly, apparently having missed my teasing tone. "Is that something you're into, dude? Because I don't remember it on your list of kinks. I can totally try, though!" He clears his throat, the serious mask he draws over his face making my lips twitch. "You gonna be good and take my cock later, son?"

Oh. My. God.

"I fucking love you," I tell him.

Brad beams. "I love you, too, man! Does this mean we're gonna be dude-bros for life? Two halves of the same man-sammie? You can be my bro-nilla milkshake, and I'll be your—"

Brad makes a startled noise when my lips press to his, but then he's kissing me back just as fiercely, his hands tugging at my shirt, mine at the back of his head as I bump him lightly into the outside of the steakhouse. My breath feels as if it's too expansive for my lungs, my eyes stinging from unshed tears. He's the wash of the ocean over my senses, lips warm like the sun, his happiness combined with my own leaving me weightless and drowning in nothing but him.

He's everything I didn't know I wanted, never thought I'd get, and can't bear to let go of.

I pull Brad away from the wall, lifting him up in my arms. He lets out a surprised sound, but it shifts quickly to a chuckle as his lips smack away from mine.

"You'll stay with me, Baby?"

His smile widens at my question, and he throws his arms out wide. "Yeah, Johnny. 'Cause I've...*haaad*—"

"Oh boy."

"—the time of my—"

"Are we really doing this?"

"—li-i-ife, and I—"

"Dude," some guy says, stopping beside us. "Are you doing *Dirty*—"

"*Dirty Dancing*, dude, fuck yeah!" Brad says, holding out his hand.

The guy slaps his palm. "Good movie."

He walks away, and Brad turns to me, eyes wide. "See? Everyone gets it."

I can't help but chuckle, so smitten it's a struggle to let Brad slide back to the ground where he's even an inch further away from me. "For the record," I say, "I'm not sure how I feel about you calling me Johnny, considering it's my uncle's name."

He winces. "Yeah. To be honest, I kinda like bub more than Baby, anyway. It's better, you know? 'Cause it's ours."

"Yeah," I answer, kissing Brad's temple, my heart clenching tight. "What would you say to going home, bub? Maybe we could do the steakhouse another night?"

"Sounds like a plan, Joey-roo. There's just one thing I need to do first."

"What's that?" I ask cautiously.

"*Owe-it-all-to-you-u-u*," Brad yells quickly before threading our fingers together. He gives my hand a squeeze, tugging me down the sidewalk at a fast clip. "Fuck, that's better."

Brad and I barely make it a step inside my doorway before he's on me. We stumble down the hall together, lips locked, me managing to kick the front door shut before we get too far. Brad heads for the stairs, pulling me along with him, but I grab the banister to halt our momentum.

"Wait," I tell him, pulling in a breath. "I need to grab something."

He squints at me. "Is it rope?"

"Not...rope. No."

"Did you find the handcuffs?"

I go still. "There are handcuffs in my house? Where?"

Brad scoffs. "Yeah, like I'm telling you that."

"What—" I stop and shake my head. "Nope. No. I'm getting sidetracked. Just...wait for me in the bedroom?"

Brad takes a step backwards, a mischievous glint in his eye. "*Ooh*, wait for you. Kinky. I like it."

"How is that kinky?" I ask slowly.

He takes another step up the stairs, winking at me.

"Dear Lord. *Please* don't be doing anything weird when I get up there," I plead.

He winks harder before turning and running up the stairs.

"Fuck," I mutter to myself, heading toward the garage. "Why'd I have to latch on to that one?"

I find what I'm looking for quickly and strip down, leaving my clothes in a pile beside the door. Then, I take a deep breath and head up the stairs.

I'm slow to push my bedroom door open, a little terrified about what I'm going to find. As it turns out, it's Brad, nude and kneeling on the bed, a fanny pack in his grip that he's dragging along one open palm like one might a flogger. We both stop dead when we see one another.

"*Holy*," Brad wheezes. "You... The tool belt, and... Naked. *Joey*... You're a slutty carpenter."

"What are you doing with that fanny pack?" I have to ask.

He throws it off the bed. "Nothing. Not a fucking thing. Get over here and drill me, dude!"

"I could certainly do that," I agree, my dick jerking as Brad's gaze rakes over me, his desire palpable. "*Or.* I took the time to get extra clean in the shower earlier, so, if you want..."

"I could drill you," he breathes.

I nod, stepping toward the bed.

"Yes. Yep. That," Brad says, reaching for me. "Why the fuck are you so far away?"

Laughing, I let Brad tug me in, and our mouths collide. He groans against my lips, his fingers slipping down my stomach to curl under the band of the tool belt. The sound he makes is strangled, his dick pressing into my stomach.

"Joey," he pants.

"Yeah?" I murmur against his mouth, my palms smoothing over his ass.

"I'm going to lie on this bed," he says.

"Okay?"

"And *you're* going to get up on this bed."

"Sure."

"And then you're going to king me."

My confusion must be written across my face because Brad goes on without my having to ask.

"Treat me like your throne, king, and sit on my motherfucking face."

The wave of lust that hits me has me grunting, my cock bucking against Brad's thigh.

"Is that a yes?" he checks.

"Yeah," I manage.

"Good," he says, letting me go and falling back against the mattress, an angel on bright white sheets. "And Joey?"

"Uh-huh," I rasp.

"Leave the belt on."

It takes me a moment to speak past my dry throat. "Whatever you want, boomer."

Brad's laugh curls inside my chest the same way the man himself managed to. He's wrapped around my heart, and no matter where we go from here, no matter where life takes us, I know that will never change.

Chapter 31
BRAD

Joey hops up onto the bed, his belt swaying with the movement in a way that has me fighting back a groan. He looks like a wet dream. A god of hardwood and hammers.

"So much better than a Halloween costume," I mutter.

"What's that?" Joey asks.

"Not important," I say, tugging on his leg. "Get over here and sit on my face, man. I want my tongue up your ass."

"*Fuck me.*"

"And then that, yes," I heartily agree.

Joey swings his leg over my head, reminding me of the times we've 69ed. This time, however, it's his ass staring me in the face instead of his cock. With a happy hum, I grab hold of his tool belt and tug him down to meet me.

Joey lets out a strangled noise, his weight settling over my face. He tries to ease upwards, to give me more space maybe, but I don't let him. I hold his belt tight and run my tongue over his asshole, my own cock throbbing at the single touch.

I've always loved having my partners ride my face. Granted, this is the first time a man is treating me like their own personal bicycle seat. Joey, specifically. But the sheer size of him, the power I know is leashed beneath my fingertips, his thick-as-fuck thighs cradling my head, and his weight all but smothering me...

I don't think it gets better than this.

Joey moans deeply as I work my tongue against him without restraint, the vibration of his pleasure like static beneath my hands. I grip the belt tighter, keeping him in place, running my tongue up and down flatly before pressing against him. His whole body shakes, a tremor, and I do it again, feeling his muscles loosen and his body go lax. Joey starts rocking against me, and I can barely breathe, but it's perfect.

Once I'm able to get my tongue inside his body, I feel triumphant. He stills, shuddering, his thighs squeezing me as they shake. I slide my hands down his hips, grabbing the sides of his ass, using him as leverage to try to push myself as deep as I can go.

Joey curses, a tortured, "Bub," leaving his lips. And it hits me—as my tongue is buried in his ass, his thighs around my head like I'm a nut he wants to crack—that I'll be hearing that *bub* for a long time to come.

I don't know if I have a commitment kink or if it's just Joey, but the mental flash of us old and gray hits me, and I have to slap the side of Joey's ass, urging him to give me an inch of room so that I can breathe. Because, suddenly, my throat is so tight getting air is difficult.

"Okay?" Joey asks immediately.

I nod and clear my throat. "Yeah. Just, uh, really love you, I guess."

He cranes around to try to look at me, but I grab his tool belt again.

"Nuh-uh," I tell him. "You're not going anywhere. Give me your balls."

"You sure?"

"Son, get those balls in my mouth. *Now.*"

Joey coughs out what I think is a laugh. "You know I don't actually have a Daddy kink, right?"

"Oh, thank fuck," I breathe. "Because honestly? I have absolutely no clue how that works."

Joey laughs outright this time, letting me tug him back down to my face, his balls in easy reach now. I run my tongue over them—his sac smoothly shaven—and take one into my mouth. Joey grunts, and I keep one hand on his belt like a leash as I slip the other under the leather pockets, finding his cock. He makes another sound of fervent approval as I rub my thumb over the top of his dick, spreading the precum there.

I'll never get sick of having Joey's cock in my hand. Feeling how hard he is for me, the way he aches, knowing I can get him off with my fist or my lips or even my ass. I suck Joey's other ball into my mouth, giving his cock a squeeze before slapping the side of his thigh lightly and letting his sac pop free.

"Feed me your dick," I demand.

Joey doesn't hesitate this time. He resituates, backing up until that glorious cock is hanging over my mouth. I take hold of it, sucking him between my lips, licking and bobbing as if he's the most delicious corn dog.

"Bub," Joey croaks.

"You ready?" I ask.

"Very."

Joey eases off of me, landing on his back on the bed. He unfastens his tool belt with an apologetic smile, and I understand. He doesn't want to make a mess of the material. It's a bummer, but he still looks gorgeous without it, his cock standing proudly, the man himself every bit a fantasy I didn't know I had until recently.

"Jesus Christ, I'm gonna drill you so good," I promise.

"Yeah?" he asks, smiling as he tosses the belt aside.

"Yeah, dude. This Brad is ready to...*fuck*. Something clever about being the hammer instead of the nail. *Oh*, I've got it. Hey, Joey. Joey. My kangaroo-boo."

"Yes?" Joey says, his lips twitching.

"You be my anchor, and I'll be your screw. Get it? 'Cause I'm going to screw—"

"Yes, bub. I get it," Joey says, his eyes crinkled in happiness.

"Fuck. You're so pretty. I can't wait to find your prostate, then poke the ever-loving fuck out of it."

Joey laughs as I grab the lube from the nightstand. I settle between his legs as he strokes his cock slowly, not enough to get off, just enough to make me jealous of his hand. I focus on my target, though, popping the lube open before grabbing a pillow. Joey takes the hint, lifting his hips enough for me to stuff the pillow underneath him.

"Okay," I whisper to myself. "Here we go."

Squeezing some lube onto my fingers, I warm the liquid a bit before rubbing it against Joey. A quick check of his face shows he's relaxed, so I ease a finger inside of him, surprised when it glides right in.

"Oh fuck," I mutter.

"Okay?" Joey asks.

"Yeah. Yep. Just, uh...having a moment here. A very warm, very *tight* moment."

Joey chuckles. "Just think what it'll feel like when it's your dick inside of me instead of your finger."

I groan, dropping my forehead to Joey's knee. "You're so cruel, and I love you."

He huffs another laugh. "Keep going, bub. Feels good."

I nod, squeezing a little more lube onto my fingers before sliding two in. I work them in and out the same way Joey has done to me, doing my best to stretch him, not wanting to hurt him once it's my cock. Pretty sure the dude has magical ass abilities because it's not long at all before I'm fitting three fingers inside his body, my own practically vibrating with a whole dam's worth of pent-up need. It's not even the idea of sinking inside the man I love, which—*whoa*. Yes, I love this dude. And yes, I do want that very much.

But it's more than that. It's the need to be closer. To bring this man comfort and the pleasure he's asking for. To make him feel good, which is something I want to do for the rest of my life. It's wanting to show him my love. To share it with him.

I've never had that level of intimacy with anyone before Joey, regardless of gender. He's the first. The first person I've fallen in love with.

If I'm lucky, he'll be my last.

"I'm going to do my absolute best not to blow in under six seconds," I tell him sincerely, pulling my fingers free. "But if I don't last, just know I'll make it up to you."

Joey snorts, his flushed cheeks making him look impossibly beautiful. "It doesn't matter how long you last, bub. It'll be perfect no matter what. Because it's you."

"Ah, fuck."

"Brad," Joey says in concern. "Are you crying?"

"No. Nope," I say quickly, wiping my cheek. "Just some condensation. Okay, ready?"

"Screw away," he says lightly, his lips quirked but his eyes so very soft.

Fuck, I love this man.

I grab the bottle of lube, coating my cock and then adding a little more just to be safe. "Just gonna..." I mumble, squeezing some over his crack.

"That's a lot of lube," Joey comments.

"Just a touch more. Don't wanna hurt you. *There*. That should be good."

"Brad," Joey says flatly, his ass positively glistening. "That was too much."

"No, see? It's fine," I tell him, wiping the excess off on his leg. "I'll just...rub it in."

"It's not lotion."

"It's *fine*," I promise, spreading it over Joey's hammies and then across the tops of his thighs. It's maybe a bit more than needed, but *there*. See? Perfectly... "*Fuck*, you're so slippery. Where do I hold on?"

Joey laughs.

"No, no. We're good," I say, abandoning my plan to tug Joey closer and shuffling forward instead. I blow out a breath, holding my cock as I rub over his perfectly oiled hole, testing a little pressure. His body gives in a way that has me groaning, the sight of him opening up for my dick as enticing as the feel of him swallowing my cockhead just like he swallowed my fingers. My voice is hoarse when I ask, "Okay?"

"Good," Joey answers. "Keep going."

I press forward, letting go of my cock to plant my hand on the bed, my other steadied against Joey's abs. I watch my dick sink into his body inch by inch, going slow to make sure it doesn't hurt him. Joey urges me on with words like *yes* and *good* and *like that, bub*, his heels pressed against my ass.

When I finally seat myself fully inside Joey's body, not a single inch between us, I let out a shuddering breath. "Fuck."

"Come here," he says softly, his hand sliding up my arm, giving me a tug.

I'm powerless to resist him. I fall forward, my face inches from his, this man who smiled at me one day in the gym and made me feel as if I were standing on the edge of a new beginning. He never once rushed me. Never tried to *change* me. He was there, waiting maybe. But a good friend to me always.

"Did you like me the whole time?" I ask, not taking my eyes off of his.

He blinks once, his legs tightening around my hips almost imperceptibly. "I tried not to."

"I set you up on so many bad dates."

"Yes."

"We took nearly naked photos together."

He swallows roughly. "That was...hard."

"Literally for you."

"Yes," he agrees.

I groan, dropping my face to his neck. "I'm so sorry."

"I'm not," he says. "Bub, I'm not. Look at me."

I do. Of course I do.

Joey's hands come up to frame my face, his callused touch gentle and warm. "I don't regret any of it. Yes, I liked you from the start. More than I probably should have without being honest with you about it. But letting myself fall, knowing the chances of you reciprocating were slim to nil? That was my decision. And I'd do it again given the choice. You're worth it."

"I'm going to make you really happy," I tell him hoarsely.

"You already do."

"I'll give you as many Joey-blowies as you want."

"Is that—"

"A Joey-specific blowjob, yes. And me and my douche bulb have come to an agreement, so anytime you wanna plow me, you just let me know. My ass is yours."

"That might be the most romantic thing anyone has ever offered me," he says, sounding fond.

I snort. "Yeah. Sure. You just wait."

His eyes narrow. "What are you plan—"

I kiss him. Hard. It's instantaneous, the way he lights me up inside, as if all that warmth he possesses sinks right into my very skin and bones. I try to show him the way he makes me feel. Try to give him back some of the same heat and comfort. And when his cock flexes against my stomach, I take a deep breath, kiss my way down his neck, and move.

Joey huffs out a breath, an airy grunt of sorts, when my hips meet his ass. He's surrounding me. His legs wrapped around my hips. His smell, manly with that underlying hint of fresh-cut pine, in my lungs. His hand on the back of my head tightening when I suck his nipple into my mouth, and his ass squeezing me as I rock inside his body.

It's everything I thought it would be. *More*. It's Joey.

When a particular angle has him moaning in a way that's distinctly new, I pop off his pec.

"There?" I ask.

"Yeah," he breathes, his head arching back as I do it again.

"Fuck yes," I mutter, keeping up at his p-spot, wanting desperately to see Joey come undone. I shift my hand to his dick, tugging in the way I know he likes, my gaze flicking between his face and where I'm fucking him, the sight so unbelievably sexy my cock throbs. "Fuck, Joey."

"Yes, you are," he pants.

Goddamn it, I'm going to walk with this man down the aisle.

"Oh, holy fuck," I gasp aloud. "There's no way I'm not going to think about this during our wedding."

"What?" Joey asks, his eyes flaring wide.

"What?!" I shout.

"Fuck, I'm gonna—"

Joey's words cut off into a groan, and he comes in a flash across my fist, painting his stomach in a dirty abstract work of fucking art as his ass clamps tight around my cock.

"*Fuuuck*," I agree, jerking him through his orgasm as my own barrels down on me with blinding speed. I suck in a breath, holding back until the last possible second, and then I crack apart.

My moan is a loud, stuttered thing as I come inside Joey's body, my hips flexing to push inside of him as far as I can go, a ridiculous biological imperative I have no control over. My release adds to the slick glide between our bodies, smooth and warm and feeling so fucking good I could weep. It seems as if it lasts forever, that blissful freefall, when realistically, I know it's only a few seconds later that I blink open my eyes.

Joey is watching me steadily.

"It was just dirty talk," I whisper, well aware it's far too soon to be discussing our...*wedding*.

Joey's lips curve into the tiniest smile, his thumb smoothing over my forehead, likely wiping off the sweat there. "You have the strangest idea of what constitutes dirty talk, bub."

"Psht. You like my mouth."

"I won't deny that," he says before looking down. "Are you... writing your name again?"

"Yep," I say, finishing the *D* on Joey's stomach and letting out a sigh. He doesn't complain when I collapse over his chest, my cock slipping out of his body. "Aw, man. I liked it in there."

He huffs a laugh, his fingers threading through my hair. "You're welcome anytime." After a minute of mutual petting and afterglow basking, he says, "You lasted more than six seconds."

"I did!" I reply happily. "And I found your prostate."

"That you did," he says on a chuckle.

"We should probably have some steak or something to celebrate," I suggest, my stomach voicing its own approval with a growl. "We did miss dinner."

"A shower would also be a good idea."

"Yeah, man. We are *covered* in lube."

"It's everywhere."

"You're probably going to need to throw out these sheets," I point out. "Maybe even your mattress. I think we wrecked the bed."

He snorts, pushing up onto his elbows. I lean back, giving him room to sit up all the way. I'm not expecting the swift slap to my ass cheek. "Come on, Bradley. Let's wash up so I can put my meat in your mouth."

"Dude," I breathe, watching Joey's ass as he walks away, the globes still glistening from lube. "I love you so much, you don't even know."

Joey's laughter beckons me to follow him down the hall. We wash up together, taking turns under the showerhead, Joey joining in when I start singing "Bohemian Rhapsody," his falsetto even more impressive than my own.

I never had a solid grasp growing up of what it meant to fall in love. I didn't have parents in my life or many role models to show me what a healthy relationship looked like. I didn't have many people who stuck around, period.

I'm not sure I could have dreamed up Joey Delgado even if I tried. Falling in love with my friend? With someone I can be silly with and be honest with, someone I can play video games with, go to the gym with, be myself with...

Like Jason said, maybe it was simply inevitable. But I sure didn't see it coming.

I guess in the end, I really crushed this whole wingman thing, didn't I? I found Joey his guy. The one who will love him for all he is and all he will be.

And, as it turns out, I found my person, too.

Chapter 32

JOEY

"You shall never defeat me! Your efforts are futile, tiny humans. Surrender now or—"

Brad cuts off on a gasp, falling to his knees as Sonny nails him with a blast from his water gun.

"No! This can't be," the love of my life says in dramatic fashion, sinking to the grass as my cousins' kids advance on him, giggling hysterically all the while. "You may have wounded me, but I will rally. You'll never win. You'll never…"

Brad makes a gurgling sound and goes still, his face pressed to the ground.

"That one?" Iggy asks.

"That one," I agree, letting out a sigh. My smile is ridiculously wide as I watch Brad feign his demise. Iggy slaps my shoulder, chuckling softly.

"Here you go, hon," my Aunt Margot says, passing me a new margarita. "He's good with them. Are the two of you thinking about having kids of your own?"

I cough into my drink, and Iggy cackles.

"If you ever want a test run," Alice calls from nearby, "just let me know. You guys can have mine for the weekend."

I look over at where Sonny is repeatedly shooting Brad in the head with water, his hair now soaked.

Oh boy.

"That's, uh, great. Thanks, Alice," I manage, heading over to Brad's sprawled form. "I think you guys got him. Why don't you head inside and grab plates and silverware for lunch?"

The kids groan but head for the house, and I squat down, running my fingers through Brad's wet hair.

"Doing all right?" I ask.

"They just kept shooting," he mutters, shifting his face toward me, a grass stain on one cheek. "Ruthless little gremlins."

I snort. "They had fun."

"So did I," he says, accepting the hand I hold out for him. He lets me tug him up and brushes loose grass off his shirt. "But now my health points are low, Joey-roo, so I'm gonna need you to feed me. What are we having for lunch? Please say meat."

"Burgers and brats," my Uncle Johnny calls, holding up his tongs. A massive brat is held in the metal.

Oh no.

"Frack yeah," Brad says, bounding toward the patio table. "*Ooh*! Whole pickles. These things are huge. Sonia! Where'd you find such big dills?"

Oh no.

Lunch is…interesting. Luckily, I don't have to try to stop myself from watching Brad as he eats, even when he manages to turn his brat into a two-biter. An impressive feat, for sure.

Once we finish up and the table has been cleared, Brad and I go change into our swimsuits. He's less hesitant this time as we get into the water, but I still stick close.

"You're doing good," I tell him, watching as he swims along the edge of the pool. He stops before long, his arm resting on the concrete perimeter.

Floating still isn't his strong suit.

"Well, see, this guy I'm dating is part fish," he says with a grin. "So I had to learn a few things."

"This fish would have happily stayed on land for you," I point out.

Brad frowns before pushing off the edge. "Incoming."

I keep the two of us buoyant as Brad wraps his legs around my waist, his arms looped loosely over my shoulders.

"I need you to listen to me," he says seriously, his light green eyes pinging between my own.

My heart thumps. "Listening."

"I never, *ever*, want to erase part of who you are. Relationships are supposed to be about compromise, right? But you have this tendency to go balls to the wall when it comes to making other people happy. The fact that you're here now, for one. And I know," he adds quickly. "You don't regret moving. I know that. But you can't tell me you don't miss New Hampshire and your mom."

I can't deny it.

"Which is why we're going to make a point of visiting when we can," he goes on. "Every few months, even when it's all cold and snowy and I get frostbite on my nips."

"Why would you be shirtless in the snow?" I question.

"I dunno, dude! Isn't polar plunging a thing?"

"Please, *please* don't do that."

He waves me off. "Naked snow angels, then. Whatever. My point is you can't leave behind the best parts of your past just to make a future with me. And I wouldn't want you to. I'm happy to learn how to swim so I can be here in the water with you. And I'll be happy to get on a big metal death trap every so often so we can visit your mom. I like spending time with your family, Joey. I like working on the house with you.

I like sharing your favorite things. So don't ever think loving you—all of you—is a hardship. Because it's not. It's the easiest thing."

"Fuck, bub," I manage, my throat tight. "You're constantly amazing me, you know that?"

He preens. "Well, I *am* pretty amazing."

"You are," I agree easily. "Thank you for...I don't know. For seeing me, I guess."

He cocks his head slightly, hand wet as his fingers drift over one of my eyebrows. "Joey Kangaroo, my guy, I may have missed a few things along the way, but I've never been able to look away from you. Logan can attest to that."

I huff a laugh, having half-forgotten about the man and our failed date at the ballpark. "You kept touching my stomach," I remember.

"It's so nice," Brad groans, his hand squeezing between our bodies to drift along my abs. "So, so nice. The best baker couldn't have crafted you."

"I...thank you?"

He hums. "Logan understood. He's been really nice about it. Wishes us well."

"You've kept in touch?" I ask in surprise.

"Oh, sure," Brad says. "We chat sometimes. I actually set him up with Lewis. Remember him?"

It takes me a moment. "Watersports Lewis?"

"Yeah, man! Turns out they're getting along really well." He huffs a laugh. "You never can tell who enjoys piss play."

Jesus.

"Well, I'm glad for them," I say.

"Me too," Brad replies dreamily. "Now be a good Joey-floaty and let me drift on you."

"Anytime, bub," I answer, propelling us through the water. "Anytime."

It's early evening when we arrive at Brad's apartment, the calendar having declared it a "Brad-pad" night. We shower off the chlorine from the pool, and then Brad retreats to the living room to order a late-night snack of chicken and waffles. I give my mom a call.

"Hi, my boy," she says in greeting. "How's my favorite Vegan?"

I groan. "We're called Las Vegans. Not *vegans*. It's a totally different vowel sound. And Brad is fine, thanks for asking."

My mom chuckles. "He said you guys are planning a trip over around Thanksgiving?"

I snort, even as my insides light. Leave it to Brad to schedule our next visit without even telling me. "We sure are. He, uh...really wants to make a habit of visiting."

She hums. "I won't lie and say that doesn't make me happy to hear. He's a good one, Joey. He's good for you."

"Yeah," I say, that lump back in my throat. "It, uh...scares me sometimes."

"Why's that?" she asks.

It takes me a minute to figure out how to answer her. I walk over to the wall as I pull the words to the surface, tracing the canvas of Brad and me from our boudoir photoshoot with my eyes and then the tip of one finger. He's so beautiful. So open, even then. It astounds me, when I think about how he grew up. It would have been easy for him to close himself off. To guard against all the hurt in the world.

Instead, he's one of the most genuine people I know. He's utterly transparent and trusting. Damn near *fearless*, as far as I'm concerned.

He doesn't have walls around his heart. And I want nothing more than to make sure that organ beating inside his chest doesn't get bruised or broken.

"I've never loved anyone the way I love him," I tell my mom. "How do I protect him? How do I keep him safe?"

"Oh, honey," my mom says softly. "You don't. It's not your job to stop everything life will throw at the two of you. You couldn't even if you tried. It's your job to hold his hand. To stay at his side and work through it together. You'll heal each other over time whenever anything bad happens. That's just how it goes. As long as he knows you're there for him, there *with* him, he'll always feel safe."

I pull in a breath, my subsequent exhale shaky. "Thanks, Mom."

"Of course, my boy. You two will be okay. I know it. Now... *Ah*, is that him I hear now?"

*"Joey-roo, my kangaroo-boo. Waffles are here, and I love—*Oh." Brad stops in the doorway, a scrunched grin on his face. "Are you on the phone?"

"It's my mom," I tell him.

"Mama D!" Brad calls, coming into the room and swiping my phone. "I tried those seaweed snacks you mentioned. You're right. They're really good, even though my brain is convinced I'm eating poison." He nods a couple times as he paces over to the window, peeking out through the curtain. "Uh-huh. Uh-huh. The chickpea ones are okay. Kinda dry, though."

I sit on the edge of the bed, a smile on my face as I watch Brad chat effortlessly with my mom. Not for the first time, I'm profoundly grateful for the woman who raised me. Not only because she's always been there for me, but because she's there for Brad without question. I think she knew he needed it from the start.

Brad comes over before long, climbing onto my lap as he continues to talk. The phone is close enough now that I can hear both sides of the conversation.

"Did you get the coffee I sent?" my mom asks.

"I did!" Brad answers. "It's really good. Thank you."

"My pleasure. I should probably get going now, but it was lovely talking to you, darling."

"Likewise. Do you want to say bye to Joey?"

"Please," my mom says.

Brad hands over the phone, settling his head on my shoulder as I bring the device to my ear.

"Mom?"

"I just wanted to say have a good night. Talk soon, and I love you."

"Love you, too," I tell her. "And thanks again. For earlier."

Brad nuzzles his nose against my neck, fingers drifting up under my shirt as my mom says, "Of course. You'll be all right, my boy."

"Yeah," I agree hoarsely.

My mom says a final *love you*, and we end the call. I set my phone aside, clearing my throat as Brad's fingers trace over my skin, a purely soothing touch on his part, not remotely sexual. Not that it stops me from reacting at least a little.

"Hey," I say gently.

"Hi," he mutters. "Waffles are waiting in the living room, but I left them boxed up so they'd stay warm."

Brad makes no move to get up and head that way, so I run my hand up and down his back, my other on the outside of his thigh. I've never been with a single other person as physically affectionate as Brad.

"I'm really lucky to have you," I tell him seriously.

He stills, pulling back to see my face. "Yeah?"

"Mhm. Are you excited for your coming-out party this weekend?"

"Oh, fuck yeah," Brad says with a grin. "Edible phalluses have been procured, porn stars have been assembled, and I'm ready to grind away on your hammies. Or your quads. Any preference on whether I'm in back or in front?"

I snort. "You can have any side of me you want, bub."

"Oh, shit. That's hot. If you happen to see a 'Property of Brad' fanny pack show up in your closet, don't worry about it, okay?"

"Um."

Brad jumps up, climbing off my lap and jogging for the door. "Waffles, Joey!"

With a laugh, I follow after him.

Brad is in the living room when I arrive, opening our boxes of chicken and waffles. "So here's what I'm thinking," he says, setting our controllers down next to our food. "We fuel up while taking out the zombies at the old textiles factory because they're easy. Then you'll have my rear once we reach the abandoned motel. I want you plastered to my back, Joey. Don't be afraid to unload everything you've got. After that, once we make it through the overrun alleyway and get to the forest cache outside the city, I'll return the favor. Bros gotta take care of each other's fannies, dude."

As Brad details our game plan, setting out silverware and drinks as he talks, there's a profound sense of peace that settles over me. This, right here, is a simple moment. It's not grandiose or accompanied by fanfare. But that doesn't make it any less important. It's Brad and me, spending our evening together. One of many more to come.

What I said to Brad is true. I've felt lucky since the moment he came into my life. When I saw him laugh and felt it like a physical blow to my sternum.

When he hugged me the first time and didn't let go.

When he became my friend, listening when I talked and sharing his own stories—his own self—with me in return.

When he asked me to kiss him because he wanted proof that what he was feeling was real.

Every time he's touched me, cuddled me, slept with his head on my chest.

Every press of his lips to mine and the way he smiles at me as if squinting into the sun.

Those eyes, so green, always laughing. Always happy and kind.

His honesty.

His goodness.

The way he loves.

I've felt lucky every day since meeting this man, and I know I'll continue being the luckiest person alive.

Because of him. All because of him.

"Joey," Brad says in amusement, snorting as he holds up a piece of chicken with his fork. It's covered in syrup from his waffles. "Look. This chicken strip looks like a peen, dude! It even has two balls, see? Well, maybe one and a half. Something definitely happened to the second one. But still." He wiggles the chicken a bit. "Think I can get it down in one bite?"

Yep, that's the one.

I'm going to spend the rest of my life loving that man.

I can't wait.

Chapter 33
BRAD

"Birdie!"

"Fuck my life," my bestie from another nestie mutters, his arms squashed at his sides as I hug him tight. "Cas. Little help here?"

Cas gives my shoulder a tap, and I turn to give him an equally hearty hug.

"...five, six," I mutter, stepping back and slapping his shoulder. "Cat-man! Thanks so much for being here."

"Like we'd miss your coming-out party," Jason says, fixing his beanie and looking around the club. "Where are the guys?"

"Up in the VIP lounge," I tell him, grabbing two candy necklaces from Joey and placing them over Jason's and Cas's heads. "There's your pass up. Super tasty, by the way. Try the green dick. It's my favorite."

"That...doesn't sound right," Jason mutters, he and Cas heading toward the stairs.

"Doing okay?" Joey asks, his voice close to my ear.

I spin so I can see his lovely face. "Sure am. Also, I know I said the green dick is my favorite, but the truth is it's Greg.

Well, you and Greg, since you're kind of a package deal. Heh. Package. Speaking of..."

"I meant because of last night," Joey says, his eyes twinkling. There's still a thread of concern there, though, and it makes me melt. Just a little.

"I'm used to bad nights of sleep," I tell him, patting his chest a couple times. Groping a little. "But I appreciate you looking out for me. If you *want*, you could wear me out so thoroughly later I'll have no choice but to sleep right through the night."

His lips twitch. "And how would you suggest I do that?"

"Uh... Was that not obvious? Sexual intercourse, my dude. Your penis. My sphincter. A happy little meet-and-greet with our friend, Mr. Lube. I sure wasn't talking about the gym. And what? Why are you laughing?"

Joey drops his hand from in front of his face, his happy smile making my chest feel light. "How do you make that sound so unsexy, bub?"

"I don't know," I groan. "I just open my mouth, and words fall out. It's a curse."

"More like a gift," he corrects, tugging me in close. "Ready to head upstairs and celebrate your bi-fabulousness? Pretty sure there's a bunch of porn stars waiting on us."

"That sounds way dirtier than I think you intended, Joey-roo, and I heartily approve. Although, just to be clear, I'm not sharing you with anyone. You're my exclusive kangaroo. No one's getting all up in your pouch except for me."

He shakes his head, even though there's a smile on his face. "My pouch is all yours."

My responding grin is huge.

When we make it up to the VIP lounge, a cheer goes up. Alex waves frantically to his boyfriend Finn, who pulls a cord near the edge of the room, releasing balloons that fall from the ceiling in colorful bundles of three. Each is shaped like a dick with balls. I can't help but laugh, amazed that these men put so much effort into this celebration for me.

Alex is the first to reach us, looping his arm with mine. "Welcome to the queer club, sweets! Officially, I mean."

"Thanks. Is there a secret handshake I should know?"

"Sure is," he says. "First, you take off your pants. Then—"

"Behave," Dixon grumbles, plucking the smaller man off me. He holds out an envelope. "Here."

"What's this?" I ask, pulling the flap open and looking inside.

"A two-year subscription for Elite 8 Studios," Niko says from Dixon's side, waggling his eyebrows. "We all chipped in."

"You guys got me online porn?" I ask, tearing up. "That's so fucking thoughtful."

"Just make sure to hydrate," Kipp calls from nearby, a grin on his face. Teddy smiles adoringly at his husband.

I nod solemnly. "I will. Promise. Where's Jason? Birdie!"

My friend ducks lower on the couch he's sitting on, Cas beside him.

"Look, Birdie! Free porn."

"Don't say it," Jason pleads.

"Now I can see your boyfriend's—*Ahh.* Joey! Get him off me. Mercy. Mercy!"

Jason drops back to the floor, punching me on the shoulder—hard—before skulking off.

"Geez," I mutter, rubbing my arm. "Strong dude. Excuse me."

Joey nods, giving the side of my neck a quick squeeze before heading over to chat with some of the guys. I watch him for a moment, smiling softly, and then I go search for my friend. I find Jason sitting at a table in the back of the room and plunk down on a stool beside him.

"You know I'd never actually do that," I tell him seriously. "I respect your relationship with Cas, and I know you don't like people objectifying him."

"You make it really hard to stay mad at you," he mumbles.

I snort. "I'm lovable. I think it's my face."

"It's something, all right," he says before sighing. He nods toward the other partygoers, and my eyes shoot straight to Joey. "You really love him, don't you?"

"Fuck, Birdie. I do. He just... He makes everything better, you know? It's like..."

"Like what?" he asks when I don't go on.

I let out a breath. "You're my big love, Jason. You know that. You've been my closest friend since kindergarten. My brother. You've always been there for me, no matter what. But Joey..."

I look at my boyfriend again, my chest feeling so damn full it's a miracle it doesn't burst.

"Joey is the person I want to spend the rest of my life with. He's my other half in a way I didn't know was possible. It's not that he completes me. We just...*work* together, like we were always meant to find one another and become something bigger than our individual wholes. Which...sounds weird when I say it like that. I'm not talking about *holes*, like our—"

"Yeah, no, I got it," Jason says quickly.

"I just love him," I go on. "Different than how I love you, but just as meaningful. He's going to be the person I live with. Start a family with, maybe. He's going to be there in the mornings as I drink my first cup of coffee and at night when I need a warm pair of arms to help me fall asleep. I'm going to grow old with that man. And I'm going to love him every step of the way."

"Goddamn it," Jason mutters, swiping at his face. "Fuck, Bee."

"I *know*. I've gone soft. Well...not *soft*. Joey makes me harder than anyone, I swear. The other day, he put on his safety goggles and proceeded to rub my hardwood until—"

"*Ahh*," Jason says, shaking his head and covering his ears. "No. Nope. I don't need to hear it."

I pull his arm down. "Let's just say my sawdust got *all* over him."

"I hate everything," he mumbles.

I give my bestie's head a pat. "Oh, look! Emil and Christian are here."

I hop out of my seat to greet the newcomers, both of whom work at Elite 8 Studios. Like Dixon and Niko, they're dating and often film together. Emil has the nerdy look down pat, glasses included, whereas Christian is a total femboy and rather toppy, from what I've heard. And like usual when I see him, he's wearing...

"Oh my God," I whisper to myself, beelining for Joey at the last second. He looks over at me as soon as I attach to his side.

"Yes?" he says in amusement.

"Joey, look," I hiss, nodding over to Christian and his thin silver belly chain. "I could *chain* you, dude."

"That sounds...concerning."

"Isn't it pretty?"

"It *is*," he says slowly. "But..."

"But what?" I prompt, letting Joey go as he reaches for the hem of his sweatshirt. My pulse spikes. "But what, Joseph?"

He tugs the material off over his head.

"*Joey*," I breathe.

My sexy-as-fuck boyfriend not only reveals a crop top that shows off every one of his challah abs, but there's also a bright yellow fanny pack secured tightly around his stomach, the front of which is bedazzled with the word *Brad*.

"You beautiful sexy beast," I growl in awe. "Were you hiding that this entire time?"

"Wore it just for you," he says, giving me a wink.

"You're so fucking hot, dude. I'm gonna ravage you later. You don't even know. My tongue is going to be in places you didn't even know it could reach."

"I'm...not sure if I should be turned on or not right now," he admits.

I stroke his beautifully adorned stomach. "Joey Kangaroo, can I twerk on you?"

He laughs, his arm coming around me as he lays his sweatshirt on the back of a chair. "You can do just about anything you want to me, bub. I'm yours, remember?"

"Fuck. For that, you can ravage *me* later. My ass is yours, dude. Take me however you want. I don't even care how filthy or depraved or—Oh, hey there, Rowan."

The shy mechanic gives us a wave before heading over to his boyfriends. Alex and Finn shift as he gets close, as if attuned to him.

"Come on," I tell Joey, sighing happily. "Let me introduce you to the guys you haven't met yet, and then we'll dance. Did you know Emil is an exhibitionist?"

Joey and I make the rounds, dick balloons at our feet and the occasional tiny candy penis finding its way into my mouth. My necklace is gone by the time we get down to the dance floor, my body buzzing with energy from this night and Joey's presence. He doesn't seem to mind me all but humping his thick thighs, and his hands are never far, on my back, in my hair, tugging me closer still.

I don't know how long we dance for, but our rambunctious *coming out* group closes down the club, all of us stumbling out the doors with promises to catch up again soon. I make sure to give Jason a big, wet smooch on the cheek before we part. He mutters a *gross*, but he loves it. I know he does.

Joey and I catch a rideshare back to my apartment. I'm half-hard when we step inside the door, Joey immediately pressing me against the wood until it closes with a click.

"Hi," I say, grinning at him.

Molten brown eyes hold my own for only a beat before Joey's mouth is on mine. He attacks me with a sort of hunger at odds with his usually calm demeanor, and I don't fight it. Not wanting to and more than ready to take whatever it is Joey has planned for me. He kisses me deeply, his hands tipping my head where he wants me to go, soft, stubble-lined lips tracking down my neck, his thumb pressing up under my jaw.

My head thunks against the door, and I pull in a breath, my stomach contracting when Joey's hand lifts my shirt, fingers trailing over skin. He tugs the material up, mouth finding my chest, my nipples, mapping a path down my stomach as he sinks to his knees.

"Fuck," I mutter, my shirt covering my view for only a second before I toss it away.

Joey looks up at me, bared to me as he always is, and slowly unzips my jeans. I try to control my breathing, try to keep myself in check, but it's hard with him staring at me with such focused intensity, as if nothing and no one could tempt him away. His hands deftly slide my pants down my legs, and then he leans in, a groan leaving his lips as he runs a hand over the length of my cock through the thin layer of my underwear. My gut clenches tight when he pulls me free.

Not a single word comes out of my mouth as Joey sucks my cock down his throat, only a low moan that rattles around inside my chest like the flapping of wings. It sure feels as if my heart could fly away given the chance, if only to find a home within this man looking at me with love in his eyes.

I don't know what I did to deserve his affections, but I won't ever take for granted this beautiful soul at my feet. I won't ever give him up. Won't ever let him question what he means to me.

"Joey," I rasp, motioning him upwards, needing him inside of me like I need my next breath. "Would you fuck me?"

His mouth meets mine again in answer, warm and soft and urgent. I nearly die when he leans back, but then he's shucking his clothes and all is forgiven. I stay his hand when he reaches for his fanny pack.

"Leave it," I tell him.

He smirks but doesn't try to remove it again. Instead, he unzips the bag and pulls out a travel-sized bottle of lube.

"Oh my God," I wheeze, my cock bucking. "That was the sexiest fucking thing I've ever seen in my life."

"Turn around," he tells me.

"Nope. That was. Jesus Christ."

I spin, Joey's lips laying kisses across my shoulders as his hand settles between my ass cheeks. He slips a lubed finger inside of me, his other hand curling around the front of my throat. I nearly sob, fingers digging into the door as my fore-head greets the wood.

"You're mine, bub."

"*Yes.*"

"And I'm yours."

"Yes," I agree again, nodding furiously against the door as Joey stretches me open.

"Anything you want, anything you need, I'll give it to you."

"Please," I croak, three of his fingers inside of me now, the stretch blooming into an ache so exquisite, I can't stop myself from shifting back against him, chasing more.

His fingers leave, and I choke out a sound. But then Joey is spinning me, hitching one of my legs over his hip and rubbing the blunt end of his cock against my ass. He presses just a little. Just enough to feel the renewed stretch.

"I love you so much it hurts," he says vehemently. "And I never want it to stop."

I keen as he pushes inside of me, the driving force of his cock making it nearly impossible to focus on anything else. Yet his words ring in my head, the aching truth of them leaving me no room for doubt.

"Love you," I say in return, my voice no more than a breath.

Joey's gaze says all the things his lips can't utter right this second, but I still hear them. Still understand. He spins the fanny pack around to his back, moving it out of the way, before hoisting me up by the backs of my thighs. I wrap both legs around him, shock a fleeting emotion as Joey presses me against the door. His grip on me is absolute, his cock pushing deeper inside of me.

He rolls his hips, and my head hits the wood.

I hold Joey's shoulders tight as the man proceeds to fuck me against the front door as if I weigh no more than a feather. There's not a single thing I can do but hang on, tears lining the backs of my eyes at the sheer blissful, overwhelming assault to my senses. He's everywhere. Holding me up. Surrounding me. Inside of me. His voice at my ear, telling me how much he loves me, how good I am, how he'll never let me go. His lips brushing my cheek, stubble like sparks against my skin. His stomach grinding against my cock as he moves, *his* cock ramping me steadily higher, that *pressure-push-pull* inside of me an intoxicating high I never knew I was missing before him.

It's *him*. He's what I was missing.

The home I never had.

I cry out when I come, my orgasm sneaking up on me. Joey fucks me through it, his "Bub" a hoarsely spoken syllable in the air. His cheek rests against mine, fingers digging into my thighs as he jerks against me, his cock throbbing out his release. I pant, still shaking, still twitching as aftershocks rumble through my system.

Neither of us moves for the longest time, the pressure of Joey's body keeping me pinned to the door, our chests heaving together as we catch our breaths.

He's the first to pull back, his eyes meeting mine. He looks almost...amused.

"What?" I ask, the one word slurred in my post-orgasmic haze.

"Nothing," he says. "It's just... This is where you'd normally make a joke."

I snort, and he chuckles with me. "You fucked all the jokes out of me, dude. I got nothing."

"Nothing about hammering you so good, the other brads are jealous?"

"Nope."

"What about our pollination efforts to help support the bees?"

"Nuh-uh. I'm just happy," I tell him, meaning it. "And maybe a little boneless."

His expression is soft as he shifts enough for his cock to slip out of me. He lowers me to the ground carefully. "Shower and bed?"

"Lead the way, Joey-roo. I've forgotten where the bathroom is."

He huffs a laugh, kissing me on the temple as he guides me down the hall. We wash the cum off our skin before falling into bed together, Joey a comfy, warm presence beneath my cheek. His arms wrap around me, holding me tight like he so often does, knowing how much I crave the connection.

It's some time later, once Joey is sound asleep but my mind is still wandering, that I slip out of bed to grab a familiar notebook. I take it with me back to the bedroom, not wanting to be far from Joey. He doesn't wake as I climb onto the mattress, sitting next to him and flipping the notebook open to the page I'm looking for.

My eyes skim down the list I started what feels like a lifetime ago, that day I met Joey in the gym. There's an ache in my chest thinking about it, about what might have happened if Joey and I had never crossed paths or become friends. Or if I'd simply never realized the depth of my feelings for him.

It's not an alternative I like to imagine.

My pen scratches lightly against the paper as I add to my list.

Step nine in Brad's Guide to Finding Himself and Falling in Love:

Follow your heart.

I close the notebook, setting it aside as I glance at the man sleeping beside me, the one my heart guided me to. Flicking off the lamp, I curl against his body, right where I belong, a smile on my face I know isn't going anywhere anytime soon.

Step nine?

Yeah.

Abso-fucking-lutely nailed it.

Epilogue
BRAD

Four Years Later

"Hey, everyone. Thanks for coming today. I know most of you are here out of the goodness of your hearts. But for those who showed up for the free drinks, the bar is at the back of the room."

The gathered crowd chuckles, some of them raising wine glasses or cocktails, others smiling, a couple letting out cheers. I smile back before going on.

"So, I have a speech I prepared that I'd like to share with you. And I know, I know. The last time I gave a speech, I got a papercut and passed out. But see? This time I came prepared."

I wave the laminated paper in the air to another round of chuckles. Taking a small breath to center myself, I run my fingers along the smooth surface.

"Here's the thing. I had this list I created a while back, right? Over four years ago actually. It was supposed to be about finding myself. About striking out on my own and figuring out what I wanted out of life. Maybe even finding my person. And I *did*. I did find my person. And, in a lot of ways, I learned more about myself along the way. It's just that none of it happened like I expected it to. Let me just...let me read it to you, and I think you'll understand."

I look down at the laminated sheet I've seen a hundred times or more before leaning toward the mic.

"Step one. Make a new friend." I huff a laugh, eyes meeting the crowd again. "That was Joey. If you know him, which I know you do, you know he's the easiest guy to befriend. He introduced himself to me at the gym one day, and we just clicked. Granted, he was trying to pick me up, and I had no clue, but it worked out fine in the end."

More chuckles. More smiles.

"I think about that day a lot," I admit. "When this guy with warm brown eyes came into my life and I went home feeling hopeful. Excited. Because I'd just made a new friend. Even still, Joey is one of my best friends. He's one of the best people I know, period. And I'm lucky that he didn't give up on me back then. If he had, well... Broey might not exist. That's Brad and Joey, in case it's not clear."

There's some more laughter, and I smile before taking a small sip of my water to wet my throat.

"Step two," I continue. "Do a good deed. *Oh Christ.* Okay, so this one is a funny story. Remember that whole *Joey thought he snagged a date* thing? Well, I felt really bad about that, so I came up with this brilliant plan. To be Joey's wingman. The *best* wingman. And, honestly, I think I smashed it. I mean, look at us now."

Cas snorts, giving me a smile when I glance back. Jason just shakes his head, but he's smiling, too. *Such good dudes.*

I focus forward again, my throat a little tight.

"I told Joey I'd find him the one. And I did, in a round-about kinda way. Which leads me to step three. Try something unexpected. Oh boy. You might want to close your ears for this one, Mama D."

Joey's mom laughs from her table not far in front of me, her smile so bright she's practically glowing. I grin right back, tossing her an air kiss before going on.

"On my journey as a wingman, I set Joey up on several dates. This was before the Broey era, of course. One of those dates happened to be a photoshoot of the...*sexy* variety. And when Joey's date didn't show, well, I stepped in. Which is why there's now a life-size canvas of the two of us in our underwear on the bedroom wall."

There are more chuckles at that, and a few rowdy porn stars in the crowd hoot and holler. I shoot them a wink.

"The thing is—I hadn't realized at that point I had feelings for Joey. It seems so obvious now, but I guess that's the benefit of hindsight, right? Emotions are complicated. Sexuality, even, is complicated. And, as Joey himself likes to remind me when I point out the two gym-bros in a semi-nude pose above our bed, there's no one right time or way to understand yourself. It's an ongoing process. And I appreciate that Joey never once made me feel bad for taking a little longer to clue in to the fact that I wanted to lick him from head to toe and back to head again, if you get what I mean."

I wince, even as a few people whistle.

"Sorry, Mama D."

Mama Delgado waves me off, but my cheeks still heat.

"Anyways, that *something unexpected* turned into a memory I know I'll carry with me forever. Same with step four. Accomplish a goal. This is a good one. A simple one really, but impactful all the same. Joey and I ran a 5k together. It was..." I let loose a breath. "There was this guy, see? My new friend. Jogging beside me. Helping me finish my first charity run. I think it's important in life to surround ourselves with people who support us. Those who encourage us and stay by our side. Joey was one of those people from the get-go. Even though... Even though he had feelings for me, he set them aside to be my friend. Incidentally, that was also when I started noticing Joey's c—*ahh*. His abs. Which led to a whole lot of gutter-related fantasies that shaped the person I am today. But I'm getting a little bit ahead of myself. Okay, let's see..."

I search my paper as the crowd laughs.

"Right. Step five. Be brave. This was a turning point. Joey and I had just gone on his date with Logan. Speaking of, where's Logan and Lewis? Ah! Hey, dudes! Glad you could make it."

The pair wave back at me, matching grins on their faces.

"So Joey and I went out with Logan. Well, *Joey* went out with Logan. I was just there. Because I was sorta jealous. And we got back to Joey's place—just me and Joey, not Logan—and I was trying to work out why it upset me so much to see my new friend on a date with another man. And it was this revelation, right? This lightbulb while we were hugging where I wanted to be...*closer*. I wanted more from Joey, and I hadn't realized it until just then. So I did what any presumably straight man would do. I hid behind the garage, called for emotional reinforcements, and then I kissed a guy for the very first time in my life."

Joey's cousin Iggy lets out a wolf whistle, and I shoot him a two-finger salute.

"My buddy Cas called me brave on that call. And I wanted to be. So, yes. I went inside and asked Joey to kiss me. And *boy* did he kiss me. That's also the moment I met Greg."

A throat clear has me hurrying along.

"Right. Uh... So that leads into step six. Wade fearlessly into the unknown. I'm just gonna give the CliffsNotes on this one. There was a tool belt. Rubbing wood. Sawdust *everywhere*. A shower and then getting dirty again. Trust me when I say I learned quite a few new things that day. But the important part was not letting fear stop me. Joey made that easy. He made it safe to leap because I knew he was there to catch me. He's always there, arms ready. It's one of my favorite things about him, really."

I find soft faces in the crowd when I lift my gaze, and I take another sip of water to shore myself up before going on.

"That brings me to step seven. Learn a new self-truth. It was obvious, really, but knowing something and *acknowledging* it are two different things. That was the point I made peace with my bisexuality. Not that I had any issues with it in the first place. But I was frustrated with myself, in a way, for taking so long to figure it out. Cas would remind me people are constantly changing and sexuality can be fluid, too. Joey would tell me everyone is different and I shouldn't compare myself to others. And Jason would probably just say *I told you so*. Which yeah, dude, you did."

Jason slides down in his chair, trying to hide. Cas gives him a consoling pat.

"But the point is I took what I knew to be true and acknowledged it. And I think that's a big part of what let me move forward with Joey. Of course, that didn't go as smoothly as I would've liked. Alex, you know what I'm talking about."

The blonde man perks up. "The blood?" he calls.

"Yeah, man, the damn blood. See, I had this plan to woo Joey. To sweep him off his feet in grand gesture style."

I wave the laminated paper in the air again.

"But papercut. Remember? So I passed out before I could ask Joey to be my forever and always kangaroo-boo. That's where step eight comes in. Never give up on your dreams. I planned a final date. A completion of my wingman promise. Because, see, at the time, Joey and I weren't officially dating. Let's just say we were like a 401k sans cash but with all the benefits."

"Get it!" someone in the crowd shouts. I huff a laugh, waiting for everyone's chuckles to die down before continuing.

"The date I planned was a massive flop, though. I won't go into the whole thing, but Joey thought I was setting him up with someone else. And that hurt him. Which wasn't what I wanted in the least. It worked out in the end, once Joey blurted that he loved me, and I was all like, *uh, dude, duh, I love you, too.* And now we're here, so win?"

This time, it's Jason snorting.

"There are always going to be bumps in the road," I say seriously. "But that doesn't scare me. Not when it comes to Joey and me. And that's because of step nine. Follow your heart. No matter what, no matter where life takes us, I'm not afraid of what the future has in store. Because through it all, I'll have him. Over four years ago, Joey Delgado became a friend. He's still that. Always will be. But he's also the love of my life. He's the person whose smile I wake up to each morning. He's the one to greet me after a long day with a hug. He's the one who can settle me with a simple press of his lips to mine.

That's love. That's what love is capable of. It's grounding. Reassuring. It's comfort and safety and that bubbling in your chest that never quite goes away. It's the reason we're here today and what led to step ten."

Letting out a slow breath, I turn in place, facing the table behind me. Joey is already watching me with tears in his eyes. My smile wobbles a little as I trace his features with my gaze. Those brown eyes I love so much. His hair, styled neatly today, and the crisp suit he's wearing that makes him look impossibly handsome.

"Step ten," I nearly whisper, the mic still picking up the sound. "Put a ring on it."

I let out a snort.

"You all know this story. How Joey and I picked out rings at the same time, unbeknownst to each other. How we got the call that they were ready...again, at the same time. How we showed up at the jewelry store, a mere minute separating our arrival. And how, as soon as we realized what was happening, it was a mad dash to drop to our knees right there in front of the display cases."

I chuckle hoarsely as the crowd laughs behind me.

"I asked Joey to be my husband that day. And he asked me to be his. It wasn't the proposal either of us had planned, but that's life. And now, here we are, husbands, celebrating our wedding with our family, friends, and coworkers. So you see?"

I lift up the laminated sheet for our guests again, even as I hold Joey's gaze.

"This list is quite possibly the best thing I've accomplished in my entire life. Because, as it turns out, it was ten ways to accidentally fall in love. And every step led me to you."

A tear slips down Joey's cheek, one he quickly wipes away. I let my own fall, not willing to look away from the man who tumbled into my life at the moment I needed him most. The one who loves me for *me* and always has.

"I thought I was finding myself," I tell my husband. "But instead, I found you. So here's to Joey Francis Delgado-Bradley."

I lift my champagne glass off the table, and behind me, I can hear our guests doing the same.

"To my husband. My gym-bro turned bestie turned partner. My confidant and supporter. My great love. Here's to a lifetime of bennies and laughter together. I love you, my Joey-roo."

"Hear, hear," our guests call out, glasses clinking, people clapping. I touch the lip of my glass to Joey's across the table before taking a sip, him doing the same.

"Get over here, bub," he says, standing. I round the table, placing the mic and my laminated list on the end, our guests chatting again now that my toast is over.

"Look," I tell him cheekily, holding up my unblemished hands. "No blood."

"You did good," he says, those big arms coming around me, his fingers sifting up into my hair. "I didn't know you were going to do that."

"I still have some surprises up my sleeve."

"Oh yeah?" he asks. "Anything else I should be aware of?"

"Well," I say slowly. "I might've booked us for a naked body painting workshop during our honeymoon. The paint is edible."

I waggle my eyebrows, and Joey huffs a laugh. "I suppose now is a good time to admit I scheduled a photoshoot for when we get back."

"*Nooo*. With Gianna?"

"Mhm," he hums, hands slipping down my back. "She's coming to our house this time. And I might've requested a...carpentry theme in front of the wainscoting."

"Joey," I breathe. "Tool belts?"

"Tool belts," he confirms.

I groan, and he laughs lightly, his lips feathering across my cheek.

"It's never boring with you," he says. "That's for sure."

"Is that what you'd hoped for? A lifetime of excitement?"

He hums, the two of us swaying slightly as if dancing to a silent beat. "Do you remember what I wished for?"

I think back, his words sparking a memory. "Happiness," I recall. "On our first non-date date, you said if you could wish for anything, it'd be happiness."

"I found that with you."

"Fuck, Joey."

His eyes catch mine, so full of love I have trouble swallowing.

"Every day with you is my new favorite day, bub. Yes, we have fun. But more than that, you make me so damn happy I have trouble remembering what that word meant before you. You made it something different. Something our own. I'm so unbelievably lucky I get to spend the rest of my days as your husband, sharing that happiness with you."

My lips tremble as I press them softly to Joey's, inhaling through my nose, the scent of freshly cut wood—of sawdust—an ever-present familiarity whenever he's near. I let it settle in my lungs, let him flow through my veins and fill my heart.

It's strange to think back to the day I met Joey. When I felt like a lone bee in search of some sort of companionship. Turns out I didn't need a flower at all. My ideal partner came with thick-as-fuck hammies and the perfect kangaroo pouch for me to sink right into, *aaand* shit. It got weird again.

No worries. Joey's my man. And he loves me, weirdness and all.

I guess it's pretty fortuitous I found myself tripping headfirst into accidental love with him. It led us here, didn't it? Walking down the aisle together. Saying our *I dos*. Sharing a kiss as husbands.

Fuck. My husband.

A familiar tune has me pulling back with a gasp, Joey's beautiful brownie eyes smiling back at me.

"*Joe*. Do you hear that? It's our song."

His lips twitch, and he takes a step away, holding out his hand. "Would you do me the honor of sharing our first dance, bub?"

"Fuck, I love you so much."

"Is that a yes?"

"Heck yes. Always."

With smiles on our faces, Joey leads me out onto the dance floor as "(I've Had) The Time of My Life" plays from speakers nearby. We mouth the words as we dance together, our friends and family joining us before long. Jason shoots me a small wink as Cas spins him in place.

Maybe our road to get here was full of twists and turns. But I'm thankful for every single step that brought me closer to Joey.

I married my friend. My kangaroo.

I guess now all that's left to do is be ridiculously happy together.

Big. Fat. Check.

The End

About the Author

Information about Emmy Sanders and her complete list of works can be found on her website. Subscribe to her newsletter, join her Facebook reader group, Emmy's Enclave, and connect via email or social media:

www.emmysanders.com

Find online:
www.facebook.com/emmysandersmm
www.instagram.com/emmysandersmm